Dear Reader:

The MacKade Brothers have always held a special place in the hearts of our readers, so we are very pleased to bring back two more classics featuring these irresistible men—*The Heart of Devin MacKade* and *The Fall of Shane MacKade*. These passionate brothers are sure to steal your heart...while getting their own stolen in the process!

For Devin MacKade it's always been Cassie Connor Dolin. But as sheriff, Devin's a staunch believer in justice and doing the right thing. So he's kept his love for Cassie hidden for twelve long years while watching her go through hell with her no-good husband. But he's through watching—now it's time for action.

And while Devin's always been a one-woman man, his brother Shane has never found a woman he didn't appreciate. And they appreciated him right back! Except one frustrating, gorgeous woman who seems impervious to his charms. Rebecca Knight appears much more interested in her academic pursuits than in him. But Shane is planning on changing all that...

It looks as if these two MacKade brothers are well on their way to falling hard and deeply in love!

The Editors
Silhouette Books

NORA ROBERTS

THE MACKADE BROTHERS:
BROTHERS:
DEVIN & SHANE

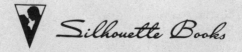

Silhouette Books

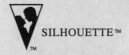 SILHOUETTE™

Recycling programs for this product may not exist in your area.

The MacKade Brothers: Devin & Shane

ISBN-13: 978-1-335-14068-5

Copyright © 2020 by Harlequin Books S.A.

The Heart of Devin MacKade
First published in 1996. This edition published in 2020.
Copyright © 1996 by Nora Roberts

The Fall of Shane MacKade
First published in 1996. This edition published in 2020.
Copyright © 1996 by Nora Roberts

This edition published by arrangement with Harlequin Books S.A.

For questions and comments about the quality of this book, please contact us at CustomerService@Harlequin.com.

Silhouette
22 Adelaide St. West, 40th Floor
Toronto, Ontario M5H 4E3, Canada
www.Harlequin.com

Printed in U.S.A.

CONTENTS

THE HEART OF
DEVIN MacKADE

For those who follow their hearts

Prologue

Devin MacKade considered the age of twenty to be an awkward time in the life of a man. It was old enough for him to be considered responsible for actions and deeds, old enough for him to make a living or love a woman. Yet in the eyes of the law it was not quite old enough for him to be considered fully adult.

He was glad it would only take twelve months to get through it.

Being the third of four brothers, he'd already watched Jared and Rafe move beyond him into adulthood, and Shane was not far behind him. It wasn't that he was in a hurry, really. He was enjoying his time and his life, but Devin had begun, in his methodical way, to make plans for what would be.

The little town of Antietam, Maryland, would have been surprised to know that he had decided to uphold the law, rather than break it. Or bend it.

His mother had pushed him into college, true, but once he arrived, Devin had decided to enjoy it. The courses in administration of justice, criminology, sociology, fascinated him. How rules were made, why, how they were upheld. It had seemed almost from the beginning that those books, those words, those ideals, had just been waiting for him to discover them.

So, in his thoughtful way, he had decided to become a cop.

It wasn't something he wanted to share with his family just yet. His brothers would rag him, undoubtedly. Even Jared, who was already on his way to becoming a lawyer, would show no mercy. It wasn't something he minded. Devin knew he could hold his own with all three of his brothers, be it with words or fists. But for now, it was a personal agenda, and he wasn't talking.

He was aware that not everything you wanted, deep inside, worked out. There was proof of that right here in Ed's Café, where he and his brothers were grabbing a quick meal before heading to Duff's Tavern to shoot pool. Yes, the proof was right here, serving him the blue plate special, flushing shyly at Rafe's easy teasing.

Five foot two, barely a hundred pounds, as delicate and fragile as a rosebud. Angel hair like a curling halo around a face that was all quiet gray eyes. A nose that tipped up just the tiniest bit at the end. The prettiest mouth in the county, with its deep dip in the top lip. Like a doll's. Small hands that he knew could juggle plates and coffeepots and glasses with a studied competence.

Hands that carried a ring with a chip of a diamond barely big enough to glint on the third finger.

Her name was Cassandra Connor, and it seemed he'd loved her forever. Surely he'd known her forever, watched her grow up with a flicker of interest that had become a full-blown crush he'd considered too embarrassing to act on.

And that was the problem. By the time he decided to act, he'd been too late. Joe Dolin had already claimed her. They would be married in June, just two weeks after she graduated from high school.

And there was nothing he could do about it.

He made sure not to watch her walk away from their booth. His brothers had sharp eyes and he would never be able to tolerate being teased about something as intimate and humiliating as unrequited love.

So he looked out the window at Main Street. That, he thought, was something he could do something about. One day he would give something back to the town that had been such an intricate and important part of his life. One day he would serve and protect here. It was his destiny. He could feel it.

The way he sometimes felt, in dreams, that he had done so before—or tried, when the town was ravaged by war, split and frayed by divided loyalties. In dreams, he could see it the way it had been, the way it was in those old Civil War photos. Stone houses and churches, horses and carriages. Sometimes he could almost hear the men gathering on corners or in the barbershop, discussing the War between the States.

Of course, he thought with cool rationality, the town, or parts of it, were haunted. The old Barlow place on the hill just outside of town, the woods, his own home, the fields he helped plow and plant every spring. There were echoes there of lives and deaths, of hopes and fears.

A man had only to listen to hear.

"Almost as good as Mom's." Shane shoveled mashed potatoes into his mouth, and the MacKade dimple flashed as he grinned. "Almost. What do you figure women do on their night out?"

"Gossip." His plate clean, Rafe leaned back and lit a cigarette. "What else?"

"Mom's entitled," Jared commented.

"Didn't say she wasn't. Old lady Metz is probably giving her an earful about us right now, though." Rafe grinned wickedly at that thought, and at the knowledge that his mother could handle even the formidable Mrs. Metz with one arm tied behind her back.

Devin looked away from his view of Main Street, back at his brother. "We do anything lately?"

They all thought about it. It wasn't that their memories were poor, it was just that they found trouble so easily, they often overlooked the results.

Anyone breezing by the big window of Ed's Café would have seen the four MacKades, dark-haired, green-eyed devils, handsome enough to raise any female's blood pressure, be she ten or eighty. Reckless enough to have most men bracing or backing away.

They argued awhile over who had done what most recently—fights picked and fought, laws broken, or at least dented. It was agreed, after the argument grew heated, that Rafe had the prize, with his race against Joe Dolin's Chevy on route 34.

They hadn't been caught, but word had gotten around. Especially as Rafe had won and Joe had slunk off muttering about revenge.

"The guy's a jerk." Rafe blew out smoke. No one disagreed, but Rafe's gaze shifted to where Cassie was busy serving a booth behind them. "What does a sweet little thing like Cassie see in him?"

"If you ask me, she wants out of the house." Jared pushed

his plate aside. "Her mother would be enough to send anyone looking for the first escape hatch. The woman's a fanatic."

"Maybe she loves him," Devin said quietly.

Rafe's opinion of that was one crude word. "Kid's barely seventeen," he pointed out. "She'll fall in love a dozen times."

"Not everyone has a flexible heart."

"A flexible heart." Shane whooped with laughter at the phrase. "It ain't Rafe's heart that's flexible, Dev, it's his—"

"Shut up, creep," Rafe said mildly as his elbow jammed hard into Shane's ribs. "You up for a beer, Jare?"

"I'm up for it."

Rafe leered nastily. "Too bad you two have to stick with soda pop. I bet Duff has a whole case of the fizzy stuff for you kids."

That, of course, insulted Shane. As it was meant to. Hot words came first, then the jostling. From her station at the counter, Edwina Crump shouted at them to take it outside.

They did, with Devin lagging behind to pay the tab.

On the other side of the window, his brothers pushed and shoved each other, more out of habit than from any real temper. Ignoring them, he smiled over at Cassie.

"Just blowing off steam," he told her, adding a tip that wouldn't embarrass her.

"The sheriff sometimes comes by about this time of night." Her voice was barely a whisper of warning. And so sweet to Devin's ears, he almost sighed.

"I'll go break it up."

He slid out of the booth. He thought his mother probably knew his feelings. It was impossible to hide anything from her. God knew, they had all tried and failed. He thought he knew what she would say to him.

That he was young yet, and there would be other girls, other women, other loves. She would mean the best by it.

Devin knew that though he wasn't yet fully an adult, he had a man's heart. And he'd already given it.

He kept that heart out of his eyes, though, because he would hate Cassie's pity. Casually he walked out of the diner to break up his brothers. He caught Shane in a head-lock, elbowed Rafe in the gut, cocked a brow at Jared and suggested amiably that they go play some pool.

Chapter 1

The town of Antietam was a pretty sight in late spring. Sheriff Devin MacKade liked to walk the uneven sidewalks and smell the freshly mowed grass, the flowers, hear the yip of dogs and shouts of children.

He liked to take in the order of it, the continuity and the little changes. Outside the bank, a bed of pink begonias was spreading. The three cars jockeying in line at the drive-in window constituted a traffic jam.

Down a little ways, in front of the post office, there were men passing the time, taking the air. Through the barbershop window, he could see a toddler experiencing his first haircut, while his mother bit her nails and blinked damp eyes.

The banners were flying for the annual Memorial Day parade and picnic. He could see several people busily scrubbing or painting their porches in preparation for the event.

It was an event he enjoyed, even with its logistical and

traffic headaches. He liked the continuity of it, the predict-
ability. The way people would plant themselves with their
folding chairs and coolers along the curb, hours before parade time, to ensure that they would have a good view of
the marching bands and twirling batons.

Most of all, he liked the way the townspeople threw
themselves into that weekend, how much they cared, how
strong their pride.

His father had told him of the ancient man who, when he
himself was a little boy, had walked creakily down Main
Street wearing Confederate gray at an earlier Memorial
Day. One of the last living testaments to the Civil War.

Dead now, as they all were, Devin mused as he glanced
over at the memorial in the town's square. Dead, but not and
never forgotten. At least not in little towns such as these,
which had once known the sound of mortar and rifle fire
and the terrible cries of the wounded.

Turning away, he looked down the street and sighed.
There was Mrs. Metz's Buick, parked, as usual, in the red
zone. He could give her a ticket, Devin mused, and she
would pay it. But when she lumbered into his office to
hand over the fine, she would also treat him to a lecture.
He blew out a breath, studied the door of the library. No
doubt that was where she was, gossiping over the counter
with Sarah Jane Poffenberger.

Devin drew together his courage and fortitude and
climbed the old stone steps.

She was exactly where he'd expected her to be, leaning
over the counter, a mountain of paperback novels at her
dimpled elbow, deep into the latest dirt with the librarian.
Devin wondered why any woman so…generously sized insisted on wearing wildly patterned dresses.

"Mrs. Metz." He kept his voice low. He'd been tossed out of the library many times in his youth by Miss Sarah Jane.

"Well, hello there, Devin." Beaming a smile, Mrs. Metz turned to him. Her elbow nearly toppled the mountain of books, but Miss Sarah Jane, for all her resemblance to an understuffed scarecrow, moved fast. "And how are you on this beautiful afternoon?"

"I'm just fine. Hello, Miss Sarah Jane."

"Devin." Iron-gray hair pulled back from paper-thin white skin, starched collar buttoned firmly to her chin, Sarah Jane nodded regally. "Did you come in to return that copy of *The Red Badge of Courage*?"

"No, ma'am." He very nearly flushed. He'd lost the damn book twenty years before, he'd paid for it, he'd even swept the library for a month as penance for his carelessness. Now, though he was a man—one who wore a badge and was considered responsible by most—he was shriveled down to a boy by Sarah Jane Poffenberger's steely eyes.

"A book is a treasure," she said, as she always did.

"Yes, ma'am. Ah, Mrs. Metz…" More to save himself now than to uphold parking laws, he shifted his gaze. "You're parked illegally. Again."

"I am?" All innocence, she fluttered at him. "Why, I don't know how that happened, Devin. I would have sworn I pulled into the right place. I just came in to check out a few books. I'd have walked, but I had to run into the city, and stopped by on my way home. Reading's one of God's gifts, isn't it, Sarah Jane?"

"It is indeed." Though her mouth remained solemn, the dark eyes in Sarah Jane's wrinkled face were laughing. Devin had to concentrate on not shuffling his feet.

"You're in the red zone, Mrs. Metz."

"Oh, dear. You didn't give me a ticket, did you?"

"Not yet," Devin muttered.

"Because Mr. Metz gets all huffy when I get a ticket. And I've only been here for a minute or two, isn't that right, Sarah Jane?"

"Just a minute or two," Sarah Jane confirmed, but she winked at Devin.

"If you'd move your car—"

"I'll do that. I surely will. Just as soon as I check out these books. I don't know what I'd do if I didn't have my books, what with the way Mr. Metz watches the TV. You check these out for me, Sarah Jane, while Devin tells us how his family's doing."

He knew when he was outgunned. After all, he was a cop. "They're fine."

"And those sweet little babies. Imagine two of your brothers having babies within months of each other. I just have to get over to see them all."

"The babies are fine, too." He softened at the thought of them. "Growing."

"Oh, they do grow, don't they, Sarah Jane? Grow like weeds, before you can stop them. Now you've got yourself a nephew and a niece."

"Two nephews and a niece," Devin reminded her, adding Jared's wife Savannah's son, Bryan.

"Yes, indeed. Give you any ideas about starting your own brood?"

Her eyes were glittering at the thought of getting the inside story on future events. Devin stood his ground. "Being an uncle suits me." Without a qualm, he tossed his sister-in-law to the wolves. "Regan has little Nate with her at the shop today. I saw him a couple hours ago."

"Does she?"

"She mentioned Savannah might be coming by, with Layla."

"Oh, my! Well..." Being able to corner both MacKade women, and their babies, was such a coup, Mrs. Metz nearly trembled at the idea. "Hurry on up there, Sarah Jane. I've got errands to run."

"Hold your horses now, I've got 'em for you right here." Sarah Jane handed over the canvas bag Mrs. Metz had brought, now pregnant with books. Moments later, when Mrs. Metz puffed her way out, Sarah Jane smiled. "You're a smart boy, Devin. Always were."

"If Regan finds out I headed her over there, she'll skin me." He grinned. "But a man's gotta do what a man's gotta do. Nice seeing you, Miss Sarah Jane."

"You find that copy of *The Red Badge of Courage,* Devin MacKade. Books aren't meant to be wasted."

He winced as he opened the door. "Yes, ma'am."

For all her bulk, Mrs. Metz moved quickly. She was already pulling out of the red zone and into the sparse traffic. Congratulating himself on a job well done, Devin told himself he could take a quick ride down to the MacKade Inn.

Just needed to check and make sure there wasn't anything that needed his attention, he told himself as he walked up the street to his cruiser. It was his brother Rafe's place, after all. It was his duty to check on it now and again.

The fact that Cassie Dolin managed the bed-and-breakfast and lived on the third floor with her two children had nothing to do with it.

He was just doing his job.

Which was, he thought as he slipped behind the wheel of his car, a huge and ridiculous lie.

He was, however, doing what he had to do. Which was to see her. At least once a day, he simply had to see her.

He just had to, no matter how much it hurt, or how careful he had to be. More careful, he reminded himself, now that she was divorced from that bastard who had beaten and abused her for years.

Joe Dolin was in prison, Devin thought with grim satisfaction as he headed out of town. And he would be there for quite some time to come.

As the sheriff, as a friend, as the man who had loved her most of his life, Devin had a duty to see that Cassie and the kids were safe and happy.

And maybe today he could make her smile, all the way to her big gray eyes.

What had been the old Barlow place—and likely would remain that forever in the mind of the town—sat on a hill just on the edge of Antietam. Once it had been the property of a rich man who enjoyed its height, its expensive furnishings, its enviable view. It had stood there while the bloodiest day of the Civil War raged around it. It had stood while a wounded young soldier was murdered on its polished grand staircase. There it had remained while the mistress of the house grieved herself to death. Or so the legend went.

It had stood, falling into decay, disuse, disregard. Its stones had not moved when its porches rotted, when its windows were shattered by rocks heaved by rambunctious children. It had stood, empty but for its ghosts, for decades.

Until Rafe MacKade had returned and claimed it.

It was the house, Devin thought as he turned up its steep lane, that had brought Rafe and Regan together. Together, they had turned that brooding old building into something fine, something lovely.

Where there had once been weeds and thorny brambles, there was now a lush, terraced lawn, vivid with flowers and shrubs. He had helped plant them himself. The MacKades always united when it came to developing dreams—or destroying enemies.

The windows gleamed now, framed by rich blue trim, their overflowing flower boxes filled with sunny-faced pansies. The sturdy double porches were painted that same blue, and offered guests a place to sit and look toward town.

Or, he knew, if they chose to sit around at the back, they'd have a long view of the haunted woods that bordered the inn's property, his own farm and the land where his brother Jared, his wife, Savannah, and their children lived.

He didn't knock, but simply stepped inside. There were no cars in the drive, but for Cassie's, so he knew the overnight guests had already left, and any others had yet to arrive.

He stood for a moment in the grand hall, with its polished floor, pretty rugs and haunted staircase. There were always flowers. Cassie saw to that. Pretty vases of fragrant blooms, little bowls and dishes with potpourri that he knew she made herself.

So, to him, the house always smelled like Cassie.

He wasn't sure where he would find her—in the kitchen, in the yard, in her apartment on the third floor. He moved through the house from front to rear, knowing that if he didn't find her in the first two, he would climb the outside stairs and knock on the door of her private quarters.

It was hard to believe that less than two years before, the house had been full of dust and cobwebs, all cracked plaster and chipped molding. Now floors and walls gleamed, windows shone, wood was polished to a high sheen. Antique tables were topped with what Devin always thought of as dust collectors, but they were charming.

Rafe and Regan had done something here, built something here. Just as they were doing in the old house they'd bought for themselves outside of town.

He envied his brother that, not just the love, but the partnership of a woman, the home and family they had created together.

Shane had the farm. Technically, it belonged to all four of them, but it was Shane's, heart and soul. Rafe had Regan and their baby, the inn and the lovely old stone-and-cedar house they were making their own. Jared had Savannah, the children and the cabin.

And as for himself? Devin mused. Well, he had the town, he supposed. And a cot in the back room of the sheriff's office.

The kitchen was empty. Though it was as neat as a model on display, it held all the warmth kitchens were meant to. Slate-blue tiles and creamy white appliances were a backdrop for little things—fresh fruit in an old stoneware bowl; a sassy cookie jar in the shape of a smiling cat that he knew would be full of fresh, home-baked cookies; long, tapered jars that held the herbed vinegars Cassie made; a row of African violets in bloom on the wide windowsill over the sink.

And then, through the window, he saw her, taking billowing sheets from the line where they'd dried in the warm breeze.

His heart turned over in his chest. He could handle that, had handled it for too many years to count. She looked happy, was all he could think. Her lips were curved a little, her gray eyes dreamy. The breeze that fluttered the sheets teased her hair, sending the honeycomb curls dancing around her face, along her neck and throat.

Like the kitchen, she was neat, tidy, efficient without being cold. She wore a white cotton blouse tucked into navy slacks. Just lately, she'd started to add little pieces of jewelry. No rings. Her divorce had been final for a full year now, and he knew the exact day she'd taken off her wedding ring.

But she wore small gold hoops in her ears and a touch of color on her mouth. She'd stopped wearing makeup and jewelry shortly after her marriage. Devin remembered that, too.

Just as he remembered the first time he'd been called out to the house she rented with Joe, answering a complaint from the neighbors. He remembered the fear in her eyes when she'd come to the door, the marks on her face, the way her voice had hitched and trembled when she told him there wasn't any trouble, there was no trouble at all. She'd slipped and fallen, that was all.

Yes, he remembered that. And his frustration, the hideous sense of impotence that first time, and all the other times he'd had to confront her, to ask her, to quietly offer her alternatives that were just as quietly refused.

There'd been nothing he could do as sheriff to stop what happened inside that house, until the day she finally came into his office—bruised, beaten, terrified—to fill out a complaint.

There was little he could do now as sheriff but offer her friendship.

So he walked out the rear door, a casual smile on his face. "Hey, Cass."

Alarm came into her eyes first, darkening that lovely gray. He was used to it, though it pained him immeasurably to know that she thought of him as the sheriff first— as authority, as the bearer of trouble—before she thought of him as an old friend. But the smile came back more quickly than it once had, chasing the tension away from those delicate features.

"Hello, Devin." Calmly, because she was teaching her-self to be calm, she hooked a clothespin back on the line and began folding the sheet.

"Need some help?"

Before she could refuse, he was plucking clothespins. She simply couldn't get used to a man doing such things. Especially such a man. He was so…big. Broad shoulders, big hands, long legs. And gorgeous, of course. All the MacKades were.

There was something so male about Devin, she couldn't really explain it. Even as he competently took linen from the line, folded it into the basket, he was all man. Unlike his deputies, he didn't wear the khaki uniform of his of-fice, just jeans and a faded blue shirt rolled up to the el-bows. There were muscles there, she'd seen them. And she had reason to be wary of a man's strength. But despite his big hands, his big shoulders, he'd never been anything but gentle. She tried to remember that as he brushed against her, reaching for another clothespin.

Still, she stepped away, kept distance between them. He smiled at her, and she tried to think of something to say. It would be easier if everything about him wasn't so… definite, she supposed. So vivid. His hair was as black as midnight, and curled over the frayed collar of his shirt. His eyes were as green as moss. Even the bones in his face were defined and impossible to ignore, the way they formed hollows and planes. His mouth was firm, and that dimple beside it constantly drew the eye.

He even smelled like a man. Plain soap, plain sweat. He'd never been anything but kind to her, and he'd been a part of her life forever, it seemed. But whenever it was just the two of them, she found herself as nervous as a cat faced with a bulldog.

"Too nice a day to toss these in the dryer."

"What?" She blinked, then cursed herself. "Oh, yes. I like hanging the linens out, when there's time. We had two guests overnight, and we're expecting another couple later today. We're booked solid for the Memorial Day weekend."

"You'll be busy."

"Yes. It's hardly like work, though, really."

He watched her smooth sheets into the basket. "Not like waiting tables at Ed's."

"No." She smiled a little, then struggled with guilt. "Ed was wonderful to me. She was great to work for."

"She's still ticked at Rafe for stealing you." Noting the distress that leaped into her eyes, Devin shook his head. "I'm only kidding, Cassie. You know she was happy you took this job. How are the kids?"

"They're fine. Wonderful." Before she could pick up the basket of linens herself, Devin had it tucked to his hip, leaving her nothing to do with her hands. "They'll be home soon, from school."

"No Little League practice today?"

"No." She headed toward the kitchen, but he opened the door before she could, and waited for her to go in ahead of him. "Connor's thrilled he made the team."

"He's the best pitcher they've got."

"Everyone says so." Automatically, she went to the stove to make coffee. "It's so strange. He was never interested in sports before...well, before," she finished lamely. "Bryan's been wonderful for him."

"My nephew's a hell of a kid."

There was such simple and honest pride in the statement that Cassie turned around to study him. "You think of him that way, really? I mean, even though there's no blood between you?"

"When Jared married Savannah, it made Bryan his son. That makes him my nephew. Family isn't just blood."

"No, and sometimes blood kin is more trouble than not."

"Your mother's hassling you again."

She only moved her shoulder and turned back to finish the coffee. "She's just set in her ways." Shifting, she reached into one of the glass-fronted cabinets for a cup and a small plate. When Devin's hand curled over her shoulder, she jerked and nearly dropped the stoneware to the tiles.

He started to step back, then changed his mind. Instead, he turned her around so that they were face-to-face, and kept both of his hands on her shoulders. "She's still giving you a hard time about Joe?"

She had to swallow, but couldn't quite get her throat muscles to work. His hands were firm, but they weren't hurting. There was annoyance in his eyes, but no meanness. She ordered herself to be calm, not to lower her gaze.

"She doesn't believe in divorce."

"Does she believe in wife-beating?"

Now she did wince, did lower her gaze. Devin cursed himself and lowered his hands to his sides. "I'm sorry."

"No, it's all right. I don't expect you to understand. I can't understand myself anymore." Relieved that he'd stepped back, she turned to the cookie jar and filled the plate with chocolate chip and oatmeal cookies she'd baked that morning. "It doesn't seem to matter that I'm happy, that the kids are happy. It doesn't matter that the law says what Joe did to me was wrong. That he attacked Regan. It only matters that I broke my vows and divorced him."

"Are you happy, Cassie?"

"I'd stopped believing I could be, or even that I should be." She set the plate on the table, went to pour him coffee. "Yes, I am happy."

"Are you going to make me drink this coffee by myself?"

She stared at him a minute. It was still such a novel concept, the idea that she could sit down in the middle of the day with a friend. Taking matters into his own hands, he got out a second cup.

"So tell me…" After pouring her coffee, he held out a chair for her. "How do the tourists feel about spending the night in a haunted house?"

"Some of them are disappointed when they don't see or hear anything." Cassie lifted her cup and tried not to feel guilty that she wasn't doing some chore. "Rafe was clever to publicize the inn as haunted."

"He's always been clever."

"Yes, he has. A few people are nervous when they come down for breakfast, but most of them are…well, excited, I guess. They'll have heard doors slamming or voices, or have heard her crying."

"Abigail Barlow. The tragic mistress of the house, the compassionate Southern belle married to the Yankee murderer."

"Yes. They'll hear her, or smell her roses, or just feel something. We've only had one couple leave in the middle of the night." For once, her smile was quick, and just a little wicked. "They were both terrified."

"But you're not. It doesn't bother you to have ghosts wandering?"

"No."

He cocked his head. "Have you heard her? Abigail?"

"Oh, yes, often. Not just at night. Sometimes when I'm alone here, making beds or tidying up, I'll hear her. Or feel her."

"And it doesn't spook you?"

"No, I feel…" She started to say "connected," but

thought it would sound foolish. "Sorry for her. She was trapped and unhappy, married to a man who despised her, in love with someone else—"

"In love with someone else?" Devin asked, interrupting her. "I've never heard that."

Baffled, Cassie set her cup down with a little clink. "I haven't, either. I just—" *Know it,* she realized. "I suppose I added it in. It's more romantic. Emma calls her the lady. She likes to go into the bridal suite."

"And Connor?"

"It's a big adventure for him. All of it. They love it here. Once when Bryan was spending the night, I caught the three of them sneaking down to the guest floor. They wanted to go ghost-hunting."

"My brothers and I spent the night here when we were kids."

"Did you? Of course you did," she said before he could comment. "The MacKades and an empty, derelict, haunted house. They belong together. Did you go ghost-hunting?"

"I didn't have to. I saw her. I saw Abigail."

Cassie's smile faded. "You did?"

"I never told the guys. They'd have ragged on me for the rest of my life. But I saw her, sitting in the parlor, by the fire. There was a fire, I could smell it, feel the heat from the flames, smell the roses that were in a vase on the table beside her. She was beautiful," Devin said quietly. "Blond hair and porcelain skin, eyes the color of the smoke going up the flue. She wore a blue dress. I could hear the silk rustle as she moved. She was embroidering something, and her hands were small and delicate. She looked right at me, and she smiled. She smiled, but there were tears in her eyes. She spoke to me."

"She spoke to you," Cassie repeated, as chills raced up and down her back like icy fingers. "What did she say?"

"'If only.'" Devin brought himself back, shook himself. "That was it. 'If only.' Then she was gone, and I told myself I'd been dreaming. But I knew I hadn't. I always hoped I'd see her again."

"But you haven't?"

"No, but I've heard her weeping. It breaks my heart."

"I know."

"I'd, ah, appreciate it if you wouldn't mention that to Rafe. He'd still rag on me."

"I won't." She smiled as he bit into a cookie. "Is that why you come here, hoping to see her again?"

"I come to see you." The minute he'd said it, he recognized his mistake. Her face went from relaxed to wary in the blink of an eye. "And the kids," he added quickly. "And for the cookies."

She relaxed again. "I'll put some in a bag for you to take with you." But even as she rose to do so, he covered her hand with his. She froze, not in fear so much as from the shock of the contact. Speechless, she stared down at the way his hand swallowed hers.

"Cassie..." He strained against the urge to gather her up, just to hold her, to stroke those flyaway curls, to taste, finally to taste, that small, serious mouth.

There was a hitch in her breathing that she was afraid to analyze. But she made herself shift her gaze, ordered herself not to be so much a coward that she couldn't look into his eyes. She wished she knew what she was looking at, or looking for. All she knew was that it was more than the patience and pity she'd expected to see there, that it was different.

"Devin—" She broke off, jerked back at the sound of giggles and stomping feet. "The kids are home," she finished quickly, breathlessly, and hurried to the door. "I'm down here!" she called out, knowing that they would do as they'd been told and go directly to the apartment unless she stopped them.

"Mama, I got a gold star on my homework." Emma came in, a blond pixie in a red playsuit. She set her lunch box on the counter and smiled shyly at Devin. "Hello."

"There's my best girl. Let's see that star."

Clutching the lined paper in her hand, she walked to him. "You have a star."

"Not as pretty as this one." Devin traced a finger over the gold foil stuck to the top of the paper. "Did you do this by yourself?"

"Almost all. Can I sit in your lap?"

"You bet." He plucked her up, cradled her there. He quite simply adored her. After brushing his cheek against her hair, he grinned over at Connor. "How's it going, champ?"

"Okay." A little thrill moved through Connor at the nickname. He was small for his age, like Emma, and blond, though at ten he had hair that was shades darker than his towheaded sister's.

"You pitched a good game last Saturday."

Now he flushed. "Thanks. But Bryan went four for five." His loyalty and love for his best friend knew no bounds. "Did you see?"

"I was there for a few innings. Watched you smoke a few batters."

"Connor got an A on his history test," Emma said. "And that mean old Bobby Lewis shoved him and called him a bad name when we were in line for the bus."

"Emma..." Mortified, Connor scowled at his sister.

"I guess Bobby Lewis didn't get an A," Devin commented.

"Bryan fixed him good," Emma went on.

I bet he did, Devin thought, and handed Emma a cookie so that she'd be distracted enough to stop embarrassing her brother.

"I'm proud of you." Trying not to worry, Cassie gave Connor a quick squeeze. "Both of you. A gold star and an A all in one day. We'll have to celebrate later with ice-cream sundaes from Ed's."

"It's no big deal," Connor began.

"It is to me." Cassie bent down and kissed him firmly. "A very big deal."

"I used to struggle with math," Devin said casually. "Never could get more than a C no matter what I did."

Connor stared at the floor, weighed down by the stigma of being bright. He could still hear his father berating him. *Egghead. Pansy. Useless.*

Cassie started to speak, to defend, but Devin sent her one swift look.

"But then, I used to ace history and English."

Stunned, Connor jerked his head up and stared. "You did?"

It was a struggle, but Devin kept his eyes sober. The kid didn't mean to be funny, or insulting, he knew. "Yeah. I guess it was because I liked to read a lot. Still do."

"You read books?" It was an epiphany for Connor. Here was a man who held a real man's job and who liked to read.

"Sure." Devin jiggled Emma on his knee and smiled. "The thing was, Rafe was pitiful in English, but he was a whiz in math. So we traded off. I'd do his—" He glanced at Cassie, realized his mistake. "I'd help him with his English homework and he'd help me with the math. It got us both through."

"Do you like to read stories?" Connor wanted to know. "Made-up stories?"

"They're the best kind."

"Connor writes stories," Cassie said, even as Connor wriggled in embarrassment.

"So I've heard. Maybe you'll let me read one." Before the boy could answer, Devin's beeper went off. "Hell," he muttered.

"Hell," Emma said adoringly.

"You want to get me in trouble?" he asked, then hitched her onto his hip as he rose to call in. A few minutes later, he'd given up on his idea of wheedling his way into a dinner invitation. "Gotta go. Somebody broke into the storeroom at Duff's and helped themselves to a few cases of beer."

"Will you shoot them?" Emma asked him.

"I don't think so. How about a kiss?"

She puckered up obligingly before he set her down. "Thanks for the coffee, Cass."

"I'll walk you out. You two go on upstairs and get your after-school snack," she told her children. "I'll be right along." She waited until they were nearly at the front door before she spoke again. "Thank you for talking to Connor like that. He's still so sensitive about liking school."

"He's a bright kid. It won't take much longer for him to start appreciating himself."

"You helped. He admires you."

"It didn't take any effort to tell him I like to read." Devin paused at the door. "He means a lot to me. All of you do." When she opened her mouth to speak, he took a chance and brushed a finger over her cheek. "All of you do," he repeated, and walked out, leaving her staring after him.

Chapter 2

Some nights, late at night, when her children were sleeping and the guests were settled down, Cassie would roam the house. She was careful not to go on the second floor, where guests were bedded down in the lovely rooms and suites Rafe and Regan had built.

They paid for privacy, and Cassie was careful to give it.

But she was free to walk through her own apartment on the third floor, to admire the rooms, the view from the windows, even the feel of the polished hardwood under her bare feet.

It was a freedom, and a security, that she knew she would never take for granted. Any more than she would take for granted the curtains framing the windows, made of fabric that she had chosen and paid for herself. Or the kitchen table, the sofa, each lamp.

Not all new, she mused, but new to her. Everything that had been in the house she shared with Joe had been sold.

It had been her way of sweeping away the past. Nothing here was from her before. It had been vital to her to start this life with nothing she hadn't brought into it on her own.

If she was restless, she could go down on the main level, move from parlor to sitting room, into the beautiful solarium, with its lovely plants and glistening glass. She could stand in the hallways, sit on the steps. Simply enjoy the quiet and solitude.

The only room she avoided was the library. It was the only room that never welcomed her, despite its deep leather chairs and walls of books.

She knew instinctively that it had been Charles Barlow's realm. Abigail's husband. The master of the house. A man who had shot, in cold blood, a wounded Confederate soldier hardly old enough to shave.

Sometimes she felt the horror and sadness of that when she walked up and down the staircase where it had happened. Now and again she even heard the shot, the explosion of it, and the screams of the servants who had witnessed the senseless and brutal murder.

But she understood senseless brutality, knew it existed.

Just as she knew Abigail still existed, in this house. It wasn't just the sound of weeping, the scent of roses that would come suddenly and from nowhere. It was just the feel of the air, that connection that she'd been too embarrassed to mention to Devin.

That was how she knew Abigail had loved a man who wasn't her husband. That she had longed for him, wept for him, as well as for the murdered boy. That she had dreamed of him, and despaired of ever knowing the joy of real love.

Cassie understood, and sympathized. That was why she felt so welcomed in this house that held so much of the past. Why she was never afraid.

No, she was grateful for every hour she spent here as caretaker to beautiful things. It had been nearly a year since she had accepted Regan's and Rafe's offer and moved her family in. She was still dazzled that they would trust her with the job, and she worked hard to earn that trust.

The work was all pleasure, she thought now, as she wandered into the parlor. To tend and polish lovely antiques, to cook breakfast in that wonderful kitchen and serve it to guests on pretty dishes. To have flowers all around the house, inside and out.

It was like a dream, like one of the fairy tales Savannah MacKade illustrated.

She was so rarely afraid anymore, hardly even disturbed by the nightmares that had plagued her for so long she'd come to expect them. It was unusual for her to wake shivering in the middle of the night, out of a dream—listening, terrified, for Joe's steps, for his voice.

She was safe here, and, for the first time in her life, free.

Bundled into her robe, she curled on the window seat in the parlor. She wouldn't stay long. Her children slept deeply and were content here, but there was always a chance they might wake and need her. But she wanted just a few moments alone to hug her good fortune close to her heart.

She had a home where her children could laugh and play and feel safe. It was wonderful to see how quickly Emma was throwing off her shyness and becoming a bright, chattering little girl. Childhood had been harder on Connor, she knew. It shamed her to realize that he had seen and heard so much more of the misery than she had guessed. But he was coming out of his shell.

It relieved her to see how comfortable they were with Devin, with all the MacKades, really. There had been a time when Emma hesitated to so much as speak to a man, and

Connor, sweet, sensitive Connor, had forever been braced for a verbal blow.

No more.

Just that day, both of them had talked to Devin as if it were as natural as breathing. She wished she was as resilient. It was the badge, she decided. She was finding it easier and easier to be comfortable with Jared or Rafe or Shane. She didn't jolt when one of them touched her or flashed that MacKade grin.

It was different with Devin. But then, she'd had to go to him, had to confess that she'd allowed herself to be beaten and abused for years, had been forced to show him the marks on her body. Nothing, not even Joe's vicious fists, had ever humiliated her more than that.

She knew he was sorry for her, and felt obligated to look out for her and the children. He took his responsibilities as sheriff seriously. No one, including herself, would have believed twelve or fifteen years before, when he and his brothers were simply those bad MacKade boys, that they would turn out the way they had.

Devin had made himself into an admirable man. Still rough, she supposed. She knew he could break up a bar fight with little more than a snarl, and that he used his fists when that didn't work.

Still, she'd never known anyone gentler or more compassionate. He'd been very good to her and her children, and she owed him.

Laying her cheek against the window, she closed her eyes. She was going to train herself not to be so jumpy around him. She could do it. She had been working very hard over the past year or so to teach herself composure and calm, to pretend she wasn't shy when she greeted the guests. It worked so well that she often didn't even feel shy anymore.

There were even times, and they were coming more and more often, when she actually felt competent.

So she would work now to teach herself not to be so jittery around Devin. She would stop thinking about his badge and remember that he was one of her oldest friends— one she'd even had a little crush on, once upon a time. She would stop thinking of how big his hands were, or what would happen if he got angry and used them against her.

Instead she would remember how gently they ruffled her daughter's hair, or how firmly they covered her son's when he helped him with his batting stance.

Or how nice it had been, how unexpectedly nice, to feel the way his finger brushed her cheek.

She curled more comfortably on the padded seat…

He was here, right here beside her, smiling in that way that brought his dimple out and made odd things happen to her insides. He touched her, and she didn't jolt this time. There, she thought, it was working already.

He was touching her, drawing her against him. Oh, his body was hard. But she didn't flinch. She was trembling, though. Couldn't stop. He was so big, so strong, he could break her in half. And yet…and yet his hands stroked so lightly over her. Over her skin. But he couldn't be touching her there.

His mouth was on hers, so warm and gentle. She couldn't stop him. She forgot that she should, even when his tongue slid over hers and his hand cupped her breast as if it were the most natural thing in the world.

He was touching her, and it was hard to breathe, because those big hands were gliding over her. And now his mouth.

Oh, it was wrong, it had to be wrong, but it was so wonderful to feel that warm, wet mouth on her.

She was whimpering, moaning, opening for him. She felt him coming inside her, so hard, so smooth, so right.

The explosion of a gunshot had her jerking upright. She was gasping for breath, damp with sweat, her mind a muddled mess.

Alone in the parlor. Of course she was alone. But her skin was tingling, and there was a tingling, almost a burning, inside her that she hadn't felt in so many years she'd forgotten it was possible.

Shame washed over her, had her gathering her robe tight at her throat. It was terrible, she thought, just terrible, to have been imagining herself with Devin like that. After he'd been so kind to her.

She didn't know what had gotten into her. She didn't even like sex. It was something she'd learned to dread, and then to tolerate, very soon after her miserable wedding-night initiation. Pleasure had never entered into it. She simply wasn't built for that kind of pleasure, and had accepted the lack early on.

But when she got to her feet, her legs were shaky and there was a nagging pressure low in her stomach. She drew in a breath, and along with it the delicate scent of roses.

So she wasn't alone, Cassie thought. Abigail was with her. Comforted, she went back upstairs to check on her children one last time before going to bed.

Devin was well into what he considered the paper-pushing part of the day by noon. He had a report to type and file on the break-in at Duff's Tavern. The trio of teenagers who'd thought to relieve Duff of a bit of his inventory had been pathetically easy to track down.

Then there was the traffic accident out on Brook Lane.
Hardly more than a fender bender, Devin mused as he hammered at the keys, but Lester Swoop, whose new sedan had
been crinkled, was raising a ruckus.

He had to finish up his report to the mayor and town
council on the preparations for crowd control on parade day.

Then, maybe, he'd get some lunch.

Across the office, his young deputy, Donnie Banks, was
dealing with parking tickets. And, as usual, drumming his
fingers on the metal desk to some inner rhythm that Devin
tried hard to ignore.

The day was warm enough that the windows were open.
The budget didn't run to air-conditioning. He could hear
the sounds of traffic—what there was of it—and the occasional squeal of brakes as someone came up too fast on
the stop light at Main and Antietam.

He still had the mail to sort through, his job, since Crystal Abbott was off on maternity leave and he hadn't come
up with a temporary replacement for her position as general dogsbody.

He didn't mind, really. The sheer monotony of paperwork could be soothing. Things were quiet, as they were
expected to be in a town of less than twenty-five hundred.
His job was to keep it that way, and deal with the drunk-and-disorderlies, the traffic violations, the occasional petty
theft or domestic dispute.

Things heated up now and again, but in his seven years
with Antietam's sheriff's department, both as deputy and
as sheriff, he'd had to draw his weapon only twice. And
he'd never been forced to fire it.

Reason and guile usually worked, and if they didn't, a
fist usually turned the tide.

When the phone rang, Devin glanced hopefully toward

his deputy. Donnie's fingers never broke rhythm, so, with a sigh, Devin answered the phone himself. He was well on his way to calming a hysterical woman who claimed that her neighbor deliberately sent her dog over into her yard to fertilize her petunias when Jared walked in.

"Yes, ma'am. No, ma'am." Devin rolled his eyes and motioned Jared to a seat. "Have you talked with her, asked her to keep her dog in her own yard?"

The answer came so fast and loud that Devin winced and held the phone six inches from his ear. In the little wooden chair across the desk, Jared grinned and stretched out his legs.

"Yes, ma'am, I'm sure you worked very hard on your petunias. No, no, don't do that. Please. There's a law against discharging a firearm within town limits. You don't want to go waving your shotgun at the dog. I'm going to send somebody over there. Yes, ma'am, I surely am. Ah…we'll see what we can do. You leave that shotgun alone now, you hear? Yes, ma'am, I've got it all down right here. You just sit tight."

He hung up, tore off the memo sheet. "Donnie?"

"Yo."

"Get on over to Oak Leaf and handle this."

"We got us a situation?" Donnie stopped his drumming, looking hopeful. Devin thought he seemed very young, in his carefully pressed uniform, with his scarecrow hair and eager blue eyes.

"We've got a French poodle using a petunia bed as a toilet. Explain about the leash law, and see if you can keep these two women from a hair-pulling contest."

"Yo!" Delighted with the assignment, Donnie took the information sheet, adjusted his hat and strode out, ready to uphold the law.

"I think he started to shave last week," Devin commented.

"Petunias and poodles," Jared said, and stretched. "I can see you're busy."

"Antietam's a real naked city." Devin got up to pour them both coffee. "Had us a *situation* down to Duff's," he added, tinting his voice with Donnie's accent and emphasis. "Three cases of beer went missing."

"Well, well..."

"Got two of them back." After handing Jared the mug, Devin eased a hip onto his desk. "The other had been consumed by three sixteen-year-olds."

"Tracked them down, did you?"

"It didn't take Sam Spade." Devin shook his head as he sipped. "They'd bragged about it right and left, took the beer out to the field near the high school and had themselves a party. They were sick as dogs when I caught up with them. Idiots. Now they've got B and E charges, larceny and an appointment with juvie."

"Seems to me I remember a couple of cases of beer and a party. In the woods."

"We didn't steal it," Devin reminded him. "We left Duff the money in the storeroom—after we'd broken in and taken the beer."

"A fine but salient point. God, we got drunk."

"And sick," Devin added. "When we crawled home, Mom made us shovel manure all afternoon. I thought I'd die."

"Those were the days," Jared said with a sigh. He sat back. Despite the trim suit and tie, the expensive shoes, there was no mistaking him for anything but a MacKade. Like his brother, he had the reckless dark good looks. A bit more groomed, a bit more polished, but reckless enough.

"What are you doing in town?"

"This and that." Jared wanted to work up to what he had to tell Devin. "Layla's getting a tooth."

"Yeah? Keeping you guys up?"

"I forgot what sleep's like." His grin flashed. "It's great. You know, Bryan changes diapers. The kid's so in love with her, Savannah says the first thing he does when he gets home from school is to go find her."

"You got lucky," Devin murmured.

"Don't I know it. You ought to try it, Dev. Marriage is a pretty good deal."

"It's working for you and Rafe. I saw him this morning, heading into the hardware with Nate strapped to his back. He looked real domestic."

"Did you tell him that?"

"I didn't want to start a fight in front of the baby."

"Good call. You know what you need around here, Dev?" Still sipping coffee, Jared looked around the office. It was utilitarian, basic. Desks, wood floors, coffeepot, a ceiling fan that he knew squeaked when it was put into use in the summer, unpadded chairs, metal file cabinets. "You need a dog. Ethel'll be dropping that litter any day now."

Devin raised a brow. Fred and Ethel, Shane's golden retrievers, had finally figured out what boy and girl dogs could do together besides chase rabbits. "Yeah, I need a puppy puddling on the floor and chewing up my papers."

"Companionship," Jared insisted. "Think how you'd look cruising around town with a dog riding shotgun. You could deputize him."

The image made Devin grin, but he set his coffee down. "I'll keep it in mind. Now why don't you tell me what you came in to tell me?"

Jared blew out a breath. He knew how Devin's mind

worked, step by meticulous step. He'd let Jared ramble, but he hadn't been fooled. "I had some business at the prison this morning."

"One of your clients not getting his full television rights?"

Jared set his coffee aside, linked his fingers. "You arrest them, I represent them. That's why it's called law and order."

"Right. How could I forget? So?"

"So. I had a meeting with the warden, and as he's aware that I'm Cassie's lawyer, he felt it reasonable to pass some news on to me."

Devin's mouth thinned. "Dolin."

"Yeah, Joe Dolin."

"He's not up for a parole hearing for another eighteen months." Devin knew the exact day, to the hour.

"That's right. It seems that after a difficult period of adjustment, during which Joe was a disciplinary problem, he's become a model prisoner."

"I'll bet."

Jared recognized the bitterness in the tone, understood it perfectly. "We know he's a bastard, Devin, but the point here is, he's playing the game. And he's playing it well."

"He won't make parole, not the first time at bat. I'll make sure of it."

"Parole's not the issue. Yet. He's been put on work release."

"The hell he has!"

"As of this week. I argued against it. I pointed out the fact that he'll be only a matter of miles from Cassie, his history of violence, his ties to the town." Feeling helpless, Jared unlinked his hands, held them palms up. "I got shot down. He'll be supervised, along with the rest of the crew.

We need the work release program, need the park and the roads cleaned and maintained, and this is a cheap way to handle it. Letting cooperative prisoners serve the community is a solid method of rehabilitation."

"And when they take a hike from trash detail?" Devin was pacing now, eyes fiery. "It happens. Two or three times a year, at least, it happens. I hauled one back myself last fall."

"It happens," Jared agreed. "They rarely get far. They're pretty easy to spot in the prison uniform, and most of them don't know the area."

"Dolin knows the damn area."

"You're not going to get any arguments from me. I'm going to fight it, Devin. But it's not going to be easy. Not when Cassie's own mother has been writing the warden in Joe's defense."

"That bitch." Devin's hands curled into fists. "She knows what he did to Cassie. Cassie," he repeated, and scrubbed his hands over his face. "She's just starting to pull things together. What the hell is this going to do to her?"

"I'm heading over there now to tell her."

"No." Devin dropped his hands. "I'll tell her. You go file papers, or whatever you have to do to turn this thing around. I want that son of a bitch locked up, twenty-four hours a day."

"They've got a crew out on 34 right now. Trash detail. He's on it."

"Fine." Devin headed for the door. "That's just fine."

It didn't take him long to get there, or to spot the bright orange vests of the road crew. Devin pulled to the shoulder behind a pickup truck where bags of trash were already heaped.

He got out of his car, leaned against the hood and watched Joe Dolin.

The sixteen months in prison hadn't taken off any of his bulk, Devin noted. He was a big man, thick, burly. He'd been going to fat before his arrest. From the look of him, he'd been busy turning that fat into muscle.

The prison system approved of physical fitness.

He and another man were unclogging the runoff on the other side of the road, working systematically and in silence as they gathered up dead leaves, litter.

Devin bided his time, waited until Joe straightened, hauled a plastic bag over his shoulder and turned.

Their eyes met, held. Devin wondered what the warden would say about rehabilitation if he'd seen that look in Joe's eyes. The heat and the hate. If he'd seen that slow, bitterly triumphant smile before Joe tossed the bag in the bed of the pickup parked on his side of the road.

Because he knew himself, Devin stayed where he was. He knew that if he got close, too close, he wouldn't be able to stop himself. The badge he wore was both a responsibility and a barrier.

If he was a civilian, he could walk across the road, ram his fists into Joe's leering face and take the consequences. If he was a civilian, he could pummel the wife-beating bastard into putty.

But he wasn't a civilian.

"Help you, Sheriff?" One of the supervisors walked over, ready to chat, officer to officer. His easy smile faded at the look in Devin's eyes. "Is there a problem?"

"Depends." Devin took out one of the cigarettes he'd been working on giving up for the past two months. Taking his time, he struck a match, lit it, blew out smoke. "You see that man there, the big one?"

"Dolin? Sure."

"You remember that name." Devin flicked his gaze down to the ID clipped to the supervisor's shirt. "And I'm going to remember yours, Richardson. If he gets away from you, even for a heartbeat, it's going to be your ass."

"Hey, look, Sheriff—"

Devin merely fixed his eyes on Richardson's face, kept them there as he pushed off the hood. "You make sure that son of a bitch doesn't wander into my town, Richardson. You make damn sure of it."

Joe watched the sheriff's car pull out, drive away. He bent his back to the work, like a good team player. And patted his pocket, where the latest letter from his mother-in-law was tucked.

He knew what it said, almost word for word. She kept him up with Cassie just fine. How the little bitch had a fancy job now at the MacKade Inn. Lousy MacKades. He was going to take care of all of them, every last one of them, when he got out.

But first he was going to take care of Cassie.

She thought she could have him tossed in a cell. She thought she could divorce him and start strutting her stuff around town. Well, she was going to think again, real soon.

Her mama was helping him out, writing him letters. They were preachy letters, and he couldn't stand the dried-up old bat, but she was helping him out. And he wrote her every week, telling her how he'd suffered, how he'd gotten religion, how he wanted to be with his family again. He made sure he went on about the kids.

He could have cared less about the kids. Whiny little brats.

It was Cassie he wanted. She was his wife—till death

do us part. He was going to be reminding her of that before too much longer.

He hauled another bag to the bed of the truck, tossed it in. Oh, yeah, he was going to remind her good, just like the old days. She would pay, in spades, for every hour he'd spent in a cell.

Curling his hand into a fist, he dreamed about his homecoming.

Chapter 3

Instead of going directly to Cassie, Devin went to the prison. He didn't doubt Jared's skill as a lawyer, but he wanted, needed, to add his weight. He forced himself to stay calm as he laid out the facts, and his opinion, to the warden.

For every protest he made, he was shown a report to offset it. Joe Dolin had indeed made himself into a model prisoner, one who showed every sign of rehabilitation. He worked hard, followed the rules, went to chapel regularly. He expressed regret over his crimes and kept up with his alcohol-abuse counseling.

When Devin left, he understood that the system he worked hard to uphold had just kicked him in the teeth. All he could do now was tell Cassie and try to reassure her.

He found her on her hands and knees in the parlor, polishing the carved wood of a gateleg table. She was so busy humming to herself, she hadn't heard him come in. She was wearing a white bib apron over her blouse and slacks, and had a plastic basket beside her filled with rags and cleaning tools.

Her wavy hair was tucked behind her ear to keep it from falling forward into her face. She'd been letting it grow some, he thought. It rippled just past her chin.

She looked so damn happy, Devin thought, and jammed his hands into his pockets.

"Cass?"

She jerked up, barely missed rapping her head on the table extension. Then blushed right to the hairline.

"Devin." She twisted her polishing rag in her hands as her nerves went into overdrive. She'd been replaying the dream in her head, the dream she'd had right here in the parlor, on the window seat. The dream where Devin had… Oh, my…

He stared at her, then stepped forward. She looked as though she'd been caught rifling the till. "What's wrong? What's the matter?"

"Nothing. Nothing." It seemed her stomach was suddenly full of bats, and she had to hold back a nervous giggle. "My mind was wandering, that's all." Was it ever. "And you startled me. That's all."

It wasn't like her to keep repeating herself, and his gaze narrowed. "Are you sure you're all right?"

"Yes, yes. Fine. Just fine." She scrambled to her feet, still twisting the rag. "The couple who are staying here went out to tour the battlefield. They're going to stay another night. They're from North Carolina. He's a battlefield junkie. That's what he said. I gave them all the pamphlets, and…and a tour of the house. They wanted to see all of it. They're excited about the idea of ghosts."

Puzzled, he nodded. She was babbling like a brook,

when he usually had to coax to get three sentences in a row out of her. "Okay."

"Do you want some coffee? I'll get you some coffee," she said, and started to bolt before he could answer. "And brownies. I made brownies this morning, and—" When he put a hand on her arm to stop her, she froze like a doe caught in headlights.

"Cassandra, relax."

"I am relaxed. I'm relaxed." His hand was firm, warm. She thought she could feel the texture of it through her skin, all the way to the bone.

"You're about to jump out of your shoes. Take a deep breath. Take a couple of them."

Obediently, she did, and felt some of the nerves settle. "I'm fine, Devin."

"Okay, we'll have some coffee." But even as he started to lead her out, his beeper went off. "Damn it." He strode to the candlestick phone on the gateleg to call in. "Mac-Kade. Yes, Donnie."

Devin pressed his fingers against his eyes. Where had the headache come from, and why the hell was Cassie staring at him as if he'd grown two pounding heads?

"I'm on a call now, Donnie. Handle it. That's what I said. Look, put the damn poodle in lockup, along with those idiot women, if you have to, but—" He broke off, cursed himself, knowing Donnie would do exactly that.

"Abort that. Be diplomatic, Donnie, and do your job. You're going to have to fine the poodle lady, but do it privately and professionally. Suggest a fence. Remind her that the leash law is there for her pup's safety, as well as the public's. There's traffic on that street, and her little dog could get himself squashed. When you've handled that, you go over to the complainant, tell her it's been dealt with and compliment her on her flowers. Suggest a fence. You know, how good fences make good neighbors. No, I didn't make that up. Go away, Donnie."

He hung up and turned to see Cassie smiling at him. "A small dog problem," he explained.

"You're so good at that, and knowing how to handle people and put things right."

"I'm a regular Solomon." He blew out a breath. "Sit down, Cassie. I need to talk to you."

"Oh." Her smile faded. "Something's wrong."

"Not necessarily. Come on, let's sit down." Because he wanted to be able to hold her hand when he told her, he chose the curvy settee that always made him feel like a clumsy giant. "I'm going to tell you first that there's nothing to worry about. That I don't want you to worry."

"It's about Joe." Her hand trembled once in his, then went still. "They let him out."

"No." He squeezed her hand gently, reassuringly, and kept his eyes steady on hers. "He's not going to be out of jail for a long time."

"He wants to see the children." She went dead pale, her eyes huge and dark and terrified. "Oh, God, Devin, the children."

"No." He cursed himself, knowing he was only making it worse by trying to cushion the blow. "It's nothing like that. It's the work release program. You know what that is."

"Yes, they let the prisoners out for a few hours to do jobs, community service. Oh." A single shudder escaped before she closed her eyes. "That's it."

"He's working on a road crew. Trash and litter pickup. That sort of thing. I wanted you to know, and not worry. I've arranged to be informed of his schedule. I'll know exactly where he is, and so will you. I don't want you driv-

ing by one day and seeing him on the side of the road and
getting scared."

"All right." The fear was there, but she could handle it.
She'd handled worse. "He's supervised."

"That's right." He wasn't going to bring up how often
they misplaced a prisoner. She'd know it already. "I'm going
to drive by, or have one of the men drive by, wherever he's
working, a couple of times a day. And, because I want you
to feel secure about this, we'll do drive-bys here, too."

And at the school, he thought, but he didn't want to bring
up the kids again.

"He's still in prison," she said, to reassure herself. "There
are guards."

"That's right. Jared's working on a protest, but I should
tell you— Damn it." He let out another breath. "Your mother's for it, and she's been writing to the warden."

"I knew that." Cassie squared her shoulders. "She and
Joe are writing each other. She's showed me his letters. It
doesn't make any difference, Devin. I'm never going back
to that. I'm never letting my children go back to that. We'll
be all right."

"You'll be fine." He was going to see to it. He tucked a
stray curl behind her ear, relieved that she didn't jolt. "I'm
sorry I scared you."

"You didn't. Not really."

"Anytime, Cassie, day or night, that you feel uncomfortable or uneasy, I want you to call me. You know I spend
most nights at the office. I can be here in five minutes if
you need me."

"I never feel uncomfortable or uneasy here. I'm hardly
ever alone." When he lifted a brow, she smiled. "Can't you
smell them?"

"The roses? Yeah." Now he smiled. "Still, I'm usually better company than a ghost. You call me."

"All right." She had to draw together all her courage. A point had to be proved. He was her friend, always had been. She had to stop being a trembling little mouse. "Thank you." She made herself smile, then laid a hand on his cheek, and touched her lips to his.

He barely tasted her, but the explosion ripped through his system like napalm. It was so unexpected, so long desired. He didn't realize his hand had tightened like a vise on her fingers, making her eyes go wide with shock. All he knew was that her lips had been on his, just for an instant.

And he couldn't stand it.

He dragged her against him, and captured that taste again, devoured it, steeped himself in it. Warm, sweet. The shape of her mouth, that deep dip, drove him crazy. He crushed it under his, traced it with a frantic tongue, then dived deep to plunder.

His heart was thundering, wild surf against jagged rocks. His blood was racing, making his head buzz. She was everything soft and small and sweet, everything he craved, everything he cherished.

It took him several desperate moments to realize her hands were trapped between them. And she was rigid in his arms. Stunned, he let her go and leaped up in one frenzied motion.

And she stared at him, eyes dark as rain clouds, one hand lifted to lie against the mouth he'd just savaged.

That was the word for it, he thought, disgusted. Savaged.

"I'm sorry." He was as pale now as she was flushed, and cursing himself viciously. "I'm sorry," he said again. "I'm... sorry. I didn't mean to— You caught me off guard." There was no excuse, he reminded himself, and his punishment for breaking her trust would be the losing of it. "That was way out of line, and it won't happen again. I don't know what I was thinking of. I have to go."

"Devin—"

"I have to go," he repeated, almost desperately, as he backed up. He nearly tripped over a table, decided that would have capped things off nicely. Because she hadn't moved an inch, he was able to escape without further humiliating himself.

She listened to the door slamming behind him. No, she hadn't moved, because she couldn't. She didn't think it would be wise to try to stand just yet.

What had just happened here? she asked herself. She had kissed him, thinking it was time she was able to make that friendly gesture.

Rafe kissed her all the time. When he came by the inn for something, he often kissed her, just the way she'd tried to kiss Devin. Lightly, casually. And after a while, she'd gotten used to it, and she no longer stiffened up.

Then Devin had kissed her. But he didn't kiss like Rafe at all. No, not at all. She still had her fingers against her lips, and could still feel the heat there. No, she'd never been kissed like that before, by anyone. As if the man's life had depended on it. She'd never imagined Devin...

Oh, but she had, she remembered, letting her unsteady hand fall into her lap. She had imagined, just the night before. Had she dreamed her way into this?

What had happened here was certainly reality. Her heart was pounding still, and her skin was hot. She'd been so shocked by what he'd done, the way he'd grabbed her, the way his mouth had covered hers, she hadn't been able to move.

How long had it lasted? Thirty seconds, a minute? She

couldn't say, but so much had happened inside her. She was still shaky from it.

He'd been sorry. Of course he had, she thought, and leaned back, closed her eyes and tried to catch her breath. He hadn't meant to kiss her. It had just been some sort of spontaneous reaction. A male reaction. Then he'd found her lacking and let her go. Apologized. He was a good and honorable man, and he'd apologized for doing something he hadn't really meant to do.

It was just a kiss, she reminded herself, but had to press a hand to her jittery stomach. Now she'd spoiled things, because she hadn't been able to shrug it off, or laugh it off like a normal woman. Any more than she'd been able to respond to him and make him want to kiss her again.

She would make an effort, Cassie ordered herself, to behave as though nothing had happened. The very next time she saw him, she would smile and make natural conversation. She was getting better at those things. She simply couldn't bear it if they couldn't be friends anymore.

She got up on still-wobbly legs to finish her polishing. And didn't think of Joe Dolin at all.

Devin worked like a fiend the rest of the day and all of the next. He drove his deputies insane, and drove out to the farm to extend the same courtesy to his younger brother.

Of course, he told himself he'd come out to work. There were crops to be tended, and several of the cows that hadn't yet calved were due to drop. He found his services welcomed when one of the cows delivered breech.

By the time it was over and the new calf was teetering on its spindly legs, Devin was a mess. His shirt was ruined, his arm was bruised from being contracted inside the cow's birth canal. And he stank.

In the stall, Shane was equally dirty, and he was whistling cheerfully as he administered inoculations to the annoyed baby. "There you go, pal. That didn't hurt much."

Disgusted, Devin stared at him. It had been a hard, messy job, and it wasn't over. The stall would have to be cleaned out and fresh hay spread, and the calf would need watching for the next couple of hours.

And there was Shane, kneeling in the muck, happy as a fool.

He'd been letting his hair grow lately, Devin noted, and he'd pulled a tail of it through the opening in the back of his grimy cap. His green eyes, shades paler than Devin's, were dreamy, and his mouth was curved next to his dimple. He was sinfully good-looking, even for a MacKade. And he was the baby of the family, even younger than Devin, which meant that his older brothers had been honor-bound to kick his butt well and often.

As he continued to whistle, Devin gave serious thought to doing so now. "What the hell are you so happy about?"

"Nice healthy calf, from the look of him." Despite the calf's strong objections, Shane was holding him still and examining his eyes and ears. "Mama's doing fine now. What's not to be happy about?"

"She damn near broke my arm."

"She couldn't help it," Shane said reasonably. "Besides, I told you I'd take that end. You insisted."

"Yeah, right. This place is a mess."

"Birthing's not neat." Shane stood and rubbed his filthy hands on his equally filthy jeans. He stepped out of the stall and leaned against the open door. "Besides, I thought this might sweat the mood out of you." His grin was cocky, confident—all the more reason for Devin to want to punch it in. "Women trouble, right?"

"I don't have women trouble."

"That's 'cause you don't have any women—which, I might add, is an embarrassment to all of us. Why don't you take one of mine? I've got plenty."

Devin answered the suggestion with the crude and expected response before he stepped over to the sink to wash his hands.

"No, really. You know who I think would be good for you? Frannie Spader. She's got all this red hair that just sort of tumbles all over the place, and the cutest smile. And when you get past the hair and the smile, she's got a body that can make a man whimper. I don't think you've done nearly enough whimpering lately."

"I'll pick my own women. I don't need your damn cast-offs."

"Just being brotherly." He slapped Devin on the back before reaching for the soap. "Of course, if you weren't so damn brotherly yourself, you could probably be making time with little Cassie—"

It was a tribute to Devin's speed, and Shane's innocence, that the blow caught Shane solidly on the jaw and sent him flying. He landed hard, shook his head. Before he could ask Devin what the devil had gotten into him, he was assaulted by a hundred and seventy-five pounds of furious, frustrated male.

They were well matched, knew each other's moves and rhythms. The barn echoed with grunts, the smack of flesh against bone, curses, as they rolled over the dusty concrete floor.

"Oh, for heaven's sake."

The female voice, and the disdain in it, didn't register on either of the combatants. Shane dropped his guard just long enough to be rewarded with a split lip, and answered it by bloodying Devin's nose.

"But, darling, it looks like they've just gotten started."

"I mean it, Rafe." With a heavy sigh, Regan MacKade shifted the gurgling baby on her hip. "Break it up."

"Women," he muttered. But he would break it up his way, which was to dive into the fray, and get in a few licks of his own. Knowing he couldn't enjoy himself for long, he managed to shove Shane aside and sit on Devin.

"Stay out of this." Swiping at blood, Shane hauled himself to his knees. "It's between him and me."

"Maybe I will." Rafe was having quite a bit of trouble holding Devin down. To prove he meant to, he covered Devin's grimy face with the flat of his hand and gave it enough of a shove to have his head rapping against the concrete. "And maybe I want to play," he added. "What's it about?"

"Ask him." Already cooling off, Shane flexed his sore hand. "I was just talking to him, and he punched me."

"Well, I want to punch you half the time you're talking to me," Rafe said reasonably, and looked down to see that Devin's eyes were clearing. He hadn't meant to rap his brother's head quite that hard. "What were you talking to him about?"

"Stuff. Women."

Devin's vision was coming back, and so was his temper. He started to heave Rafe aside when Regan's firm, no-nonsense voice stopped him.

"That's just enough of this ridiculous behavior, Devin. You should be ashamed of yourself."

Still on top of him, Rafe looked down and grinned. "Yeah, Dev, you should be ashamed of yourself."

"Get the hell off me."

"You going to be a good boy?" With a laugh, Rafe leaned over and kissed him. He was quick, and agile, and sprang away before Devin could retaliate.

"A fine thing," Regan said from the doorway of the barn, making Devin think twice about jumping Shane again. She stood there in tailored slacks and a crisp spring blazer, a wide-eyed baby on her hip, a polished leather shoe tapping. "Wrestling in the barn like a couple of bad-tempered boys. Look at the two of you—you're filthy, bloody, and your clothes are torn."

"He started it." Wisely, Shane held back a laugh, and tried to look humble. "Honest, Regan, I was just defending myself."

"I'm not interested in who started it," Regan said regally, and deflated her brother-in-law with one snippy look. "I believe we were invited to dinner."

"Oh, yeah." Shane had forgotten about that. "We had a little trouble with a birthing. Breech calf. We just got finished."

"Oh." Instantly Regan was all concern. Tossing back a curtain of honey-brown hair, she hurried inside. "Is it all right?"

"Just dandy. Hey, Nate."

"No, you don't." Even as the cooing baby held out his arms to his uncle, Regan turned aside. "You're filthy. The two of you go clean up."

Devin eyed Shane narrowly, then hissed out a breath. "I felt like pounding somebody. You were available. You also have a big mouth."

Shane dabbed at the blood on his lip. "You sucker-punched me."

"So?"

"So I owe you one."

"That's it, boys, kiss and make up."

When both Shane and Devin turned on Rafe, Regan gritted her teeth. "Stop right there. If nobody punches anyone else, I'll cook dinner."

"Good deal," Shane decided.

"But you're not coming in the kitchen until... What's that noise?"

"What noise?" Devin unclenched his ready fist and listened. The whimpering sound was soft, barely audible over little Nate's babbling. Homing in on it, he strode halfway down the barn and looked into another stall. "Looks like it's the day for birthing. Ethel's having her babies."

"Ethel." Like a frantic papa, Shane bolted down the barn, and all but fell into the stall beside his laboring pet. "Oh, honey, why didn't you call me? Jeez, she's already had two."

"Fred's probably out passing out cigars." At the entrance to the stall, Rafe leaned over and kissed his wife, then his son. "I know just how he feels."

Seeing the panic in Shane's eyes, Devin shook his head. They'd witnessed or assisted in countless births with the stock over the years, but that meant nothing now. This was Ethel, and she was as close to a true love as Shane had ever known. He stepped in, crouched down beside his brother.

"She's doing fine." He hooked an arm over Shane's shoulders.

"You think?"

"Sure. She's a MacKade, isn't she?" Devin glanced up at Regan and winked. "MacKade women are the best there is."

After the birthing, the cleaning up, the cooking and the celebrating of Fred and Ethel's six healthy puppies, Devin drove back to the office. He was too restless to stay at the farm. Though he had taken a long, soaking bath to soothe out the worst of the aches his scuffle with Shane had caused, he still wasn't able to fully relax.

He slowed down as he passed the inn, saw lights shining on the second and third floors. Grimly he punched the gas again and headed into town.

She wasn't going to forgive him easily, he thought. He wasn't going to forgive himself. He'd acted like a maniac. He'd been rough and demanding when she deserved, and should have expected, a gentle touch.

No wonder she'd looked at him as though he'd lost his mind, her eyes round in shock, her soft, pretty mouth trembling.

He'd make it up to her somehow, eventually. He knew how to bide his time, didn't he? He'd been waiting for her nearly half his life already.

Joe Dolin was also biding his time. His cell was dark, but he wasn't sleeping. He was planning. He knew most people thought he wasn't very smart, but he was going to show them, all of them, soon. He'd learned how to play the game, to say what the guards and the psychiatrists and the fat-faced warden wanted to hear. He'd learned how to act as they wanted him to act.

He could be humble. He could be repentant. He could be anything he had to be. As long as it got him out.

Devin MacKade thought he'd proved something, driving by the work site, flashing his badge. Oh, he owed Devin MacKade. Big-time. He hadn't forgotten the way Devin had come after him, had cuffed him and tossed him into a cell. No, he hadn't forgotten what he owed Devin. There would be payback.

But Cassie would come first, because he owed her most of all. Everything would have been fine if she'd stayed in her place. But she'd gone whining to MacKade, sniveling about their personal business.

A man had a right to punish his wife, to give her the back of his hand or let her feel his fist when she needed it. And Cassie had needed it a lot. She still did.

No fancy divorce papers changed that. She was his wife, his property, and he was going to be reminding her of that before too much longer.

Till death do us part, he thought, and smiled into the dark.

Chapter 4

Parade day was a tactical nightmare. That was to be expected. Over and above his usual reasons, Devin was looking forward to it, because it would keep him too busy to think about any personal problems.

The parade would kick off at twelve sharp—which meant anytime between noon and twelve-thirty—with the usual speeches at the square and the ceremonial laying of the wreath at the memorial.

As sheriff, he was required to be there, in full uniform. He could handle it. There were only a handful of days out of the year when he had to drag out the dress khakis and tie and shiny black shoes.

Of course, that meant dragging out the ironing board, as well, which he hated. It was the only domestic chore he truly despised, and the only one that jittered his nerves.

But by 8:00 a.m. he was pressed and dressed and out on the street. Already there were eager beavers claiming their spots, holding spaces along the curbs and sidewalks for others with lawn chairs and coolers.

Most of the storefronts and shops along the parade route were closed for the day, but he could count on Ed's being open for breakfast.

He sauntered down the sidewalk, knowing he had the best part of an hour before he had to worry about crowd control or making certain the concessionaires were in their proper places with their balloons and hot dogs and ice cream.

Summer had decided to make its debut on parade day. It was already hot, and he tugged irritably at his collar.

He imagined the tar on the street would be soft and melting by afternoon. He hoped the little girls who did their tumbles and cartwheels in their spangled uniforms were prepared.

He made a note to make certain there was plenty of water along the route for the marchers. He didn't want anybody fainting on him.

It might be a holiday, but Ed's was doing a brisk business. He could smell ham frying, coffee brewing. The scent reminded him that he'd been off his feed for the past couple of days.

After exchanging a few greetings with patrons in booths, he sidled up to the counter and took a stool.

"Sheriff." Ed winked at him. As usual, her rhinestone glasses were dangling on a pearl-studded chain against her scrawny chest. She wore a splattered apron, but beneath it she was ready for the celebration in a snug, midriff-baring top as red as her hair, and shorts that barely met the limits of the law.

She had bright blue shadow all the way up to her penciled brows, and her mouth was stop-sign red. Poppies dangled from her ears and were pinned to her apron.

Devin grinned at her. Only Edwina Crump could get away with an outfit like that.

"Ham and eggs, Ed, and keep the coffee coming."

"You got it, sweetie." Though she was old enough to be his mother, she fluffed her hair and flirted. "Don't you look handsome in your uniform!"

"I feel like an aging Boy Scout," he grumbled.

"One of my first beaus was a Boy Scout." She wiggled her brows as she took the clear plastic top off a plate of doughnuts and chose one for him. "He was surely prepared, let me tell you. On the house," she added, casting a sharp eye over her two scrambling waitresses.

She left Devin with his coffee and doughnut before heading back into the kitchen.

He tried not to brood, really. To keep himself sane, he set his clipboard on the counter and read over his notes and itinerary. A half hour later, he was doing some fine-tuning and trying to enjoy Ed's very excellent ham and eggs.

"Hi there, Sheriff. Locked anybody up lately?"

He swiveled on the stool and looked into the stunning and not altogether friendly face of his sister-in-law. Savannah MacKade always made a statement, Devin thought. When that lush siren's body sauntered into a room, men's hearts stopped. There was all that thick black hair falling past her shoulders, those almond-shaped eyes the color of sinful chocolate and those ice-edged cheekbones against gold-dust skin.

And there was, Devin mused, all that attitude.

"As a matter of fact, no, not lately." He grinned at the boy beside her—his nephew, whether Savannah liked it or not. Tall for his age, and as dark and handsome as his mama, Bryan was sporting his baseball uniform and fielder's cap. "Riding in the parade today?"

"Yeah. Me and Con and the guys are riding in the coach's pickup. It'll be cool."

"Kind of early, aren't you?"

"We had some things to pick up," Savannah supplied. "Including Connor. We're on our way to get him as soon as Bryan here fills his stomach."

"I'm starving," the boy claimed and, eyeing the plate of doughnuts, he leaped onto the stool beside Devin.

"Hey, Ed, you got a starving boy out here."

"I'm coming." She slapped the swinging door of the kitchen open and strolled out. Her grin flashed at Bryan. "Well, it's my champ." As sponsor of the Antietam Cannons, Ed preened with pride. "Hell of a game Saturday." She saluted Savannah, leaned over the counter long enough to coo at the baby in the stroller, then fell into a deep and serious discussion with Bryan about food and baseball.

Devin didn't ask. He'd be damned if he would. He slid off the stool long enough to pick up his niece, then settled back down with the wide-eyed Layla on his lap.

Beneath the frilly sun hat, Layla's hair curled thick and dark. Her mouth—her mother's mouth, Devin mused—was serious as she watched him out of big eyes that were already easing from birth blue to MacKade green.

"Hello, beautiful." He bent over to kiss her, and was pleased to see that pretty mouth curve. "She smiled at me."

"Gas."

Devin looked up into Savannah's bland eyes. "The hell it is. She smiled at me. She loves me. Don't you, Layla? Don't you, darling?" He traced a finger over her hand until she gripped it. "She's got MacKade eyes."

"They're still changing," Savannah claimed. But she was softening. Despite the badge, and the fact that she tried to resist him, she grew fonder of Devin every day. "They might turn brown."

"Nah. MacKade eyes." He looked up again, smiled at her. "You're stuck with them. With us."

"Apparently."

His grin only widened. He knew she liked him, no matter how cool she tried to be. "Want a doughnut?"

"Maybe." She gave up and slid onto a stool. "You don't have to hold her."

"I want to hold her. Where's Jared?"

"Doing some lawyer thing. He's going to meet us at the inn about nine-thirty."

"So, you haven't been by yet," Devin said casually, very casually, as he shifted Layla to his shoulder and rubbed her back.

"No." Savannah bent down to take a cloth from the stroller and smoothed it over Devin's shoulder. "I nursed her right before we left. She's liable to spit up all over that pretty cop suit."

"Then I wouldn't have to wear it. You're just picking up Connor?"

"Mmm-hmm…" With an expert's eye, Savannah selected her own doughnut. "Rafe and Regan are swinging by later to get Cassie and Emma. Shane's going to drive Jared in so we don't have so many cars when we head to the park for the picnic."

She glanced over, saw that her son was well on his way to demolishing the two doughnuts Ed had given him. "You angling for a ride?"

"No. I've got to take the cruiser so I can pretend I'm working."

"I didn't see you at the game Saturday."

"I swung by for a couple of innings." He'd spotted Cassie

in the stands, and he hadn't wanted to make her uncomfortable.

"You didn't make it to Sunday dinner yesterday at the farm."

"Did you miss me?"

"Not particularly." But there was something in his eyes that wiped the sneer off her face. "Is something wrong, Devin?"

"No."

"Jared told me about Joe Dolin, the work release. It's bothering you."

"That's a mild term for it. I'm keeping my eye on him," he murmured, and turned his face into Layla's sweet-smelling neck to nuzzle.

"I'll bet you are," Savannah murmured. She brushed a hand over her daughter's head, then let it rest on Devin's shoulder in a gesture of affection and support that surprised both of them.

"Am I growing on you, Savannah?"

She let her hand drop, but the corners of her mouth quirked up. "Like you said, I'm stuck with you. Now give me my kid."

Devin settled Layla in her mother's arms, then kissed Savannah, firm and quick, on the mouth. "See you. See you, Bry," he added as he rose.

Bryan mumbled something, hampered by a mouthful of apple-filled doughnut.

"Damn MacKades," Savannah said under her breath. But she was smiling as she watched Devin stride away.

By noon, the town was bursting at the seams. People crowded the sidewalks and spilled over porches and front yards. Kids raced everywhere at once, and the bawling of fretful babies rose through the air like discordant music.

Several streets were barricaded to keep the parade route clear. Devin posted himself at the main intersection so that he could soothe travelers who had forgotten about parade day, or were from far enough out of town that they'd never heard of it.

He offered alternate routes, or invitations to park and join the festivities.

The two-way radio hitched to his belt belched and squawked with static or calls from deputies placed at distant points along the route.

Across the street from him, at the corner of the gas station, a clown sold colorful balloons. Half a block down, ice cream and snow cones were big sellers. They melted in the heat almost as soon as they were passed from hand to hand.

Devin looked at the wrappers, the spills, the bits of broken toys and balloons. Cleanup was going to be a bitch.

Then, in the distance, he heard the first of the marching bands approaching the square. The brassy music, the *click-clack* of booted feet, had his practical frame of mind shifting into the pleasures of his youth.

What the hell—there was just nothing like a parade.

"Officer! Officer!"

Resigned, Devin turned back to the barricade, where another car had pulled up. With one look, he summed up the middle-aged couple in the late-model sedan as hot, frazzled and annoyed.

"Yes, ma'am." He leaned down to the open window and gave them his best public-servant smile. "What can I do for you?"

"We have to get through here." The driver's irritated tone carried the flavor of the North that went with his Pennsylvania tags.

"I told you not to get off the highway, George. You just had to take the scenic route."

"Be quiet, Marsha. We have to get through," he said again.

"Well, now." Devin ran his hand over his chin. "The problem here is that we've got a parade going on." To prove it, the marching band let out a blare of trumpets, a boom of drums. Devin pitched his voice over the din. "We won't be able to open this road for another hour."

That sparked a heated domestic argument, demands, accusations. Devin kept the easy smile on his face. "Where y'all headed?"

"D.C."

"Well, I'll tell you what you can do, if you're in a hurry. You turn around and head straight up this road for about five miles. You're going to see signs to route 70. Take the eastbound. You'll hit the Washington Beltway—that's 495—in just about an hour."

"I told you not to get off the highway," Marsha said again.

George huffed. "How was I supposed to know some little one-horse town would block off the streets?"

"If you're not in a hurry," Devin continued, calm as a lake, "you can turn around and pull into that field where there's a sign for parking. It's free. We got a nice parade here." He glanced over as a junior majorette tossed up her baton and snagged it, to the forceful applause of the crowd. "I can give you a nice, pretty route into D.C."

"I haven't got time for any damn parade." Puffing out his cheeks, George slapped the sedan in Reverse. Devin could hear them arguing as he jockeyed the car into a turn and headed off.

"Ain't that a shame..." Devin muttered, and turned,

nearly knocking Cassie over. He grabbed her instinctively, then let her go as if her skin had burned his hands. "Sorry. Didn't see you."

"I thought I should wait until you'd finished being diplomatic."

"Yeah. George and Marsha don't know what they're missing."

Smiling, she watched the senior majorettes twirl and tumble. But in her mind she was still seeing Devin in his uniform. So competent and male. "I know. You must be hot. Would you like me to get you a drink?"

"No, I'm fine. Ah…" His tongue was in knots. He didn't know the last time he'd seen her in shorts. And over the years he'd done his best not to think about her legs. Now here they were, all long and smooth, showcased by neat little cuffed shorts the color of plums. "Where's Emma?"

"She's made friends with the little McCutcheon girl, Lucy. They're in her yard." It was easier to talk to him if she wasn't looking at him, so Cassie concentrated on the slow-moving convertible and its passenger, the waving and flouncily dressed current agriculture princess. "Are you angry with me, Devin?"

"No, of course not." He stared so hard at the princess that she flashed him a brilliant, hopeful smile, and a very personal wave. But it was Cassie he saw, looking shocked and delicate. And beautiful.

"You've flustered Julie," Cassie murmured, noting the exchange.

"Julie? Who's Julie?"

Her quick laugh surprised them both. Then they were staring at each other. "Are you sure you're not mad?"

"No. Yes. Yes, I'm sure." He jammed his hands into his

pockets, where they would be safe. "Not at you. At me. Like I said, I was out of line the other day."

"I didn't mind."

The blare of the next band rang in his ears. He was sure he hadn't heard her correctly. "Excuse me?"

"I said I—" She broke off when his two-way squawked.

"Sheriff. Sheriff, this here's Donnie. We got a little situation down in quadrant C. You there, Sheriff?"

"Quadrant C, my butt," Devin muttered. "He's at the elementary school. Watching too many *Dragnet* reruns."

"I'll let you go," Cassie said quickly as he whipped out his two-way. "You're busy."

"If you'd—" He cursed again, because she was already hurrying through the cheering crowd. "MacKade," he snapped into the receiver.

The little situation turned out to be a harmless brawl between overly loyal students at rival high schools. Devin broke it up, snarled at Donnie, then helped a mother deal with her terrified daughter, who had lost her breakfast over the idea of twirling her baton in public.

By the time the last marching boot clicked, the last flag waved and the last balloon drifted into the sky, he had to oversee the traffic headed for the park and the cleanup detail, and help a couple of weeping lost children find their way back to Mama.

He took his time cooling off under the stingy spray of his office shower, then gratefully retired his uniform until the next official event. By the time he made it to the park and snuck the cruiser in behind a trail of cars, the picnic, with its grilling food and boisterous games, was well under way.

There was softball, horseshoes, pitching contests, egg-throwing contests, three-legged races. He saw Shane nuzzling Frannie Spader, the curvy redhead he had so generously offered Devin a few days before.

There was Rafe, stepping up to bat, and Jared winding up to pitch. Regan and Savannah were spread out in the shade with their babies.

There were dogs and kids, big-bellied men sitting in lawn chairs, discussing sports and politics, old women fanning themselves and laughing. There was Cy, the town mayor, looking ridiculous as always, sporting a pair of violently checkered Bermuda shorts that exposed far too much of his hairy legs.

Mrs. Metz was shouting encouragement to her grandchildren, gnawing on a chicken leg and gossiping with Miss Sarah Jane.

Good God, Devin thought, he really loved them. All of them.

He wandered over the grass, stopping here and there to chat or listen to a complaint or a snippet of news. With his hands tucked in his back pockets he watched solemnly with old Mr. Wineburger as horseshoes were tossed and clanged against the pole.

He was debating different techniques of horseshoe pitching when Emma came up quietly and held out her arms. He picked her up, settled her on his hip while Wineburger wheezed out opinions. But Devin's mind had begun to wander.

Little Emma smelled like sunshine and was as tiny as a fairy. But she was nearly seven now, he recalled with a jolt. Soon she wouldn't want to be picked up and held. She would, like the young girls he saw over at the edge of the field, be flirting with young boys, want to be left alone to experiment with being female.

He sighed and gave her a quick squeeze.

"How come you're sad?" she wanted to know.

"I'm not. I'm just thinking that you're growing up on me. How about a snow cone?"

"Okay. A purple one."

"A purple one," he agreed, and set her down. Hands linked, they walked toward the machine manned by the American Legion. He bought two, then settled down with her on the grass to watch the softball match.

"Come on, Dev!" From his position at second, Rafe shouted to his brother. "Batter up!"

"I'm not moving. I've got me a pretty girl here," he shouted back.

"Mama says I'm pretty, too."

He smiled at Emma, ruffled her hair. "That's because you are."

"Mama's pretty."

"She sure is."

Emma cuddled closer, knowing his arm would come around her, just the way she liked it. "She hardly ever cries anymore." In her innocence, she licked at the snow cone and didn't notice the way Devin's arm went taut. "She used to cry all the time, at nighttime. But now she doesn't."

"That's good" was all Devin could manage.

"And we got to have Ed the kitten, and a brand-new house, and nobody yells and breaks things or hits Mama now. Connor gets to play baseball and write stories, and I can have Lucy come right to my room to play. I've got pretty curtains, too, with puppies on them. And new shoes."

She wiggled her pink sneakers for Devin's benefit.

"They're very nice."

"It's 'cause you made him go away, the bad man. Connor said you arrested him and sent him to jail and now he can't hit Mama and make her cry." She looked up at him, her mouth circled with sticky purple, her eyes wide and clear. "I love you."

"Oh, Emma…" Undone, he lowered his brow to her soft golden curls. "I love you, too. You're my best girl."

"I know." She puckered her purple lips and planted a sticky kiss on his cheek. "I'm going to get Lucy now. She's my very best friend." She got to her feet, smiled her mother's soft smile. "Thank you for the snow cone."

"You're welcome."

He watched her dance off, pretty as a pixie, then rubbed his hands over his face. It was hard enough being in love with the mother. What the hell was he going to do with this need for the child?

Was he going to have to settle—always—for protecting, for watching over, for being the dependable friend, the favored honorary uncle?

He was getting damn sick of it, of holding in, of holding back.

This time, when Rafe called out, Devin got to his feet. Yeah, he thought, he'd batter up, all right. God knew he needed to hit something.

There was something intrinsically satisfying about smacking a little white ball with a slim wooden bat. It was the connection, the way the power of it sang up the arms. It was the sound, the solid crack, the whoosh of air, the rising cheers as the ball lifted.

He was feeling human by the time he rounded third and headed for home. More than human, since it turned out to be Shane guarding the plate. His lips peeled back in a feral grin matching his brother's as he went into a hard, bruising headfirst slide.

There was the brutal collision of flesh and bone, the swirl of choking dust, the hysterical screams of fans and teammates. He heard Shane grunt as his elbow whipped around to catch his brother in the ribs, beside the padded catcher's vest. He saw stars as some bony part, probably Shane's knee, caught him beside the ear.

But what he heard over it all was the glorifying call of "Safe!"

"I'll be damned." Shane had managed to hold on to the ball that Jared had bulleted to him, even after the nasty collision. "I tagged the sucker," Shane insisted, waving the ball for emphasis.

Cy, the umpire, hung tough. "You weren't on the plate, Shane. Devin was. You didn't get the tag in time."

That, of course, was tantamount to a declaration of war.

From the sidelines, Savannah watched the very polished attorney Jared MacKade go nose-to-nose with the town's mayor, while her brothers-in-law shouted at each other, and anyone else who happened to get in the way.

"I love picnics," Savannah commented.

"Mmm… Me, too." Regan stretched her arms. "They're so relaxing." She smiled up at Cassie, who stepped under the shade with them. "Don't worry," she said, noting the way Cassie hugged her arms. "They won't hurt each other. Very much."

"I know." She tried not to be so poor-spirited. The MacKades were always yelling. But she hugged herself tighter when she saw Connor and Bryan race up to get a piece of the action.

"Don't worry," Regan said again.

"No, I won't."

It was good, wasn't it, that Connor could race and shout that way? He'd been too quiet for too long. Too worried, she thought guiltily. He was coming into himself more and more every day. And if picking sides over a baseball call made him happy, then no, she wouldn't let herself worry.

It was over soon enough, with vows of revenge and retaliation. She watched Bryan do a victory boogie, then nag until he was allowed up to the plate. Devin picked up a mitt, bent over and said something that had Connor goggling with pleasure. Her son raced into the outfield and joined the game.

"He's awfully good with children," Cassie murmured. "Devin," she added.

"Every time he comes by the house, he has Nate on his hip the minute he steps through the door." Regan smiled down at her son, who was busy chewing on a bright red teething ring. "He's bleeding."

Alarmed, Cassie looked down at Nate. "Where?"

"No, I meant Devin. His mouth's bleeding. Anyone got a tissue?"

"I do." Cassie pulled one out of her pocket.

As she hurried over to where Devin was walking to the outfield, Regan grinned. "She hasn't figured it out yet, has she?"

"Nope." Savannah leaned back against the tree. Layla was napping, and that seemed like a wonderful idea. "He's going to have to do something a little more obvious for her to realize he's crazy about her."

"He's the only MacKade I know who moves slow."

Savannah arched a brow before she closed her eyes. "I'll bet he moves fast enough when the time comes. Cassie won't have a chance."

"No," Regan said softly. "She'll have the best chance of her life."

Out of breath from the effort of catching up with his long strides, Cassie called out, "Devin! Wait a minute!"

He glanced around, saw her rushing after him and did what he'd trained himself to do. He put his hands in his pockets. "What?"

"Your mouth. Gosh, you must be all leg," she managed, puffing, when she stopped in front of him.

"My mouth?"

"It's bleeding." In practiced maternal gestures, she dabbed at the corner of his mouth. "I saw you dive headfirst into Shane. I had to close my eyes. You're lucky you only cut your lip doing something that crazy. It's only a game."

"It's baseball," he reminded her, and struggled not to groan as her fingers gently soothed the wound he hadn't even been aware of. "I got the run."

"Yes, I know. I'm learning all the rules and terms. RBIs and ERAs. Connor's so excited about playing. It was sweet of you to let him go into left field."

"Right. Right field," Devin managed as his heart jitter-bugged in his chest. He kept his hands balled into fists in his pockets. "Cassie, I'm fine."

It was the tone, the sharp impatience in it, that had her stopping. "You are mad at me."

"I'm not mad at you. Damn it, I'm not mad. Look." Frustrated beyond belief, he snatched the blood-spotted tissue from her hands. "What's this?"

"It's blood. I told you your mouth—"

"Blood," he said, interrupting her. "That's what I've got in my veins. Blood, not ice water. So if you're going to keep leaning up against me and putting your hands on my face, I—" He cut himself off, clenched his teeth. "I'm not mad," he said, more calmly. "I need to take a walk."

Cassie gnawed at her lip as he strode away into the little grove of trees that lined the east side of the park. The idea of losing his friendship gave her all the courage she needed to follow him.

He stopped, turned, and the heat in his eyes was like an arrow in her heart. "I'm sorry," she said quickly. "I'm sorry, Devin."

"Don't say you're sorry to me, Cassie, you have nothing to apologize for." Where the hell was everybody? he asked himself. Why weren't there people in the grove? He couldn't risk being alone with her now, when he didn't have himself under complete control. "Go on back, Cassie. Go on, now."

She started to. It was second nature for her to do as she was told. But she couldn't, not this time. Not when it was so important. "If you're not mad, then you're upset. I don't want to be the cause of that."

It was hard, almost terrifying, to step forward, when there was still temper simmering in his eyes. She knew he wouldn't hurt her, of course she knew, but there was a part of her that couldn't be entirely sure. But for Devin she'd risk it.

"It's because I kissed you," she blurted out. "I didn't mean anything by it."

The temper drained from his eyes. They were blank now, carefully blank. "I know you didn't."

"You kissed me back." Her heart was pounding so hard she could barely hear herself speak. "You said you were angry with yourself for doing it, but I don't want you to be. I didn't mind."

"You didn't mind," he repeated, spacing out the words. "Okay. We'll put it aside. Go on back now."

"Why did you kiss me like that?" The words ended on a whisper as her courage began to flag.

"Like I told you, you caught me off guard." When she only continued to stare at him with those big, soft eyes, he felt something snap. "Damn it, what do you want from me? I apologized, didn't I? I said it wouldn't happen again. I'm trying to stay away from you, and it's killing me. I've waited to kiss you for twelve years, and when I do I practically eat you alive. I didn't mean to hurt you."

Her knees were starting to shake, but it didn't feel like fear. She knew fear well enough to recognize it. But whatever this was that was working through her was unfamiliar.

"You didn't hurt me." She had to swallow. "I didn't mind. I don't mind."

He was trying to get a bead on her, but wasn't sure of his aim. "I want to kiss you again."

"I don't mind," she repeated, because it was the best she could do.

She didn't move as he stepped toward her, had no idea if she should touch him. She would have liked to run her hands up those arms, they were so strong. But she wasn't sure.

Then she didn't have to worry, or think, or try to guess. He laid his hands on her cheeks, framing her face, and lowered his mouth to hers, so gently, so patiently.

Her heart fluttered, and the sensation was sweet, like something flying silently out of a cage when the door has been opened unexpectedly. When he drew her closer, just a little closer, she thought she floated toward him. Her lips parted on a sigh of quiet wonder.

This was what he meant to do, always. Show her tenderness and care. Let himself slide into her, slowly, gently. The dappled shade was perfect, sweetened by the call of birds and the tang of wildflowers.

This was what he'd meant to do, he thought hazily, and deepened the kiss with patient skill until she sighed again.

And all the years he'd waited and wanted seemed like minutes, now that she was here, with him.

The sound of the shouts and laughter from the field beyond was like the buzz of happy bees in her head. She didn't realize she'd lifted her hands, curled them around his wrists, until she felt the strong quick beat of his pulse against her fingers. She held on as lovely colors began to revolve in her head, as the kiss went on and on, spinning out time.

He didn't let her go until her hands had slipped weakly from his wrists to fall to her sides.

Her eyes were still closed when he lifted his head, when he moved his hands from her face to her shoulders. As he watched, she pressed her lips together, as if to draw in that last taste, and savor it.

"Cassie."

She opened her eyes, and they were heavy and clouded and confused. "I don't know what to say now." Yes, she did, she realized. "Will you kiss me again?"

Twelve years of repression kept him from groaning out loud. "Not just this minute," he said, and held her at arm's length. Any closer, and he might just toss her over his shoulder and carry her off behind some handy rock. He wasn't sure either of them was ready for that. "I figure we ought to spread it out a little."

"No one's ever kissed me like that. Made me feel like this."

"Cassie." The words had his libido growing fangs. Snapping down on it, he took her hand. "Let's go back. I... haven't had lunch."

"Oh, you must be starving."

"Right." He could almost laugh at himself as he pulled her back onto the field.

Chapter 5

"I really appreciate this, Cassie." Regan tucked a giggling Nate into his portable swing, then bent over to kiss him as he bounced gleefully. "With out-of-town clients coming into the shop this morning, I just can't keep him with me. And Rafe's got two crews to supervise."

"It's a real hardship," Cassie said from the sink. "I can't think of anything more annoying than having to play with the baby."

"He is wonderful, isn't he? I can't believe he's already five months old." When she cranked up the music on the swing, Nate began to kick his feet in delight. "I nursed him an hour ago, and I've got plenty of bottles here, and diapers, and two changes of clothes, and—"

"Regan, I know what to do with a baby."

"Of course you do." Grinning foolishly at Nate, Regan swept her hair back. "It's just that I know you're so busy with the inn."

"You and Rafe are slave drivers, it's true, but I'm learning to bear up."

Amused, Regan cocked her head. "You're joking, and you're smiling, and I'm pretty sure I heard you singing when I came in."

"I'm happy." Cassie loaded plates into the dishwasher. The breakfast hour was over, and the guests were either gone or relaxing in their rooms. "I didn't know I could be this happy. This is the most wonderful house in the world."

Regan handed Nate a ring of colorful plastic to jiggle. "So working here makes you happy?"

"Absolutely. Not that I wasn't happy working for Ed, but... I love living here, Regan." She beamed at the view from the window. "The kids love living here."

Regan ran her tongue around her teeth. "And that's why you were singing?"

Cassie bent over a little farther, busied herself arranging dishes. "Actually, there is something else. I guess you've got to go open the shop."

"I've got a few minutes. One of the perks of running my own business."

If there was anyone she could talk to, it was Regan. Cassie straightened, took a deep breath. "Devin—it's about Devin. That is, I'm probably making too much of it. Or not making enough of it. It's just, well... Do you want some coffee?"

"Cassie."

"He kissed me," she blurted out, then slapped a hand to her mouth when a laugh bubbled out. "I mean, *kissed* me. Not like Rafe kisses me, or Shane or Jared. I mean, like... My hands are sweating."

"It's about time," Regan said, with feeling. "I thought he'd never get to it."

"You're not surprised."

"Cassie, the man would crawl naked over hot coals for you." She decided she would have some coffee, and walked over to the stove to pour it herself. "So, how was it?"

Regan's statement had Cassie running a nervous hand through her hair. "How was what?"

With a chuckle, Regan sipped and leaned back against the counter. "I have to figure that he has more in common with Rafe than a quick temper and great looks. So it must have been a pretty terrific kiss."

"It was at the picnic, two days ago. My head's still buzzing."

"Yep. That's a MacKade for you. What are you going to do about it?"

"I don't know what to do." Brow creased, Cassie picked up a damp rag and began to wipe the counter. "Regan, I started going with Joe before I was sixteen. I've never been with anyone else."

"Oh." Regan pursed her lips. "I see. Well, it would be only natural to be a little nervous over the idea that you might be heading toward a physical relationship."

Because her palms were indeed damp, Cassie set down the cloth and rubbed them on her apron. "I don't like sex," she said flatly, rattling dishes again so that she didn't note the lift of Regan's brow or the concern in her friend's eyes. "I'm not any good at it, and I just don't like it, anyway."

"Cassie, I know the counseling helped you."

"Yes, it did, and I'm grateful for you persuading me to go. I feel better about myself, and I'm more confident about a lot of things. I know I didn't deserve to be abused, that I didn't cause it, and that I did the right thing by getting out." She let out a breath. "This is a different matter. Not all women are built to enjoy sex. I've read about it. Anyway," she continued before Regan could comment, "I'm getting ahead of myself. But I'm not stupid, Regan. I know that Devin has needs, and I'm prepared to meet them."

"That is stupid," Regan snapped. "Making love is not supposed to be a chore like—like..." Flustered, she gestured to the sink. "Like doing the damn dishes."

"I didn't mean it that way." Because Regan was her friend, she smiled. "What I meant was that I care for Devin. I always have. This is a different level. I didn't know he was attracted to me. I'm so flattered."

Regan's response to that was a muttered curse that only made Cassie's smile widen.

"Well, I am. He's so beautiful, and he's kind. I know he won't hurt me."

"No," Regan said quietly. "He wouldn't hurt you." But, she thought, would you hurt him?

"Kissing him was lovely, and I think having sex with him would be nice."

Wisely, Regan covered her cough with a sip of coffee. If Devin was anything like Rafe, *nice* was hardly the word. "Has he asked you to bed?"

"No. He wouldn't even kiss me again when I asked him to. That's what I wanted to ask you about. How do I go about letting him know I don't mind being with him— that way?"

It was a tribute to her willpower that Regan didn't goggle. Carefully she set the coffee cup aside. "This goes against the grain for me, Cassie, against every feminist cell in my body, but I have to trust my instincts here, and go with what I know about you and about Devin. I'm going to advise you to let him set the pace, at least initially. Take your cues from him. Just relax and enjoy the ride. I think you can count on him to get you both where you want to go. When you're ready, Cassie. It's important to think of yourself, too, not just Devin."

"So I really shouldn't do anything?"

"Do what seems right to you. And do this—don't compare him with Joe. And don't compare the woman who lived with Joe with the woman you are now. I think you're in for a few surprises."

"I've already had one." Cassie touched a fingertip to her lips. "It was wonderful."

"Good. Keep an open mind." She gave Cassie a quick kiss, bent down to fuss over Nate one last time. "And, Cass, I really wouldn't mind if you sort of kept me up-to-date with the progress."

By mid-afternoon, Cassie had finished the guest rooms, and the laundry, and had Nate tucked in a portable crib in Emma's room for a nap. She'd slipped a chicken in the oven to roast and was giving some thought to tackling the mending when she heard the quick rap on her door.

Her heart did a little flip at the hope that it might be Devin stopping by. But settled again when she saw her mother through the screen.

"Hello, Mama." Dutifully Cassie opened the door and pecked her mother's dry cheek. "It's nice to see you. I've just made some iced tea, and I have some nice cherry cobbler."

"You know I don't eat sweets in the middle of the day." Constance Connor scanned the living area of her daughter's quarters. She wrinkled her nose at the cat that curled under the table. Animals belonged outside.

The curtains were drawn back, which would surely fade the upholstery with that strong sunlight. But it was neat. She'd taught her daughter to be neat.

After all, cleanliness was next to godliness.

Still, she didn't care for the bright colors, or all the fol-derols sitting about. It was showy. She sniffed to indicate her disapproval and sat down on one of the living room chairs, her back broomstick-straight.

"I'll say again, it's a poor choice for you to live in a man's house who isn't your husband."

It was an old argument, and Cassie answered by rote. "I lived in Mr. Halleran's house for nearly ten years."

"And paid good rent."

"I earn my keep here. What's the difference?"

"You know very well the difference, so I'll not mention it again."

Until the next time, Cassie thought wearily. "Would you like some iced tea, Mama?"

"I can get through an hour without sipping or snacking." Constance set her purse firmly on her lap, crossed her ankles above her sensible shoes. "Sit down, Cassandra. The children are in school, I take it."

"Yes. They're doing very well. They'll be home in about an hour. I hope you'll stay and see them."

"It's you I've come to see." She unsnapped her bag with fingers adorned with only a thin gold band. There was no glint to it, no shine. As, Cassie thought, there had been no glint or shine to her parents' marriage. She often thought, after a visit with her mother, that her father had died sim-ply to escape it.

But she said nothing, waiting as her mother drew out an envelope. She didn't have to see the handwriting to know who it was from.

"This is the latest letter I received from your husband. It came in this morning's mail." Constance held it out. "I want you to read it."

Cassie folded her hands in her lap, linked her fingers. "No."

Eyes narrowed with righteous anger, Constance studied her daughter. "Cassandra, you will read this letter."

"No, ma'am, I won't. He's not my husband."

Constance's thin, pale face went dark with temper. "You took vows before God."

"And I've broken them." It was hard, so hard, to keep her voice and hands from trembling, to keep her eyes level.

"You take pride in that? You should be ashamed."

"No, not pride. But you can't make me sorry for breaking them, Mama. Joe broke them long before I did."

She refused to look at the letter, refused to feel this bitter anger, that even so small a part of him had come into her home. Instead, she kept her eyes on her mother's face.

"Love, honor, cherish. Did he love me, Mama, when he beat me? Did he honor me when he used his fists on me? Did he cherish me when he raped me?"

"You will not speak that way about your husband."

"I came to you when I had nowhere to go, when he'd hurt me so badly I could hardly walk, when my children were terrorized. And you sent me away."

"Your place was at home, making the best of your marriage."

"I made the best of it for ten years, and it nearly killed me. You should have been there for me, Mama. You should have stood up for me."

"I stood up for what was right." Constance's mouth was a thin line. "If you forced him to discipline you—"

"Discipline me!" Stunned, even after all the time that had passed, Cassie leaped to her feet. "He had no right to *discipline* me. I was his wife, not his dog. And not even a dog deserved to be treated the way I was. He would have disciplined me to death, if I hadn't finally found the courage to do something about it. Would that have satisfied you, Mama? I'd have kept my vows then. Till death do us part."

"You're overdramatizing. And whatever happened before is done. He's seen his mistakes. It was the drink, the women who tempted him. He's asking for your forgiveness, and hopes that you will keep your vows, as he intends to."

"He can't have my forgiveness, and he can't have me. How can you do this to me? I'm your daughter, your only child." Cassie's eyes were no longer haunted, but steely. "How can you take the side of a man who hurt me and betrayed me and made my life a misery? Don't you want me to be happy?"

"I want you to do what's expected of you. I expect you to do as you're told."

"Yes, that's all you ever wanted from me. To do what I was told, to be what you expected me to be. Why do you think I married him, Mama?"

Cassie couldn't believe the words were coming out of her mouth, but they wouldn't be stopped. Just as the emotions that pushed them from her heart to her throat and through her lips wouldn't be stopped.

"It was to get away from you, to get out of that house, where nobody ever laughed, nobody ever showed any affection."

"You had a good home." This time it was Constance whose voice trembled. "You had a decent Christian upbringing."

"No, I didn't. There's nothing decent or Christian about a house where there's no love. My children won't be raised that way, not anymore." Cassie spoke calmly now, amazed that she could, fascinated that she felt nothing at all. "You're my mother, and I'll give you all the respect that I can. All

I'm asking is for you to give me the same. I don't want you corresponding with Joe anymore."

Constance got to her feet. "You would dare tell me what to do?"

"Will you stop writing him, Mama? Will you stop writing the prison authorities?"

"I will not."

"Then you're not welcome in my home. We have nothing else to say to each other."

Staggered, Constance could only stare. "You'll come to your senses."

"I have come to them. Goodbye, Mama."

Cassie walked to the door and held it open. She stiffened when Constance swept by. And then the trembling began.

Slowly, unsure of her footing, Cassie walked to the table. She braced herself on it as she lowered herself into a chair. Wrapping her arms tight around her body, she began to rock.

She was still sitting there when Devin came to the door, ten minutes later. He started to give a friendly rap on the wooden slat of the screen. But then he saw her, saw the way her shoulders were hunched and curled and the quick, monotonous rocking of her body, as if she were trying to still something inside herself. Or comfort it.

He'd seen her like that before, sitting in his office with her face battered. All he knew was that she was hurt, and he was through the door like a bullet.

"Cassie."

She sprang to her feet. He saw alarm mix with the hurt. Even as he reached out, she scooted back, out of his way.

"Devin, I didn't hear you come up. I was— I should—" Her mind raced for excuses, for the barrier of appearances. As always. Pale with grief, her eyes swimming with it, she stared at him. Then she began to move quickly. "Let me get you some iced tea. It's fresh." She was hurrying for glasses, for the pitcher, her movements jerky. "I've got some cobbler. I just made it this morning."

She jolted like a spring when his hands came down on her shoulders, and the glass she had just filled smashed on the tiles. The cat that had been napping under the table took off in a blur of fur.

"Oh, God, look what I've done." Her breathing hitched, and the feeling in her chest tightened. She couldn't stop it. "I have to— I have to—"

"Leave it." He struggled to keep his voice easy as he turned her to face him. She was shaking hard, trying to pull back. *Not this time* was all he could think. *Not this time.* "Come here," he murmured. "Come on now."

The instant he drew her into his arms, the dam broke. She wept against his shoulder, the fast, hot tears soaking his shirt. He kissed her hair, stroked her back. "Tell me. Tell me what's wrong, so I can help."

It wasn't coherent, nor was it complete, but he understood the gist when she stuttered out words between sobs. Bitter fury curled inside him as he soothed her, kissing her wet cheeks.

"You did what you had to do. You did what was right."

"She's my mother." Cassie lifted her ravaged face to his. "I sent her away. I turned my mother away."

"Who turned who away, Cass?"

Her breath sobbed out again, and her hands balled into fists on his shoulders. "It's not right."

"Get away from her." The screen door slammed as Connor burst through it. His own hands were fisted, and his face was flushed with fury, taut with violence. All he saw was a man holding his mother, and his mother crying. "If you touch her I'll kill you."

"Connor!" Shock had Cassie's voice ringing sharp. Was this her baby, with his fists raised and his eyes fierce? She caught a glimpse of Emma at the door, her frightened face pressed to the screen. "Don't speak that way to Sheriff MacKade."

Every cell on alert, Connor stepped forward. "Take your hands off my mother."

Intrigued, Devin merely lifted a brow and let his arms fall to his sides.

"I said not to speak that way," Cassie began.

"He was hurting you. He made you cry." Connor bared his teeth, a ten-year-old warrior. "He better leave right now."

"He wasn't hurting me." Though she was shaken to the core, Cassie stepped between them. "I was upset— Grandma upset me—and Sheriff MacKade was helping to make me feel better. I want you to apologize, this minute."

Devin saw the boy's arms drop, and knew when the angry flush on Connor's cheeks turned to shame. With his eyes on the boy, he laid a hand on Cassie's shoulder.

"I'd like to talk to Connor. Alone." Anticipating her protest, he gave Cassie's shoulder a quick squeeze. "Cass, the baby's crying. Why don't you and Emma go see to him?"

"Nate. I forgot." At her wits' end, Cassie dragged a hand through her hair.

"Why don't you go on?" Devin said, giving her a gentle nudge. "Con and I are going to take a walk."

"All right. Come on, Emma, Nate's crying." But she took a deep breath as she held out a hand for her daughter. "I expect you to apologize, Connor. You understand?"

"Yes, ma'am." With his chin on his chest, Connor turned to go outside.

He knew what was coming. He was going to get whipped. His father had always done the hitting away from the house, away where his mother couldn't see and wouldn't know. He'd get a beating now for sure, and it would be worse than anything his father had ever done to him. Because he'd tried to do what was right, and he'd been wrong.

Devin said nothing at all, just walked with the boy across the lawn, toward the woods that bordered it. He chose the path without thinking. The woods were as familiar to him as the town, as his own home, as his own mind. Beside him, Connor walked stiffly, his head drooped in shame, his back braced.

Because he knew he had to gauge his timing, and his moves, Devin resisted the urge to drape his arm over those thin little shoulders. Instead, he led the way down a path and stopped at the cluster of rocks where two soldiers had once met and doomed each other.

He sat, and the boy stood rigid and waiting.

"I'm awfully proud of you, Connor."

The words—the last he'd expected to hear—had the boy's head whipping up. "Sir?"

Casually Devin took out a cigarette—the first of a very long day. "I have to tell you, it's a relief to me. I worry about your mother some. She's had a bad time of it. Knowing you're there to look after things makes my mind a lot easier."

Connor's confusion was too huge for him to feel any pride. He stared at Devin, his eyes still wary. "I—I sassed you."

"I don't think so."

"You're not going to hit me?"

Devin's hand stiffened, hesitated. Very slowly he tossed

the barely smoked cigarette on the ground and crushed it under his heel. As he would have liked to crush Joe Dolin.

"I'm never going to raise my hand to you, not today, not any day." He spoke deliberately, his eyes level with Connor's, as a man would speak to another man. "I'm never going to raise it to your mama or to your sister." But he held out that hand, and waited. "I'm giving you my word, Connor," he said, when the boy simply stared at the hand being offered. "I'd be grateful if you'd take it."

Dumbfounded, Connor put his hand in Devin's. "Yes, sir."

Devin gave the hand a little squeeze, tugged the boy a little closer. And grinned. "You'd have torn right into me, wouldn't you?"

"I'd have tried." The emotions swirling inside Connor were frightening. Most of all, he was afraid he would cry now and show Devin he was just a stupid little boy after all. "I never helped her before. I never did anything."

"It wasn't your fault, Connor."

"I never did anything," Connor repeated. "He hit her all the time, Sheriff. All the time."

"I know."

"No, you don't. You only know about when one of the neighbors would call you, or when he'd get so drunk he'd hit her someplace where it would show. But there was more. It was worse."

Devin nodded. There was nothing else he could do. And drew the boy down on the rocks beside him. "He hit you, too."

"When she couldn't see." Bravery forgotten, Connor pressed his face into Devin's side. "When she didn't know."

Devin stared off into the trees, eaten away by a useless anger at what he hadn't been able to prevent. "Emma?"

"No, sir. He never paid much attention to Emma, because

she was just a girl. Don't tell Mama. Please don't tell her he hit me. She'd just feel bad."

"I won't."

"I hate him. I'd kill him if I could."

"I know how you feel." When the boy shook his head, Devin drew him back, looked deep into his eyes. "I do know. I'm going to tell you something. I used to fight a lot."

"I know." Connor sniffled, but was profoundly grateful he'd controlled the tears. "People talk about it."

"Yeah, I know they do. I used to like it, and I used to think there were lots of people I wanted to rip into. Sometimes I had reason for it, sometimes I didn't. Anyway, I had to learn to take a step back. It's important, that step. Now, you figure you owe your father some grief—"

"Don't call him that," Connor snapped out, then flushed darkly. "Sir."

"All right. I figure you owe him some, too. But you've got to take that step back. Let the law handle it."

"I'm not ever going to let him or anybody hurt her again."

"I'm with you there." Studying Connor's determined face, he decided the boy deserved to know the situation. "I'm going to give it to you straight, okay?"

"Yes, sir."

"Your grandma got your mama real upset today."

"She wants him to come back. It's never going to happen. I won't let it happen."

"Your mama feels the same way, and that's why she sent your grandma away. That was hard for her, real hard, Connor, but she did it."

"You were helping her. I'm sorry I—"

"Don't apologize," Devin said quickly. "I mean it. I know Cassie thinks you should, but we know how things stand. You did exactly right, Connor. I'd have done the same."

No compliment he'd ever received, no praise from a teacher, no high five from a teammate, had ever meant more. He had done what Sheriff MacKade would do.

"I'm glad you want to help her. I'll do anything you want me to do."

That kind of trust, Devin thought, was worth more than gold. "I need to tell you that they've given Joe work release."

Connor's face tightened up. "I know about it. Kids at school say things."

"They giving you a rough time?"

He moved a shoulder. "Not as much as they used to."

Learning to handle yourself, Devin thought with an astonishing sense of pride. "What I want is for you not to worry too much, but more, I want you to keep your eyes open. You're smart, and you notice things. That's why you write good stories."

Connor wriggled with pleasure. "I like to write."

"I know. And you know how to look at things, how to watch. So I know you're going to watch out for your family. If you see something, hear something, even feel something that doesn't sit right, I want you to come to me. I want your word on that."

"Yes, sir."

"Do you have to call me sir all the time? It makes me feel creaky."

Connor flushed, and grinned. "I'm supposed to. It's like a rule."

"I know all about rules." Devin decided they could deal with that little matter later. "A man would be lucky to have you for a son, Connor."

"I don't ever want to have a father again."

The hand that had lifted toward Connor's shoulder stiffened. Biting back a sigh, Devin ordered it to relax. "Then

I'll say a man would be lucky to have you for a friend. Are we square here?"

"Yes, sir."

There were those eyes again, Devin thought, filled with trust. "Your mama's probably worried you're beating me up." When Connor giggled at the idea, Devin ruffled his hair. "You go on back now and tell her we straightened it all out. I'll talk to her later."

"Yes, sir." He scrambled off the rocks, then had to bite his lip to spark that last bit of courage. "Can I come to your office sometime, and watch you work?"

"Sure."

"I wouldn't get in the way. I'd just—" Connor tumbled over his own words and skidded to a halt. "I can?"

"Sure you can. Anytime. It's mostly boring."

"It couldn't be," Connor said with giddy pleasure. "Thanks, Sheriff. Thanks for everything."

Devin watched the boy race off, then settled back. He wished briefly for a cigarette before reminding himself he was quitting. Then he reminded himself that sooner or later he intended to have those two children, and maybe another on the way.

Connor didn't want another father, and that would be a tough one. So, Devin mused, he'd just have to find the right path to take, and step carefully.

The first step, of course, was Cassie. One step, then the next. Direction always took you somewhere. If he was careful, she would be taking those steps with him.

Chapter 6

It was supposed to be Devin's day off, but he spent two hours in the morning dealing with a small crisis at the high school. The smoke bomb had failed in its mission. When it landed in the girl's locker room, it hadn't put out much of a cloud, and, more important, hadn't made the girls come rushing out screaming in their underwear.

The one he'd put together a short lifetime ago had had far more satisfying results. Not that he'd mentioned that particular incident to the two offenders he collared.

Once he had it under control, and the juvenile chemists shaking in their basketball shoes, he headed straight for the inn.

He had a surprise for Cassie, one he hoped would make her smile. And one he hoped would ease the way into that next step.

He supposed he had an unfair advantage. He knew her so well, had watched and observed for years. He knew every expression of her face, every gesture of her hands. He knew her weaknesses and her strengths.

She knew him, he thought, but not in the same way, or in the same detail. She'd been too busy surviving to notice. If she had noticed, she would have been able to see that he was in love with her.

It was just as well she didn't see. Not until he'd finished laying the foundation. He could take his time about that, Devin mused as he turned up the lane toward the inn. But once he had that foundation in place and solid, he was going to move fast.

Twelve years was a damn long time to wait.

Because there was a car parked in one of the guest slots, he opted to go into the inn first. He was delighted to find her there, fully occupied with two snowy-haired women.

She'd forgotten to take her apron off. The new arrivals had come unexpectedly, and they had wanted a full tour, and the history of the inn. Cassie was grateful she'd finished the breakfast dishes, even though she'd been caught in the middle of vacuuming.

The two women were sisters, both widowed, and were eager to hear about the Barlow legend. Cassie led them back down the stairs after the tour of the second floor, and was well into her spiel when Devin walked in.

"...the bloodiest single day of the Civil War. The Antietam battlefield is one of the most pristine parks in the country. The visitors' center is only four miles from here, and very informative. You'll find— Oh, hello, Devin."

"Don't let me interrupt. Ladies."

"Mrs. Berman, Mrs. Cox, this is Sheriff MacKade."

"Sheriff." Mrs. Cox adjusted her glasses and beamed through the lenses. "How exciting."

"Antietam's a quiet town," he told her. "Certainly more

quiet than it was in September of 1862." Because tourists inevitably enjoyed it, Devin grinned. "You're standing right about on the spot where a Confederate soldier was killed."

"Oh, my goodness!" Mrs. Cox clapped her hands together. "Did you hear that, Irma?"

"Nothing wrong with my ears, Marge." Mrs. Berman peered down at the stairs, as if inspecting for blood. "Mrs. Dolin was telling us something of the history. We decided to visit the inn because we read one of the brochures that claimed it was haunted."

"Yes, ma'am. It surely is."

"Sheriff MacKade's brother owns the inn," Cassie explained. "He can tell you quite a bit about it."

"You can't do better than to hear it from Mrs. Dolin," Devin corrected. "She lives with the ghosts every day. Tell them about the two corporals, Cassie."

Though she told the story several times each week, Cassie had to struggle not to feel self-conscious in front of Devin. She folded her hands over her apron.

"Two young soldiers," she began, "became separated from their regiments during the Battle of Antietam. Each wandered into the woods beyond the inn. Some say they were looking for their way back to the battle, others say they were just trying to go home. Still, legend holds that they met there, fought there, each of them young, frightened, lost. They would have heard the battle still raging in the fields, over the hills, but this was one on one, strangers and enemies because one wore blue, and the other gray."

"Poor boys," Mrs. Berman murmured.

"They wounded each other, badly, and crawled off in different directions. One, the Confederate, made his way here, to this house. It's said he thought he was coming home, because all he wanted, in the end, was his home and his family. One of the servants found him, and brought him into the house. The mistress here was a Southern woman. Her name was Abigail, Abigail O'Brian Barlow. She had married a wealthy Yankee. A man she didn't love, but was bound to by her vows."

Devin's brow lifted. It was a new twist, a new detail, to the legend he had known since childhood.

"She saw the boy, a reminder of her own home and her own youth. Her heart went out to him for that, and simply because he was hurt. She ordered him to be taken upstairs, where his wounds would be tended. She spoke to him, reassured him, held his hand in hers as the servant carried him up these stairs. She knew that she could never go home again, but she wanted to be sure the boy could. The war had shown her cruelty, useless struggle and the terrible pain of loss, as her marriage had. If she could do this one thing, she thought, help this one boy, she could bear it."

Mrs. Cox took out tissues, handed one to her sister and blew her own nose hard.

"But her husband came to the stairs," Cassie continued. "She didn't hate him then. She didn't love him, but she'd been taught to respect and obey the man she had married, and the father of her children. He had a gun, and she saw what he meant to do in his eyes. She shouted for him to stop, begged him. The boy's hand was in hers, and his eyes were on her face, and if she had had the courage, she would have thrown her body over his to protect him. To save not only him, but everything she'd already lost."

Now it was Cassie who looked down at the stairs, sighed over them. "But she didn't have the courage. Her husband fired the gun and killed him, even as she held the boy's hand. He died here, the young soldier. And so did she, in her heart. She never spoke to her husband again, but she learned how to hate. And she grieved from that day until she died, two years later. And often, very often, you can smell the roses she loved in the house, and hear her weeping."

"Oh, what a sad, sad story." Mrs. Cox wiped at her eyes. "Irma, have you ever heard such a sad story?"

Mrs. Berman sniffed. "She'd have done better to have taken the gun and shot the louse."

"Yes." Cassie smiled a little. "Maybe that's one of the reasons she still weeps." She shook off the mood of the story and led the ladies the rest of the way down the steps. "If you'd like to make yourselves at home in the parlor, I'll bring in the tea I promised you."

"That would be lovely," Mrs. Cox told her, still sniffling. "Such a beautiful house. Such lovely furniture."

"All of the furnishings come from Past Times, Mrs. MacKade's shop on Main Street in town. If you have time, you might want to go in and browse. She has beautiful things, and offers a ten-percent discount to any guest of the inn."

"Ten percent," Mrs. Berman murmured, and eyed a graceful hall rack.

"Devin, would you like to have some tea?"

It took an effort to move. He wondered if she knew that Connor got his flair for telling a story from his mother.

"I'll take a rain check on that. I have something in the car for upstairs. For your place."

"Oh."

"Ladies, nice to have met you. Enjoy your stay at the MacKade Inn, and in the town."

"What a handsome man," Mrs. Cox said, with a little pat of her hand to her heart. "My goodness. Irma, have you ever seen a more handsome young man?"

But Mrs. Berman was busy sizing up the drop-leaf table in the parlor.

* * *

By the time Cassie had settled the ladies in with their tea, her curiosity was killing her. She had chores to see to, and she scolded herself for letting them lag as she hurried around to the outside stairs.

Halfway up, she saw Devin hooking up a porch swing. "Oh." It made a lovely picture, she thought, a man standing in the sunlight, his shirtsleeves rolled up, tools at his feet, muscles working as he lifted one end of the heavy wooden seat to its chain.

"This seemed like the spot for it."

"Yes, it's perfect. Rafe didn't mention that he wanted one."

"I wanted one," Devin told her. "Don't worry, I ran it by him." He hooked the other end and gave it a testing swing. "Works." Bending, he gathered up the tools. "Going to try it out with me?"

"I really have to—"

"Try it out with me," Devin finished, setting the tools aside in their case. "I put it up because I figured it was a good way to get you to sit with me on a summer afternoon. A good way for me to kiss you again."

"Oh."

"You said you didn't mind."

"No, I didn't. I don't." There it was again, that flutter in her chest. "Aren't you supposed to be working?"

"It's my day off. Sort of." He held out a hand, then curled his fingers around hers. "You look pretty today, Cassie."

Automatically she brushed at her apron. "I've been cleaning."

"Real pretty," he murmured, drawing her to the swing, and down.

"I should get you something cold to drink."

"You know, one of these days you're going to figure out that I don't come around so you can serve me cold drinks."

"Connor said you worried about me. You don't have to. I was hoping you'd come by so I could tell you how much I appreciate what you did for him the other day. The way you made him feel."

"I didn't do anything. He earned what he felt. You've got a fine boy in Connor."

"I know." She took a deep breath and relaxed enough to lean back against the seat. The rhythm of the swing took her back, far back, to childhood and sweet days, endless summers. Her lips curved, and then she laughed.

"What's funny?"

"It's just this, sitting here on a porch swing, like a couple of teenagers."

"Well, if you were sixteen again, this would be my next move." He lifted up his arms, stretched, then let one drape casually over her shoulders. "Subtle, huh?"

She laughed again, tilted her face toward his. "When I was sixteen, you were too bad to be subtle. Everybody knew how you snuck off to the quarry with girls and—"

The best way to stop her mouth was with his. He did so gently, savoring the quick tremor of her lips, of her body.

"Not so subtle," he said quietly. "Wanna go to the quarry?" When she stuttered, he only laughed. "Some other time. For now I'd settle for you kissing me back. Kiss me back, Cassie, like you were sixteen and didn't have a worry in the world."

With someone else, anyone else, he might have been amused by the concentration on her face. But it struck his heart, the way her mouth lifted to his, that hesitant pressure, the unschooled way her hands lifted to rest on his shoulders.

"Relax," he said against her mouth. "Turn off your head for a minute. Can you do that?"

"I don't..." She didn't turn it off. It shut off when his tongue danced lightly over hers, when his hands skimmed down her sides and up again. Down and up, in firm, steady strokes that had the heels of his hands just brushing the sides of her breasts.

"I love the taste of you." He pressed his lips to her jaw, her temples, back to her lips. "I've dreamed of it."

"You have?"

"Most of my life. I've wanted to be with you like this for years. Forever."

The words were seeping through that lovely haze of pleasure that covered her whenever he kissed her. "But—"

"You got married." He trailed his lips down her cheek. "I didn't move fast enough. I got drunk the day you married Joe Dolin. Blind, falling-down drunk. I didn't know what else to do. I thought about killing him, but I figured you must have wanted him. So that was that."

"Devin, I don't understand this." If he'd stop kissing her, just for a minute, she might be able to understand.

But he couldn't seem to stop, any of it. "I loved you so much I thought I'd die from it. Just keel right over and die."

Panic and denial had her struggling away. "You couldn't have."

He'd said too much, but the regrets would have to come later. Now, he'd finish it. "I've loved you for over twelve years, Cassandra. I loved you when you were married to another man, when you had his children. I loved you when I couldn't do anything to help you out of that hell you were living in. I love you now."

She got up and, in an old defensive habit, wrapped her arms tight around her body. "That's not possible."

"Don't tell me what I feel." She jolted back a full step at the anger in his tone, making him clench his teeth as he rose. "And don't you cringe away from me when I raise my voice. I can't be what I'm not, not even for you. But I'm not Joe Dolin. I'll never hit you."

"I know that." She let her arms drop. "I know that, Devin." Even as she said it, she watched him struggle to push back the worst of his temper. "I don't want you to be angry with me, Devin, but I don't know what to say to you."

"Seems like I've already said more than enough." He began to pace, his hands jammed in his pockets. "I'm good at taking things slow, thinking them through. But not this time. I've said what I've said, Cass, and I can't—won't—take it back. You're going to have to decide what you want to do about it."

"Do about what?" Baffled, she lifted her hands, then let them fall. "You want me to believe that a man like you had feelings for me all these years and didn't do anything about it?"

"What the hell was I supposed to do?" he tossed back. "You were married. You'd made your choice, and it wasn't me."

"I didn't know there was a choice."

"My mistake," he said, bitterly. "Now I've made another one, because you're not ready, or you don't want to be ready. Or maybe you just don't want me."

"I don't—" She lifted her hands to her cheeks. She honestly didn't know which, if any, of those alternatives was true. "I can't think. You've been my friend. You've been, well, the sheriff, and I've been so grateful—"

"Don't you dare say that to me." Devin shouted the words, and was too twisted with pain and fury to notice that she went white as death. "Damn it, I don't want you to be grateful. I'm not playing public servant with you. I don't deserve that."

"I didn't mean… Devin, I'm sorry. I'm so sorry."

"The hell with being sorry," he raged. "The hell with gratitude. You want to be grateful I locked the son of a bitch up who was pounding on you, then be grateful to the badge, not to me. Because *I* wanted to break him in half. You want to be grateful I've been coming around here being the nice guy, like some love-whipped mongrel dog, don't. Because what I've wanted to do is—"

He bit that back, his eyes cutting through her like hot knives. "You don't want to know. No, what you want is for me to keep my voice down, my feelings inside and my hands to myself."

"No, that's not—"

"You don't mind if I kiss you, but then, you're so damn grateful it's the least you can do."

Her stumbling protest fell apart. "That's not fair."

"I'm tired of being fair. I'm tired of waiting for you. I'm tired of being torn up in love with you. The hell with it."

He strode by her, and was halfway down the stairs before her legs unfroze. She raced after him. "Devin. Devin, please don't go this way. Let me—"

He jerked away from her light touch on his shoulder, whirled on her. "Leave me alone now, Cass. You want to leave me be now."

She knew that look, though she had never expected to see it aimed from his eyes into hers. It was a man's bitter fury. She had reason to fear it. Her stomach clenched painfully, but she made herself stand her ground. He would never know how much it cost her.

"You never told me," she said, fighting to keep her voice slow and even. "You never let me see. Now you have, and you won't give me time to think, to know what to do. You don't want to hear that I'm sorry, that I'm grateful, that I'm afraid. But I'm all of those things, and I can't help it. I can't make myself into what anyone else expects me to be ever again. I'll lose everything this time. If I could do it for anyone, I'd do it for you. But I can't."

"That's clear enough." He knew he was wrong—not completely wrong, but wrong enough. It just didn't seem to matter, compared with this ragged, tearing hurt inside of him. "The thing you've got twisted around, Cass, is that I don't want you to be anything but what you are. Once you figure that out, you know where to find me."

She opened her mouth again, then closed it when he strode away. There was nothing else she could say to him now, nothing else she could do. She felt raw inside, and her throat hurt.

And it was hurt that had been in his eyes, she thought, closing her own. Hurt that she had caused, without ever meaning to.

Devin MacKade loved her. The idea left her weak with terror and confusion. But bigger even than that was the idea that he had loved her all this time. Devin MacKade, the kindest, most admirable man she knew, loved her, had loved her for years, and all she had to give in return was gratitude.

Now she had lost him, the friendship she'd come to cherish, the companionship she had grown to depend on. She'd lost it because he wanted a woman, and she was empty inside.

She didn't weep. It was too late for tears. Instead, she rose, reminded herself to square her shoulders. She went back into the inn through the kitchen. There were chores to see to, and she could always think more clearly when she was working.

Her latest guests had gone off, eager to hunt antiques, so Cassie went back upstairs and turned on the vacuum she'd abandoned when the guests arrived.

She worked methodically, down the hallway, room by room. The bridal suite—Abigail's room—was her favorite. But she paid little attention now to the lovely wallpaper with its rosebuds, the graceful canopy bed, the wash of sunlight through the lace curtains.

She reminded herself to bring up fresh flowers. Even when the room wasn't occupied, there were always flowers on the table by the window. She'd forgotten them that morning.

Yet the room smelled of roses, powerfully. A sudden chill had her shivering. She felt him, and turned toward the door.

"Devin." Relief, confusion, sorrow. She experienced them all as she took a step toward the doorway.

But it wasn't Devin. The man was tall, dark-haired and handsome. But the face wasn't Devin's, and the clothes were formal, old-fashioned. Her hand went limp on the handle of the vacuum, and the sound of it buzzed in her ears.

Abigail, come with me. Take the children and come with me. Leave this place. You don't love him.

No, Cassie thought, I've never loved him. Now I despise him.

Can't you see what this is doing to you? How long will you stay, closed away from life this way?

It's all I can do. It's the best I can do.

I love you, Abby. I love you so much. I could make you happy if you'd only let me. We'll go away from here, away

*from him. Start our lives over, together. I've already waited
for you so long.*

How can I? I'm bound to him. I have the children. And
you, your life is here. You can't walk away from the town,
your responsibilities, the people who depend on you. You
can't settle for another man's wife, another man's children.

*There's nothing I wouldn't do for you. I'd kill for you.
Die for you. For God's sake, Abigail, give me the chance
to love you. All these years I've stood by, knowing how
unhappy you were, knowing you were out of reach. That's
over now. He's gone. We can leave and be miles from here
before he comes back. Why should either of us settle for
less than everything? I don't want to sit in the parlor with
you and pretend I don't love you, don't need you. I can't
keep being only your friend.*

You know I value you, depend on you.

Tell me you love me.

I can't. I can't tell you that. There's nothing inside me
any longer. He killed it.

Come with me. And live again.

Whatever was there, whoever was there, faded, until
there was only the doorway, the lovely wallpaper and the
strong, sad scent of roses. Cassie found herself standing, almost swaying, with one hand reaching out to nothing at all.

The vacuum was still humming as she sank weakly to
the floor.

What had happened here? she asked herself. Had she
been dreaming? Hallucinating?

She laid a hand on her heart and found it was beating
like a wild bird in a cage. Carefully she let her head drop
down to her updrawn knees.

She had heard the ghosts before, felt them. Now, she realized, she had seen one. Not one of the Barlows, not the

poor doomed soldier. But the man Abigail had loved. The man who had loved her.

Who had he been? She thought she might never know. But his face had been compelling, though filled with sorrow, his voice strong, even when it was pleading. Why hadn't Abigail gone with him? Why hadn't she taken that hand he reached out to her and run, run for her life?

Abigail had loved him. Cassie drew in a deep breath. Of that she was sure. The emotions that swirled through the room had been so powerful, she felt them still. There had been love here. Desperate, helpless love.

Is that why you weep? Cassie wondered. Because you didn't go, and you lost him? You didn't reach out, and then there was nothing to hold on to?

You were afraid to love him, so you broke his heart.

Just as she had broken Devin's heart today.

With a shudder, Cassie lifted her head. Why? she asked herself. Out of fear and doubt. Out of habit. That was pathetic. All Devin had wanted was affection. But she hadn't told him that she cared. Hadn't showed him she cared.

Would she close herself away, as Abigail had, or would she take the chance?

Hadn't she been a coward long enough?

Wiping her damp face, she got to her feet. She had to go to him. She would go to him. Somehow.

Of course, such things are never simple. She had children, and could hardly leave them to fend for themselves. She had guests at the inn, and a job to do. It took her hours to manage it, and with every minute that passed, the doubts weighed more heavily.

She combated them by reminding herself that it didn't

matter how clumsy she was. He wanted her. That would be enough.

"I'm so grateful, Ed. I know it's a lot to ask."

"Hey—" already settled down in front of the television with a bowl of popcorn, Ed waved a hand "—so I closed a little early. I get a night off."

"The kids are asleep." But still Cassie fretted. "They hardly ever wake up after they're down."

"Don't you worry about those angels. And don't worry about the people downstairs," she added, anticipating Cassie. "They want anything, they'll call up here and let me know. I'm going to watch this love story I rented, then hit the sack."

"You take the bed. You promised," Cassie insisted. "I'll just flop down on the couch when I get back."

"Mmm-hmm…" Ed was betting that wouldn't be until dawn. "You say hi to Devin for me, now."

Cassie twisted the collar of her blouse in her fingers. "I'm just going over to his office for a little while."

"If you say so, honey."

"He's angry with me, Ed. He's so angry with me, he might just boot me out."

Ed stopped the videotape she was watching, turned around on the couch and gave Cassie one long, summing-up look. "Honey, you look at him like that, and he's not going to boot you anywhere but into that cot he's got in the back room." When Cassie wrapped her arms around her body, Ed only laughed. "Oh, you stop that now. Devin's not going to push you into anything. A man like that doesn't have to push. He just has to be."

"How did you know I was going over there to…to try to…"

"Cassie, honey, look who you're talking to here. I've

been around this block plenty. You call me, ask if I'd settle in here for the night because you need to see Devin, I'm going to figure it out. And it's long past time, if you ask me."

Cassie looked down at her plain cotton blouse and simple trousers. Her neat flat-heeled shoes. Hardly the garb of a femme fatale. "Ed, I'm no good at this sort of thing."

Ed cocked her head. "I'd wager Devin's plenty good at it, so don't you worry."

"Regan said I should let him set the pace. Maybe I shouldn't be going over there."

"Sweetie pie, sometimes even a real man needs a little kick. Now you stop second-guessing yourself and wringing your hands. Go on over there and get him."

"I should do something with my hair," Cassie fretted. "And I've chewed off my lipstick, haven't I? Maybe I should put on a dress."

"Cassie." Ed tipped down her rhinestone glasses, peered over them. "You look fine. You look fresh. He doesn't care what you're wearing, take my word for it. He's only going to care that you're there. Now go get him."

"All right." Cassie squared her shoulders, picked up her purse. "I'm going. I'm going now. But if you need anything, just—"

"I won't need a thing. Go."

"I'm going."

Ed wiggled her bright red brows as Cassie went out the door. Poor kid, she thought. She looked like she was walking out in front of a firing squad. With a cackle, Ed tipped her glasses back up and flipped the video back on.

Her money was on Devin MacKade.

Chapter 7

He really should just give it up and go back and crawl into his cot. That was what Devin told himself, but he kept right on sitting at his desk with his nose in a book. The story just wasn't holding his interest. It wasn't the fault of the author; nothing could have held his interest just then.

He knew it was foolish, and useless, but he'd had nothing and no one to vent his temper on. So there it was, still curdling inside him. He'd actually considered heading out to the farm and picking a fight with Shane. It would have been easy. Too easy. So he'd decided against it.

He told himself it was because he was a better man than that. He'd have done that sort of thing in his teens—hell, in his twenties. The fact was, he'd probably have done it last week.

But it just didn't suit his mood now.

He was just going to sit here, in his quiet office, with

his feet up on his desk and the chair kicked back, and read. Even if it killed him.

It was after ten on a weeknight, which meant it was doubtful any calls were going to come in to liven things up. He didn't have to be there, but he liked the solitude of his office at night, the familiarity of it. And the fact that he could be there, behind the desk instead of behind the bars.

He hadn't even turned the radio on, as he often did to bring a little music and company into the night. The only light was the one on his desk, the metal gooseneck lamp aimed at the book in his hands. The book he wasn't reading.

He considered getting up and brewing coffee, since he wasn't going to bed. But it seemed like too much effort.

It was the first time in his life he could remember being so angry and so tired at the same time. Usually temper energized him, got his blood up and his adrenaline sizzling. Now he was sapped. He supposed it was because most of the anger was self-directed, though he still had plenty left over for Cassie.

When a woman hurt a man, it was the most natural thing in the world to cover it with anger.

He'd told other women he loved them. He wouldn't have denied it. The fact was that he'd tried to love other women. He'd worked hard at it for a space of time. The last thing he'd wanted to do was moon around over something he couldn't have.

Which was just what he was doing now.

Sulking, his mother would have called it, he thought with a grimace. He missed her more just now than he had since she'd died. And he'd missed her quite a bit over the years.

She'd have given him a cuff on the ear, he supposed, or she'd have laughed. She'd have told him to get his sorry butt up and do something instead of brooding over what he should have done. Or shouldn't have done.

Well, he couldn't think of anything to do, except count his losses. He'd moved too quick, pushed too hard, and he'd stumbled over his own heart.

The hell with it, Devin thought again, and let the book lie on his chest. Shifting in the chair, he closed his eyes and ordered himself to think about something else.

He needed to talk to the mayor about getting a stop sign out on the end of Reno Road. Three serious accidents there in a year was reason enough to push for it. Then there was the talk he'd promised to give at the high school for the last assembly before summer hit. And he really had to help Shane with the early haying...

The dream snuck up on him, sly and crafty. Somehow he'd gotten from the hayfield to her bedroom door. Cassie? No, that wasn't Cassie. Abigail. Love and longing stirred in him. Why couldn't she see that she needed him as much as he needed her? Would she just sit there with her hands folded in her lap over her embroidery, her eyes tired and lost?

It seemed nothing he could say would convince her to come with him, to let him love her, as surely he'd been born to do. No, she would close herself off from him, from everything they could have. Should have.

Anger stirred along with the love, along with the longing. He was tired of coming begging, with his hat in his hand. *I won't ask again,* he told her, and she just watched him. *I won't come to you again and have you break my heart. I've waited long enough. If this is the way it has to be, I'm leaving Antietam. I can't keep running the law here, knowing you're here, always out of reach. I have to pick up whatever pieces are left of my life and go.*

But she said nothing, and he knew when he stepped

back, walked down the hall and down the stairs that it was the end. Her weeping drifted to him when he left the house.

Cassie stood on the other side of the desk, twisting the strap of her purse in her fingers. She hadn't expected to find him asleep, didn't know if she should wake him or leave as quietly as she had come.

There was nothing peaceful about him. There should have been, the way his feet were propped on the desk, crossed at the ankles, the way the book was lying open against his chest, the desk lamp slanting light over it.

But his face was hard and tense, his mouth grim. She wished she had the courage to smooth those lines away and make him smile.

Then again, courage had always been her problem.

He opened his eyes and had her jumping like a rabbit. "I'm sorry. I didn't mean to wake you."

"I wasn't asleep." At least he didn't think he'd been asleep. His brain was fuzzy and full of the scent of roses, and for a moment he'd thought she was wearing some full-skirted blue gown, with lace at the throat.

Of course, she wasn't. Just her tidy little blouse and slacks, he thought, dragging a hand through his hair.

"I was just going over some things in my head. Town business."

"If you're busy, I can—"

"What do you want, Cassie?"

"I…" He was still angry. She had expected that, was prepared for it. "I have some things to say to you."

"All right. Go ahead."

"I know I hurt you, and that you're furious with me. You don't want me to apologize. You get mad when I do, so I won't."

"Fine. Aren't you going to make me coffee?"

"Oh, I—" She'd already turned to the pot before she caught herself. She drew a breath, turned back and faced him. He had a brow lifted. "No."

"Well, that's something."

"I'm used to waiting on people." Now she was irritated, a not entirely unpleasant sensation, even if an unfamiliar one. "If it annoys you, I can't help it. Maybe I like waiting on people. Maybe it makes me feel useful."

"I don't want you to wait on me." He could see the irritation clearly enough. It added a snap to her eyes that fascinated him. "I don't want you to feel obliged to me."

"Well, I do feel obliged. And I can't help that, either. And the fact that I do feel obliged and do feel grateful— Don't shout at me, Devin."

Impressed with her no-nonsense tone, he closed his mouth, then added, "I might yet."

"At least wait until I've finished." It wasn't so hard, she realized. It was like dealing with the children, really. You just had to be fair and firm, and not allow yourself to be sidetracked. "I have good reasons to feel obliged to you, and grateful to you, but that doesn't mean that beyond that, or besides that... It doesn't mean I don't have other feelings, too."

"Such as?"

"I don't know, exactly. I haven't had real feelings for a man in—maybe never," she decided. "But I don't want to lose your friendship and...affection. Next to the children, there's no one I care for more than you, Devin. Being with you..." She was going to fumble now, and she hated herself for it. "The way we were today, this afternoon, before you got mad, was so nice, it was so special."

She was cutting right through his temper, slicing it to

ribbons, the way she was standing there, twisting her purse strap and struggling to find a way to put things right between them.

"Okay, Cassie, why don't we—"

"I came here to go to bed with you."

His jaw dropped. He was sure he heard it hit the edge of the desk. Before he could pick it up again, the door burst open and Shane strolled in.

"Hey, Dev. Hey there, Cassie. Thought you might want to go down to Duff's and shoot a couple games. Why don't you come along, Cassie? It's about time you learned how to shoot pool."

"Go away, Shane," Devin muttered, without taking his eyes off Cassie's face.

"Come on, Dev, you've got nothing to do around here except read another book and drink stale coffee." Experimentally he picked up the pot and sniffed. "This stuff'll kill you."

"Get lost now, or die."

"What's the problem? We'll just—" All innocence, Shane turned back. The tension in the air struck him like a fist, the way his brother was staring at Cassie. The way she was staring back. "Oh. Oh," he repeated, drawing out the word on a mile-wide grin. "Well, son of a gun. Who'd have thought?"

"You've got ten seconds to get out the door before I shoot you."

"Well, hell, I'm going. How was I supposed to know you and Cassie were—"

"Tomorrow," Devin said evenly, and finally managed to get his feet off the desk and onto the floor, "I'm going to break you into very small pieces."

"Yeah, right. I guess you two don't want to play pool, so

I'll be going. Ah, want me to lock this?" he said, winking as Devin snarled at him. But he was obliging enough to flip the latch and shut the door snugly behind him.

"You're not really going to fight with him?" Cassie began quickly. "He didn't mean anything, and..." Tongue-tied, she let her words trail off as Devin walked slowly around the desk.

"What did you say to me before my idiot brother came in?"

"That I came here to go to bed with you."

"That's what I thought you said. Is this your way of mending fences and keeping my friendship? Some new way of apologizing?"

"No." Oh, she was making a mess of it. He didn't look amorous, just curious. "Yes, maybe. I'm not sure. I know, at least, I thought you wanted to. Don't you?"

"I'm asking what you want."

"I'm telling you." Lord, hadn't she just said it, out loud, in plain words? "I came here, didn't I? I called Ed, and she's staying with the kids, and I'm here." She shut her eyes briefly. "It isn't easy for me, Devin."

"I can see that. Cassie, I want you, but what I don't want is for you to think this is necessary to make things up with me."

She did what she had done once before. It had worked then. Cupping her hand on his cheek, she leaned up and kissed him.

"Now you're waiting for me to jump you," Devin murmured.

"Oh, I'm no good at this." In disgust, she tossed her purse into a chair. "I never have been."

"At sex?"

"Of course at sex. What else are we talking about?"

"I wonder," he said quietly, but she was off and running in a way he'd never seen or heard before.

"I don't know what you want, or how to give it. If you'd just do whatever you usually do, it would be all right. It's not that I won't like it, I will. I'm sure I will. It's not your fault that I'm clumsy or stiff, or that I don't have orgasms."

She broke off in horror, and saw that he was gaping at her.

"Excuse me?"

Someone else had said that, she thought frantically, looking everywhere but at him. Surely someone else had said that. All she could do to cover the overwhelming tide of horrid embarrassment was to rush on.

"What I mean is, I want to go to bed with you. I know it'll be nice, because it's nice when you kiss me, so I'm sure the rest will be, too. And if you'd just *do* something, I wouldn't be feeling so stupid."

What the hell was he supposed to do? He knew very well the woman standing there was the mother of two, had been married for a decade. And he'd just realized she was as close to a virgin as anyone he'd ever touched.

It scared the living hell out of him.

He started to tell her that they would take a step back, take it slow. Then he knew that was the wrong way to go. It was painfully obvious that so much of her had been crushed already. What he would know was patience, she would see as rejection.

"I should do what I want with you?"

Enormously relieved, she smiled. "Yes."

It was an offer that had the juices flowing hot. He knew if he wanted this to work he had to clamp down on needs— and on nerves. "And I'll tell you what to do, and you'll do it."

"Yes." Oh, it was really so simple. "If you just don't expect too much, and you—"

"Why don't we start this way?" He put his hands on her shoulders and lowered his mouth gently to hers. "There's something I want very much, Cassie."

"All right."

"I want you to say you're not afraid of me, that you know I won't hurt you."

"I'm not. I know you won't."

"And I want you to promise something." He skimmed his lips up her jaw, felt her shoulders relax under his hands.

"All right."

"That you'll say stop if you mean stop, if I do something you don't like."

"You won't."

His lips cruised around to her ear and made something quake inside her. "Promise me."

"I promise."

He took her hand and led her through the door into the small room he used at night. It was dark. It held little more than a narrow bed, a rickety table, an ashtray he rarely used anymore.

"It shouldn't be here. I should take you somewhere."

"No." If it wasn't now, she'd lose her nerve. What difference did atmosphere make, when it was dark and her eyes were closed? "This is fine."

"We'll make it better than fine."

He lit one of the station's emergency candles, so at least there was soft light. She couldn't know how arousing she was, standing there, tidy and terrified, prepared to give herself. To sacrifice herself, he thought grimly.

He would show her different.

"I love you, Cassie." It didn't matter that she didn't believe him. She would. He kissed her again, slowly, deeply, patiently, putting his heart into it.

And moment after moment there was nothing but the kiss, the taste of it, the meeting of lips, the way she softened against him.

"Hold me," he murmured.

Obedient, wanting to please, she wrapped her arms around him. There was a little shock when she felt how hard he was, how strong. How odd it was to hold him tight against her. While his mouth moved over hers, she stroked her hands over his back.

"I want to see you." He continued to rub his lips over her throat, even as her hands tensed on his back. He didn't mind her being shy. He found it endearing. "You have such a lovely face." His eyes stayed on it as he slowly undid the buttons of her blouse. "Eyes like fog, and that sexy mouth."

She blinked, thrown off enough to make no protest when he parted her blouse. No one had ever called her sexy. Then his gaze shifted downward, and the sound that rumbled in his throat had something curling hard in her stomach.

He was cupping her breasts in his hands, holding them as if they were delicate glass that could be shattered by a careless touch.

"Lovely."

"I'm small."

"Perfect." He lifted his gaze to hers again. "Just perfect." He watched her lashes flutter when he circled her breasts, brushed his thumbs over her nipples. And his blood heated when they stiffened, when she shuddered, when her eyes opened again in surprise and went dark.

What was he doing? Why wasn't he squeezing or pulling? She felt her head spin before it fell back. Heard, with a kind of dull shock, her own moan.

"Do you have to close your eyes?" he asked her. It wasn't so difficult to keep his hands easy, after all, not on skin that was soft as silk. "I like to watch them go cloudy when I touch you. I love to touch you, Cassie."

"I can't breathe."

"You're breathing. I can feel your heart." He lowered his lips to her shoulder before straightening to pull off his shirt. "Feel mine."

My oh my, Cassie thought. He looked like something in one of those glossy magazines. All muscles and firm smooth skin. With only the slightest of hesitations, she laid a hand on his chest, and smiled. "It's pounding. Are you ready?"

"Oh, Cassie." Biting back a groan, he drew her into his arms, cradled her there, savored the feel of her flesh pressed against his. "I haven't even started."

Because she thought he meant something entirely different, her brows drew together and she swallowed her distaste and reached courageously for his crotch.

With a ripe oath, he jerked back, stuttering, as she covered herself and gaped.

"I thought you wanted… I thought you meant…" Good God, he'd been hard as rock. And huge.

He decided laughing would be better than screaming. "Darlin', you do that again, I'm going to embarrass myself, and we'll have to start all over. If it's all the same to you, I'd just like to touch you for a while."

"I don't mind, but you're…"

"I know what I am. You said you'd do what I want," he reminded her, fighting to keep his voice from growing rough with need. "I want you to look at me, look right at me now."

When she did, he skimmed his hands over her breasts

again. He could see surprised pleasure ripple over her face, hear it in her quickening breaths. So he began to murmur to her, endearments, foolishness, gauging her reaction.

When her eyes closed, he lifted her slowly off her feet, holding her suspended, trailing his mouth down from hers and over her throat, her collarbone, and at last to her breast.

Her hands clamped on his shoulders and her body arched as arrows—bullets—of hot sensation pierced through her flesh and straight to her center to burn. She shook her head, struggling to clear it.

"Devin."

He laved his tongue over her. "Do you want me to stop?"

"No. No."

"Thank God."

When she was quivering, when her hands were clutching and flexing on his skin, he lowered her to the floor again, until his mouth was fixed on hers. Her hands were fisted in his hair, her breath was coming fast. Her lips were hot.

And still she stiffened, just for an instant, when he unhooked her slacks.

She wouldn't spoil it. That she promised herself. Whatever came now didn't matter, because what came before had been so lovely. She'd never felt these pulls, these yearnings. Or she'd somehow forgotten them. His hands were hard, the palms rough, but he used them so gently on her. She would have been happy to have him go on touching her, just like this, forever. She could blissfully have drowned in those wonderful ripples of sensations.

Now he was uncovering the rest of her, and she knew it would be over soon. But he would hold her when he was done. He would hold her close and warm, she was sure of it. That would be enough.

When he picked her up and cradled her against his chest,

she smiled. The candlelight was lovely, and she felt an intense sense of tenderness, of sweetness. He'd made her feel wanted. She laid her lips against his, curled her arms around his neck, keeping them there as he lowered her to the cot so that the springs squeaked under their weight.

She opened her eyes in confusion when he didn't push inside her. Instead, he was curved beside her, his eyes on her face, his hand stroking up and down her torso.

"Don't rush me," he said mildly. "I'm enjoying myself."

To her astonishment, he began to talk to her about her body, her skin, her eyes, her legs. And the things he was murmuring sent flashes of new heat inside her.

She was grateful he didn't seem to need her to talk back. She was having trouble breathing again.

She was so incredibly sweet, so amazingly innocent. That was what kept his need locked away, kept his hands from taking quickly. Twelve years, he thought, listening to the way her breath caught, then burst out, when he skimmed a finger up the inside of her thigh. When a man had waited so long, he could be as patient as a saint, though his blood churned like a riptide.

He lowered his mouth to her breast again. So small, and firm, and smelling like spring. Under his lips he felt her heart thundering, felt her skin quiver. And knew he pleasured her.

He wanted to give her more, to give her everything, to know she craved as he did. So he stroked and suckled, arousing himself and her until she began to writhe under him and he knew she was climbing toward the edge. And he would be the one to show her that the fall was sweet.

It was too hot. She was burning from the inside out and couldn't keep still. She ached, and nothing she could do seemed to soothe the throbbing. Something inside her was racing for something else, and she strained away from it. It was too big, too huge, too terrifying. The air was thick, the sensations were too fast and too many. She moaned and bit down on her lip to stop the sound.

"You can yell," Devin told her, his own voice ragged. "You can scream if you want. Nobody can hear but me. Just let go, Cassie."

"I can't."

He dipped his fingers inside her, and his head spun. She was hot and wet and more ready than she knew. "Don't ask me to stop," he murmured against her mouth. "Don't ask me."

"No. No, don't."

She did scream then, a sound that should have shocked her, it was so wild and wanton. But her body was too busy rearing up toward him, poised on a spear of dark, drenching pleasure such as she'd never known. Everything inside her came to a fist, tensed violently, painfully, then burst free. She collapsed, weak as water, and thought she heard him groan.

"Again." He was greedy now. He kept a hand fisted in the tousled sheet to keep himself sane, and urged her up, urged her over. She strained against his hand, poured into it, and the arms she'd wrapped around him slid bonelessly to the mattress.

Surrender, he thought. More, fulfillment. But now he would give her himself.

He covered her, slipped inside her, holding himself back as her eyes fluttered open on fresh shock. He took her slowly, drawing out each stroke, each pulse. His heart almost burst from the strain of control when she convulsed again. Deliberately, patiently, he stirred her, gaining unimagined joy as he felt her begin once more to tremble and race.

The shudder worked through him, ripping, demanding. This time he knew he would go with her. Finally, with her. He clenched at the hand she'd fisted in the sheet, covered it. And took the fall.

She couldn't stop shuddering. But she wasn't cold. Not cold at all. The heat from her body, and from Devin's, which lay over her, seemed to rise in waves that were all but visible. He was breathing hard, like a man who'd been racing, and his full weight was on her, pinning her to the mattress so that she could feel the springs pushing against her back.

It was lovely.

She understood, for the first time in her life, the secrets of the dark.

"I know I'm crushing you," he managed. "I'm trying to move."

"You can stay." She wrapped her arms around him to keep him there. He was still inside her, still there. It felt wicked and wonderful. "I like it this way."

"I appreciate you putting up with all that, seeing as you're not big on sex."

The dry tone alerted her, but she was too delighted to mind being teased. "I didn't mind," she said, and smiled against his throat. "Devin, it was wonderful. I actually—"

"I know. Several times. I counted."

She laughed, and didn't feel at all embarrassed. "You did not."

"I certainly did." He found the energy to lift his head and look down at her. "You can thank me later."

Her smile sweetened. She'd never had a man look at her like that, all hazy-eyed and satisfied and sleepy. "It was all right." Incredibly moved, she lifted a hand to his cheek. "Wasn't it?"

"It was worth waiting for." He turned his lips into her palm. "But I'm not waiting another twelve years to have you again."

"I don't want you to." Everything inside her was dreamy and disjointed. "You're so handsome."

"The curse of the MacKades."

"I mean it." She lifted her other hand, framing his face. It was so easy to touch him now, to let her finger trace that wonderful dimple beside his smile. "Do you remember how I used to come out to the farm sometimes when I was a girl, to visit with your mother?"

"Sure. You were a pretty little thing, skinny, and I didn't pay you much mind. My mistake."

"I used to watch you. In the summer, especially. When you'd be working with your shirt off."

His grin flashed. "Well, well, little Cassie..."

"I had a terrible crush on you for a while, and these really imaginative fantasies." She chuckled. "Well, I thought they were imaginative, until now. Nothing came close. I can't believe I'm saying this, talking to you like this."

"Under the circumstances, you can say pretty much anything." He was hoping she would. He could feel himself hardening inside her.

"I was about twelve, and you were always nice to me. All of you were. I loved coming out there, just to be there. But it was a bonus when it was summer and you'd be bare-chested and sweaty. Like you are now." Experimentally, she traced a finger over his shoulder. "All those muscles shiny with damp. Your body...it's so beautiful. Sometimes you'd come into Ed's, and when you'd go out, if there were women in there, they'd roll their eyes and sigh."

"Come on."

"Really. Of course, if one of your brothers came in, they'd do the same thing."

"Don't spoil it."

She laughed, lifting a hand to push tousled hair from her cheek. "Okay. They sighed louder, and longer, for you."

"That's better."

"And Ed would say something like 'That Devin Mac-Kade's got the best buns in three counties.'" She caught herself on a giggle, her eyes going wide. "I shouldn't have said that."

"Too late. Besides, I know Ed's partial to that particular part of the anatomy. She's told me."

"She's shameless." With a long sigh of her own, Cassie wound her arms around him again, let her hands wander down. "But you do have an exceptional seat."

"Now you've done it." As her fingers brushed over his hips, he began to move inside her. Nothing could have pleased him more than seeing the way her eyes rounded in surprise.

"But how can you— Oh, my God!"

"It's no trouble," he assured her. "It's my pleasure."

And after, a long time after, he curled up beside her on the cot, his face buried in her hair, his legs tangled with hers. As she had hoped, as she had needed, he held her.

Chapter 8

It was barely dawn when Cassie crept into her own kitchen. She felt giddy, like a teenager sneaking home after curfew. Not that she'd ever broken curfew, she thought now. Not that she'd ever done anything except exactly what was expected of her.

It made her hushed, secret return all the more liberating.

She'd just spent the night, all night, with the most exciting, beautiful, the most gentle man she'd ever known.

She, Cassandra Connor Dolin, was having an affair.

She had to slap her hand over her mouth to muffle a burst of laughter. Her heart was still racing, her head still swimming, and her body...her body felt as though it had been polished with flower petals.

She was sure she looked different, and tried to see her reflection in the chrome of the toaster. Because she was alone, she allowed herself three quick spins before putting the kettle on for coffee.

Then, being a mother, she padded toward the bedrooms to make sure her children were snug and asleep. Turning from Connor's room, she stifled a gasp. There was Ed, her fire-engine hair done up in squashy pink rollers, wearing a wildly flowered robe of pink and blue.

"I'm sorry," Cassie whispered. "I didn't mean to wake you."

"You were quiet as a little mouse. I was listening out for you." Ed took a long, measuring look, and liked what she saw. "Well, well, I believe you're feeling good and smug this morning. About time, too."

Cassie cast a last look at her sleeping son, then backed down the short hallway toward the kitchen. "The kids didn't give you any trouble, did they?"

"Of course not. Never heard a peep out of either of them." Grinning, Ed followed Cassie into the kitchen, watched while she busied herself measuring out coffee. "You going to tell me about it, or am I going to have to use my imagination? I got a damn good one."

The heat rose to Cassie's cheeks, but it was from pleasure as much as embarrassment. "I stayed with Devin."

"I figured that out, sweetie pie." Very much at home, Ed popped bread into the toaster. "From the look on your face, the two of you didn't discuss world events until morning." Sighing a little, she poked around in the refrigerator. "I'm not just being nosy. I guess I want to make sure you're as okay on the inside as you look on the out."

"I'm fine." Cassie turned, smiled. There was Ed, holding a jar of preserves in one hand and a gallon of milk in the other, her thin face shiny with night cream, her hair exploding on rollers, her outrageous robe falling over legs the shape of toothpicks.

This, Cassie realized, was the mother of her heart. Cassie

set the steaming kettle down again and dashed over to throw her arms around Ed.

Surprised, moved, Ed pressed her lips to Cassie's hair. "There, baby…"

"I feel…different. Do I look different?"

"You look happy."

"My stomach's still jumping." Laughing at herself, Cassie drew back and pressed a hand to it. "But it feels good. I didn't know it could be like that. I didn't know I could be like that." Casting a quick look at the hallway, she went back to the coffee. Her children were asleep, and would be for another half hour. After all these years, Cassie thought, she would have a mother to listen.

"I've never been with anyone but Joe."

"I know that, baby."

"Before we were married, I wouldn't let him. I wanted to be married first, I wanted it to be right." She poured coffee for both of them, then sat at the table. "I was nervous on our wedding night, but excited, too. You'd given me a white nightgown for my shower. It was so pretty, so perfect. It made me feel like a bride. When we got to the motel, I asked Joe to give me an hour to myself. I wanted to take a long bath and…well, you know."

"The female ritual. Yeah, I know."

"He came back—it was closer to two hours—and he was drunk. It wasn't the way I'd always dreamed. He ripped the gown, and he pushed me onto the bed. It all happened so fast, and he hurt me. I knew it was supposed to hurt some the first time, but it was more than some. He fell asleep right after, and I just laid there. I didn't feel anything."

"A man's not supposed to treat a woman that way." Even if she hadn't already despised Joe Dolin, Ed would have despised him now. "That's not how it's supposed to be."

"It was the way it was. Always. I never felt anything, Ed. Ever. He didn't always hurt me, but it was always quick, and mostly a little mean. I figured it was my fault—he told me it was often enough. It got better when I was carrying Connor, because he left me alone most of the time. I didn't know he was cheating on me then. I guess I was too stupid."

"Don't you call yourself stupid," Ed said fiercely. "I don't want to hear that."

"Maybe I just didn't care enough to know, or want to know. I was wrapped up in becoming a mother, then in being one. He was already hitting me. We hadn't been married long when that started, but I didn't think there was anything I could do about it. My mother said…well, it doesn't matter what she said. I stayed, then Emma came along. He only wanted me a couple of times after Emma… He forced me."

"Oh, Cassie. Honey, why didn't you tell me?"

"Ed, I was too ashamed. He was my husband, and I had it in my head that he had a right to do what he did. I know different now." She took a long breath. "You see, when I went to Devin last night, I didn't think… I knew he wouldn't hurt me, at least not like Joe had. I thought going to bed with him would make him happy, and it didn't matter to me. I mean, I thought he would just…that I would just…"

"You had yourself a real man last night," Ed finished. "And it changed things."

"Yes." Relieved, Cassie smiled. "He was so gentle, so patient. You know, it mattered to him what I was feeling. It really mattered. And he made me feel beautiful. Ed…" She bit her lip, even as it curved again. "It matters to me now. I'm already thinking about next time."

Ed let out a cackling laugh and squeezed Cassie's hand. "Good for you."

"He says he loves me," Cassie said quietly. "I know men say those things when they want you, or they think you need to hear it. But do you think he could?"

"I think Devin MacKade's a man who says what he means. What about you?"

"I don't know. That part of me is so confused. I didn't love Joe, Ed. I never did. I used him."

"Cassandra—"

"No, I did. I used him to get out of the house, because I wanted to have a family of my own, and he was there. I wasn't fair to him. I don't mean that gave him the right to beat me," she added, noting the warrior gleam in Ed's eye. "Nothing gave him that right. But I didn't love him, not the way a woman should love her husband."

"He didn't do anything to deserve love."

"No, he didn't. With Devin, I feel so many things, so many different things, and I don't know if one of them is that kind of love."

"Then you take all the time you need to sort it out. Don't you let anyone push you into anything you're not ready for. Not even Devin."

"How will I know?"

"Sweetie pie, when the time comes you'll know. Take my word for it, you'll know."

While Cassie was talking with Ed over coffee, Devin was pulling up at the farm. He'd felt a need for home. The sky was losing its dawn haze when he walked into the milking parlor. Shane and two of the 4-H students he often took on as help were finishing up the morning routine.

Patiently Shane showed one of the boys how to detach

cow from machine without causing irritation. The parlor smelled of warm milk, animal and hay.

"You're going to check her teats after, just like you did before, to make sure there's no infection." He did so himself, demonstrating. "When she's dry, you see to her feed." He cocked a brow at Devin. "You can see the sheriff wanders in when most of the work's done. Y'all lead them out now."

Devin gave the cow an easy swat, then helped Shane clean and disinfect the machines. It was routine, companionable work.

"Remember when Dad had us milking by hand?" Devin asked.

"He figured we'd better know. Machines break down, but cows fill up regular. You're up early," Shane commented. "And you've got a stupid grin on your face. Looks like you got lucky."

Devin only angled his head. "I'm feeling too good to pound on you this morning."

"Good, because I've got to finish up here and get to the hens before breakfast. You and Cassie," he said, grinning again. "Who'd have thought it?"

"I've been thinking about it for a long time." Devin helped Shane secure the fresh milk in the stainless-steel tanks. "I've been in love with her a long time."

Shane straightened, winced. "Man, don't start that. Every time I turn around, somebody's falling in love. It's giving me nightmares."

"Well, get used to it. I'm going to ask her to marry me."

Shane rubbed his hands over his face, pulled off his cap, dragged hands through his hair. "What is it? Something in the water around here? First Rafe, then Jared. Now you. I turn my back for a minute and everybody's getting married, having babies. Get a hold of yourself, Dev."

"Afraid it's going to rub off?"

"Hell, I'm going to start to take shots. Look, Cassie's as sweet as they come, and as pretty as fresh milk, but let's not go crazy."

"I love her," Devin said, so simply Shane groaned. "It seems I always have. There's nothing I could do about it even if I wanted to."

"You know what kind of trouble this is going to cause me? Don't you have any consideration?" Shane demanded. "I'll be the only one of us left. Women home in on things like that. I won't be able to get myself a snuggle without the woman thinking it's going to lead to orange blossoms."

"You'll have to tough it out."

"What in sweet hell's so appealing about marriage?" Grumbling, Shane headed out of the milking parlor. "I mean, think about it, Dev. Really think. You've got one woman for the rest of your life. Just one. And there're so many out there. Tall ones, short ones, round ones."

Amused, Devin slapped a hand on Shane's shoulder as they walked toward the chicken coop. "And with me out of the way, there'll be more for you."

"There is that." Taking it philosophically, Shane shrugged. "I guess it'll be up to me to maintain the MacKade legend. I'll just have to make the sacrifice."

"You're up to it, bro."

Cassie never lingered in the library. She was much too conscientious to skim over her cleaning there, but most often she tried to arrange her schedule so that someone was in the house when she dealt with that room.

There was no one in the house now. Her children were in

school and the guests were busy with their sightseeing for the afternoon. She made excuses in her head for why she should see to a dozen other things besides that one room. But she knew the library had been used the day before. She knew there were books that needed to be put back on the shelves, plants that needed watering, windows that needed washing.

She told herself it was foolish. She knew the emotions and moods of the house better than she knew her own. There was nothing here that could hurt her. In fact, the house had changed her life, and all for the better.

Armed with her cleaning basket, she went in. If she left the door open wide behind her, it was only because she wanted to be able to hear if one of the guests returned and wanted anything.

It wasn't because she was afraid.

She set the basket aside and tidied the books first. She knew guests often liked to borrow one to read on a rainy afternoon or to help them drift off to sleep at night. Rafe and Regan had provided a variety of books for a variety of tastes. She, too, was free to borrow any she liked, whenever she liked. But she rarely did.

Nor, she thought suddenly, did Connor, though he was a voracious reader. It occurred to her that he, too, avoided this room, even though he was thoroughly at home in the rest of the inn.

It was a feeling, she supposed. Something that lingered in the air. Shaking it off, she carried her basket over to the twin philodendrons that trailed their leaves from pots set in stands by the tall window that overlooked the side garden.

They needed to be dusted. She'd been putting it off.

As she began, she felt the chill, down to the bone.

And knew she wasn't really alone.

She thought she could see him, out of the corner of her

eye. The big body going to fat, the wide face set in hard, dissatisfied lines.

Joe.

The terror came so quickly, she dropped the basket at her feet as she whirled around.

He wasn't there. Of course he wasn't. No one was. But it was so bitterly cold. With numb fingers, she reached for the window to open it to the warm breeze.

She fumbled, couldn't work the latch and discovered her breath was coming in short gasps.

You let him touch you, didn't you? Whore.

She hunched her shoulders automatically against a blow that didn't come.

Did you think I wouldn't know? Did you think you could cuckold me in my own house? You, with your innocent face and fancy Southern manners. Nothing but a slut.

Shaking, she backed slowly away from the window. Her eyes darted around the room, searching corners. There was no one there. But how could she hear the voice so clearly in her head?

Know this. You'll never leave me. I'll see you dead first.

You don't love me, Cassie wanted to say. You despise me. Let me go. But the words wouldn't come.

I'll kill you both. Remember that. Till death do us part. And death is your only escape.

"Cassie."

On a strangled shriek, she spun around. Devin was just inside the door, his eyes narrowed in concern. Without a thought, she ran into his arms.

"Devin. Devin, you have to go. Go quickly, before he sces you. He's going to kill you."

"What are you talking about? God, you're shaking like a leaf. It's freezing in here."

"You feel it?" Her teeth were all but chattering as she drew back. "You can feel it?"

"Sure I can. It's like an icebox." He rubbed her hands in his to warm them.

"I thought it was Joe. I swear I saw his fist coming toward me, and then—" The room spun; her knees buckled. The dizziness lasted only an instant, but she was already up in Devin's arms. "I'm all right. It's gone."

The room was warm again, sunny and bright, with the scent of roses and polish. Very gently, he laid her down on the soft leather sofa. "Let me get you some water."

"No, I'm all right." She thought she might jump out of her skin if he left her alone there. "It's just this room." She steadied herself, sat up. "I thought it was Joe, but it wasn't. It was Barlow."

She was still too pale, Devin thought, but her eyes had cleared. His heart had dropped to his knees when he'd seen them roll back in her head. "Has this happened before?"

"Not like this. Not this strong. I'm never very comfortable in this room. Even his bedroom is easier. But this time, I heard... You're going to think I've lost my mind."

"No, I won't." He cupped her face in his hands. "Remember who you're talking to."

"All right." She blew out a breath. "I heard him talking, in my head, I think. It sounded so much like Joe—the tone, the meanness in it. He called me—her—a whore, a slut. He knew she was in love with someone else, but he wasn't going to let her go, ever. He said he'd kill her first, kill both of them."

"Come on, let's get out of here. Let's go upstairs."

"I haven't finished—"

"Leave it, Cassie. Just leave it." He would have carried

her, but she got to her feet. Still, her hand reached for his. "The other day, when you were talking to the old ladies?"

"Mrs. Cox and Mrs. Berman, yes."

"You talked about Abigail being in love with someone. I thought you'd made it up, to add a little romance to the story."

"No. I can't explain it, Devin. I just know it's true. I saw him."

He paused at the back stairs that led up to her apartment. "You saw who?"

"The man she loved. I was in her room, and then I looked and he was at the door. He was looking right at me, talking to me as if I were Abigail. I could feel her there. Her heart was broken, but she let him go. Made him go. Devin... Devin, I think she killed herself."

He sat her down in a chair in her living room. "Why do you think that?"

"I can't explain that, either. Just a feeling. She didn't know how else to get free. And maybe because I thought about it once."

The blood drained from his face. "Good God, Cassie."

"Not for very long," she said quickly. "And not very seriously. I had the kids to think about. If I hadn't had them, I might have thought about it longer. When you're trapped, Devin, you get crazy ideas about escape."

Nothing he knew about her had ever frightened him more. "I would have helped you. I wanted to help you."

"I wouldn't let you. I wouldn't let anyone. You, Ed, Regan. There were others, too, others who were willing to do whatever they could. I was wrong not to accept the help, but that's over now." She curled her hands over his. "I'm not telling you this to upset you, but to try to help you understand how I know she did it. She didn't have people to help her. He'd seen to that. He made sure she was cut off from the women in town, made sure the servants were too frightened to do anything but stand back."

Somewhere in her mind, she could almost feel it, see it. "He hit her, too. It was his fist I saw today. Not Joe's. But it's the same, you see. So much the same. When he killed that boy in front of her, she knew he was capable of anything. She gave up, Devin. Eventually even her children weren't enough to keep her from escaping in the only way she knew."

"It's not you, Cassie."

"It could have been."

"But it's not," he said firmly. "You're here, you're with me. There's nothing for you to be afraid of."

"I'm tired of being afraid." She closed her eyes, let her head rest on his shoulder as he crouched in front of her. "I'm glad you're here." She let out a deep sigh. "Why are you here?"

"I worked it so I could clear out for an hour. I wanted to see you. I wanted to be with you."

"I thought about you all morning. I nearly put coffee in Emma's thermos for school, because I was thinking about you instead of what I was doing."

"Really?" He couldn't think of a more satisfying compliment. When she lifted her head, he could see that the color was back in her cheeks. "Were you thinking that you'd like to make love with me again?"

"Yes, I was."

"I've still got most of an hour," he murmured, rising and bringing her to her feet.

She blinked. "It's the middle of the day."

"Uh-huh." He drew her toward the hall.

"Devin, it's daylight."

"That's right." He unhooked the belt that held his beeper and weapon, hung them over the doorknob.

"It's…" Her heart stumbled as he reached out to unbutton her blouse. "It's barely noon."

"Yeah, I'm going to miss lunch." As he slipped the blouse from her shoulders, lowered his mouth toward hers, he smiled. "Do you want me to stop, Cassie?"

Her head rolled back on her shoulders. "I guess I don't," she said, weak, willing.

She forgot that the sun was shining and the birds were twittering. She forgot that traffic was cruising by on the road, and that people were going about their business in town.

It was so easy, so powerfully easy, to let it all happen again. It was so easy to enjoy the way his hands moved tenderly over her, the way his mouth coaxed hers to warm. He felt so good against her when she curled her arms around him, so solid, that she forgot to feel self-conscious because the sun was pouring through the windows.

He undressed her, completely, taking his time over it, drawing out each moment just to look at her. To look at what was finally his. The softness. The sweetness. He kissed her, soothing and arousing her, as he undressed himself. His hands were gentle, because he knew it was what she needed. His mouth was patient, allowing her to set the pace. And the pace was slow and dreamy.

He lowered her to the bed she'd made so neatly that morning, gave himself the quiet delight of brushing her hair with his fingers until it was all tangled golden curls over the plain white quilt. Her eyes were closed, and already her cheeks carried the faint flush of stirred passions.

Last night there had been only the light from a practical and unscented emergency candle, a narrow bunk and a room that smelled of old coffee.

Today there was sunlight, birdsong and the perfume of the flowers by her window. And today, he thought, she knew there would be pleasure.

He gave her pleasure. Rivers of it. She floated on it, glided on it, immersed herself in it without reserve. All hesitancy, all shyness, vanished under a warm haze of gently lapping sensations.

The texture of his callused fingers, the friction of them as they moved over her skin caused little sparking shocks that speeded her pulse. The taste of his mouth as it moved to her flesh, then back to her lips, was drugging. She could hear his breathing quicken, or those little hums of pleasure in his throat, whenever he touched some new part of her. He was so beautiful to her—not just his incredibly stunning outward good looks. More, it was the beauty inside that drew and seduced her—the kindness, the strength, the patience.

It delighted her to be able to squeeze her hands over his biceps, feel the coil of strength in them, in the muscles of his back. She adored the shape and weight of his body, the way it pressed hers deep into the mattress. The light scrape of his teeth on her shoulder gave her a quick, jittery thrill. To answer it, she nipped at his while her hands grew bold enough to journey down.

He hissed out a breath, jolted. Her eyes flashed open when his head reared up. For an instant, for an eternity, she saw something dark and edgy and dangerous in those moss-green eyes. Something that had her blood leaping high and her pulse scrambling.

He yanked himself back into control, the way he would have yanked a wild dog on a thick leash. His muscles knotted. He could have sworn he felt the sweat burst out of his pores.

"Don't worry." His voice was raw, but he lowered his mouth gently to hers again. "Don't be afraid."

She wanted to tell him she wasn't, couldn't be, afraid of him. That she would be afraid of nothing that happened between them. That she wanted to know what had come into his eyes. But he was kissing her into oblivion again, into that misty place where there was nothing but warm, quiet pleasures.

Her moan was long and deep when he eased her to a peak. Long and deep when he gave her more. She let the current take her, opening for him, letting him fill her. Nothing was more stunning than moving with him, feeling his body mesh and mate with hers.

Then his mouth was at her ear, and through her own gasping passion she heard him say her name. Just her name, before he pulled her with him.

"I love you." He still ached for her, even as he shifted his weight and drew her against his side. "I want you to get used to hearing that."

"Devin—"

"No, I don't expect it yet. I will, but I don't expect it yet." He turned his face into her hair and breathed in the scent of it and her, a scent that always reminded him of sunlight on a meadow. "You just get used to hearing it. You tell me when you're used to it, because then I'm going to ask you to marry me."

She went rigid. "I can't. How can I think about that? This is happening too fast."

"Not for me." He wouldn't be angry, he wouldn't even allow himself to be discouraged by the shock in her voice. Instead, he stroked a hand down her arm and spoke with quiet confidence. "I've gotten good at waiting, so I can wait a while longer. But I figured you should know where I'm heading here. I want you, I want the kids, I want a life, but I can wait until you're ready."

"I might never be ready. Devin, you have to understand, I don't know if I can ever make those promises again."

"You've never made them to me. That's all that counts." He rose up on his elbow so that he could study her face. He'd frightened her, he noted. But it couldn't be helped. "I love you. You let that settle in, and we'll see what happens next."

"Don't you see that—"

"I only see you, Cassie." Persuasively, he kissed her, until the hand she'd lifted to push against his shoulder went lax. "Only you."

A few miles away, Joe Dolin was policing a picnic area on the battlefield for litter. As he worked, his eyes scanned the fields, the hills, the road below. There were large, shady trees, stone walls. He was going to pick his time, and his spot. This wasn't it.

Eventually the crew would work their way down toward the bridge where General Burnside had screwed up during the Battle of Antietam. There the ground was uneven, rocky and thick with brush. There was a creek to hide his scent, trees to cover him.

He'd often poached in those woods, jacklighting deer illegally with some of his drinking buddies. He had plenty of time now to calculate how long it would take him to travel through them, where he could hide, who he could go to for a little help.

In the meantime, he was making himself a busy little bee, picking up the soft drink cans and wrappers tossed aside by lousy tourists or kids hooking school. His supervisor wasn't a fool, but Joe never gave him any lip, any trouble, and made sure he was first in line to volunteer for any of the harder or messier jobs.

He was building himself a damn good rep in prison, something he'd never had on the outside. Something, he thought as he wiped sweat from his brow, that was going to help him get out of the cage.

And get back to Cassie. Get to Cassie.

The little bitch was going to pay for every day he'd spent behind bars. Every hour he'd had to go without a drink or a woman.

When he was finished with her, he was going after MacKade. Maybe all four of the stinking MacKades. He'd had plenty of time to plan it out, to work out the mistakes, to dream about it.

He hoped he had to kill one of them. He hoped it would be Devin. And when he was finished, he was going to Mexico, taking whatever was left of his wife with him.

All he needed was money, a car and a gun. He knew exactly where he was going to get all three.

Chapter 9

Connor tried to take in everything at once. He knew Bryan was getting restless, wandering around the sheriff's office, trying to get a look at the cells in the back. But for himself, he thought nothing was more fascinating than watching the sheriff handle calls and type up reports.

He was going to write a story about it, and he had to get everything just right. The way the office looked, with the dust dancing in the sunlight through the windows, the scars on the desk from feet or cigarettes, the way the ceiling fan squeaked overhead.

He took a deep sniff and filed away in his mind the scent of coffee—really strong, and a little harsh—and the smell of the dust that sort of tickled the nose.

He tried to remember just how the phone sounded when it shrilled on the sheriff's desk, how the sheriff's chair scraped against the floor, how the deputy scratched his head, then his cheek, as he put papers away in the file cabinet.

He already had the sound of the sheriff's voice. It was deep and slow, and there was a hint of something in it. Humor, Connor thought, when he answered some of the calls. Other times it was brisk, kind of official. Once or twice he'd seen lines form between the sheriff's brows.

He sure did drink a lot of coffee, Connor thought, and he wrote a lot of things down. Connor had a million questions, but he held them in because he knew the sheriff was working.

Devin glanced up and saw the boy watching him. Like an owl, he thought. Wise and patient. A look at his watch told him he'd kept the kids hemmed in for most of their Saturday morning. He imagined Connor could sit there, quiet as a mouse, for hours yet. But he recognized the signs of trouble brewing in Bryan.

It was time to give them all a break.

"Donnie, you take over here. We're going to get some lunch at Ed's."

"Yo."

"The state boys call about the Messner case, you tell them I'll have the report to them by Monday."

"Yo," Donnie said again, and crushed his brows together over the filing.

"I'll pick up lunch for Curtis. Tell him, if he starts to make noises back there."

"You got a prisoner?" Suddenly all of Bryan's boredom was washed away in the thrill of it. "You didn't tell us."

"Just somebody sleeping off a night on the town." He was almost sorry he couldn't tell them it was a mad psychopath. "I could use a burger."

"All right!" Bryan darted out of the door. "I'm starving. Extra fries, right, Con?"

"I guess." Connor could hardly think about food with all the questions in his head. "Ah, Sheriff, how come you have that police radio on all the time? I mean, it has fire department stuff, and things from out of your jurisdiction."

"Because you can never be sure what might come over that you'd have to pay attention to."

"When you know somebody, does it feel funny to have to lock them up?"

"Sometimes if you know them it makes it easier to settle things before they get out of hand."

"Have you ever had anybody break out?" Bryan wanted to know as he danced backward on the sidewalk. "Like, conk you over the head and run for it?"

Devin ran his tongue around his teeth. He had a wonderful image of poor old Curtis going over the wall. "Nope, can't say as I have."

"If they did, you'd have to shoot them, right?" The excitement of it leaped in Bryan's eyes. "Like in the leg."

"If they did, it's likely I'd know who they were, so I'd just go to their house and bring them back."

"What if they resisted arrest?"

Devin knew what was expected of him. "I'd have to rough 'em up."

"Slap the cuffs on him," Bryan said with a hoot. "And back into the cage. Wham!"

"The town's quiet," Connor said, "because the sheriff keeps it quiet."

Touched, Devin flipped a finger over the bill of Connor's ball cap. "Thanks. We aim to serve."

"Sheriff."

Devin turned and watched with an inner sigh as the ancient and wiry owner of the general store and sub shop approached. The man could talk the bark off a tree.

"Afternoon, Mr. Grant. How's business?"

"Oh, up and down, Sheriff, up and down." Mr. Grant paused, flicked a bit of lint from the front of his wrinkled brown shirt. "I thought I should let you know, Sheriff... not that I poke my nose into what's not my business... With me, it's live and let live..."

That ended the statement, which Devin knew was habitual. Mr. Grant's mind wandered freely from pillar to post. "Let me know what, Mr. Grant?"

"Oh, well, I was just taking a little air and happened to walk by the bank. Just past closing time, you know."

"Yes, I know."

"Seemed to me somebody was holding up the bank."

"Excuse me?"

"Seemed to me," Mr. Grant repeated, in his ponderous way, "somebody was holding up the bank. Had a gun, sure enough. Looked to me to be a .45. Could be I'm wrong about that. Might be a .38."

Before either boy could comment, Devin slapped a hand on each of their shoulders. "Go on up to Ed's. Stay there."

"But, Devin—"

"Do it, Bryan. Go on now, both of you. Stay there, and don't say anything." He stared hard at Connor. "Don't say anything," he repeated. "We don't want people getting upset and getting in the way."

"What are you going to do?" Connor said in an awed voice.

"I'm going to take care of it. Get up to Ed's. Move. Now."

When they ran off, Devin kept one eye on them, to be sure they obeyed. "Mr. Grant, I wonder if you'd come along with me. Let's just take a look at this."

"Fine by me."

The bank was across the street and another half a block up. An old brick building with elaborate ironwork, it sat catty-corner from Ed's Café. A quick look showed Devin that the boys had indeed gone in. They had their faces pressed up to the window.

Devin scanned the street. It was Saturday, and there was considerable traffic. Enough, in any case, to cause a problem if there was trouble. He didn't intend to have any of his people hurt.

"Did you get a look at the man, Mr. Grant?"

"Some. Young, 'bout your age, I expect. Can't say as I recognized him. Looked a little like the Harris boy, but wasn't."

Devin nodded. He spotted a dirty white compact with Delaware tags at the curb in front of the bank. "Recognize that car there?"

Mr. Grant thought it over. "Can't say as I do. Never seen it around here."

"Stay here a minute." Unsnapping the flap covering his weapon, Devin sidestepped up to the bank. The door was festooned with curvy ironwork. Through it, he could make out one teller behind the wide counter. And the man across from her, nervously waving a gun.

It was a .45, he noted. Grant had been dead-on.

He slipped away from the door. "Mr. Grant, I'd like you to get on down to the office, tell Donnie I need some backup here at the bank. We've got an armed robbery in progress. I want you to tell him that, straight out. And that I don't want him coming up here blaring sirens or coming into the bank. I don't want him coming into the bank. Have you got that?"

"Why, sure I do, Sheriff. Be happy to oblige."

"And stay down there yourself, Mr. Grant. Don't come back up here."

He'd just started to move again when he saw Rafe approaching. Before his brother could lift a hand in greeting, Devin snagged him. "You're deputized."

"Hell, Devin, Regan just send me out for more diapers. I haven't time to play deputy."

"See that car? White compact, Delaware plates?"

"Sure, I got eyes."

"Put it out of commission."

Now Rafe's brows lifted, and his grin flashed. "Gee, Devin, I don't know as I remember how."

"Do it," Devin said, and the sharp impatience got through.

"What's going on?"

"Somebody's robbing the bank. Put the car out of commission in case he gets past me. And do what you can to keep people out of the way without getting them stirred up."

"You're not going in there alone."

"I've got the gun, you don't," Devin pointed out. "And I've got the badge. Be a pal, Rafe, and deal with the car. As far as I can tell, there's only one perp. I'm going in. If he comes out waving that damn gun, don't be a jerk. Get out of the way."

The hell he would, Rafe thought, but he crouched down to move around to the driver's side of the car while Devin took out his weapon.

Devin wanted to keep it simple, and safe. He tucked his gun into the back of his belt, slipped his badge off and into his pocket. He strolled into the bank, smiled at the teller.

"Hey there, Nancy. Thought I'd be too late to make my deposit. Lucky for me you're still open."

Though her face was frozen in fear, she managed to gape at him. "But— But—"

"The wife'll have my hide if I forget to put the money in. We got that automatic withdrawal on our insurance, you know." He strolled up to the counter, one hand reaching down.

"Are you crazy?" the man with the gun shrieked out, nerves in every syllable. "Are you out of your mind? Get down on the floor! Down! Now!"

"Hey, I'm not butting in line," Devin said reasonably. "Just trying to do some business." He kept his eyes on the man's face, his hand still going down and back, where a man kept his wallet.

"I'll show you some business!"

To Devin's relief, the man shifted the gun from Nancy and toward him. "Put your damn money on the counter. I'll take that, too."

As if he'd just noticed the weapon, Devin held up a hand in peace. "Holy hell, you robbing the bank?"

"What does it look like I'm doing, Einstein? Let's have the money."

"Okay, okay. I don't want any trouble here. You can have it." But instead of his wallet, Devin came out with his gun. "Now, are we going to stand here and shoot each other, or what?"

The man's eyes went wild. "I'll kill you! I swear I'll kill you!"

"That's a possibility." A remote one, since the idiot was waving the gun like a flag on the Fourth of July. "It's just as likely I'll kill you. You drop that gun on the floor and step back from it. You've already got armed robbery, you don't want to add shooting a police officer."

"A cop, a damn cop! Then I'll just shoot her!" Furious, he swung the gun back toward the teller.

Devin didn't hesitate, he didn't even bother to curse. Nancy was just where she should be. On the floor, out of the line of fire. And since he was close enough, Devin used his fist instead of his gun.

"Damn idiot."

The man managed to get off one shot at the ceiling before the gun flew out of his hand. Ignoring it, Devin put his own between the man's eyes.

"What you want to do now," he said calmly, "is roll yourself over and put your hands behind your head. If you don't, I'm going to have to blow your head right off, and this carpet's only a year old."

"Damn cop. Damn lousy one-horse town."

"You got that right." With a bit more force than was strictly necessary, Devin jerked the man's hands down, cuffed them. "You shouldn't mess with small towns. We're real careful about them. Anybody hurt back there? You all right, Nancy?"

As a chorus of breathless, excited voices exploded from behind the counter, he glanced back, knowing Rafe was behind him. And grinned at the crowbar his brother was slapping against his palm.

"I told you I'd handle it."

"This was just in case. What did you do, Dev, scalp him?"

Idly Devin picked up the wig that had been dislodged during the scuffle. "Looks that way. Might as well give him a shave while I'm at it." None too gently, he pulled the man's head back and ripped off the fake mustache. "In case you haven't figured it out, you're under arrest. You have the right to remain silent…" he began as he hauled the man to his feet.

He finished Mirandaizing him on the way to the door. "Y'all get up from behind there now. I'm going to send Donnie in to get your statements."

From their station at the diner window, both boys watched Devin come out, dragging a balding man with a bloody lip.

"He got him," Bryan said, awed. "Devin got an honest-to-God bank robber."

"Of course he did." Connor beamed. "He's the sheriff."

There was talk of little else but the attempted bank robbery. In the way of small towns, unofficial reports leaped over the wires far ahead of official ones. In many of the phone and backyard-fence conversations, it was said that Devin had burst into the bank, gun drawn, eyes blazing. In others, he had taken out the robber, who'd been armed to the teeth with automatic weapons, bare-handed.

By the end of the day, Devin found himself the recipient of enough homemade baked goods that he could have opened his own restaurant. They made up for the endless official reports he had to type and file. They nearly made up for the phone calls he was forced to field, from concerned citizens, the mayor, the bank manager and a number of women who thought he might need a bit of comfort after his ordeal.

He was deflecting one of the offers when his brothers walked in.

"No, Annie, I wasn't wounded." He rolled his eyes as all three of his visitors grinned at him. "No, he didn't shoot me. Sharilyn's exaggerating. Ah…" A little baffled by the offer presented to him, he cleared his throat. "That's nice of you, Annie, and I appreciate the thought, but— No, I don't think I'm going to suffer from delayed stress syndrome. Yeah, I've heard of it, but— No, no, really, I'm just fine. And I'm a little tied up right now. Yeah, official business. That's right. You take care now. Uh-huh. You bet. Bye."

He let out a long breath, shaking his head briskly as he replaced the receiver. "Holy hell."

"Was that Annie 'The Body' Linstrom?" Shane wanted to know.

"She was hitting on me," Devin said with a snort of laughter. "Women are a puzzle. There's no way around it."

Jared sat on the corner of Devin's desk. "The way I heard it, bullets bounce off your chest."

"Nah." Shane sniffed at one of the pies sitting on a crowded shelf. "I heard he eats bullets. Betty Malloy bake this lemon meringue?"

"Yeah." Devin winced when the phone rang again. "Where the hell is Donnie?"

"Last I saw, he was strutting down Main Street trying to look like Supercop." Rafe cocked his head. "Aren't you going to answer it—Sheriff?"

Devin swore and picked up the phone. "Sheriff's office. MacKade."

He leaned back, closed his eyes. It was the press again. Every small paper and news bureau within fifty miles had picked up on the botched robbery. By rote, he gave the official line, danced around the demand for a more in-depth interview and hung up.

"You're good at that," Jared decided. "Real stern and authoritative."

"I'm beginning to wish I'd kicked that jerk in the head," Devin muttered. "He's caused me a lot of trouble. Now I'm stuck here, answering the damn phone, typing reports, with some out-of-town idiot who couldn't hold up a lemonade stand in the back. He whines all the time."

"At least you won't starve," Shane said, and helped himself to one of the cookies on a plate by the pie. "We thought we'd take you down to Duff's, buy you a drink."

"Can't leave the prisoner unattended."

"Rough," Jared said, without sympathy. "You know, Bryan was about to jump out of his socks when he got home. You're better than Rambo."

Amused, Devin scratched his cheek. "Don't tell him the last robbery I had to deal with was when a couple of kids stole underwear off Mrs. Metz's clothesline." He shuffled papers on his desk. "Have you been by the inn, Rafe? Everything okay there?"

"Everything's fine. Cassie was a little upset. Word travels," he added unnecessarily. "But I told her it was all blown out of proportion, and you didn't do anything much."

"Thanks a lot."

"No problem. Connor was already writing a story about you."

"No kidding?" The grin all but split his face.

"'A Day in the Life of Sheriff MacKade.'" Rafe helped himself to coffee. "The boy's nuts about you."

"Good thing." Shane took another cookie. "Since Devin's going to marry his mama."

Rafe bobbled the coffee, spilled it on his hand and swore. "Cassie? Little Cassie?"

"Shane's getting ahead of himself," Devin said, in a mild tone that belied the gleam in his eye. "As usual."

"Hey, you're the one who said it. Me, I figure you've just lost your mind. Like these two."

"Shut up, Shane." Jared kept his eyes on Devin's face. "You and Cassie?"

"So what?"

"So...that's interesting."

"Are you speaking as her attorney?" Devin pushed back from the desk. If the phone rang again, he thought he might just rip it out of the wall. To get himself back under control, he went to the coffee.

"He's got it bad," Rafe observed. "Didn't you have a thing for her about ten, twelve years ago?" When Devin didn't answer, merely poured the coffee, sipped it steely-eyed, Rafe grinned. "Never got over it, did you? Son of a gun. Why, that's practically poetic, bro. It gets me, right here." He thumped a hand on his chest.

"Keep ragging me, it'll get you somewhere else."

"It's getting so every day's Valentine's Day in Antietam." In disgust, Shane shoved another cookie in his mouth. "A man's not safe."

"Cassie's a sweetheart," Rafe said pointedly.

"Sure she is." Gamely, Shane swallowed, so that he could make his point. "She's as good as they come, and pretty with it. But why does that mean he has to marry her? You see all this stuff?" With a sweep of his hand, he indicated all the pies, cakes, tarts, cookies. "Women are going to fall all over him, and he's tossing them off because he's gone cross-eyed over *one* woman. It's not only stupid, it's...well, it's selfish."

Rafe gave Shane a thump on the back of the head that would have felled a grizzly. "Man, I love this guy. He's going to carry the MacKade legend into the next millennium."

"Damn right," Shane agreed. "No woman's going to tie

me down. I mean, with all the flowers out there, why pick one when you can have a bouquet?"

"Now that's poetry." Rafe thumped him again. "Let's go get that beer."

"You two go on." Jared stayed where he was. "I need to talk to Devin a minute."

They left, arguing about who was buying. When the room was quiet again, Devin took his coffee back to his desk. "You got a problem?"

"No." Jared shifted so that they were face-to-face. "But you might. Have you talked to Cassie about marriage?"

"A little. Why?"

"Joe Dolin."

"They're divorced. It's done."

"They're divorced." Eyes steady, Jared rested a hand on his knee. "But done's another thing. He'll get out eventually, Devin. He'll come back."

"I'll handle it."

"Yeah, I figure you can handle Joe, one-on-one. But there's the law."

Unconsciously Devin brushed a finger over his badge. "He tries to touch Cassie again, just tries, and I'll have him back behind bars before he can blink."

"And that's part of the problem. You're the sheriff, but you won't be objective. You can't be."

Devin set his coffee aside, leaned forward. "I've been in love with her most of my life. At least it seems that way. And I had to stand back and do little more than nothing while he hurt her. While I knew what he was doing to her inside that house. She wouldn't let me help, so the law tied my hands. Things are different now, and nothing's going to stop me from taking care of her. He lifts his hand to her again, and he's dead. Problem solved."

Jared nodded. He didn't take the statement lightly. He knew what it was to need to protect the woman you loved from any sort of harm. And he knew Devin was a man who said exactly what he meant.

"I'm talking about a situation that could develop if he's smart enough not to lift his hand to her. What if, after he serves his time, he moves back here, stays clean. How are you going to handle that?"

"One step at a time, Jared, like always. Of course, the first thing I'd have to do is keep Rafe from going after him because of what he tried to do to Regan."

That was true enough, Jared thought. And Rafe wouldn't be the only one who wouldn't welcome Joe Dolin back into the community. "Dev, I know what Cassie's been through. Exactly. I know because I'm her lawyer, I handled the divorce. We're talking about a textbook case of spousal abuse. A pitiful phrase, *textbook case,* for that kind of horror. Therapy's helped her, the town's helped her, and her own backbone's helped her. But she's got scars she's never going to get rid of."

"I'm being careful," Devin said slowly. "For God's sake, Jared, I've given her time—even after the divorce, I waited and gave her time. I'm trying to give her more."

"Devin, I'm just trying to show you the whole package. Believe me, I can't think of anyone I'd rather see you with than Cassie. Anyone I'd rather see her with than you. God knows she deserves somebody decent. But it's not just the two of you. There are two kids here. Joe Dolin's kids."

Devin's eyes darkened, narrowed. "You can say that to me, when you've got Bryan? Are you going to tell me it matters they're another man's blood, when I know damn well Bryan's as much yours as Layla?"

"That's not what I'm saying." Jared's voice was low and

calm. "I've seen you with them. I didn't have a clue how you felt about Cassie. You kept that covered well. But anybody with eyes can see you're crazy about those kids, that you've been good for both of them. They deserve you," he added, and nipped Devin's temper before it could bloom. "They deserve a father who loves them, and a home where they can just be kids."

"Fine. That's what I'm going to see they have."

"But it's not like Bryan, Dev. His biological father isn't around, isn't an issue. Dolin is."

"He doesn't give a damn about those kids, never has."

"No, but he'll have a right to them." Knowing that the frustration he felt didn't help, Jared spread his hands and took a deep breath. "The law says he does. And if he can't get to Cassie, he may just come up with the notion to get to her through them. Once he's out, he'll have a legal right to see them, to have visitation, to be part of their lives. You won't be able to block that."

Devin hadn't thought of it. Maybe he hadn't let himself. Now that it was there, right in the front of his mind, his blood went cold. "You're the lawyer. You block it."

"Parental rights are a sticky business, Dev. You know that. Until and unless he does something to put them in jeopardy, until and unless we can prove he's not just unfit, but dangerous to them, he'll have the law on his side."

Already Jared was thinking it through, working it out. "We may be able to put the pressure on for supervised visitations only, but blood still counts heavy in court."

"He beat Connor."

Jared's brows drew together. "I didn't know anything about that."

"Connor didn't tell Cassie, didn't want to make it worse on her."

"I might be able to use that, if the time comes. But once he's considered rehabilitated, a lot of the slate gets erased. He's going to be in for a long time yet, but I want you to know what you're up against here."

"I've got a clear picture of what I'm up against. Nothing's going to stop me from making Cassie and the kids mine. Not Joe Dolin, not the law, not anything."

"Well, then." Jared rose. "I'll state the obvious. I'm behind you. Rafe and Shane are behind you."

"I appreciate it."

"If you get yourself out from behind that desk for an hour, come down to Duff's. I'll buy you a beer." Satisfied, Jared headed for the door, then paused. "She's a terrific woman, Dev. Sweet, like Shane says, but tougher than you might think. Tougher than she thinks. If you convince her she wants you as much as you want her, you'll handle whatever comes down. I've got one piece of advice."

"You always do," Devin said dryly.

"For Cassie, it's not enough to let her know you love her, you want her. You let her know you need her. That's a woman who'd go to the wall for a man who needed her."

He did need her, Devin thought when Jared had shut the door behind him. But he didn't know how to show her, and wasn't entirely sure he should. Wasn't that just the kind of pressure he was struggling not to put on her?

He didn't want Cassie to go to the wall for him. He only wanted her to feel safe and happy. No, it was up to him to see that she was never hurt again, to protect her, to shield her and the children.

His need could wait.

Chapter 10

Cassie told herself it was foolish to worry. Devin was fine. Rafe had told her the story himself, and she knew that his version of the attempted bank robbery was much more accurate than those she'd heard over the phone. Even Connor's report, given in fits and starts of desperate excitement, had been less dramatic than the gossip spewing out of the town.

So there was no need to worry.

She was so worried, she jumped each time the phone rang. If she'd been able to leave the inn and the children for an hour, she'd have dashed into town to check every inch of Devin herself.

One thought, one fact, kept running in a loop in her brain. He'd faced down a man with a gun.

She shuddered again, and gave up trying to block the picture from her mind. He'd walked into an armed robbery, risked his life to protect others. His badge had never taken on such huge proportions for her before. He'd risked his life. In the day-to-day business of a town like Antietam, a sheriff's work was more diplomacy—or so she'd imagined—than risk.

Of course, now, she began to see that had been foolish of her. There were fights, drunks, break-ins, hot tempers between neighbors and families. She had personal knowledge of the dangers of domestic disputes—that tidy term for the violence that could happen behind closed doors.

He was in charge. And while Connor might see him as a hero, she began to see just how vulnerable the badge made him.

Because she did, she also realized that the worry that ate at her all through the long afternoon and evening wasn't just for a friend, a lover, not just for a man she admired and cared for. It was for the man she loved.

It had taken something unexpected, shocking, to open her eyes. Now that they were open, she could look back. Almost as far back as she could remember, Devin had been there. She had depended on him, admired him and in some ways, she supposed, taken his place in her life for granted.

It had been humiliating to go to him and admit what Joe had done to her, to show him the marks, to describe how she had come by them. Not just because he'd been the sheriff, she thought now. Because he had been Devin.

She'd always been more shy around him than around his brothers. Because, she thought again, he'd been Devin. Part of her heart had always been set aside for him. So she had never been able to look at him as just one of the MacKades, or just her friend, or just the sheriff.

She'd always felt something more. Now she was free, and she could let those feelings out. She could admit that it wasn't just part of her heart that belonged to him, but all of it.

All of her.

Through the worry came the wonder, and with it the joy. She loved.

When the phone rang, she raced to it like a madwoman, then struggled to keep her voice calm when Savannah greeted her.

"Hi, I guess you've heard the big news by now."

"No one's talking about anything else." To calm herself, Cassie reached over to the refrigerator and took out a pitcher of juice. "Have you seen Devin since it happened?"

"Not personally. Jared has. He says our big, bad sheriff is annoyed with all the glory. A television crew came down from Hagerstown, and the paper's been here." Because she understood Cassie's silence perfectly, she softened her voice. "He's fine, Cassandra. Not a scratch. Just grumbling because this whole business is going to keep him tied up for a while. Are you all right?"

"Me?" Cassie stared at the juice she'd poured. "I'm fine. I'm just concerned."

"I know. I have to admit that by the time Bryan finished giving me the play-by-play, I was pretty concerned myself. But the one thing we can all be sure of is that Devin Mac-Kade can handle himself."

"Yes." Cassie picked up the glass, set it down again. "He can. I guess there's no one who needs anyone worrying about him less than Devin." But why hadn't he called?

"Listen, I really called to ask you a favor."

"Sure. What can I do?"

"You can give my temper a break and send Connor over for the night. Bryan's been nagging me since he got home from the great bank robbery."

"Oh." Cassie peeked out the window into the yard, where Connor and Emma were playing with the cat. "He'd love it, if you're sure."

There was a crash, and Cassie could hear Savannah yell,

"Bryan MacKade, if you break a window with that base-ball, you're not only out of the game, you're suspended for the season!

"Yes, I'm sure," she said to Cassie, with feeling, when she returned to talk in the receiver. "But there's more. Can we have Emma, too?"

"Emma? You want Emma to spend the night?"

"Jared has this idea that we'd better start practicing with girls. We sure know boys, and he started thinking that once Layla starts growing up, we'll be lost." She laughed, and Cassie heard the baby coo. "So, how about giving us Emma for the experiment? We swear we'll turn her back over in one piece."

"She'd be thrilled. But, Savannah, you'd have four to deal with."

"Yeah. We've decided that's our magic number. If you know what I mean."

"Four?" It was Cassie's turn to chuckle. "Well, you're going to need plenty of practice, then."

"Let's just see how we survive one night. Pack them up, will you, Cassie? Jared will walk over through the woods and get them."

"On one condition. You'll call, anytime, if you want to bail out."

"You've got my word on that one." There was another crash, and something shattered. "All right, Bryan, now you have to die. Hurry, Cassie—I have to believe there's safety in numbers."

Though it tugged at her heart a little, Cassie supervised the overnight packing, while her children bristled with excitement. They were so eager to go, and she tried not to fret that it was Emma's first sleepover.

She made certain they had clean clothes, toothbrushes, instructions on how to behave. They even took the cat.

When they trooped off toward the woods with Jared, she was completely, utterly alone.

With too much time, she realized, to think, to brood, to worry.

She went down to the inn, found the handful of guests well occupied and content. Still, she set up cake and coffee in the parlor, offered complimentary wine to those playing cards in the sunroom.

Seeing that she wasn't needed, she set the table for breakfast, and checked her pantry and refrigerator, though she knew she was well supplied for the large Sunday breakfast the inn was becoming renowned for.

At loose ends, she wandered outside. She wasn't used to having nothing to do, no one to look after. Certainly, she had often fantasized about how she would spend an evening alone. A bubble bath, a book, a late movie on television.

That was what she would do, she told herself. As soon as she ran into town and made sure Devin was really fine.

She dashed up the stairs, then let out a yelp when she saw the shadowy figure on the porch swing.

"I saw you were busy," Devin said. "Thought I'd wait."

She still had a hand against her speeding heart. "I thought you had to stay in town."

"I dragooned Donnie into staying at the office. It's the least he can do, after he left me with the phones all damn afternoon." He held out a bouquet of yellow tea roses. "I brought you flowers. I was going by the florist and remembered I'd never brought you flowers. I know you like them."

"They're beautiful."

"Are you going to sit down with me?"

"All right." She sat and held the roses in her arms as she would have a child. "They're beautiful," she said again. "I should put them in water."

"They'll keep a minute." Curious, he tucked a hand under her chin and turned her face to his. "What is it?"

"It's nothing. I was so worried," she blurted out. "I couldn't leave, and kept waiting for you to call. Devin, why didn't you call? I'm sorry," she said immediately. "I shouldn't nag you."

One of the scars, he mused, and kept his fingers firm when she would have looked away. "Don't be sorry. I did call, several times. Your phone was busy."

"Everyone's been calling. I've heard a dozen different stories."

"The truth's probably less exciting."

"He had a gun, didn't he? You knew he had a gun when you went into the bank."

"I had to do my job, Cass. He wasn't going to get anywhere, and even if he did, there was a canister inside the moneybag that would have spewed red paint all over him and the bills." His grin spread. "Actually, I'm kind of sorry we couldn't play that part out. It would have been some show. But he might have hurt someone."

"He might have hurt you."

"Well, then, you didn't hear about how bullets bounce off me."

Instead of laughing, she pressed her face into his shoulder. "I'm so glad you're all right. I'm so glad you're not hurt. I'm so glad you're here."

"I'm happy to be all of those things." Slipping an arm around her, he set the swing in motion. "I'd have come sooner, if I could."

"I know. You were on the news."

"Yeah. So I hear."

"You didn't see." She turned her head. "They'll show it again at eleven."

"I know what I look like."

Studying his face, she found something endearing. "You're embarrassed."

"No, I'm not." He shifted. "Maybe. Some."

Not just endearing, she realized. Adorable. "I'm awfully proud of you," she murmured, and brushed her lips over his. "Actually, we taped the broadcast. Connor was so excited. We can watch it, if you want."

"I'll pass. I don't—"

She interrupted him with her lips again, and experienced an odd, sweet power when she felt his heart jump. "I've watched it three times. I thought you looked like a movie star."

"You don't get out enough." His palms were damp, so he eased off the swing. A little distance, MacKade, he warned himself, before you explode. "I've been thinking about that, too. I haven't ever taken you out. To dinner, or anywhere."

"You took us down to the zoo in the spring, and to the fair last summer."

Why was she looking at him like that? he wondered. She'd never looked at him like that before. With... Was that amusement, or lust, or— God.

"I meant you and me. I love having the kids, but—"

"I don't have to go out on dates, Devin. I'm happy with the way things are."

"Still and all." He couldn't seem to think very clearly, not when she was just sitting here, smiling at him, a bouquet of flowers in her arms. "I, ah, brought all this food. Pies and cookies and cakes. People have been bringing them by the office all afternoon."

"They're grateful." With her heart tripping lightly, she rose. "They want to show it."

"Yeah, well, I'd never be able to eat it all. I gave some to Donnie, but I figured the kids might..." He backed up when she stepped forward. "They might want some. I didn't see them when I came up. It's a little early for them to be in bed on a Saturday night, isn't it?"

"They're not here." She blessed Savannah and Jared, and fate. "They're spending the night at the cabin."

"They're not here."

"No. We're alone."

He'd been prepared to leave, to spend a little time with her, then go. He wouldn't have asked to stay with her through the night, with the children in the next room. None of them were ready for that.

Now they were alone, and the night had just begun. A slap of desire whipped through him, painfully. He braced against it, and managed an easy smile.

"Then I'll take you out."

"I don't want you to take me out," she murmured. "I want you to take me to bed."

It closed his throat. "Cassie." His hand was very gentle on her cheek. "I don't expect that every time I come here. That's not the only reason I want to be with you."

"I know." She turned her lips into his palm. "It's what I'd like tonight. I'm going to put these in water."

She left him, churning and speechless, on the dark porch. More than a little dazed, he followed her inside.

"I bought this at Regan's shop." Briskly Cassie filled a green Depression glass pitcher with water. "I'm still getting used to having a little extra money to buy pretty things. I don't even feel guilty about it anymore."

"You shouldn't feel guilty about anything."

"Oh, a few things." With hands as gentle as they were efficient, she arranged the roses in the pitcher. "But not this. And not you." Her eyes lifted. "Do you know what I feel about you, Devin? About us?"

He thought it was best not to try to speak just then, not with the way the blood was draining out of his head.

"Dazzled," she murmured. "You dazzle me. You make me feel things, and want things I never knew I could have. I'm almost twenty-nine, and you're the only man who's really touched me. I want you to touch me."

He would, as soon as he could be sure he had his hands, and his needs, under control. If it had been anyone but Cassie, he would have thought she was seducing him.

Because he said nothing, made no move toward her, she was afraid she was doing it all wrong. It wasn't nerves now that plagued her, so much as doubt. And doubt had her shifting her gaze back to the flowers.

"If you'd rather not right now…if you don't want me—"

"God." It exploded out of him, made her head whip up in alarm, made him bite back whatever might have come out next. "Let's go for a drive," he said quickly. "It's a pretty night, the moon's coming up. I'd like to go for a drive with you."

She was sure she'd made some foolish mistake, but couldn't put her finger on it. All she was sure of was that her system was in overdrive, and his wasn't. As a seductress, she thought, she was a miserable amateur.

"All right, if you like."

He recognized that tone, the bright and false cheerfulness. He would have slit his throat before he did anything to cause that. "Cassie, it's not that I don't want to make love with you. I do. It's just that… Maybe I'm a little more revved from this morning than I thought. I need to smooth out some of the edges before I… I can't touch you now," he ended, his tone too sharp, too quick.

"Why?"

"Because I'm a little too needy right now, and it doesn't

help for you to keep looking at me that way. I wouldn't be able to— I'd hurt you."

"You're angry with me?"

"No." He swore, ripely, showing her some portion of his frustration in the way he whirled around and paced. "When I'm angry with you, you'll know it. You're driving me crazy. Look at the way you're standing there, with your hands folded and those big, gorgeous eyes watching every move I make. I can't breathe when you look at me like that. I used to be able to." He shot the words out like an accusation. "But that was before, and I just can't handle it as well now that we've been together. We've got to get out of here before I eat you alive."

"We're not going anywhere." It surprised them both, how firm and settled her voice was.

"I'm telling you—"

"Yes, I believe you are trying to tell me. You think I'm too fragile to handle it. To handle you. Well, you're wrong."

"You haven't got a clue what you're dealing with, not with me."

"Maybe I don't. Maybe you haven't let me." Suddenly strong, suddenly sure, she walked to him. "Every time we've made love, it hasn't been for you."

"Don't be ridiculous. Of course it was for me."

"It was for me," she said firmly. Strong, she thought. Strong face, strong eyes, strong hands. Not a picture in a magazine, or a white knight fantasy. A strong man, with strong needs. "You were so careful, so patient. No one's ever been careful with me before."

"I know." Because he did, his hand was gentle when he lifted it to brush the golden curls of her hair. "You don't have to worry anymore."

"Don't treat me like a child, Devin." Boldly she took his face in her hands, that familiar and compelling face. "You were holding back. Every time, you were holding back. I've been too dazzled to realize it."

"Cassie, you need tenderness."

"Don't tell me what I need." Her voice had a snap to it, there was a spark in her eyes. "I've had enough of that in my life. Yes, I need tenderness, but I also need trust and respect, and to be treated like a woman. A normal woman."

As carefully as he could, he wrapped his fingers around her wrists. "Don't push me here, Cassie." He pressed his lips to her brow, and infuriated her.

"Kiss me like you mean it," she demanded, then crushed her lips to his. She felt his jolt, the burst of heat, then his struggle for control. "Show me what it's like," she said against his mouth. "I want to know what it's like, what you're like when you stop thinking."

With an oath, he devoured her mouth. It was like that first shocking kiss, she realized as her blood burst inside her veins. The first and the last time he had given her a glimpse of real hunger.

There was that surge of power again, that odd, whippy sensation that she could do or be anything. She strained against him when he tried to draw back.

"Damn it, Cassie."

"Again." Surprisingly strong, she dragged his dark head back to hers. "Kiss me like that again." Her eyes, slumberous, aware, stayed on his. "Show me what it's like," she murmured. "I've waited my whole life to know." She ran her hands over his chest, felt the wild beat of his heart, the rigid edge of his control. "Take me. Don't be kind tonight, Devin. Just take me. That's what I want."

His hands, shaking now, were tensed and rough as he wrapped her hair around them and dragged her head back. He plundered her mouth, ravishing it with lips and teeth and tongue. A part of him hung back still, waiting for her to object. He told himself he would stop—could stop—the moment he frightened her.

But as her taste seeped into him, he was afraid it was a lie. Just look at her, he thought, the sunbeam hair, the cloudy eyes, the rose petal skin.

"Cassie—"

"No. Just show me." She was almost delirious with new knowledge, with the force of her desire and her utter lack of fear. "Show me."

He could have sworn he heard himself snap, heard an echo of brittle control breaking. The wildness overcame him, primitive, almost brutal, making all the years of patience nothing.

In his rush to taste her flesh, he ripped her blouse. The sound of the seam tearing would have snapped him back, but she moaned and wrapped herself around him. Instinctively he recognized the quiver of her body as desire, not fear. It clawed at him.

"I can't...stand it."

"Then don't," she murmured, thrilling when his arms clamped around her, when he lifted her off her feet so that she was pressed hard against him, heat to heat. "Touch me." She fisted her pale hands in his dark hair, amazed at the hunger that swarmed through her. "I'll go crazy if you don't."

Nearly stumbling, his mouth racing over her face and throat, he headed for the bedroom. But she wrapped her legs tight around his waist and shot new fire into his blood. By the doorway, he pressed her against the wall, using it to brace her. His desperate mouth clamped over her breast, suckling hard through her tattered blouse. Her response was to throw back her head and rock against him.

"More." She couldn't believe what was coming out of her mouth, couldn't believe this vicious need had been in either one of them. With a groan, she reached down and tore her own blouse aside so that his mouth could take her.

She climaxed the instant his teeth closed over her, shocking herself with the power of it. For an instant she was like a moth, pinned, quivering helplessly, and then she was alive, bursting with life.

Mindless as coupling animals, they dragged each other to the floor.

She pulled at his shirt, he yanked at her slacks. Speech was impossible as they rolled over the floor in the narrow hallway, groping for each other. There were only gasps and moans. No sighs now, no murmurs, only hissing breath and thundering pulses.

Craving drove him, a craving long suppressed and denied. He yanked her hips high and ripped her practical cotton panties to shreds. And made her scream with his greedy mouth.

She bucked, then stiffened into a quaking bridge, her arms straining as her body arched up toward him. He drove her ruthlessly, relentlessly, until throaty growls rumbled in her throat.

"More." This time it was he who demanded it, he who groaned, as her nails scraped up his back and dug crescents into his shoulders. When her hand closed around him, his vision grayed, and the drumbeat of his pulse scrambled.

She was moving under him, writhing. Her eyes were nearly black, and blind with pleasure, when he fused his mouth to hers again. It was greed, rather than control, that kept him from ending it, that had him sliding sleekly down her body again, tasting and taking and touching until they were both mad.

He reared up, clamped his hands over hers, then plunged into her. Beyond all reason, he pumped and thrust, angling her rocking hips so that he could immerse himself in her, deep, then deeper. His mind had gone dark, leaving only snarling sensations as he rammed into that hot, wet pleasure with a feral force that had them both gasping.

She couldn't hold on. She tried, for him. How could she have known he needed like this? That she was capable of needing like this? How could she have known until he finally showed her? But she was being tossed too high now to fight her way back. Her hands slid off his damp skin, rapped hard on the wooden floor. She gave herself willingly to the last savage stab of pleasure, going weak as he continued to hammer himself into her.

Then that wonderful hard body heaved, went rigid. She saw him throw his head back as if in pain, saw with wonder that it was he who was lost. When he shuddered, shuddered and cried out her name, she wept with the joy of it.

He felt the tears against his shoulder the moment his sated body collapsed on hers. He would have levered himself away instantly, but her arms came around him.

"Don't. Please don't move."

"I'm sorry." There was nothing he could say to her that would be good enough, nothing he could say to himself that would be bad enough. "I hurt you. I promised I wouldn't."

"Do you know what you did?" Her lips were curved, but he couldn't see. All he could see was his own careless treatment of the most precious thing in his life. "You forgot."

"Forgot?" Again he tried to shift, again she held him tight.

"You forgot to be careful, you forgot to worry, you forgot everything. I didn't know I could make you do that. It makes me feel—" a long, satisfied sigh "—powerful."

"Powerful?" His throat was bone-dry. He wanted to lift her up off the floor. God, he'd taken her on the floor. He wanted to tuck her into bed and soothe her. But the word she'd used, and the tone, baffled him.

"Strong, sexy." At last she lifted her arms, stretched them above her head in a long, lazy movement. "Powerful. I've never felt powerful before. I like it. Oh, I really like it." Eyes closed, lips curved, she hummed in her throat.

And that was his first glimpse of her when he lifted his head, the smug smile and erotic glow of a woman who'd just discovered a dangerous and exciting secret. His blood stirred all over again. She looked…triumphant, he realized. Just who, he wondered, had ravaged who?

"You like it," he repeated.

"Mmm… I want to feel this way again. And again and again. I want to feel cherished, too, the way I do when you're gentle. I want to feel everything. I made you forget." She opened her eyes again and laughed when she saw the stunned and sated look in his eyes. "I seduced you. Didn't I?"

"You destroyed me. I tore your clothes."

"I know. It was exciting. Will you do it again?"

"I…" He shook his head, but when it didn't clear he gave up and lost himself in her eyes. "Anytime."

"Can I rip yours?"

Words failed him. He managed a couple of strangled sounds before clearing his throat. "We'd better get off the floor."

"I like it here. I like knowing you wanted me so much you couldn't wait." She lifted a hand to toy with the dark curls that fell, damp, over his forehead. "I like the way you're looking at me right now. It's probably wrong, and

I don't care, but I like knowing you wanted me for years. That you watched me, and wanted me. Like this."

"I didn't exactly picture it like this."

Her lips curved again, a sly, knowing smile that made his blood swim. "Didn't you?"

"Well, maybe." His brain was still numb. It was the only part of him that seemed to have shut down. "Once in a while."

She pressed her lips together, ran the tip of her tongue over them. "I can still taste you."

"Oh, God."

A quick and delicious tremor coursed through her as she felt him move inside her. "I'm doing it again."

"Huh?"

"Seducing you."

He couldn't get his breath. "Looks like that."

She felt powerfully a woman, a normal, competent, well-loved woman. "Tell me you love me, Devin. While you're filling me, while you're wanting me, tell me you love me."

He couldn't keep himself from hardening again, from driving deep into her, from groaning as her body rose and fell with him.

"I love you." Helpless, he buried his face in her hair. Somehow she'd taken the reins from him. He could do nothing but ride. "I can't stop."

She absorbed it all, the love, the passion, the power, willingly matching his fast and desperate pace. When she knew he was falling off the edge with her, when they were both defenseless, she turned her lips to his ear.

"I love you, Devin. I love you. I think I always have."

When he could speak again, he gathered her up, cradled her in his lap. "I've wanted to hear that for a long time."

"I meant it. I couldn't have said it unless I did."

"I know." And it left him shaken and without defenses. "You've tossed my master plan into the Dumpster, Cass."

"How?"

"Well, I had it plotted out, you see. By my reckoning, I'd get you to fall in love with me by Christmas. Then I'd keep things at a nice, steady pace, and talk you into marrying me by spring."

"Let's not talk about marriage, Devin. Not yet. Not now."

He tipped her head back. "When?"

"I don't know." There was worry in her eyes again, and in her voice. "Marriage isn't always the right answer."

"It is for people like you and me." He nearly spoke of the children, but stopped himself. It wasn't right to use them to press his case. "I'd make you happy."

"I know you would." She turned her face into the curve of his neck. "Let this be enough for now. It's so much more than I ever thought I'd have. Let it be enough for now."

"For now." He contented himself with the scent of her hair. "Why don't we do this? Get ourselves some wine, some of that pie, have a little picnic?"

"I'd like that." She leaned back, smiled. "I'll get a couple of plates." But when she reached for her slacks, his hand closed over hers.

"You're not going to need those," he said, his eyes dark and wicked.

She laughed. "I'm not going to serve pie buck-naked." Then she blinked, felt a quick skitter of her pulse. "Am I?"

"Why don't we see?"

Chapter 11

School was out, and that made life for two ten-year-old boys close to perfect. The haunted woods that fringed between Bryan's cabin and the inn beckoned. There they could search for ghosts, listen for the pounding of mortar fire, or hunt for more tangible remnants of war in the dirt and brambles. Even after more than a century, old shells could be unearthed.

Connor had a collection Bryan envied, stubby bullets that looked like they were made of clay, an old brass button that had survived the uniform it belonged to and, best of all, the metal triangle of a stirrup Cassie had unearthed in the garden of the inn.

The boys had decided it had belonged to a Union general and his trusty steed.

Connor viewed this stretch of summer in a way he never had before. The last year had been exciting when they moved into the new apartment, but he'd still worried often that it would all end. Now he'd come to believe, now he could anticipate the long, hot days, the companionship of his best friend and a home where no one stumbled in drunk with fists raised.

He watched his mother still. Her eyes no longer looked so tired, and she laughed so much more than she had ever laughed before. He liked the way she put pretty things around the house, the flowers, the pale green glass she'd begun to collect from Regan's shop. But he kept quiet about that, because he knew the guys would rag on him for liking something as lame as flowers or glass bowls.

But not Bryan. Bryan was the best of friends, and didn't even mind if Emma tagged along with them. Bryan liked to listen to Connor's stories. Bryan could keep secrets. Bryan was his brother, his blood brother. They had held a solemn ceremony in the woods, pricking their fingers and mixing their blood together to seal the bond.

They spent some of those early days of freedom from books and classrooms in the tree house Jared had built on the edge of the woods nearest the cabin. Some they spent in the yard of the inn, practicing baseball. They would also cut through the trees and visit Shane at the farm. As Bryan said, Shane was very cool, and he never minded if they wanted to play with the dogs and the puppies or hang out in the hayloft of the big old barn.

But almost every day, it was the woods that pulled at them. And tonight they had finally wangled permission to camp out, just the two of them, deep in the haunted woods.

They had pitched Devin's old tent. It was Devin, Connor knew, who had turned the tide. His mother had worried over the idea of letting the two boys loose for a night, but Devin had talked to her about rites of passage and memories and friendships. He owed the most important night of his life to Sheriff MacKade.

They had built a fire carefully, in a circle of stones on clear ground, as Devin had shown them, and they had hot dogs and marshmallows to roast over it. Cassie had given them a big jug of juice, but Devin had slipped them a six-pack of soda and told them to take the empty cans, along with the other trash, over to the farm in the morning for disposal.

Their sleeping rolls were spread out in the tent, the moon was high and bright overhead, and owls were hooting. The fire crackled, and the scent of scorched meat stung the night air. The sweet, gooey taste of marshmallow was in Connor's mouth. And he was in heaven.

"This is the best," he said.

"It's pretty cool." Bryan watched his hot dog turn black on the end of his stick, just the way he liked it. "We should do it every night."

Connor knew it wouldn't be special if they did it every night, but didn't say so. "It's great here. Sheriff MacKade said that he and his brothers used to camp out in the woods all the time."

"Dad likes to walk in the woods." Bryan loved using that word. *Dad*. He tried to use it often, without making it a big deal. "Mom, too. They sure kiss a lot." He made smacking noises with his lips so Connor would laugh. "Beats me why kissing's supposed to be so damn neat. I think I'd gag if a girl tried to put her mouth on me. Disgusting."

"Revolting. Especially the tongue part."

At that, Bryan executed very realistic vomiting sounds that had both boys rolling with laughter.

"Shane's always kissing girls." Connor rolled his eyes. "I mean, *always*. I heard your dad say he's got an addiction."

Bryan snorted at that. "It's weird. I mean, Shane knows all there is to know about animals and machines and stuff, but he likes having girls hang around. He gets this funny look in his eye, too. Like Devin does with your mom. I figure some girls must zap some guys' brains. Like a laser beam."

"What do you mean?" Connor had gone very still.

"You know, zap!" Bryan demonstrated with a pointed finger and cocked thumb.

"No, about Sheriff MacKade, and my mom."

"Jeez, he's really stuck on her." The hot dog was thoroughly burned. Concentrating, Bryan blew on the end before biting it and filling his mouth with charcoal. "He hangs around her all the time and brings her flowers and junk. That's what my Dad did with Mom. He'd bring her flowers, and she'd go real dopey over them." He shook his head. "Screwy."

"He comes around because he's looking out for us," Connor said, but the sweet taste in his mouth had gone sour. "Because he's the sheriff."

"Sure, he looks out for you." Involved with his hot dog, Bryan didn't see the panic in his pal's eyes. "Maybe that's how he got stuck on her in the first place, but man, he's gone. I heard my mom and dad talking the other night, and Mom said how she got a kick out of seeing the big, bad sheriff—that's what she calls him—out of seeing him cow-eyed over Cassie. *Cow-eyed.*" Bryan snickered at the term. "Hey, if they get married, we'd be cousins *and* blood brothers. That'd be great."

"She's not getting married." Connor's voice lashed out so fast and furious that Bryan nearly bobbled the rest of his dinner.

"Hey—"

"She's not going to marry anyone, ever again." Connor leaped to his feet, fists clenched. "You're wrong. You're making it up."

"Am not. What's your problem?"

"He comes around because he's the sheriff, and he's looking out for us. That's it. You take it back."

He might have, but the martial glint in Connor's eyes sparked one in his own. "Get real. Anybody can see Devin's got the hots for your mom."

Connor was on him like a leech, knocking Bryan back, rolling over the dirt. Surprise and panic gave him the first advantage as his fists pummeled at Bryan's ribs. But it was his first fight, and Bryan was a veteran.

Within a few sweaty moments, Bryan had Connor pinned. Both of them were scraped and filthy and breathing hard. In reflex, Bryan bloodied Connor's lip, snarling like a young wolf. "Give up?"

"No." Connor jabbed an elbow out and had Bryan grunting. Into the brambles they rolled, gasping out threats and curses.

Again Bryan pinned him, and again he raised his fist. He stopped, froze. He would have sworn he heard something, something that sounded like a man dying, but it didn't sound of this world.

"You hear that?"

"Yeah." Connor didn't loosen his grip on Bryan's ripped T-shirt, but his eyes darted left and right. "It didn't sound real, though, it sounded like..."

"Ghosts." The word came through Bryan's cold lips. "Jeez, Con. They're really here. It's the two corporals."

Connor didn't move a muscle. He didn't hear it anymore, just the owls and the rustle of small animals in the brush. But he felt it, and he suddenly understood. That was what war was, he thought, stranger against stranger, brother against brother. Fighting. Killing. Dying.

And he was ashamed, because Bryan was his brother and he'd raised his fist to him. Raised his fist, he thought as tears stung his eyes, as Joe Dolin had done to Mama, and to him.

"I'm sorry." He couldn't stop the tears, just couldn't, not even when Bryan stared down at him. "I'm sorry."

"Hey, it's okay. You hit good." Uncomfortable, he patted Connor's shoulder before he levered himself to his feet. Systematically he tugged aside brambles and picked thorns out of his clothes and flesh. "You just got to work on your guard, is all."

"I don't want to fight. I hate fighting." Connor sat up and curled himself into a ball of misery.

Bryan cast around for something to say. "Man, we're a mess. You're going to have to come up with a good story for how we got our clothes torn and stuff. Maybe we could say we were attacked by wild dogs."

"That's stupid. Nobody'd believe that."

"You come up with one, Con," Bryan coaxed. "You're real good at stories."

Connor sighed, kept his head on his knees. He didn't want to lie. He hated lying as much as he did fighting. But he didn't think he could stand seeing disappointment in his mother's eyes. "We'll say we lost the baseball in the blackberry bushes and got all caught up in the thorns."

It was simple, Bryan decided. And sometimes simple was best. "How about your lip? It's going to puff up real good."

"I guess I fell down."

Bryan wiped his hands on his dirty jeans. "Does it hurt? You can put one of the soda cans on it."

"It's okay."

"Look, Con, I didn't mean anything by what I said.

Nothing bad about your mom, I mean. She's great. If I thought somebody was saying something bad about my mom, I'd beat the hell out of them."

"It's okay," Connor said again. "I know you weren't."

"Well, what'd you go at me like that for?"

Calmer now, Connor rested his chin on his knees. "I thought Sheriff MacKade was coming around because he liked me."

"Well, sure he likes you."

"He's coming around for my mother. He's probably been kissing her, and maybe even more. You know?"

Bryan shrugged. "Well, since he's stuck on her..."

"Everything's been good. Everything's changed, and it's so great the way it is. We've got the apartment, and Mama's happy, and *he's* locked up. Now everything's going to be ruined. If she marries the sheriff, it'll ruin everything."

"Why? Devin's cool."

"I don't want a father, not ever again." Dark eyes dominated Connor's dirty, tear-streaked face. "He'll take over, and things will change back. He'll start drinking and yelling, and hitting."

"Not Devin."

"That's what happens," Connor said in a fierce whisper. "It'll all be his instead of ours, and it'll all have to be his way. And if it isn't, he'll hurt her and make her cry."

He had an image of Devin making a vow, offering his hand on it, right here in the woods. But he pushed it aside.

"That's what fathers do."

"Mine doesn't," Bryan said reasonably. "He'd never hit my mom. He yells, but she yells back. Sometimes she yells first. It's pretty cool."

"He hasn't hit her yet. She just hasn't made him mad enough."

"She makes him real mad sometimes. One time, she made him so mad I thought smoke was going to come out of his ears, like in a cartoon. He picked her right up and threw her over his shoulder."

"See."

Bryan shook his head. "He didn't hurt her. They started wrestling around on the grass, and she was yelling at him and swearing. Then they started laughing. Then they started kissing." Bryan rolled his eyes. "Man, it was embarrassing."

"If he'd really been mad—"

"I'm telling you, he was. His face gets real hard, and his eyes, too. He was really steaming."

"Did it scare you?"

"Nah." Then Bryan moved his shoulders again. "Well, maybe it does just a little, when I do something to make him really mad at me. But it's not because I think he's going to belt me or anything." Bryan let out a long breath, then shifted so that he could drape an arm over Connor's shoulders. "Look, Con, Devin's not like Joe Dolin."

"He fights."

"Yeah, but not with girls, or kids."

"What's the difference?"

Connor was about the smartest person he knew, Bryan thought, but he could be so dopey. "You just socked me, right? Are you going to go home and whip up on Emma?"

"Of course not. I'd never—" He broke off, brooding. "Maybe it's different. I have to think about it."

"Cool." Satisfied, Bryan rubbed his sore ribs. "Let's break out a soda, and you can make up a ghost story. A really gruesome one."

Because Devin had awakened early, he was up and feeding the pigs when he spotted the two boys crossing from the woods with their gear and bag of trash. He lifted a hand in greeting, then cocked a brow when he saw the scrapes, bruises and ripped shirts.

"Must have been some night," he said mildly. "Run into bears?"

Bryan chuckled and greeted the exuberant Fred and Ethel. "Nah. Wolves."

"Umm-hmm..." He studied Connor's puffy lip. "Looks like you put up a hell of a battle." He started to reach out for Connor's chin, but the boy jerked back.

"We lost the baseball in the berry bushes," Connor said flatly. "We got tangled up, and I fell."

"Your mothers'll probably buy that," Devin decided. "Your dad won't," he told Bryan. "But he'll let it slide." He emptied the bucket of grain into the trough and had the pigs squealing greedily. "How'd it go otherwise?"

"It was great." Bryan stepped onto the bottom rung of the fence to watch the pigs. "We ate hot dogs and marsh-mallows and told ghost stories. We even heard the ghosts."

"Sounds eventful."

"Thank you for the tent," Connor said stiffly.

"No problem. Why don't you hang on to it? I imagine you'll use it again before I will."

"I don't want it," Connor said, with a lack of courtesy so out of character, Devin only stared. "I don't want any-thing." He dropped the tent on the ground. "I have to go." He stood for a moment, chin jerked up, waiting for Devin to show him what happened when you sassed.

But Devin only studied his face, and there was puzzle-ment, rather than anger, in his eyes. "Put some ice on that lip."

Shoulders stiff, Connor turned and walked quickly away, without a word to his friend.

"I'll keep the tent, Devin." Mortified, and irritated,

Bryan shot Connor's back a seething look. "He doesn't mean to be a jerk."

"He's ticked at me. Do you know why?" When Bryan kept his head down, his hands in his pockets, Devin sighed. "I don't want you to break a confidence, Bry. If I've done something to hurt Connor, I'd like to make it right."

"I guess it's my fault." Miserable, Bryan scuffed his shoe in the dirt. "I said something about how you were stuck on his mom, and he went nutso."

Devin rubbed a hand over his suddenly tensed neck. "Is that what you fought about?" No answer again, and Devin nodded. "Okay. Thanks for telling me."

"Devin." Loyalty had never been a problem for Bryan before. Now he felt himself tugged in different directions. "It's just—he's just scared. I mean, Con's not a wimp or anything, but he's scared that if you have, you know, like a thing going with Mrs. Dolin, things'll be like they were. Before, you know. He's got it stuck in his mind that you'd start punching out on his mom the way that bastard—I mean the way Joe Dolin did." Bryan looked around, but Connor had already disappeared into the woods. "I tried to tell him he was off, but I guess he didn't really believe me."

"Okay. I got it."

"He'll probably hate me for telling you."

"No, he won't. You did right, Bryan. You're a good friend."

"You're not mad at him, are you, for talking back?"

"No, I'm not mad at him. You know how Jared feels about you, Bryan?"

Pleasure and embarrassment mixed, tinted his cheeks. "Yeah."

"I feel pretty much the same way about Con, and Emma. I just have to give him time to get used to it."

* * *

She'd tried not to worry. Really she had. But when she looked out the window and saw Connor crossing toward the inn, the relief was huge. Cassie set aside the flour she'd taken out for pancakes and went to the kitchen door of the inn.

"I'm down here, Connor. Did you have—" She saw the bruised face, the torn clothes, and her heart froze in her chest. She was outside like a bullet, terror seeping out of every pore. "What happened? Oh, baby, who hurt you? Let me—"

"I'm all right." Still seething, Connor jerked away from her. The look he aimed at her was one she'd never seen from him before. It was filled with fury and disdain. "I'm just fine. Isn't that what you always told me after he hit you? I fell down, I slipped. I walked into the damn door."

"Connor."

"Well, I'll tell you the truth. I had a fight with Bryan. I hit him, he hit me."

"Honey, why would you—"

Again he jerked away from her hands. "It's my business why. I don't have to tell you everything, just like you don't tell me everything."

It was rare, very rare, for her to have to discipline the boy. "No, you don't," she said evenly. "But you will mind your tone when you speak to me."

His swollen lip trembled, but he kept his eyes steady. "Why didn't you ever tell him that? Why didn't you ever tell him to mind his tone when he spoke to you? You let him say anything he wanted, do anything he wanted."

Her own shame at hearing the bald truth from her son swamped her. "Connor, if this is about your father—"

"Don't call him that. Don't *ever* call him my father. I hate him, and I'm ashamed of you."

She made some sound as tears sprang to her eyes, but she couldn't speak.

"You're going to let it happen again," Connor raged on. "You're just going to let it happen."

"I don't know what you're talking about, Connor. Come inside and sit down and let's straighten this out."

"There's nothing to say. I won't stay if you marry Sheriff MacKade. I won't stay and watch when he hits you. I won't let you make me have a father again."

She sucked in a harsh breath, forced it out again. "I'm not going to marry him, Connor. I'd just started to think about it, but I would never have made a decision on something that important without talking to you and Emma. And I'd never marry anyone if you were against it. I couldn't."

"He wants you to."

"Yes, he wants me to. He loves me and wants us to be a family. He deserves a family." When she said it, she realized how true it was, how selfish she'd been to ask him to wait. "He cares for us. I thought you cared for him, Connor."

"I don't want a father. I'm not ever going to have one, no matter what you do. Everything's good now, and you're going to ruin it."

"No, I won't." She blinked the tears back. "Go upstairs now, Connor, and get cleaned up."

"I won't—"

"Do as you're told," she said sternly. "However you feel about me, I'm your mother and I'm in charge. I have to fix breakfast down here. You clean up and keep an eye on Emma until I'm finished."

She turned and walked back into the kitchen.

Somehow she got through it, the cooking, the serving, the conversations. When she'd finished clearing up, she checked on the children, suggested that they play in the yard while she tidied the guest rooms.

She refused Connor's stiff offer to help, and left them to play. She was changing the linens on the bed in Abigail's room when she heard the front door open and close.

She knew it was Devin. She knew he'd come.

She didn't know that Connor had heard the car and, demanding a vow of silence from Emma, crept into the hallway.

"Can I give you a hand with that?" Devin asked.

"No." Cassie smoothed the contoured sheet out, then reached for the top one. "I've got it."

"I saw Con and Bry over at the farm this morning. You're not upset with him, are you? Boys get into tussles."

"No, I'm not upset about that."

"About what?"

She drew a breath. She'd gone over it in her mind countless times already that morning. She'd let her children down all their lives. Whatever it cost, she would never do so again.

"Devin, I need to talk to you."

"I'm here."

"Connor's very upset, very hurt." She kept her hands busy, tucking the sheet, folding it down, smoothing it. "He's sensed, or been told, something about us, and—"

"I know. I told you I saw him this morning. I'd say what he is, Cassie, is mad."

"Yes, he is. And upset, and hurt. Frightened," she added, pressing her lips together to steady them. "Most of all, frightened. I can't let him be frightened, Devin. Not after what he's already been through."

"You didn't cause it."

"Didn't I?" Meticulously she fluffed and patted the pillows into place. "Doing nothing to stop it all those years is the same as causing it. The first eight years of his life were a nightmare I didn't put an end to. I thought I was shielding him. I told myself I was. But he knew. He's ashamed of me."

"That's not true, Cassie." Devin moved to her, took her hands. "If he said that, it was because he was angry with me, and you were the nearest target. He adores you."

"I've hurt him, Devin, more than I ever realized. Maybe Emma, too. I see now that I've just started to make things right, make things up to them. Now I'm letting it change before they can adjust, before they can trust. I can't do that, Devin. And I can't see you anymore."

Panic reared up, echoed clearly in his voice. "You know that's not the answer. I'll talk to him."

"I don't want you to do that." Cassie tugged her hands from his. "I have to handle this, Devin. I need to prove to Connor that I can, and that he and Emma come first."

"I'm not asking to come ahead of them, damn it, just to be a part of your life. Of their lives. I love you, Cassie."

"I know. I love you. I always will. But I can't be with you. Don't ask me to choose."

"What are you asking me to do?" he demanded. "To just walk away? I've waited for you for twelve years. I can't keep waiting for everything to be perfect. It's never going to be perfect, it just has to be right. We're right, Cassie. You mean everything to me. So do the kids. I need you. I need all of you."

That cut her heart out. "Devin, if things were different—"

"We'll make them different," he insisted, taking her by the shoulders. "We'll make it work."

"I'm not going to ask you to wait." She stepped back, turned toward the window. "You need me, and hearing you say that is wonderful, even more wonderful than when you first told me you loved me. But Connor needs me, too. And he's just a little boy. He's my little boy, and he's frightened."

She took a deep breath, so that she could get it all out cleanly. "You want marriage, family, and you're entitled to that. You're entitled to have someone who's free to give you what you want and need. But I'm not free, and I may never be free. I can't give you what you're entitled to, so I can't be with you, Devin."

"You expect me just to step back, as if nothing's happened between us? Just step back and wait?"

"No. It's time you stopped waiting."

"There's no one but you."

Her heart ripped in two ragged pieces—one for the man, one for the boy. "You haven't let there be. I let you hold on to me, Devin. I think part of me always knew you'd be there. And that was so unfair. I'm trying to be fair now, to everyone."

"Fair? It's fair to toss me, all of what we have together, aside, because a ten-year-old boy demands it? When the hell are you going to take charge, Cassie?"

It was the first time he'd ever hurt her. She faced it, accepted it. "That's what I'm trying to do. Taking charge doesn't always mean doing what you want. Sometimes it means doing what's right for the people you love."

"Damned if I'll beg you." Suddenly bitter, suddenly furious, he bit off each word. "Damned if I'll ask you again, Cassie. I've had enough of standing on the sidelines and breaking my heart over you. I've stripped myself bare for the last time."

"Hurting you is the last thing I want, Devin. But I can't give you what you need most, so I can't give you anything."

His eyes cut into her, as hard and searing as his voice.

"It's time it was down to all or nothing. You've made your choice. Looks like I've made mine."

She listened to his receding footsteps, heard the door slam downstairs. This, she knew, was what Abigail had felt when she sent the man she loved away. This emptiness, this emptiness that was too huge for grief.

Cassie sat on the edge of the bed, buried her face in her hands and sobbed.

In the corner of the hallway, Connor kept his hand tight on his sister's.

"Mama's crying," Emma whispered.

"I know." It wasn't Joe Dolin that had made her cry either, Connor thought. And it wasn't Sheriff MacKade.

It was him, and only him.

While Cassie wept and Connor crept downstairs with grief and guilt heavy on his shoulders, Joe Dolin took his chance. He'd waited, oh, he'd waited so patiently, for just the right moment.

The creek rushed under the Burnside Bridge with a harsh bubbling sound. The trees were thick with leaves. His supervisor was gesturing to one of the other men, his attention distracted by a nest of copperheads they'd unearthed.

That was all it took.

Joe bent to gather litter, working his way toward cover, step by careful step. And then he melted into the trees. As he walked quickly through the woods he stripped off his orange vest and tossed it into the brush beside the creek.

He didn't run, not right away. He still had trouble with the peripheral vision in his right eye, thanks to an injury he'd received when he attacked Regan MacKade. So he moved carefully at first, deliberately turning his head to judge his ground, and his distance.

Then he sprinted, wild as a dog, over rocks, through brush and finally into the creek. Breathing hard, he kept to the water, following its curves and angles. Before long, he was wet to the waist, but he kept going, pushing himself.

Panting, he scrambled up the side of the bank, using rocks and vines to heave himself clear. Then he took a deep gulp of freedom. He would use the sun, and the direction of the creek, to show him the way he wanted to go.

When Devin made up his mind, he was as hard to swerve as a six-ton truck. So when Rafe wandered into his office, saw Devin sitting behind his desk, typing furiously with his face set in stubborn lines, he knew there was trouble.

"I'm supposed to ask you to dinner," Rafe said easily.

"Beat it."

"Regan wanted to have the whole family over tomorrow, plus Cassie and the kids."

"I'm going to be busy. Now get the hell out of here."

"I didn't mention what time," Rafe continued, and walked over to look over Devin's shoulder. "What the hell's this?"

"Just what it looks like."

"Looks like a resignation to me. What wild hare do you have up your—?"

"Get off my back."

Rafe did the brotherly thing and ripped the paper out of the typewriter. "Chill out." Before Devin could lunge to his feet, Rafe slapped a hand on his shoulder. "Look, we can pound each other, I don't mind, but why don't we get the preliminaries out of the way? What the hell are you doing resigning as sheriff?"

"What I should have done a long time ago. I'm getting the hell out of this town. I'm tired of being stuck here in the same damn rut, with the same damn people."

"Dev, you like nothing better than a rut." Rafe tossed the paper aside. "What happened with Cassie?"

"Nothing. Leave it."

"Aren't you the one who came breathing down my neck and made me face up to what I felt for Regan? One good turn."

"I don't have to face what I feel for Cassie. I've faced it for years. What I have to do is get over it."

"She turn you down?" The vicious gleam in Devin's eyes didn't frighten Rafe; it touched him. "Go ahead, take a shot at me. I'll give you a free one."

"Forget it." Deflated, Devin dropped back into his chair.

"Want to talk about it?"

"I'm talked out." He rubbed his hands over his face. "I'm tired. Connor doesn't trust me, she doesn't trust me. It comes down to neither of them wanting me enough. I can't keep trying to prove myself."

"The kid's come a long way, Dev. So has Cassie. Give them a little time."

"I've run out of time. I need something back, Rafe." Devin drew a deep breath. "I just can't keep hurting like this. It's killing me. I'm getting out."

Before Rafe could speak, the phone rang. Devin snagged the receiver and all but spit into it, "Sheriff's office. Mac-Kade." He was on his feet in a flash, swearing violently. "When? That's over a damn hour ago. Why in hell wasn't I notified? Don't give me that crap." He listened for another minute, then slammed down the receiver.

"Dolin's out." He strode over to the gun cabinet, unlocked it and pulled out a rifle. "You're deputized."

Chapter 12

Joe stayed hunkered in the ravine across from the little rancher where his mother-in-law lived. He doubted they'd look for him there, not right away. They'd go to his friends, check on Cassie. Maybe, just maybe, MacKade or one of his horse-faced deputies would swing by.

But his mama-in-law wasn't home. There was no car in the drive, and the curtains were drawn tight over the front windows.

The ranch house sat on the edge of a dead-end road, and was perfect for his purposes. He kept his eyes peeled, then scurried out of the ravine, keeping low. The far side of the house faced nothing but trees, so he used that for his entry. With an elbow, he shattered a window.

Once inside, he headed toward the main bedroom. He needed fresh clothes, and knew she kept some of her dead husband's things hanging in the closet like shrouds.

The old bag was morbid.

She was also paranoid.

That was how he knew there would be a pistol in her nightstand drawer, fully loaded. The only thing he wouldn't find in the house was a drink. But he'd see to that soon enough.

Instead, in dry clothes too small for his frame, he settled down to wait.

He heard her drive up, listened to her fiddling with the locks and bolts on the front door. He smiled as he rose and walked out into the darkened living room.

She was carrying a bag of groceries in one arm, a cheap purse in the other. Her eyes widened when she saw him.

"Joe, what in the world—"

He did what he'd wanted to do for years. He swung out and knocked her flat with the back of his hand.

Actually, he thought about killing her. But he wanted to save that for his darling little wife. As she moaned and flailed at him weakly, he tied her with a clothesline, gagged her. Once she was secured, wriggling like a fish on the floor, he dumped out her purse.

"Twenty lousy bucks," he complained. "I shoulda known." He stuffed the bills in his pocket and picked up her keys. "I'm going to borrow your car, need to take a little trip. A little trip with my wife. A wife's bound to go where her husband tells her to go, isn't that right?"

He grinned as she rolled her eyes, as sick panic dulled them. "It was real obliging of you to write all those letters to the prison. Real obliging. That's why I'm not going to mess you up too bad. I want to show you how I appreciate it."

He laughed when Constance moaned and babbled against the gag. "Now, Cassie's a different thing, isn't she? She didn't stick by her husband like a proper wife, did she? But I'm going to take care of that. I'm going to teach her a real good lesson. Want to hear what I'm going to do to your daughter, old woman? Want to hear what I got planned for her?"

Because he was enjoying the panic in her eyes, Joe hunkered down and told her.

Devin squealed to a halt at the inn. His eyes scanned every bush, every tree, as he hurried around to the back and up the stairs. He didn't stop praying until he opened the door and saw Cassie at the stove.

He couldn't help it. He grabbed her, dragged her hard against him and just held on.

"Devin—"

"Sorry." Clamping down on every emotion, he drew back and became a cop again. "I have to talk to you." He flicked a glance to the living room, where Connor and Emma sat staring at him. He started to tell Connor to take Emma to her room and stay there, then realized he was thinking like a father, not a cop. "Joe walked off work release just over an hour ago."

Cassie's knees buckled. Devin held her up and guided her to a chair. "Sit down, and listen. I've got people checking on his known associates, the places where he used to hang out. We'll pick him up, Cassie. Does he know you're living here?"

"I don't know," she said dully. "My mother might have— I don't know."

"We won't chance it. I want you to get whatever you need. I'm going to take you over to the cabin."

"The cabin?"

"You'll stay with Savannah. I need Jared. I need Shane, too, or I'd have taken you over to the farm. Pull it together, Cassandra," he said, sharply enough to have her eyes clearing.

"I can't go to the cabin, Devin. I can't put Savannah and her children in danger."

"Savannah can handle it."

"So can I. Give me a minute." She needed to take a breath. "Connor and Emma will go wherever you think they'll be safe."

"No, ma'am." Connor curled his trembling hand over Emma's. "I'm not going anywhere without you. I'm not leaving you."

"Nobody's leaving anybody. You're all going where I tell you to go. Get your things," Devin snapped. "Or do without them."

"Savannah is not responsible for me and mine," Cassie said slowly. "I am."

"I don't have the time to be patient with you. I can't stay here and take care of you, so you're going."

He whirled around. Connor, his stomach queasy, saw a kind of fury he'd never seen before, not even in Joe Dolin's eyes. "Get downstairs, into the car."

"I can take care of my mother."

"I'm counting on it, but not here. Do as I tell you, Connor."

"Devin, take the children, and—"

"The hell with this." He spun around again, picked Cassie up bodily and flung her over his shoulder. "Out!" he shouted at Connor, then swore when the boy's blood drained out of his face. "Damn it, boy, don't you see I'd die before I'd hurt her? Before I'd hurt any of you?"

And Connor did, so clearly that the shame of it burned color back into his cheeks. "Yes, sir. Come on, Emma."

"Put me down, Devin." Cassie didn't bother to struggle. "Please, put me down. We'll go."

He set her on her feet, keeping his hands on her shoulders for a moment. "You have to let me take care of you. You have to let me do that, at least. Trust me, Cassie."

"I do." She reached for Connor's hand. "We do."

"Make it quick." He put a hand on the screen door, scanned quickly before stepping out. "We've got roadblocks," he began. "Helicopters are on the way. Odds are we'll have him before nightfall. How many at the inn?"

"No one. We have a family coming in tonight, but—"

"I'll take care of it. Just don't—"

When the shot rang out, it was so sudden, so shocking, Cassie could do nothing but gasp. Devin collapsed at her feet.

"Hi, honey." Joe walked forward, a grin on his face, a gun in his hand. "I'm home."

She did the only thing she could do. She shoved the children behind her and faced him.

She saw the changes in him. His face was thinner, harder, as his body was. There was a scar beside and beneath his right eye, puckered and white. But the eyes themselves were the same. Brutal.

"I'll go with you, Joe." She knew Devin was breathing, but there was blood on his temple where the bullet had streaked. He needed help, an ambulance. The only way to save him and her children was to surrender herself. "I'll go wherever you want. Just don't hurt my babies."

"I'll do whatever I want with your brats, bitch. And you'll do just what I tell you." He looked down at Devin, sneered. "Not so tough now, is he? I should have aimed better." He squinted, laughed. "Got a little problem with the eye, but I'll do a lot better close up."

As if in a dream, she saw his face, saw the gun lower. The cold came over her, the cold and the knowledge that this had happened before. Only then it had been a young, wounded soldier and a woman too weak, too frightened, to save him.

"No!" She screamed, threw herself over Devin's body. "He's hurt!" She knew those words were useless, and struggled to find others. "If you kill him, Joe, and they catch you, you'll never get out again. Do you know what happens when you kill a police officer? It isn't worth it. I said I'd go with you."

"You stay there, I'll just shoot through you. Then, maybe…" He smiled again, shifted his gun toward Connor.

"Stay away from my babies!" Like a woman possessed, she lunged, threw herself at him with a fire and fury that nearly knocked him over. Even when he hit her, she clung like a burr. Then Connor was on him, pummeling, shouting.

Joe swatted him off like a fly.

"I'll teach you manners, you little brat." Before he could strike out with the butt of the gun, he heard the sound of sirens. "Later," he said as Connor scrambled to his feet. "I'll be back for you later." He had am arm around Cassie's throat, choking her, the gun to her temple.

His only escape, he saw, was the woods. "I'll kill her!" he shouted to anyone who could hear. "Anyone comes after me, she's dead!"

He dragged her away, trampling flowers.

On the ground, Emma squeezed Devin's hand. "Please wake up. Please wake up."

Connor crawled to him as Rafe and a deputy rushed around the house. "He shot him, he shot him and he took Mama!"

Grim-faced, Rafe bent over his brother. "It's not as bad as it looks." It helped to say it. He pulled a bandanna out of his pocket and stanched the blood. "He's coming around," he murmured, and relief washed through him in a flood as Devin stirred. "Connor, go in and call an ambulance. Hurry."

"No." Devin's eyes fluttered open. He batted his brother's hand away. "I'm okay. Cassie—"

"You're shot, you idiot." But even as Rafe tried to hold him down, Devin was fighting his way up.

His vision wavered, grayed. A short stream of oaths helped steady it again. "Where'd he take her?"

"To the woods." Connor bit his lip. "He took her into the woods. He was hurting her. I tried to stop him."

"Take care of your sister," Devin ordered. "I want men posted around the woods. Notify Jared, tell him to get back to the cabin. He might go there. You stay with these kids," he ordered his deputy. "Get them inside."

"I'm going in with you," Rafe stated.

"You can go in." Eyes cold, Devin drew his weapon. "But he's mine."

Cassie did whatever she could to slow him down now that he was away from her children and Devin. She would not be a silent victim again. She scratched, she bit, she kicked.

"Forgot who's boss, didn't you? Thought you could lock me up in a cage and forget who was in charge." Cursing her, he shoved the gun into his waistband, so that he could use both hands to drag her. "I'm going to have a good time reminding you."

"They'll find you. They'll catch you and lock you up for good this time."

"Maybe they'll catch me, maybe they won't." He stumbled along, hauling her after him and losing his direction in his fury. He hated these damn woods, the MacKade woods. "I've had a lot of time to think about this. I know just what we're going to do. We're going to get us a car. That's what we're going to do."

He cursed the fact that he'd had to leave the one he'd already stolen behind.

"I've got friends," he muttered. "I've got plenty of friends who'll help me out."

"You've got no one. You never did. Devin'll come after you, Joe, and he'll never stop."

"He's lying on his back and bleeding to death."

"He'll never stop," she said again. "Nothing you do to me will come close to what he'll do to you."

"Got something going with him, don't you?" Joe stopped, breathless, and dragged her head back by the hair. He thought he heard voices in his head, voices saying the words just before he did. "You whore. I own you. Don't you forget it. I own you. Till death do us part."

"You're a miserable, drunken bully." Defiance bolted through her like lightning. "You don't own anything, not even yourself. You're pathetic." She barely winced when he yanked mercilessly on her hair. "The only thing you can beat is something weaker than you. Go ahead, Joe, hit me. It's the only thing you know how to do. But this time, damn you to hell, you're in for a fight."

He released her hair, using that hand to knock her sprawling on the path. The pain only energized her. Eyes hot and deadly, she got to her feet, her fists clenched.

He stepped forward, and she braced, ready, even eager, to defend herself.

"If you touch her, if you breathe on her, I'll put a hole in you."

Slowly Joe turned. Devin was less than three yards back on the path, his weapon drawn and aimed. Rafe MacKade was behind him. As Joe's eyes darted in search of an escape, Shane stepped out of the trees. And Jared moved up the path behind Cassie.

"Drop the gun, Dolin, take it out slow and drop it, or I'll kill you."

"You're plenty brave, MacKade." Joe wet his lips as he took the gun out with two fingers, stooped to set it on the ground. "When you've got four guns on me, and your brothers standing by."

"Kick it this way."

"Yeah, a real hero, long as it's not one-to-one." Joe gave the gun a shove with his foot. "You've been helping yourself to my wife, haven't you?"

"You don't have a wife." Devin turned, handed his gun to Rafe. "Stay back," he demanded, then skimmed a glance over his other brothers. "All of you." He looked at Cassie briefly, saw the bruises already forming. And felt hatred wash through him. "Get to the cabin, Cassie. Savannah will take you back to the kids."

"You don't have to do this."

"Oh, yeah. I do." And he smiled. "Let's go, Joe. It's been a long time coming."

"What's to stop one of your brothers from shooting me in the back once I beat you to a pulp, MacKade?"

"Nothing." Now the smile turned feral. "This is the last shot you're going to get at me, though, you yellow son of a bitch. So make it good."

Joe shouted ferociously as he lunged. All Devin had to do was pivot and pump upward with a fist to send Joe reeling back.

"Tougher when it's somebody near your own size, isn't it?" Devin taunted. "Tougher when it's not a woman, or a little boy. Come on, you bastard. Try again."

Blood spilling from his lip, Joe came at him like a bull.

The woods cracked with the sound of bare knuckle against bone, of men grunting. Cassie forced herself not to cover her face with her hands.

It was for her. Each blow Devin threw or received was for her. So she would watch.

All the fear she'd felt of Joe ebbed as she did. He was exactly what she had called him. A pitiful bully. His size, and the wildness of his attack, helped him land a few blows. Certainly, it was that size that had him overbalancing Devin to the ground.

But even there, even outweighed, Devin dominated. His fists were fast, brutal, and the look on his face was so concentrated, she knew he felt none of the hits he took.

She didn't turn her face away from the blood, hold her hands over her ears to block out the sound. This was the end, finally the end, and she needed to bear witness.

The rage was on him so thick, so cold, that he could see nothing but Joe's face. Each time his fist hammered down, each time the power of it sang up his arms, he felt nothing but dark, deadly pleasure. His knuckles were raw, his shirt was splattered with blood, some of it his own, but he couldn't stop his fist from pumping.

"That's enough." Jared stepped forward to pull Devin off, and nearly got a fist in the face for his trouble. "That's enough," he repeated, but it took all three of them to drag Devin to his feet.

"That's a satisfying sight," Rafe commented, studying Joe's battered and unconscious face. "I guess I can't be too ticked you didn't leave a piece of him for me."

"Looks like he resisted arrest, right, Jare?" Shane shouldered his rifle, scratched his chin.

"That's the way I saw it. Come on, Dev, let's haul this carcass in. You need a beer and an ice pack."

But the rage hadn't faded away, not completely. Devin jerked his brother's hand from his shoulder. "Leave me alone." He turned, looked to where Cassie still stood, pale, bruised, eyes wide with shock. "I'm finished." He took off his badge, tossed it into the dirt. "Take him. I'm going home."

"Devin."

When Cassie started forward, Jared put out a hand to stop her. "Give him some time," he murmured, watching Devin cut through the woods, toward the farm. "He's hurting."

She tried. She went to her children and comforted them. She let Regan and Savannah come to her and fuss over her bruises. She spoke to her mother, briefly, on the phone and reassured herself that, though her mother had been bruised and terrified, there was no serious damage. And, perhaps, there was some understanding between them that they'd never shared before.

In the end, she gave in and took the sedative that was pushed on her and slept like the dead through the night.

But in the morning she knew she hadn't finished facing her demons. She let Regan deal with breakfast and readied herself to go to the farm and face Devin.

The only thing she needed to take, she tucked into the pocket of her slacks.

"You're going to see Sheriff MacKade." Connor stepped into her bedroom doorway. His eyes were swollen and shadowed, there was a faint bruise on his cheek, and he was still so very pale. Cassie wanted badly to gather him close, but he was standing so stiff.

"Yes. I need to talk to him, Connor. I need to thank him for what he did."

"He'll say it was his job."

"Yes, I know he will. That doesn't mean I don't have to thank him. He could have been killed, Connor, for us."

"I thought he was dead at first." When his voice broke, he sucked in a breath and steadied it again. "When he fell, and there was all the blood. I thought we were all going to be dead."

She shuddered, tried to keep the tears out of her voice. "I'm sorry, Connor, for what I did, for what I didn't do. I hope one day you'll forgive me."

"It wasn't your fault. It wasn't ever. I shouldn't have said those things." He wanted to look away, but he knew that would make him a coward. He knew what cowards were like now. "It wasn't true, and it wasn't the way I really felt. I said it to hurt you, because I felt bad."

"Connor." She held her arms out, closing her eyes tight when he raced into them. "That part of our lives is over. I promise you it's over."

"I know. You were pretty brave."

Unbearably touched, she kissed the top of his head. "So were you."

"This time." He sucked in a deep breath. "Sheriff MacKade stood up for us. Emma and I want to go with you. We talked about it. We want to see the sheriff."

"It might be better if I talked to him alone, just now. He's feeling… He's upset."

"I have to talk to him. Please."

How could she deny her child the same closure she needed for herself? "All right. We'll go together."

From his seat on the front porch of the farm, Devin saw them come out of the woods. He nearly got up and went inside, but it seemed a small and petty revenge.

They looked like a unit, he realized, and he supposed, however much it hurt him, that was what they needed to be.

His head was still aching, and his hands burned. But that was nothing compared to the pain in his gut as he watched Cassie and the children cross the wide front lawn.

There were bruises on her face, and on the boy's. Fury flashed in his blood like lightning. Then Emma broke away from Cassie's hand and raced to him.

"We came to thank you because you took the bad man away." She crawled right into his lap, as if she belonged there. "You have hurts." Solemnly she touched her puckered lips to the cuts and bruises, to the white bandage on his temple. "Is that better now?"

He gave in for a moment and pressed his face into her hair. "Yeah, thanks." Before Cassie could speak, he shifted Emma onto his knee. "If they haven't contacted you, I can tell you they've already transferred him to the state prison. With the new charges—the escape, the assaults, grand theft auto, the weapons possession, assault with a deadly weapon and—" he ran his fingers over his ripped knuckles "—and resisting arrest, he's not going to see the light of day again. You and your family have nothing to worry about."

"Are you all right?" was all Cassie could manage.

"I'm fine. You?"

"Just fine." Her fingers curled and uncurled over Connor's. "We wanted to come and thank—"

"I was doing my job."

"I told her you'd say that," Connor said, and earned a mild glance from Devin.

"So, I'm predictable." He looked back at Cassie. "You handled yourself well, Cass. You want to remember that. I've got work to do."

As he started to set Emma down, Cassie moved forward. "Devin, please, don't."

"He hurt you." The words burst out of him. "He hurt all of you, and I didn't stop him."

"You were shot, for God's sake. You were lying there unconscious and bleeding."

"The bad man was going to shoot you again," Emma told him. "But Mama wouldn't let him. She lay on top of you so he couldn't."

Every ounce of his hot blood went cold at the thought of it. "Damn it, Cassie, are you crazy?"

"You needed me." She let out a shaky breath. "I couldn't stand back, Devin. I did what I had to do. Now I'm going to ask you to do what you know is right." She took his badge out of her pocket. "Don't give this up, Devin. Don't go."

He stared at the badge in her hand, then into her face again. "You know what it's like to see something you want, you need, day after day, and know you can't have it? I'm not living like that anymore, not even for you. You won't let me be part of your life. You won't marry me, and I can't go on being your friend and nothing else."

"I'll marry you." Emma curled into him. "I love you."

His heart simply shattered. He held Emma tight, then set her gently on her feet. "I can't handle this, Cassie." He rose blindly. "Go home and leave me be."

"Sheriff MacKade." Connor bolted forward, then skidded to a halt. "I'm sorry."

"You've got a right to your feelings," Devin said steadily. "And no need to apologize for them."

"Sir, I got something to say."

Devin rubbed a hand over his face, dropped his arms. "All right, get it out, then."

"I know you're mad at me. Yes, sir, you are," Connor

said, keeping his eyes level when Devin started to correct him. "I was mad, too, because I thought you'd come around just for me, or mostly, and then I found out it was because of Mama. And I thought if she'd let you, you'd change things, and they'd get bad again, even though you'd given your word. Bryan told me they wouldn't, but I didn't believe him. I didn't want to."

He had to take a deep breath. "Yesterday, when you came to make us go to the cabin, and Mama said she wouldn't, you were mad. You were already mad, and then you were madder than anything. Weren't you?"

"That's right."

"You yelled."

"Yeah, I did."

"I thought this is it, this is when he's going to hit her. You knew I was thinking it, but you weren't going to. You told me you'd never hurt her, not for anything. I knew you meant it. I knew when you went into the woods after her, you'd do anything to save her. It wasn't just because it was your job. It was because it was her. Because it was us."

He gathered the rest of his shaky courage and climbed the steps until he stood face-to-face with Devin. "Even after she sent you away, even after I made her send you away, you wouldn't hurt her."

"I couldn't hurt her, Connor, if my life depended on it. That's how it is."

"Yes, sir. And she cried." He ignored the murmur of protest from his mother and kept his eyes on Devin's. "After she sent you away, she cried, like she used to when she was hurt and she thought I couldn't hear. But this time I made her cry, and I want to tell you I'm sorry. I want to tell you that I don't want a father. I can't help it."

"All right." Devin knew he would fall apart in a minute. "It's all right."

"I don't want a father," Connor hurried on. "Except if he was you."

The hand Devin had laid on Connor's shoulder tightened painfully. But it was a good, solid feeling, and gave him the boost he needed to finish.

"Please, I want you to be with us all the time, like families are supposed to. I know you might not want me now, after what I did, but I swear I won't get in your way. I was stupid, and I sassed you and Mama, and you can punish me, but don't go away. You don't have to love me anymore, if you'd just—"

The boy's breath whooshed out, along with hot tears as Devin hauled him hard against his chest. "You're too smart to say stupid things," Devin murmured shakily. "I haven't stopped wanting you. I couldn't stop loving you."

"Don't go away." Connor held on for his life. "Please, don't go away and leave us."

"I'm not going anywhere. I'm staying right here, okay?"

"Yes, sir."

"Stop calling me sir all the damn time." He pressed a kiss to Connor's damp brow. Gently he used his thumb to wipe the boy's cheeks as Emma wriggled between them.

"Hold me, too," she demanded. "I want you, too."

So he rose, the girl boosted in one arm, the boy wrapped under the other. Whatever happened now, he had no choice but to follow his heart.

She was standing there, her own eyes swimming, his badge clutched in one hand, the other pressed to her lips.

It wasn't the way he'd pictured it, asking her with two weepy children looking on. But it was going to have to do.

"No one's ever going to love you the way I do, Cassie. No

one's ever going to love these children more or work harder to give them a good life. The fact is, I can't live without you, without all of you. You're my heart. For God's sake, Cassie, marry me."

He couldn't know what it meant to her, to hear those words, to have him say them, so simply, so plainly, while he held the children as if they were already his.

Of course, they were. How foolish she'd been to ever think otherwise.

How foolish she'd been to think about doing what Abigail had done, turning away love.

She walked up the steps, took one of Connor's hands, one of Emma's. "You are the most remarkable man I've ever known, and I love you. If you have a fault, it's that you're too patient, Devin."

"I'm running low right now."

"Then I'll make this simple. We've kept you waiting long enough."

She released Connor's hand only long enough to pin the badge back on Devin's shirt. Then, linked again, she lifted to her toes and kissed the man she loved in front of her children.

"We'd love to marry you, Devin. Soon." She laid her head on his heart. "I think all of us have waited long enough. Very, very soon."

* * * * *

THE FALL OF
SHANE MacKADE

For those who've taken the fall

Prologue

Ice covered the shoveled walk from the house to the milking barn, and the path was slick with it. The predawn air was cupped by a dark sky chiseled with frosted chips of white stars. Each gulp was like sipping chilled razor blades that sliced, then numbed, the throat before being expelled in a frigid steam.

Wrapped in a multitude of winter layers, from long johns to knitted muffler, Shane MacKade headed toward the milking parlor and the first chores of the day. Unlike his three older brothers, he was whistling between his teeth.

He just plain loved the frosty and still hour before a winter sunrise.

His oldest brother, Jared, was nearly seventeen, and went about the business of running a farm like an accountant approaching a spreadsheet. It was all figures to him, Shane knew, and he supposed that was well enough. They had lost their father two months before, and times were rough.

As for Rafe, his restless fifteen-year-old soul was already looking beyond the hills and fields of the MacKade farm. The milking and feeding and tending of stock was simply something to get through. And Shane knew, though they never really talked about it, that their father's death had hit Rafe the hardest.

They had all loved their father. It would have been impossible not to love Buck MacKade, with his big voice and big hands and big heart. And everything Shane knew about farming—everything he loved about the land—had come straight from his father.

Perhaps that was why Shane didn't grieve as deeply. The land was there, so his father was there. Always.

He could have talked about that thought with Devin. At fourteen, Devin was already the best of listeners, and the closest to Shane's own age. Shane was going to make the big leap to thirteen next Tuesday. But he kept the thought—and the feeling—to himself.

Inside the milking parlor, the first of the stock shifted and mooed, tails swishing as they were prepped. It was a simple enough process, could even be considered a monotonous one. The cleaning, the feeding, the attaching to machines that would pump the milk from cow to pipe, from pipe to tank for storage. But Shane enjoyed it, enjoyed the smells, the sounds, the routine. While he and Devin dealt with the second line of stock, Rafe and Jared led those already relieved of milk outside again.

They made a good team, quick and efficient despite the numbing cold and early hour. In truth, it was a job any one of them could have handled alone, or with very little help. But they tended to stick together. Even closer together these days.

Still, there were chickens and pigs to see to yet, eggs to

gather, muck to shovel, fresh hay to spread. And all this before they gobbled down breakfast and climbed into Jared's ancient car for the drive to school.

If he could have, Shane would have skipped the school part entirely. You couldn't learn how to plow and plant, how to harvest or judge the weather by tasting the air, from books. You couldn't learn from books how to look into a cow's eyes and see that she was ailing.

But his mother was firm on book learning, and when she was firm, she was immovable.

"What the hell are you so happy about?" Grumbling, Rafe clanged stainless-steel buckets together. "That whistling's driving me crazy."

Shane merely grinned and kept on whistling. He paused only long enough to talk encouragingly to the cows. "That's the way, ladies, you fill her up." Content as any of his bossies, Shane moved down the line of milkers, checking each one.

"I'm going to pound him," Rafe announced to no one in particular.

"Leave him be," Devin said mildly. "He's already brain-dead."

Rafe smiled at that. "It's so damn cold, if I hit him, my fingers would probably break off."

"Going to warm up some today." Shane patted one of the cows waiting in the stanchions to be hooked for milking. "Get up into the thirties, anyway."

Rafe didn't bother to ask how Shane knew. Shane always knew. "Big deal." He strode out of the milking parlor, toward barn and hayloft.

"What's eating him?" Shane muttered. "Some girl dump him?"

"He just hates cows." Jared stepped back in, smelling of grain.

"That's stupid. You're a sweetheart, aren't you, baby?" Shane gave the nearest cow an affectionate swat.

"Shane's in love with cows." Devin flashed the wicked MacKade grin, which had a dimple flickering at the corner of his mouth. "He has better luck kissing them than girls."

Immediately insulted, Shane narrowed his eyes. "I could kiss any girl I wanted to—if I wanted to." Under the layers of clothing, his lean, rangy body was on full alert.

Recognizing the signs, Jared shook his head. He just didn't feel like a tussle now. There was too much work to do, and he had a big test in English Lit to worry about. Devin and Shane were too evenly matched, and a fight between them could go on indefinitely.

"Yeah, you're a regular Don Juan." He said it only to focus Shane's attention, and temper, on him. "All the little girls are puckered up and waiting in line."

Devin made a long, loud kissing noise that made Jared want to slug him. As Shane pivoted to do just that, Jared stepped between them. "But before you make their hearts flutter, lover boy, the water trough's iced over. These cows are thirsty."

Aiming a glance that promised Devin retribution, Shane stomped outside.

He could kiss a girl, Shane thought as he hacked at the ice. If he wanted to. He just wasn't interested.

Well, maybe he was a little interested, he admitted, blowing on his fingers to warm them. Some of the girls he knew were starting to get pretty interesting shapes. And he'd felt an odd sort of tingling under his skin when Jared's girl, Sharilyn, wiggled up against him when they were packed into the front seat of Jared's car the other day.

He could probably kiss her, if he wanted. He set the iron bar aside, looking toward the milk barn as the stars winked out overhead. That would show Jared a thing or two. They all figured he didn't know what was what because he was the youngest. But he knew plenty. At least he was starting to imagine plenty.

Hauling up the bar again, he clumped over the slippery, snow-packed ground to the pig shed.

He knew how sex worked, all right. He'd grown up on a farm, hadn't he? He knew how the bull went crazy and white-eyed when he smelled a cow in heat. He just hadn't thought the whole thing looked like a whole hell of a lot of fun…but that had been before he began to notice how girls filled out their clothes.

He hacked away the layer of ice for the pigs and, leaving his brothers to finish up the milking, dealt with the feed.

He wished he was grown-up. He wished he could do something to prove he was—besides holding his own in a fight. As it was, all he could do was simply wait until he was older, and know that then he could take control of his life.

The land was his. He'd felt that in his bones, as long as he could remember. As if at birth someone had whispered it in his ear. The farm, the land. That was what really mattered. And if he wanted a girl, too—or a whole platoon of them—he'd get that, too.

But the farm was what counted most.

The land, he thought, looking over the snow-coated fields as the sky grayed with dawn and turned explosive at the tips of the eastern mountains. The land his father had worked, and his father before that. And before that. Through droughts and floods. Through war.

They'd planted their crops, and brought them in, he

thought, dreaming a little as he walked toward the fields. Even when war came, right here, with Confederate gray and Union blue clashing in these very fields, and in the thick woods just beyond, the farm had stayed whole.

He knew just what it would have been like, turning the rocky soil behind a horse-drawn plow, your back and shoulders aching, your hands raw. But the crops would be planted, and you would see them grow. Corn springing up, spreading, hay waving and going gold with summer.

Even when the soldiers came, even when their mortars and black powder singed the drying cornstalks, the land stayed. Bodies had dropped here, he thought as a chill crept up his spine. Men had screamed and crawled through their own blood.

But the land they had fought over, fought for, didn't change. It endured.

He flushed a little, wondering where that word had come from, that word and the strong, almost dizzying emotion behind it. He was glad he was alone, glad none of his brothers could see. He didn't know how to tell them that he knew the farm had been his responsibility before, and would be again.

But he knew.

When he heard the sound behind him, he stiffened and, shouldering the bar again, turned with his face carefully closed, free of emotion.

There was no one there.

He swallowed hard. He was sure he'd heard a sound, a movement, then a small, weak cry. It wasn't the first time he'd heard the ghosts. They lived here, as he did—in the fields, in the woods, in the hills. But they terrified him nonetheless.

Gathering all his young courage, he moved around the

shed, toward the old stone smokehouse. It was probably Devin, he told himself, or Rafe, or even Jared, trying to get a rise out of him, trying to make him bolt, as he'd nearly bolted the time they spent the night in the old Barlow place, on the other side of the woods. The haunted house, where ghosts were as thick as cobwebs.

"Get a life, Dev," he said, loudly, loudly enough to calm his speeding heart.

But when he rounded the building, he didn't see his brother, or even any tracks in the snow. For an instant, just a quick, tripping heartbeat, he thought he saw a figure there. Crumpled, spilling blood over the ground, the face as white as the untouched snow, the eyes dulled with pain.

Help me. Please help me, I'm dying.

But when he stepped forward there was nothing. Nothing at all. Even the words that rang in his head faded away in the wind.

Shane stood there, a young boy with his whole life a wonderful mystery yet to unfold, and stared at the unbroken ground. He stood there, shuddering, as the cold reached through the layers of clothes, through his flesh and into his bones.

Then he heard his brothers laughing, heard his mother call from the kitchen door that breakfast was ready and to get a move on or they'd be late for school.

He turned away, closed his frightened mind off to what he had seen and what he had heard.

He walked back to the farmhouse, and said nothing of that one jolting moment to anyone.

Chapter 1

Shane MacKade loved women. He loved the look of them, the smell of them, the sound of them, the taste of them. He loved them, without reservation or prejudice. Tall, short, plump, thin, old, young, their wonderful and exotic femaleness pulled him, drew him in. The slant of an eyelash, the curve of a lip, the sway of a shapely female bottom, simply delighted him.

He had, in his thirty-two years on earth, done his very best to show as many women as possible his boundless appreciation for them as a gender.

He considered himself a lucky man, because the ladies loved him right back.

He had other loves. His family, his farm, the smell of bread baking, the taste of a cold beer on a hot day.

But women, well, they were so varied, so different and so delicious.

He was smiling at one now. Even though Regan was his

brother's wife, and Shane had nothing but the most innocent and brotherly feelings for her, he could appreciate her
considerable female attributes. He liked the way her deep
blond hair curved around her face. He adored the little mole
beside her mouth, and the way she always looked so sexy
and so tidy at the same time.

He thought if a man had to pick one woman and tie himself down, Rafe couldn't have done better.

"Are you sure you don't mind, Shane?"

"Mind what?" He caught her quirked brow as she lifted
the newest MacKade onto her shoulder. "Oh, the airport
run. Right. I was just thinking how pretty you look."

Regan had to laugh. She was frazzled, Jason MacKade,
her youngest son, was squalling, her hair was a mess, and
she was afraid she smelled more like Jason's diapers than
the scent she'd dabbed on that morning.

"I look like a madwoman."

"Nope." To give her a breather, Shane took Jason from
her and jiggled the three-week-old baby into hiccups. "Just
as pretty as ever."

She glanced over to the playpen she'd set up in the
back room of her antique shop, where her toddler, Nate,
napped through the chaos. He had the look of his father,
she thought, with a burst of love. Which meant, of course,
that he had the look of his uncle Shane.

"I appreciate it. I can use the flattery. I really hate to
ask you, though."

Shane watched her pour tea and resigned himself to
drinking it. "It's not a problem, honey. I'll pick up your
college pal and get her back to you safe and sound. A scientist, huh?"

"Hmm..." Regan handed him a cup, knowing he could
juggle that and his infant nephew and a few more things

besides. "Rebecca's brilliant. Over-the-top brilliant. I only roomed with her one year. She was fifteen, and already a sophomore. She ended up graduating, summa cum laude, a full year ahead of me and the rest of her class. Pretty intimidating."

Regan sampled the tea, and the relative quiet now that Shane had Jason calmed down to bubbling coos. "It seemed she was always in some lab, or the library."

"Sounds like a barrel of laughs."

"She was—is—a serious type, and tended to be shy. After all, she was years younger than anyone else in school. But we got to be friends. She'd have come for the wedding, but she was in Europe, or Africa." Regan waved vaguely. "Somewhere."

Shane was thinking nostalgically of his own fifteenth year, when he had learned the intricacies of the back-hook bra. In the dark. "It's nice you've got a pal coming to visit."

"Well, it's kind of a working visit for her." Regan gnawed her lip. She hadn't mentioned Rebecca's purpose, except to Rafe. She supposed if she was going to dragoon Shane into meeting her friend at the airport, she ought to make it clear.

She studied him as he made faces at the baby, then nuzzled Jason. All the MacKades were stunners, she thought, but there was something about Shane. Just an extra slice of charm, she supposed.

He had the looks, of course. That thick, midnight-black hair that he now wore in a stubby ponytail. The thin, bony, mouth-watering face, with its angles and planes, lush mouth, flashing dimple and thickly lashed green eyes. His shade of green was dreamy, the shade of an ocean at twilight.

He had the build—tall, rangy, muscled. Broad shoulders, narrow hips, long, long legs. It showed to advantage in jeans and work boots and flannel.

He had the charm. All four MacKades had it to spare, but Regan thought there was an extra dollop in Shane. Something about the way his eyes lingered on a woman, the quick, appreciative grin when he spoke to one, be she eight or eighty. That easygoing, cheerful manner that could explode into temper, then, just as quickly, edge away into a laugh.

He'd probably scare the hell out of poor, shy Rebecca.

"You're awfully good with him," she murmured.

"You keep making babies, honey, I'll keep loving them."

Amused, she angled her head. "Still not ready to settle down?"

"Now why would I want to go and do that?" He looked up from Jason, and his eyes danced with humor. "I'm the last single MacKade. I'm honor-bound to hold the fort until the nephews start springing up."

"And you take your duty seriously."

"You bet. He's asleep." Shane lowered his head and kissed Jason's brow. "Want me to put him down?"

"Thanks." She waited until Shane had Jason settled in the antique cradle. "Rebecca's expecting me. I wasn't able to catch her before she left for the airport." Frazzled all over again, Regan ran her fingers though her hair. "The babysitter canceled, Rafe's in Hagerstown getting building material. Cassie's got a full house over at the inn, Emma's got the sniffles, and I just couldn't ask Savannah to help out."

"Last time I saw her, she looked ready to pop." To demonstrate the condition of Jared's wife, Shane made a wide circle with his arms in front of his flat belly.

"Exactly. She's too pregnant to drive a three-hour round

trip, and with a furniture delivery being rescheduled for this afternoon, I didn't know who else to call and impose on."

"It's no trouble." To prove it, he kissed the tip of her nose. "I don't suppose she's as pretty as you, is she?"

Regan chuckled at that. "How am I supposed to answer that and not sound like a jerk? In any case, I haven't seen her in…five years, I guess. The last time was on a quick trip to New York, and she was hip-deep in some paper she was writing. She's four years younger than I am and has two doctorates. Maybe more. I can't keep up."

Shane didn't wince. He liked women with brains as much as he liked women without them. But he knew the old routine about smarts and wonderful personalities. He didn't think he was going to be picking up a beauty queen at the airport.

"Psychiatry and U.S. history for sure," Regan continued. "Kind of an odd mix, but then, Rebecca's unique. I remember she minored in some sort of complex math, and there was science, too. Physics, chemistry…she did post-grad work on that at MIT."

"Why?" Shane wondered out loud.

"With Rebecca it would be more a matter of why not. She's got what they call a photographic memory. Sees it, reads it, files it up there," Regan said, tapping her head.

"And she's a shrink?"

"She doesn't have a private practice. She consults, writes papers, lectures. I know she used to donate a day a week to a clinic. She wrote a definitive paper on…well, some psychosis or other. Or maybe it was a phobia. I'm a business major. Anyway, Shane—" Regan smiled brightly and patted his hand "—she's into parapsychology. As a hobby."

"Into what? Is that like ghostbusting?"

"It's the study of the paranormal. ESP, psychic phenomena, ah…hauntings…"

"Ghosts," Shane concluded, and this time he did wince. "Don't we have enough of that around here already?"

"That's the point. She's interested in the area, the legends. It's different for you, Shane," Regan hurried on, knowing her brother-in-law's aversion to local legends. "You grew up with it all. The Barlow house, the two corporals, the haunted woods. The whole idea of hauntings is one of the main reasons Rafe and I have been able to make such a success out of the inn. People love the idea of staying in a haunted house."

Shane only shrugged. Hell, he *lived* in one. "I don't mind all that. It's just when tourists want to go tramping around the farm that—"

The look in her eye stopped him, made him narrow his own. "She wants to tramp around the farm."

"She wants the whole picture, and I know she'd like to spend some time out there. But that's totally up to you," Regan said quickly. "You need to get to know her a little. She's really a fascinating woman. Anyway, I wrote down her flight number and so forth." Regan offered him a sheet of paper.

"You still haven't told me what she looks like. I doubt she's going to be the only woman off that flight from New York."

"Right. Brown hair, brown eyes. She used to wear it just sort of pulled back, or…hanging down. She's about my height, thin—"

"Skinny or slim? There's a difference."

"I guess more on the skinny side. She may be wearing glasses. She uses them to read, but she used to forget to take them off and she'd end up running into things."

"A skinny, clumsy brunette with glasses. Got it."

"She's very attractive," Regan added loyally. "In a unique way. And, Shane? She's shy, so be nice."

"I'm always nice. To women."

"All right, be good then. If you don't spot her, you can have her paged. Dr. Rebecca Knight."

Airports always entertained Shane. People were in just as much of a hurry, it seemed to him, to get where they were going as they were to get back from wherever they'd been. Everyone hit the ground running, loaded down with carry-ons. He wondered what it was about the places people chose to leave that didn't appeal enough to keep them there.

Not that he was against travel. He just figured he could get anywhere he really wanted to go by sitting behind the wheel of his pickup. That way, he was in charge of time and distance and speed.

But it took all kinds.

He also figured he could spot Regan's college pal— since she was a woman, and he knew women. She'd be in her mid-twenties, about five foot five, skinny, brown hair, brown eyes, probably behind thick glasses. From Regan's brief rundown, he didn't imagine Rebecca Knight had a great deal of style, so he would look for a plain, intellectual type, with a briefcase and practical shoes.

He loitered at the gate, eyeing a pair of flight attendants who were waiting for a change of crew. Now that, he mused, was a profession that drew pretty women. It almost made a man feel there'd be some advantage in being stuck in a flying tin can for a few hours.

As passengers began to pour out of the gateway, he judiciously shifted his attention. Businessmen, looking harried, he noted. The suit-and-tie brigade. No amount of money could convince him that it would be worth wearing a suit for eight to ten hours a day. Nice-looking blonde in sleek red slacks. She gave him a quick, flirtatious smile as she passed, and Shane pleased himself by drawing in the cloud of scent she left behind.

Pretty brunette with a long, ground-eating stride and big, wide gold eyes. They reminded him of the amber beads his mother had kept in her good jewelry box.

Here came Grandma, with an enormous shopping bag and a huge, misty-eyed grin for the trio of children who raced up to hug her knees.

Ah, there she is, Shane decided, spotting a slump-shouldered woman with brown hair scraped back in a frowsy knot. She carried an official-looking black briefcase and wore thick, laced shoes and square glasses. She blinked owlishly behind them, looking lost.

"Hey." He gave her a quick, flashing smile, and a friendly wink that had her backing up three steps into a frazzled man lugging a bulging garment bag. "How's it going?" He reached down to take her briefcase and had her myopic eyes going round with alarm. "I'm Shane. Regan sent me to fetch you. She had complications. So how was the flight?"

"I—I—" The woman pulled her briefcase protectively against her thin chest. "I'll call security."

"Take it easy, Becky. I'm just going to give you a ride."

She opened her mouth and made a squeaking noise. When Shane reached out for her arm to reassure her, she gave him a solid thwack with the briefcase. Before he had decided whether to laugh or swear, he felt a light tap on his arm.

"Excuse me." The pretty brunette cocked a brow and gave him a long, considering study. "I believe you may be looking for me." Her mouth, which Shane noted was wide and full, curved into a dryly amused smile. "Shane, you said. That would be Shane MacKade?"

"Yeah. Oh." He glanced back at the woman he'd accosted. "Sorry," he began, but she was already darting off like a rabbit pursued by wolves.

"I imagine that's the most excitement she's had in some time," Rebecca commented. She thought she knew just how the poor woman had felt. It was so miserable to be shy and plain and not quite in step with the rest of the world. "I'm Rebecca Knight," she added, and thrust out a hand.

She wasn't quite what he'd expected, but on closer study he saw he hadn't been that far off. She did look intellectual, if you got past those eyes. Rather than practical shoes, it was a practical haircut, as short as a boy's. He preferred hair on a woman, personally, but this chopped-off do suited her face, with its pointy, almost foxlike features.

And she was probably skinny. It was just hard to tell, with the boxy, shape-disguising jacket and slacks, all in unrelieved black.

So he smiled again, taking the long, narrow hand in his. "Regan said your eyes were brown. They're not."

"It says they are on my driver's license. Is Regan all right?"

"She's fine. Just some domestic and professional complications. Here, let me take that." He reached for the big, many-pocketed bag she had slung over her shoulder.

"No thanks, I've got it. You're one of the brothers-in-law."

"Yeah." He took her arm to steer her around toward the terminal.

Strong fingers, she noted. And a predilection for touching. Well, that was all right. She wouldn't squeak, as the other woman had—as she herself might have a few months before, when faced with a pure, unadulterated male.

"The one who runs the farm."

"That's right. You don't look much like a Ph.D.—on first glance."

"Don't I?" She sent him a cool sidelong look. She'd done a lot of mirror-practicing on that look. "And the woman who is probably even now hyperventilating in the nearest ladies' room did?"

"It was the shoes," Shane explained, and grinned down at Rebecca's neat black canvas flats.

"I see." As they rode down the escalator toward baggage claim, she turned to face him. Flannel shirt open at the collar, she noted. Worn jeans, scarred boots, big, callused hands. Thick black hair spilling out of a battered cap, on top of a lean, tanned face that could have been on a poster selling anything.

"You look like a farmer," she decided. "So how long a drive is it to Antietam?"

He debated whether or not he'd been insulted or complimented and answered, "Just over an hour. We'll get your bags."

"They're being sent." Pleased with her practicality, she patted the bag over her arm. "This is all I have at the moment."

Shane couldn't get over the sensation—the uncomfortable sensation—that he was being observed, sized up and dissected like a laboratory frog. "Great." It relieved him when she took shaded glasses from her jacket pocket and slipped them on.

He was used to women looking at him, but not as though he were something smeared on a slide.

When they reached his truck, she gave it a brief look,

then gave him another as he opened the door for her. She granted him one of those cool smiles, then tipped down her glasses to peer at him over them.

"Oh, one thing, Shane…"

Because she'd paused, he frowned a little. "Yeah?"

"Nobody calls me Becky."

With that she slid neatly onto the seat and set her bag on the floor.

She enjoyed the ride. He drove well, and the truck ran smoothly. And she couldn't help but get a little glow of satisfaction at having annoyed him, just a bit. Men who not only looked as good as Shane MacKade but had the extra bonus of exuding all that sex and confidence weren't easy to take down a peg.

She'd spent a lot of her life being intimidated on any kind of social level. Only in the past few months had she begun to make progress toward holding her own. She'd become her own project, and Rebecca thought she was coming along very well.

She gave him credit for making easy conversation on the trip, annoyed or not. Before long they were off the highway and driving on winding back roads. It was a pretty picture, hills and houses, pastures and trees that held their lush summer green into the late, hazy August, an occasional horse or grazing cow.

He'd turned the radio music politely low, and all she could really hear from the speakers was the throb of the beat.

The cab of the truck was neat, with the occasional strand of golden dog hair drifting upward, and the scent of dog with it. There were a couple of scribbled notes attached by magnet to the metal dash, a handful of coins tossed into the ashtray. But it was ordered.

Perhaps that was why she spotted the little gold twist of a woman's earring peeking out from under the floor mat. She reached down and plucked it up.

"Yours?"

He flicked a glance, caught the glint of gold and remembered that Frannie Spader had been wearing earrings like that the last time they...took a drive together.

"A friend's." Shane held out his hand. When the earring was in it, he dropped it carelessly amid the coins.

"She'll want it back," Rebecca noted idly. "It's fourteen-karat. So...there are four of you, right?"

"Yep. Do you have any brothers, sisters?"

"No. But you run the family farm?"

"That's the way it worked out. Jared has his law practice, Rafe's into building, Devin's the sheriff."

"And you're the farm boy," she finished. "What do you farm?"

"We have dairy cattle, pigs. Grow corn—feed mostly, but some nice Silver Queen—hay, alfalfa." He could see she was taking it all in with those big intense eyes, and he added, very soberly, "We've had ourselves a nice crop of potatoes."

"Really?" In unconscious sympathy with the beat whispering through the speakers, she drummed her fingers on her knee. "Isn't that a lot of work for one man?"

"My brothers are there when they're needed. And I take on some 4-H students seasonally." He moved his shoulders. "I've got a couple of nephews coming up. They're eleven now. I can usually con them into believing they're having fun when they're feeding the stock."

"And is it fun?"

"I like it." This time he looked at her. "Ever been on a farm?"

"No, not really. I'm an urbanite."

"Then you're in for a surprise with Antietam," he murmured. "Urban it's not."

"So Regan tells me. And, of course, I know the area through my studies. It must have been interesting growing up on one of the major battlefields of the Civil War."

"Rafe was always more into that than me. The land doesn't care if it's historical, as long as it's tended."

"So you're not interested in the history?"

"Not particularly." The truck rumbled over the bridge that spanned the piece of the Potomac River between Virginia and Maryland. "I know it," he added. "You can't live there all your life and not know it. But I don't give it a lot of attention."

"And the ghosts?"

"I don't give them a lot of attention, either."

A smile shadowed her mouth. "But you know of them."

Again he moved his shoulders. "Part of the package. You want to talk to the rest of the family about that. They're more into it."

"Yet you live and work on a farm that's supposedly haunted."

"Supposedly." He didn't care to talk about it, or think about it. "Look, Regan mentioned something about you coming out to do whatever it is you do—"

"To study and record any paranormal activity." Her smile spread. "It's just a hobby."

"Yeah, well, you'd be better off at the old Barlow place, the house Rafe and Regan put back together. It's a bed-and-breakfast now—one of my other sisters-in-law runs it. It's lousy with ghosts, if you believe in that sort of thing."

"Mmm… It's on my list. In fact, I'm hoping they can squeeze me in for a while. I'd like to stay there. And from what Regan told me, you have a large house. I'd like to stay there, too."

He wouldn't mind the company, but the purpose didn't sit well with him. "Regan didn't mention how long you were planning on being around."

"That depends." She looked out the window as he took a route through a cut in the mountains. "It depends on how long it takes me to find what I want to find, and how long it takes to document it."

"Don't you have, like, a job?"

"I'm taking a sabbatical." The word had such marvelous possibilities, she closed her eyes to savor them. "I have all the time in the world, and I intend to enjoy it." Opening her eyes again, she saw the glint from the little gold earring in the ashtray. "Don't worry, farm boy. I won't cramp your style. When the time comes, you can tuck me into some little room in the attic. I'll do my thing, you can do yours."

He started to comment, but she made some soft, strangled sound and sat bolt upright in the seat. "What?"

She could only shake her head, absorbed in the jarring sense of déjà vu. The hills rose up, grass green against outcroppings of silver rocks. In the distance, the higher mountains were purple shadows against hazy skies. Fields, high with green stalks of corn, thick with summer grains, rolled back from the road. On a sloping embankment, black-and-white cows stood as still as if they were on a postcard.

Woods, dark and thick, ranged along a field, while a winding creek bubbled along the verge.

"It looks just as it should," she murmured softly. "Exactly. Perfect."

"Thanks. It's MacKade land." He slowed the truck a little, out of pride. "You can't see the house this time of year. Trees are too thick. It's back down that lane."

She saw the rough gravel road, the way it swung left and followed the line of trees. With her heart thudding dully in her breast, she nodded.

Come hell or high water, she thought, she was going back there. And she would stay until she found all the answers to all the questions that plagued her.

She took a deep breath, turned to him. "How far to town?"

"Just a few miles now." His eyes narrowed with concern. She'd gone dead pale. "You all right?"

"I'm fine." But she did open the window to take a deep gulp of late summer. "I'm just fine."

Chapter 2

Through the display window of her shop, Regan saw the truck pull up to the curb. With a child in each arm, she dashed outside.

"Dr. Knight."

"Mrs. MacKade." Rebecca slid out of the cab of the truck and let out a cry of pure pleasure, then launched herself at her friend as her vision blurred.

Gone was the cool and the clinical, Shane noted, and he found himself grinning at the way the two women babbled and embraced. He'd had some reservations about Rebecca Knight—and maybe he'd keep a few of them. But there was no doubt as to the depth of affection here.

"Oh, I've missed you. I've missed you," Rebecca said over and over as tears stung her eyes. "Oh, Regan, you're so gorgeous, and look at these. Your babies."

She let the tears come. She'd never had to hold back

or feel foolish with Regan. Sniffling, she touched Nate's cheek, then stroked a finger along the baby's soft head.

"I don't see you for a few years, and look what you do. Married and the mother of two. I've got to hold one."

Always willing, Nate held out his arms.

"You must look like your daddy," Rebecca commented, delighted when Nate puckered up for a kiss.

"Daddy," Nate agreed. "Play ball. Shane!" He bounced up and down like a spring. "Shane, gimme ride."

"Shows what you know, choosing your uncle over a lady." But Shane hauled Nate onto his shoulders, where the toddler could squeal and grip his hair.

"You found each other." Regan beamed at both of them. "I'm sorry I couldn't get away to pick you up myself."

"I'd say you had your hands full." Rebecca turned to give Shane a mild smile. "And your brother-in-law managed just fine. All in all."

"You must be tired. Come into the shop. I'm just closing up. Shane, come in for some tea."

"I have to get back, thanks anyway. Down you go, Nate." He swung the boy around, inciting a series of rolling belly laughs.

Wise to her son, Regan clutched Nate's hand firmly in hers the minute his little feet hit the ground. "Thanks." She kissed Shane lightly on the lips. "I owe you one. I want to give Rebecca a welcome dinner tomorrow, when she's had time to catch her breath. You'll come, won't you?"

"A free meal." He winked. "Count on it. See you."

"Thanks for the lift. Farm boy."

Shane paused at the driver's-side door. "Anytime. Becky."

Regan lifted a brow as he drove away. "Becky?"

"Just a little joke." Objectively she looked up and down

the street, noted the light traffic, the old stone buildings, the people loitering in front of doorways. "I'm trying to picture Regan Bishop as resident and shop owner of Small Town, U.S.A."

"It was home the minute I saw it. Come inside," she said again. "Tell me what you think of the shop."

Now she could picture it, Rebecca realized the moment she stepped into Past Times. The style, the elegance of gleaming antiques, lovely old lamps and glass and statuary. There was a smell of spice and baby powder that made her smile.

"Mama," she said after turning around in a circle. "How does it feel?"

"Incredible. I can't wait for you to meet Rafe." She moved into a back room, setting the baby in a bassinet, then lifting Nate into a high chair, where he occupied himself with a cookie. It gave her time to take a breath. "Of course, you've seen Shane, so you've got a fairly good idea of the MacKade looks."

"Are they all like that?"

"Tall, dark and ridiculously handsome? Every one of them. With bad-boy reputations to match." She leaned back, took a long survey. "Rebecca, it's always what people say when they haven't seen each other for a while, but I have to say it anyway. You look wonderful."

Rebecca smiled as she tugged on a short tress of chestnut-brown hair. "I got the nerve to have this hacked off when I was in Europe a few months ago. You were always trying to coax me into doing something with my hair."

"I'd have never been that brave, or inventive. Boy, it suits you, Rebecca. And—"

"The clothes?" Her smile widened. "That was Europe, too. I had a crisis of style, so to speak. I was walking along the Left Bank and happened to catch a glimpse of this woman reflected in one of the shop windows. She looked like an unkempt scarecrow. Her hair was tangled and hanging down in her face, and she had on the most dreadful brown suit. I thought, *Poor thing, to look like that in a city like this.* And then I realized it was me."

"You're too hard on yourself."

"I was a mess," Rebecca said firmly. "A cliché, the dowdy prodigy with a sharp brain and bad shoes. I walked into the nearest beauty salon, gave myself no time to think, to rationalize, to intellectualize, and threw myself on their mercy. Who'd have thought a decent haircut could make such a difference to the way I felt? It seemed so shallow. I told myself that even when I walked out with several hundred dollars' worth of skin creams."

She laughed at herself as she realized that, after all this time, she was still savoring that moment. "Then I realized that if appearances weren't important, it couldn't be a problem to present a good one."

"Then I'll say it again. You look wonderful." Regan reached out for Rebecca's hands. "In fact, since you're happy with the change, I'll be perfectly honest and tell you I wouldn't have recognized you. You're absolutely striking, and I'm so glad to see you looking so fabulous."

"I have to say this." She gave Regan's hands a hard squeeze. "Regan, you were my first real friend."

"Rebecca."

"My very first, the only person I was close to who didn't treat me like an oddity. I've wanted to tell you for a long time what that meant to me. What you meant to me. But even with you, I had a hard time getting that kind of thing out."

"You're making me cry again," Regan managed.

"There's more. I was so nervous coming here, worrying that the friendship, the connection, might not be the same. But it is. Hell." Rebecca gave a lavish sniff. "Got any tissue?"

Regan dived into a diaper bag and pulled out a travel pack. She handed a tissue to Rebecca, used one herself. "I'm so happy," she said, weeping.

"Me, too."

Rebecca decided the rambling old stone house just outside of town suited Regan and Rafe MacKade perfectly. It had the rough, masculine charm of Rafc MacKade, and the style and feminine grace of Regan, all rolled into one.

She would have spotted Rafe as Shane's brother from a mile away with one eye closed, so powerful was the resemblance. So she wasn't surprised when he pulled her into his arms for a hard hug the moment he saw her.

She'd already gleaned that the MacKades liked women.

"Regan's been fretting and fussing for two weeks," he told Rebecca over a glass of wine in the big, airy living room.

"I have not been fussing or fretting."

Rafe smiled and, from his seat on the sofa, reached up to stroke his wife's hand as she sat on the arm near him. "She polished everything twice, vacuumed up every dog hair." He gave the golden retriever slumbering on the rug an affectionate nudge with his foot.

"*Most* of the dog hair," Regan corrected.

"I'm flattered." Rebecca jolted a little when Nate knocked over his building blocks and sent them scattering.

"Attaboy," Rafe said mildly. "If it's not built right, just tear it down and start again."

"Daddy. Come play."

"It's all in the foundation," Rafe said as he got up and ranged himself on the floor with his son. They began to move blocks, Rafe's big hands moving with Nate's small, pudgy ones. "Regan says you want a close-up look at the inn."

"I do. I want to stay there, at least for a while, if you have a vacancy."

"Oh, but...we want you here, Rebecca."

Rebecca smiled over at Regan. "I appreciate that, and I do want to spend time here, as well. But it would really help if I could stay a few nights there, anyway."

"Ghostbusting," Rafe said, with a wink at his son.

"If you like," Rebecca returned coolly.

"Hey, don't get me wrong. They're there. The first time I got a good hold of Regan was when I caught her as she was fainting in the hallway of the inn. They'd spooked her."

"That's not entirely true," Regan said. "I thought Rafe was playing a prank, and when I realized he wasn't, I got... overwrought."

"Tell me about it." Fascinated, Rebecca leaned forward. "What did you see?"

"I didn't see anything." Regan blew out a breath. Her son was too involved with his blocks to notice the subject of the conversation. And, in any case, he was a MacKade. "It was more a feeling...of not being alone. The house had been deserted and empty for years then. Rafe hadn't even begun the renovations. But there were noises. Footsteps, a door closing. There's a spot on the stairs, a cold spot."

"You felt it?" Rebecca's voice was flat now, that of a scientist assessing data.

"Right to the bone. It was so shocking. Rafe told me later that a young Confederate soldier had been killed there, on the day of the Battle of Antietam."

"The two corporals." Rebecca nodded at Regan's surprised look. "I've been researching the area, the legends. Two soldiers, from opposite sides, met in the woods on September 17, 1862. It's thought they were lost, or perhaps deserting. They were both very young. They fought there, wounded each other badly. One made his way to the home of Charles Barlow, now the MacKade Inn. The mistress of the house, Abigail, was a Southern woman, wed to a Yankee businessman. She had the wounded boy brought inside, and was having him carried upstairs to be tended. Instead, her husband came down and shot and killed him, there on the stairs."

"That's right," Regan agreed. "You'll often smell roses in the house. Abigail's roses."

"Really." Rebecca mulled the information over. "Well, well... Isn't that fascinating." Her eyes went dreamy for a moment, then sharpened again. "I managed to contact a descendant of one of the Barlow servants who was there at the time. It seems Abigail did her best to take care of the boy, even after his death. She had the servants search his pockets and they found some letters. She wrote to his parents and arranged for his body to be taken back home for burial."

"I never knew that," Regan murmured.

"Abigail kept it as quiet as possible, likely to avoid her husband's wrath. The boy's name was Gray, Franklin Gray, corporal, CSA, and he never saw his nineteenth birthday."

"Some people hear the shot, and weeping. Cassie—that's Devin's wife—runs the inn for us. She can tell you more."

"I'd like to see the place tomorrow, if I can. And the woods. I need to see the farm, too. The other corporal, name unknown, was buried by the MacKades. I hope to find out more. My equipment should be here by late tomorrow, or the next day."

"Equipment?" Rafe asked.

"Sensors, cameras, temperature gauges. Parapsychology is best approached as a science. Tell me, have there been any reports of telekinetic activities—the movement of inanimate objects? Poltergeists?"

"No." Regan gave a quick shudder. "And I'm sure we'd have heard."

"Well, I can always hope."

Baffled, Regan stared at her. "You used to be so…"

"Serious-minded? I still am. Believe me, I'm very serious about this."

"Okay." With a quick shake of her head, Regan rose. "And I better get serious about dinner."

"I'll give you a hand."

Regan arched a brow as Rebecca stood. "Don't tell me you learned to cook in Europe, too."

"No, I can't boil an egg."

"You used to say it was genetic."

"I remember. Now I think it's just a phobia. Cooking's a dangerous business. Sharp edges, heat, flame. But I remember how to set a table."

"Good enough."

Late that night, when Rebecca settled into her room, she snuggled up on the big padded window seat with a book and a cup of Regan's tea. From down the hall she dimly heard the sound of a baby's fretful crying, then footsteps padding down the hall. Within moments the quiet returned as, Rebecca imagined, Regan nursed the baby. She'd never imagined the Regan Bishop she'd known as a mother. In college, Regan had always been bright, energetic, interested in everyone and everything. Of course, she'd attracted male companionship, Rebecca remembered with a small smile. A woman who looked like Regan would always draw men. But it was not merely Regan's beauty, but her way with people, that had made her so popular with both men and women.

And Rebecca, dowdy, serious-minded, out-of-place Rebecca, had been so shocked, and so dazzled, when Regan offered her friendship. She'd been so miserably shy, Rebecca thought now, staring dreamily out the window while the cup warmed her hands. Still was, she admitted, beneath the veneer she'd developed in recent months. She'd had no social skills whatsoever then, and no defense against the fast-moving college scene.

Except for Regan, who had found it natural to take a young, awkward, unattractive girl under her wing.

It was something Rebecca would never forget. And sitting there, in the lovely guest room, with its big four-poster and lovely globe lamps, she was deeply, warmly happy that Regan had found such a wonderful life.

A man who adored her, obviously, Rebecca thought. Anyone could see Rafe's love for his wife every time he looked in her direction.

A strong, handsome, fascinating man, two delightful children, a successful business, a beautiful home. Yes, she was thrilled to find Regan so content.

As for herself, contentment had been eluding her of late. Academia, which had encompassed her all her life, had lately become more of a prison than a home. And, in truth, it was the only home she had ever known. Yet she'd fled from it. For a few months, at least, she felt compelled to explore facets of herself other than her intellect.

She wanted feelings, emotions, passions. She wanted to take risks, make mistakes, do foolish and exciting things.

Perhaps it was the dreams, those odd, recurring dreams,

that had influenced her. Whatever it was, the fact that her closest friend had settled in Antietam, a place of history and legend, had been too tempting to resist.

It not only gave her the opportunity to visit, and re-cement an important relationship, it offered her the chance to delve more deeply into a hobby that was quickly becoming a compulsion.

She couldn't really put her finger on when and how the study of the paranormal had begun to appeal to her. It seemed to have been a gradual thing, an article here, a question there.

Then, of course, the dreams. They had started several years before—odd little snippets of imagery that had seemed like memories. Over time, the dreams had lengthened and increased in clarity.

And she'd begun to document them. After all, as a psychiatrist, she understood the value of dreams. As a scientist, she respected the strength of the unconscious. She'd approached the entire matter as she would any project—in an organized, precise and objective manner. But her objectivity had been systematically overcome by pure curiosity.

So, she was here. Was it coincidence, imagination or fate that made her believe she'd come to a place she was meant to come to? Had been drawn to?

She would see.

Meanwhile, she would enjoy it. The time with Regan, the beauty of the countryside, the professional and personal delight of standing on historic land. She would indulge herself in her hobby, work on her confidence and explore the possibilities.

She thought she'd done well with Shane MacKade. There had been a time, not so terribly long ago, when she would have stammered and flushed, or mumbled and hunched her shoulders in the presence of a man that...male. Her tongue would have thickened and tied itself into knots at the terrifying prospect of making conversation that wasn't academic in nature.

But she'd not only talked with him, she'd held her own. And, for the most part, she'd felt comfortable doing so. She'd even joked with him, and she thought she might try her hand at flirting next.

What could it hurt, after all?

Amused at the idea, she got up and climbed under the wedding-ring quilt. She didn't feel like reading, and refused to feel guilty that she wasn't going to end the day with some intellectual stimulus. Instead, she closed her eyes and enjoyed the feel of the smooth sheets against her skin, the soft, cushiony give of down-filled pillows under her cheek, the spicy scent of the bouquet in the vase on the dresser across the room.

She was teaching herself to take time to enjoy textures, scents, sounds. Just now she could hear the wind sigh against the windows, the creak and groan of boards settling, the gentle swish of her leg moving over the sheet.

Small things, she thought with a smile ghosting around her mouth. The small things she had never taken time to appreciate. The new Rebecca Knight took the time and appreciated very much.

Before snuggling deeper, she reached out to switch the lamp off. In the dark, she let her mind wander to what pleasures she might explore the next day. A trip to the inn, certainly. She was looking forward to seeing the haunted house, meeting Cassie MacKade. And Devin, she mused. He was the brother married to the inn's manager. He was also the sheriff, she mused. Probably a good man to know.

With luck, they would have a room for her, and she could

set up her equipment as soon as it arrived. But even if not, she was sure she could arrange for a tour of the inn, and add some stories to her file.

She wanted a walk in the woods, again reputedly haunted. She hoped someone could point out the area where the two corporals had supposedly met and fought.

The way Regan had explained the layout, Rebecca thought she might slip through the woods and get a first-hand look at the MacKade farm. She wanted badly to see if she had a reaction to it, the way she had when Shane drove by the land that bordered the road.

So familiar, she thought sleepily. The trees and rocks, the gurgle of the creek. All so oddly familiar.

It could be explained, she supposed. She had visited the battlefield years before. She remembered walking the fields, studying the monuments, reenacting every step of the engagement in her head. She didn't remember passing that particular stretch of road, but she might have, while she was tucked into the back seat of the family car being quizzed by her parents.

No, the woods wouldn't have beckoned to her then. She would have been too busy absorbing data, analyzing it and reporting it to take note of the shape and color of the leaves, the sound of the creek hurrying over rocks.

She would make up for that tomorrow. She would make up for a great many things.

So she drifted into sleep, dreaming of possibilities…

It was terrible, terrible, to hear the sounds of war. It was heart-wrenching to know that so many young men were fighting, dying. Dying as her Johnnie had—her tall, beautiful son, who would never smile at her again, never sneak into the kitchen for an extra biscuit.

As the sounds of battle echoed in the distance, Sarah forced back fear, forced herself to go on with the routine of stirring the stew she had simmering over the fire. And to remind herself that she had had Johnnie for eighteen wonderful years. No one could take her memories of him away. God had also given her two beautiful daughters, and that was a comfort.

She worried about her husband. She knew he ached for their dead son every day, every night. The battle that had come so frighteningly close to home was only one more cruel reminder of what war cost.

He was such a good man, she thought, wiping her hands on her apron. Her John was strong and kind, and her love for him was as full and rich as it had been twenty years before, when she took his ring and his name. And she never doubted his love for her.

After all these years, her heart still leaped when he walked into the room, and her needs still jumped whenever he turned to her in the night. She knew all women weren't as fortunate.

But she worried about him. He didn't laugh as freely since the terrible day they'd gotten word that Johnnie had been lost at Bull Run. There were lines around his eyes, and a bitterness in them that hadn't been there before.

Johnnie had gone for the South—rashly, idealistically— and his father had been so proud of him.

It was true enough that in this border state of Maryland, there were Southern sympathizers, and families ripped in two as they chose sides. But there had been no sides in the MacKade family. Johnnie had made his choice with his father's support. And the choice had killed him.

It was that she feared most. That John blamed himself,

as well as the Yankees. That he would never be able to forgive either one, and would never be truly at peace again.

She knew that if it hadn't been for her and the girls, he would have left the farm to fight. It frightened her that there was the need inside him to take up arms, to kill. It was the one thing in their lives they never discussed.

She arched her back, placing the flat of her hand at the base of her spine to ease a dull ache. It reassured her to hear her daughters talking as they peeled potatoes and carrots for the stew. She understood that their incessant chatter was to help block the nerves that jumped at hearing mortar fire echo in the air.

They'd lost half a cornfield this morning—the fighting had come that close. She thanked God it had veered off again and she wasn't huddled in the root cellar with her children. That John was safe. She couldn't bear to lose another she loved.

When John came in, she poured him coffee. There was such weariness in his face, she set the cup aside and went over to wrap her arms around him instead. He smelled of hay and animals and sweat, and his arms were strong as they returned the embrace.

"It's moving off, Sarah." His lips brushed her cheek. "I don't want you fretting."

"I'm not fretting." Then she smiled as he arched one silver-flecked black brow. "Only a little."

He brushed his thumb under her eye, over the shadows that haunted there. "More than a little. Damn war. Damn Yankees. What gives them the right to come on my land and do their killing? Bastards." He turned away and picked up his coffee.

Sarah sent her daughters a look that had them getting up quietly and leaving the room.

"They're going now," she murmured. "The firing is getting farther and farther away. It can't last much longer."

He knew she wasn't talking about this one battle, and shook his head. The bitterness was back in his eyes. "It'll last as long as they want it to last. As long as men have sons to die. I need to go check things." He set down the coffee without having tasted it. "I don't want you or the girls setting foot out of the house."

"John." She reached for his hand, holding the hard, callused palm against hers. What could she say? That there was no one to blame? Of course there was, but the men who manufactured war and death were nameless and faceless to her. Instead, she brought his hand to her cheek. "I love you."

"Sarah." For a moment, for her, his eyes softened. "Pretty Sarah." His lips brushed hers before he left her.

In sleep, Rebecca stirred, shifted and murmured.

John left the house knowing there was little he could do. In the distance, drying cornstalks were blackened and hacked. He knew there would be blood seeping into his ground. And didn't want to know whether the men who had died there had been taken away yet or not.

It was his land, his, damn them. When he plowed in the spring, he knew, he would be haunted by the blood and death he turned into the earth.

He reached into his pocket, closing his hand over the miniature of his son that he always carried. He didn't weep; his eyes were dry and hard as they scanned the land. Without the land, he was nothing. Without Sarah, he would be lost. Without his daughters, he would willingly die.

But now he had no choice but to live without his boy.

Grim-faced, he stood there, his hands in his pockets,

his eyes on his land. When he heard the whimpering, his brows drew together. He'd already checked the stock, secured them. Had he missed a calf? Or had one of his dogs broken out of the stall he'd locked them in to keep them from being hit by a stray bullet?

He followed the sound to the smokehouse, afraid he would have a wounded animal to tend or put down. Though he'd been a farmer all his life, he still was struck with guilt and grief whenever it was necessary to put an animal out of its misery.

But it wasn't an animal, it was a man. A damn bluebelly, bleeding his guts out on MacKade land. For an instant, he felt a hot rush of pleasure. Die here, he thought. Die here, the way my son died on another man's land. You might have been the one to kill him.

Without sympathy, he used his boot to shove the man over onto his back. The Union uniform was filthy, soaked with blood. He was glad to see it, coldly thrilled.

Then he saw the face, and it wasn't a man. It was a boy. His soft cheeks were gray with pain, his eyes glazed with it. Then they fixed on John's.

"Daddy? Daddy, I came home."

"I ain't your daddy, boy."

The eyes closed. "Help me. Please help me. I'm dying..."

In sleep, Shane's fist curled in the sheets, and his restless body tangled them.

Chapter 3

It was one of the most exciting moments of Rebecca's life—just to stand in the balmy air, a vivid blue sky overhead and the old stone house spreading out in front of her. She could smell early mums, the spice of them mixing with the fragrance of the late-summer roses.

She'd studied architecture for a time, and she'd seen firsthand the majestic cathedrals in France, the romantic villas of Italy, the ancient and glorious ruins of Greece.

But this three-story building of native stone and wood, with its neat chimneys and sparkling glass, touched her as deeply as her first sight of the spires of Notre Dame.

It was, after all, haunted.

She wished she could feel it, wished some part of her was open to the shadows and whispers of the restless dead. She believed. Her dedication to science had taught her that there was much that was unexplained in the world. And as a scientist, whenever she heard of some unexplained phenomenon, she needed to know what, how, when. Who had seen it, felt it, heard it. And whether she could see, feel, hear.

It was like that with the old Barlow house, now the MacKade Inn. If she hadn't heard the stories, didn't trust Regan implicitly, Rebecca would have merely seen a beautiful house, an inviting one, with its long double porches and delightful gardens. She would have wondered how it was furnished inside, what view she might have from the windows. She might have pondered a bit over who had lived there, what they had been, where they had gone.

But she knew all that already. She had spent a great deal of time researching the original owners and their descendants.

Now she was here, walking toward that inviting porch with Regan beside her. And her heart drummed in her breast.

"It's really beautiful, Regan."

"You should have seen it before." Regan scanned the house, the land, with pride. "Poor old place, falling apart, broken windows, sagging porches. And inside..." She shook her head. "I have to say, even though he is my husband, Rafe has a real talent for seeing what could be, then making it happen."

"He didn't do it alone."

"No." Her lips curved as she reached for the door. "I did one hell of a job." She opened the door. "See for yourself."

One hell of a job, Rebecca thought. Beautiful wide planked floors gleamed gold with polish and sunlight. Silk-covered walls, elegantly trimmed. Antiques, both delicate and majestic, were placed in a perfect harmony that looked too natural to have been planned.

She turned into the doorway of the front parlor, with its curvy double-backed settee and Adam fireplace. Atop its carved pine mantel were gorgeous twin vases holding tall spires of larkspur and freesia and flanking silver-framed tintypes.

"You expect to hear the swish of hooped skirts," Rebecca murmured.

"That was the idea. All of the furnishings, all of the color schemes, are from the Civil War era. Even the bathrooms and kitchen reflect the feeling—even if they are modernized for comfort and convenience."

"You must have worked like fiends."

"I guess we did," Regan said reflectively. "Mostly it didn't seem like work at all. That's the way it is, I suppose, when you're dazzled by that first explosion of love."

"Explosion?" Rebecca smiled as she turned back. "Sounds scary—and violent."

"It was. There's very little calm before or after the storm when you're dealing with a MacKade."

"And apparently that's just the way you like it."

"Apparently it is. Who'd have thought?"

"Well, to tell you the truth, I always imagined you'd end up with some sophisticated, streamlined sort of man who played squash to keep in shape. Glad I was wrong."

"So am I," Regan said heartily, then shook her head. "Squash?"

"Or polo. Maybe a rousing game of tennis." Rebecca's laugh gurgled out. "Well, Regan, you were always so...tidy and chic." She lifted a brow and gestured to indicate the knife pleat in Regan's navy trousers, the polished buttons on the double-breasted blazer. "Still are."

"I'm sure you mean that in the most flattering way," Regan said dryly.

"Absolutely. I used to think, if I could just wear the kind

of clothes you did—do—get my hair to swing just that way, I wouldn't feel like such a nerd."

"You were not a nerd."

"I could have given lessons in the art. But—" she ran a hand down the side of her unconstructed jacket "—I'm learning to disguise it."

"I thought I heard voices."

Rebecca looked toward the stairs and saw a small, slim blonde with a baby snuggled into a sack strapped over her breasts. Rebecca's first impression was of quiet competence. Perhaps it was the hands, she mused, one lying neatly on the polished rail, the other gently cupping the baby's bottom.

"I wondered if you were upstairs." Regan walked over to get a peek at the sleeping baby. "Cassie, you've been changing linens with the baby again."

"I like to get it done early. And Ally was fussy. This must be your friend."

"Rebecca Knight, girl genius," Regan said, with an affection that made Rebecca grin, rather than wince. "Cassandra MacKade, irreplaceable manager of the MacKade Inn."

"I'm so glad to meet you." Cassie took her hand off the rail to offer it.

"I've been looking forward to coming here for weeks. This must be quite a job, managing all this."

"It hardly ever feels like one. You'll want to look around."

"I'm dying to."

"I'll just finish upstairs. Give me a call if you need anything. There's coffee fresh in the kitchen, and muffins."

"Of course there is." Regan laughed and brushed a hand over Ally's dark hair. "Take a break, Cassie, and join the tour. Rebecca wants stories."

"Well..." Cassie glanced upstairs, obviously worrying over unmade beds.

"I'd really appreciate it," Rebecca put in. "Regan tells me you've had some experiences I'd be interested in hearing about. You actually saw a ghost."

"I..." Cassie flushed. It wasn't something she told many people about—not because it was odd, but because it was intimate.

"I'm hoping to document and record episodes while I'm here," Rebecca said, prompting her.

"Yes, Regan told me." So Cassie took a deep breath. "I saw the man Abigail Barlow was in love with. He spoke to me."

Fascinating, was all Rebecca could think as they wandered through the inn, with Cassie telling her story in a calm, quiet voice. She learned of heartbreak and murder, love lost and lives ruined. She felt chills bubble along her skin at the descriptions of spirits wandering. But she felt no deep stirring of connectedness. An interest, yes, and a full-blooded curiosity, but no sense of intimacy. She'd hoped for it.

She could admit to herself later, as she wandered alone toward the woods, that she had hoped for a personal experience, a viewing or at least a sensing of some unexplainable phenomenon. Her interest in the paranormal had grown over the years, along with her frustration at having no intimate touch with it. Except in dreams—and Rebecca knew they were merely the work of the subconscious, sometimes fraught with symbolism, sometimes as simple as a thought—she'd never been touched by the otherworldly.

Though the house had unquestionably been lovely, though it had brought back echoes of a lost past, she had seen only the beauty of it. Whatever walked there had not spoken to her.

She still had hope. Her equipment would be in by the end of the day, and Cassie had assured her she was welcome to set up in a bedroom, at least for a few days. As the anniversary of the battle drew nearer, the inn would be full with reservations already booked.

But she had some time.

When she stepped into the woods, Rebecca felt a chill, but it was only from the thick shade. Here, she knew, two young boys had fought, essentially killing each other. Others had sensed their lingering presence, heard the clash of bayonets, the cries of pain and shock. But she didn't.

She heard the call of birds, the rustle of squirrels scrambling for nuts to hoard, the faint buzz of insects. The day was too still for the air to stir the leaves, and the leaves themselves were a deep green, not even hinting of the autumn that would come within a month.

Following Cassie's competent directions, she found the stand of rocks where the two corporals were reputed to have met. Sitting down on one, she took out her notebook and began to write what she would transpose onto a computer disk later.

There have been only mild, and perhaps self-induced, sensations of déjà vu. Nothing that equals that one swift and stunning emotion at seeing the edge of the MacKade farm from the road. It's wonderful seeing Regan again, being able to view firsthand her happiness, her family. I think it must be true that there is indeed the perfect mate for some people. Regan has certainly found hers in Rafe MacKade. There's a sense of strength, of self, an arrogance, an underlying potential for physical action, in him that's oddly appealing, particularly, I would think, to a female. Offsetting it, perhaps enhancing it, is his obvious love and devotion to his wife and his children. They've made a good life, and the inn they have created is successful due to their vision. Its location and history, of course, add to its success. Undoubtedly their choice of chatelaine was also inspired.

I found Cassie MacKade to be competent, organized and anything but aloof. There's a... I want to say innocence about her. Yet she is a grown woman with three children, a demanding job and, from what Regan has related to me, a miserable past. Perhaps sweetness is more accurate. In any case, I liked her immediately and felt very much at ease with her. This ease isn't something that I feel with a great many people.

I'm looking forward to meeting Devin MacKade, her husband, who is also the sheriff of Antietam. It will be interesting to see how much he resembles his brothers, not only physically, but in that less tangible but equally strong aspect of personality.

Shane MacKade has a personality that is impossible to forget. That arrogance again, though he is perhaps a bit more good-natured than his older brother Rafe. I would theorize that Shane is a man who has great success with women. Not only due to his unquestionably stunning looks, but there's also a high degree of charm—and a blatant sexuality. Is it an earthiness, I wonder? And if so, is it due to his choice of profession?

I found myself attracted in an immediate way I'd not experienced before. All in all, it wasn't an unpleasant sensation, but one I believe it would be wise to keep to myself. I don't think a man like Shane needs any sort of encouragement.

Rebecca stopped, frowned, shook her head. Her notes, she thought with some amusement, were anything but scientific. Then again, she mused, this was more a personal journal of a personal odyssey.

In any case, I experienced nothing out of the ordinary during my tour of the MacKade Inn. Cassie and Regan showed me the bridal suite, which had once been Abigail Barlow's room, a room where she had lived in virtual seclusion the last years of her life. A room where she had died, in Cassie's opinion, by her own hand, out of despair. I walked through the master's room, Charles Barlow's room, into the nursery that is now a charming bedroom and sitting area. I explored the library, where both Regan and Cassie claim to have had strong experiences of a paranormal nature. I don't doubt their word, I merely envy their openness to such things.

It seems that despite my efforts to the contrary, I remain too rooted in the rational. Here, in woods that have been haunted for more than a century, I feel only the cool shade, see only the trees and rocks. Perhaps technology will help me. I'll see when my equipment arrives. In the meantime, I have an urge to see the MacKade farm. I'm not sure of my welcome. My impression was that Shane is as closed-minded about the paranormal as I am determined to experience it. But welcome or not, I'll cut through the woods as Cassie instructed me. If nothing else, it will be interesting to see the ins and outs of a working farm firsthand.

And, on a personal note, it won't be a hardship to get another close-up look at the farmer. He is quite beautiful.

Smiling to herself, Rebecca folded her notebook, slipped it back in her shoulder bag. She thought Shane would probably enjoy being called beautiful. She imagined he was used to it.

Her first glimpse of the farmhouse came across a fallow field that smelled strongly of manure. She didn't mind the scent, in fact it intrigued her. But she was careful to watch where she walked.

It was a peaceful scene—blue sky, puffy, harmless clouds, an old spreading willow gracefully draped near a narrow creek. At least she assumed there was a creek to her right, as the sound of gurgling water came across clearly. She saw stands of corn, row after row spearing up to the sun. Fields of grain going gold. There was a big weathered barn with those odd windows that looked like eyes, and a pale blue tower she assumed was a silo.

More silos, sheds, paddocks and pens. Cows, she thought with the ridiculous grin of the urbanite at the sight of them grazing in a green field with rocks scattered gray throughout the pasture.

From a distance it was a postcard, a quiet and remote rural scene that looked as though it were always just so. And the house, she thought, at the core of it.

Her heart was beating fast and sharply before she realized it. She stopped where she was, breathing carefully as she studied the house.

It was stone, probably from the same quarry as the inn.

In this building the stone looked less elegant, more sturdy and simple. The windows were boxy and plain in the two-story structure, and the wide rear porch was a faded gray wood. She wondered if there was a front porch, and assumed there was. There would be a rocker on it, perhaps two. There would be an overhang for shade and to keep the rain off during a storm so that you could sit out and watch the clouds roll in.

Through a buzzing in her head, she heard the barking of dogs, but it barely registered. She studied the chimneys, then the gray shutters that she was sure were functional, rather than merely decorative. She could almost picture herself reaching out, drawing them in to secure the house against the night's chill—stoking the kitchen fire so that there would still be embers in the morning.

For a moment, the house was so clear, almost stark in its lines and colors against the sky, it might have been a photograph. Then she blinked and let out the breath she hadn't been aware she was holding.

That was it, of course, she realized. A photograph. Regan had described the farm to her, given her such a detailed picture of it, Rebecca decided it was her own memory of that, and her ability to project and retain, that made it all so familiar. So eerily familiar.

She laughed at herself and continued to walk, hesitating only briefly when two large yellow dogs bounded toward her. Regan had told her Shane had dogs, the parents of Regan's golden retriever. Rebecca didn't mind animals. Actually, she rather liked them, in a distant sort of way. But, obviously, these dogs had no intention of keeping their distance. They raced around her, barking, tongues lolling, tails batting back and forth in a flurry of fur.

"Nice dogs." At least she hoped they were and held out

a testing hand. When her fingers were sniffed, then licked lavishly, rather than taken off at the knuckle, she relaxed. "Nice dogs," she repeated more firmly, and drummed up the nerve to rub each yellow head. "Nice, big dogs. Fred and Ethel, right?"

In agreement, each dog gave a throaty bark and raced back toward the house. Taking that as an invitation, Rebecca followed.

Pigs, she thought, and stopped by the pen to study them clinically. They weren't nearly as sloppy as she'd imagined. But they were certainly larger than she'd imagined a pig to be. When they grunted and snorted and crowded near the fence where she stood, she grinned. She was bending down to stick a hand through the slats of the fence to test the texture of pig hide when a voice stopped her.

"They'll bite."

Her hand snapped back out like a rocket. There was Shane, standing two yards away, carrying a very large wrench. Her mind went utterly blank. It wasn't fear, though he did look dangerous. It was, she would realize later, absolute sexual shock.

There were smears of grease on his arms, arms that gleamed with sweat and rippled with muscle. Arms, she thought dazedly, that were stunningly naked. He wore a thin tank-style undershirt that had probably once been white. It was a dull, washed-out gray now, snug, ripped and tucked into low-slung jeans that were worn white at the knees. He had a blue bandanna wrapped around his forehead as a sweatband, with all that wonderful black hair curling over it in a glorious tangle.

And he was smiling. A smile, Rebecca was sure, that reflected an easy knowledge of his effect on the female system.

"Bite," she repeated, fighting off the erotic cloud that covered her like fine rain.

"That's right, sweetie." He tucked the wrench into his back pocket as he walked to her. She looked so cute, he thought, standing there in her shapeless jacket, those gold eyes squinting against the sun. "They're greedy. If you don't have food in your hand when you stick it in, they'll make do with your fingers." Casually he took her hand in his, examined her fingers one by one. "Nice fingers, too. Long and slim."

"Yours are dirty." She was amazed the words didn't come out in a croak.

"I've been working."

"So I see." She managed a friendly smile as she drew her hand free. "I don't mean to interrupt."

"It's all right." He ruffled the dogs, who had come back to join the company. "The rake needed some adjustment, that's all."

Her brows shot up. "You get that dirty fixing a rake?"

His dimple flashed. "I'm not talking about a stick with tines on the end, city girl. Been over to the inn?"

"Yes. I met Cassie. She showed me through. She's going to give me a lift back to Regan's when I'm ready. Since I was in the neighborhood..." She trailed off and looked back into the pen. "I've never seen pigs close up. I wondered what they felt like."

"Mostly they feel like eating." Then he smiled again. "They're bristly," he told her. "Like a stiff brush. Not very pettable."

"Oh." She would have liked to see for herself, but wanted to keep her fingers just as they were. Instead, she turned around and took a long scan of the farm. "It's quite a place. Why haven't you planted anything over there?"

"Land needs to rest for a season now and again." He glanced toward the fallow field near the woods. "You don't really want a lecture on crop rotation, do you?"

"Maybe." She smiled. "But not right now."

"So…" He laid a hand on the fence beside her. A standard flirtation ploy, Rebecca thought, and told herself she was above such maneuvers. "What *do* you want?"

"A look around. If I wouldn't be in your way." Instinct urged her to hunch her shoulders, shift away, but she kept her chin up and her eyes on his.

"Pretty women aren't ever in the way." He took off the bandanna, used it to wipe his hands before sticking it in his pocket. "Come on."

Before she could evade, or think to, he had her hand in his. The texture of his palm registered. Hard, rough with calluses, strong. As they skirted around a shed, she had a glimpse of a large, dangerous-looking piece of machinery with wicked teeth.

"That's a rake," he said mildly.

"What were you doing to it?"

"Fixing it."

He headed toward the barn. Most city people, he knew, wanted to see a barn. But when they passed the chicken coop, she stopped.

"You raise chickens, too. For eggs?"

"For eggs, sure. And for eating."

Her skin went faintly green. "You eat your own chickens?"

"Sweetie, at least I know what goes into my own. Why would I pick up a pack of chicken parts at the market?"

She made some sound and looked back over her shoulder, toward the pigpen. Reading her perfectly, Shane grinned. "Want to stay for dinner?"

"No, thank you," she said faintly.

He just couldn't help himself. "Ever been to a hog butchering? It's quite an event. Real social. We usually hold one out here once a year, hook it up with a fund-raiser for the fire department. Hog butchering and all-you-can-eat pancake breakfast."

She pressed a hand to her unsteady stomach. "You're making that up."

"Nope. You haven't tasted sausage until—"

"I'm thinking about becoming a vegetarian," she said quickly, but pulled herself together. "That was nicely done, farm boy."

"It was a little too hard to resist." Appreciating her quick recovery, he gave her hand a quick squeeze. "You had this look in your eyes like you were calculating every squeal and cluck, filing it away somewhere for a report on the average American farm."

"Maybe I was." She shielded her eyes with the flat of her hand so that she could study his face. He really was a most remarkable-looking male. "Details interest me. So do reports. Enough details, and you have a report. A good report equals a clear picture."

"Seems to me somebody who's into details, reports and clear pictures wouldn't be out chasing ghosts."

"If scientists hadn't been interested in explaining the unknown, you'd still be working your land with a stone ax and offering sacrifices to the sun god."

With that she stepped into the barn. Stalls and concrete floors that sloped. Hay, motes of dust that tickled the nose. The light was dimmer here, and the scent of animal stronger.

Rebecca strolled toward the stalls, then let out a shriek

as an enormous bovine head poked over a door and mooed at her.

"She's got an infection," Shane said, and wisely disguised a chuckle with a cough. "Had to separate her from the rest of the stock."

Rebecca's heart was slowly making its way from her throat back down to its proper place. "Oh. She's huge."

"Actually, she's on the small side. You can touch her. Here, top of the head." Taking Rebecca's reluctant hand, he held it between his and the cow. Rebecca was hard-pressed to decide which texture was tougher.

"Will she be all right?"

"Yeah, she's coming along."

"You treat the stock yourself? Don't you use a vet?"

"Not for every little thing." He liked the feel of her hand under his, the way it tensed, then slowly relaxed. The way her fingers were spread now and stroking curiously over the uninterested cow. "You don't run to the doctor every time you sneeze, do you?"

"No." She smiled, turned her head. "But I don't imagine you can find cow antibiotics at the local pharmacy."

"Feed and grain store carries most of what you need." But what he was interested in at the moment was the way she looked at him. So cool, so objective. She presented a challenge he couldn't resist. Deliberately he skimmed his gaze down to her mouth. "What do you do with all those degrees Regan says you have?"

"Collect them." With an effort, she kept her voice light. "And use them like building blocks, to get to the next."

"Why?"

"Because knowledge is power." Remembering that, and using the knowledge that he was teasing her with his easy sexuality, gave her the power to step aside. "You know, I am interested in the farm itself, and when we've got more time I hope you'll show me more of it. But what I'd really like to see now is the house and the kitchen where the young soldier died."

"We mopped up the blood a long time ago."

"That's good to hear." She cocked her head. "Is there a problem?"

Yeah, there was a problem. There were a couple of them. The first was that she was flicking him off as if he were a fly. "Regan asked me to cooperate, so I will. For her. But I don't much care for the idea of you poking around my house looking for ghosts."

"Certainly you're not afraid of what I might find."

"I'm not afraid of anything." She'd touched a nerve. A raw one. "I said I just don't like it."

"Why don't we go in, you can offer me a cold drink, and we'll see if we can come to some sort of compromise?"

It was hard to argue with reason. He took her hand again, more out of habit than in flirtation. By the time they reached the back door, he'd decided to give flirtation another shot. She smelled damn good, for a scientist.

He'd never kissed a scientist, he mused. Unless you counted Bess Trulane, the dental hygienist. He had a feeling that cool, sarcastic mouth of Rebecca's would be quite tasty.

"Got some iced tea," he offered.

"Great." It was all she said as she stood just inside the door, looking around with dark, seeking eyes.

Something. She was sure there was something here, some sensation just out of reach, blocked, she thought, by that almost overpowering male aura Shane exuded. It clouded things, she thought, annoyed. It certainly clouded the brain.

But there was something here, amid the scrubbed tiles, the spotless counters, the old but sparkling appliances.

It was a good-size kitchen, homey, with its glass-fronted cupboards showing the everyday dishes. What she imagined one would call a family kitchen—plenty of elbow room, big wooden table, sturdy chairs with cane seats. The morning paper was still on the table, where he had left it, she supposed, after reading it with his morning coffee.

There were little pots of green plants on the windowsill. She recognized them by scent, as well as sight. Rosemary, basil, thyme. The man grew herbs in his kitchen. It would have made her smile, if she hadn't been trying to get beyond him into what the room held for her.

Shane held two glasses filled with golden tea as he frowned at her. Those eyes of hers were sharp, as alert as a doe's. And her shoulders, under that oversize jacket, were stiff as boards. It made him nervous, and just a little angry, that she was studying his things and seeing something that he didn't.

"Never seen a kitchen before?"

Pasting a cool smile on her face, she turned to him. She needed to be alone here, she decided. A few minutes alone, and maybe she would get beyond that block. "It's amazingly sexist of me, but I didn't expect to find it so tidy and organized. You know, the cheerful bachelor, living alone, entertaining willing women and poker buddies."

This time he lifted a brow. "I don't usually entertain them at the same time." He handed her the glass. "My mother was pretty fierce about keeping the kitchen clean. You eat here, you cook here. It's like making sure the milk house is sanitized."

"The milk house." It had a charming sound to it. "I'd like to see that next time."

"Come by about 6:00 a.m., you can see it in operation. Don't you want to take off that jacket? It's warm." And he wanted to see what was under it.

"I'm fine." She moved to the back window. "Lovely view. All the windows I've looked out of since I've been here have lovely views. Do you get immune to them?"

"No. You get proprietary." To please himself, he skimmed a finger over the back of her neck. She went as still as a stone. "You've got pretty hair, Rebecca. At least, what there is of it. Of course, chopped off like this, it shows the line of your neck, and it's a nice neck. Long and white and smooth."

She recited a chunk of the periodic table in her head, so that she was calm when she turned to him. Thinking it a defense rather than a challenge, she cocked a brow, and her lips curved into an amused smile.

"Are you hitting on me, farm boy?"

Damned if he didn't want a piece of her, he realized with more than a little irritation. He particularly wanted that piece that made her voice so cool and smug.

"I've got a curiosity." He set his glass on the counter behind her, then took hers and placed it beside his. In a smooth, well-practiced move, he caged her in. "Don't you?"

"Scientists are innately curious."

He could smell her now, clean, clear soap and a hint of citrus. "How about an experiment?"

She refused to fumble, to stammer, to let him see even for an instant that she was in way, way over her head. "Of what sort?"

"Well, I do this…"

Chapter 4

He circled her waist with his hands—a surprisingly small waist—then ran them up her ribs, over to skim up her back. The punch of arousal wasn't particularly surprising. He'd certainly felt it before. But he hadn't expected quite the force of this, not with her.

Still, he enjoyed it, slid comfortably into it. When she didn't object, in fact didn't move a muscle, he aligned his body to hers until he felt her curves—not much in the way of curves—meet the angles of his.

Suddenly he really wanted to kiss her, to have a good, solid taste of that mouth. Not simply because it was female and thus desirable, but because it was Rebecca's and set in firm, almost disapproving lines.

He enjoyed being disapproved of.

But when he started to lower his head, she lifted her chin, just enough to put him off-balance.

"An experiment? What's your hypothesis?"

"Huh?"

"Your hypothesis," she repeated, relieved to have interrupted him. She'd have time enough to brace now, she decided. Time to prepare herself. "Your theory as to the outcome of your experiment."

"Theory, huh?" He kept his eyes on her mouth. It was a truly fascinating pair of lips, if a man took the time to really look at them. "How about mutual enjoyment? Is that good enough, Doc?"

"Sure." She was careful not to gulp. It would have been embarrassing, and certainly would have ruined her attempt at cool sophistication. "Why not? You want to kiss me, farm boy. Go ahead."

"I was going to." But he bypassed her mouth, just for a moment, and closed his teeth lightly over her jaw. She had the cutest little pointed chin.

Then he touched his lips to hers, just a whisper. He always liked to draw the pleasure out, for himself and the woman involved. He nibbled at them, testing their shape, their softness, and found them delightfully full, delightfully moist and giving.

Perhaps that was why he stopped thinking long enough to lose himself, to sink into that soft, wet mouth. To trace it with his tongue, tease her cool lips apart and explore.

Dark and deep was her taste, yet oddly familiar. He wondered how it could be that he was kissing her for the first time, yet he could be sure, deadly sure, that he had experienced her taste before. And the familiarity was impossibly exciting, desperately arousing.

She was so tiny. Taut little muscles, slim back, small, firm breasts yielding erotically against him. And the flavor of her, a cool, damp meadow, a quiet, shadowy glade, stirred his blood. Stirred it so that several dizzy minutes passed before he realized she hadn't moved. She wasn't touching him, her lips weren't sliding under his. She had made not one single sound.

The absolute absence of response was as effective as a slap. He stepped back, the first movement jerky before he could get a hold of himself. With his brows drawn together hard, he studied her passive face, the faintly interested eyes, the amused quirk of that luscious mouth.

"That was very nice," she said, in a tone so mild he nearly snarled. "Was that your best shot?"

He only stared at her, his gorgeous sea-toned eyes molten. He could handle rejection. A woman had every right to reject a man's advances. But he wouldn't tolerate snickering. And, damn it, he knew she was snickering under that placid exterior.

To keep from humiliating himself further, he latched tight to control. Without it, he would have hauled her into his arms again and loosed some of the hot, violent passion she'd managed to incite in him without the least effort.

"Let's just say, as experiments go, that one was a dud. I've got work to do." With some dignity, he nodded toward the wall phone. "Go ahead and give Cass a call whenever you're done here."

"Thanks. See you tonight at dinner."

At the door, he turned, glared at her. She continued to stand there, leaning back against the counter. Her pretty cap of hair wasn't even mussed.

"You're a cool one, Rebecca."

"So I'm told. Thanks for the drink, farm boy. And the experiment."

The moment the door slammed behind him, she sagged against the counter. She wanted to sit, but was very much afraid her legs would buckle before she managed to cross the three feet of tile to a chair.

She'd never known that anyone, anywhere, could kiss like that.

Her head was still reeling. Now that she was alone, she pressed a hand to her jumping heart and took several long, deep breaths that echoed in the room like those of a diver hitting the surface. That was apt, she supposed. She felt as though she'd been dragged into some deep, dark, airless space and escaped just in the nick of time.

Obviously, the man was a danger to female society. No woman could be safe around him.

She picked up her drink, watched the ice cubes clink musically together as she brought it to her assaulted lips with a shaky hand.

But she'd held together, she reminded herself. Held herself aloof and distant by desperately reciting Henry V's Saint Crispin's Day speech. God knew where that had come from, but it had kept her from whimpering like a starving puppy. True, she'd begun to lose her concentration by the time she reached "We few, we happy few," but then Shane had ended it.

If he'd kept it up for another ten seconds, she'd never have finished the speech, unless it was in incoherent mewings.

"Oh, boy," she managed now, and downed every drop in the glass. The chilly tea cooled the heat in her throat, if not in her blood.

This kind of passion was a new experience. She imagined Shane MacKade would hoot in unholy amusement if he knew just how violently he'd affected her. Her. Dr. Rebecca Knight, professional genius, perennial virgin.

She could congratulate herself that she'd maintained her composure, that she'd maintained at least the appearance of composure while the top of her head was spinning around a good six inches above her cranium. If he had even a hint of her stupidity in the ways of men and women, the slightest clue of her dazzled reaction to him personally, he would certainly press his advantage.

Not only would she get nothing done during her stay, she was dead certain she would leave with a bruised heart.

She was sure wiser women than she had fallen hard for the charm of Shane MacKade. That kind of chemistry could only result in fiery explosions. The safest position was to keep herself aloof, to annoy him if and when it was necessary and never to let him know she was attracted.

Safe, Rebecca thought with a sigh as she set her empty glass in the sink. She had good reason to know just how tedious safety could be. But she had come to Antietam to prove something to herself. To explore possibilities and to add to her reputation.

Shane wasn't a part of the plan.

His house was, however. She drew another deep breath, tried to settle her jolted nerves. There was something here for her, she was sure of it. She couldn't feel it now, not when her system was sparkling like hot, naked wires.

She would have to come back, she decided. She would have to come back and make sure she had time to explore the possibilities here. The only way to manage that, she decided, was to simultaneously charm Shane and keep him at arm's length.

Dinner at Regan's would be a good start.

It seemed to Rebecca that there were children everywhere—babies, toddlers, older kids, all going about the business of cooing, squabbling, racing. Toys were spread all over the living room rug, where Regan's Nate could compete with his cousin Layla for the best and brightest building block.

She knew who belonged to whom now. Layla, who held her own with her slightly older cousin, belonged to Jared and Savannah, as did the slim, dark-haired boy, Bryan. She knew Jared was the oldest of the MacKade brothers, a lawyer who seemed very at home in his loosened tie.

His wife was quite possibly the most stunning woman Rebecca had ever seen. Hugely pregnant, her thick black hair twisted back in a braid, dark eyes sultry and amused, Savannah looked, to Rebecca's mind, like some well-satisfied fertility goddess.

Connor was about Bryan's age, as fair as his cousin was dark, and with Cassie's slow shy warmth in his eyes. There was Emma, a golden pixie of about seven, who squeezed into the chair beside her stepfather. Rebecca found it both sweet and telling to see the easy way Devin MacKade's arm curled around the little girl while he held his sleeping baby in the crook of the other.

Wild and tough the MacKade brothers might be, but Rebecca had never seen any men so deeply entrenched in family.

"So, what do you think of Antietam so far?" Rafe stepped expertly over dog, toys and children to top off Rebecca's glass of wine.

"I think a lot of it," she said, and flashed him a quick smile. "It's charming, quiet, bursting with history."

He cocked a brow. "Haunted?"

"No one seems to doubt it." She cast an amused look at Shane, who'd settled down next to Savannah to pat her belly. "Almost no one."

"Some people block their imagination." Casually Savannah shifted Shane's hand to the left, where the baby was kicking vigorously. "There are some places in this area with very strong memories."

It was an intriguing way of putting it, Rebecca mused. "Memories."

Savannah shrugged. "Violent death, and violent unhappiness, leave marks, deep ones. Of course, that's not very scientific."

"That would depend on what theory you subscribe to," Rebecca answered.

"I guess we've all had some experience with the ghosts, or leftover energy, or whatever you choose to call it," Jared began.

"Speak for yourself." Shane tipped back his beer. "I don't go around talking to people who aren't there."

Jared only grinned. "He's still ticked off about when I scared the hell out of him when we were kids, spending the night in the old Barlow place."

Recognizing the look in Shane's eye, Devin decided to step in as peacemaker. "Scared the hell out of all of us," he said. "Rattling chains, creaking boards. I imagine you're looking for something a little more subtle, Rebecca."

"Well, I'm certainly looking." It surprised and pleased her when Nate toddled over and crawled into her lap. She hadn't been around children enough to know whether she appealed to them, or they to her. "I'm anxious to get started," she added as Nate toyed with the tourmaline pendant she wore.

"Dinner in five," Regan announced, her face prettily flushed, as she hurried in from the kitchen. "Let's round up these kids. Rafe?"

"Jason's asleep. I already put him down."

"I'll get Layla." Shane shot Savannah a wicked grin.

"It's going to take Jared at least five minutes to haul you up from the couch."

"Jared, make sure you punch him after we eat."

"Done," Jared assured his wife, and rose to help her up.

As exits went, it was a noisy one, as was the meal that followed. The big dining room, with its tall windows, held them all comfortably, the long cherrywood table generous enough to make room for the necessary high chairs.

The choice of spaghetti with marinara sauce, platters of antipasto and crusty bread was, Rebecca thought, inspired. There was enough for an army, and the troops dug in.

She wasn't used to family meals, to spilled milk, scattershot conversations, arguments or the general, friendly mess of it all. It made her feel like an observer again, but not unhappily so. A new experience, she thought, one to be enjoyed, as well as assessed.

She found it oddly stimulating that, while not everyone talked about the same things, they usually talked at the same time. Both toddlers smeared sauce lavishly on themselves and over their trays. More than once during the meal, she felt the warm brush of fur against her legs as the dog searched hopefully for dropped noodles or handouts.

She couldn't quite keep up as conversations veered from baseball to the late-summer harvest, from teething to town gossip, with a variety of unconnected subjects in between.

It dazzled her.

Her memories of family dinners were of quiet, structured affairs. One topic of conversation was introduced and discussed calmly and in depth for the course of the meal, and the meal would last precisely one hour. Like a class, Rebecca mused now. A well-organized, well-constructed and well-ordered class—at the end of which she would be firmly dismissed to attend to her other studies.

As the careless confusion swirled around her, she found herself miserably unhappy with the memory.

"Eat."

"What?" Distracted, she turned her head and found a forkful of pasta at her lips. Automatically she opened her mouth and accepted it.

"That was easy." Shane rolled another forkful, held it out. "Try again."

"I can feed myself, thanks." Struggling with embarrassment, she scooped up spaghetti.

"You weren't," he pointed out. "You were too busy looking around like you'd just landed on an alien planet." He reached for the wine bottle and topped off her glass before she could stop him. She never drank more than two glasses in an evening. "Is that what the MacKades look like, from a scientific viewpoint?"

"They look interesting," she said coolly. "From any viewpoint. How does it feel to be a member of such a dynamic family?"

"Never thought about it."

"Everyone thinks of family, where they come from, how they fit in, or don't."

"It's just the way it is." Shane helped himself to another generous serving from the communal pot.

"But, as the youngest, you'd—"

"Are you analyzing me, Doc? Don't we need a couch and a fifty-minute clock?"

"I'm just making conversation." Somehow, she realized, she'd gotten out of rhythm. And she'd been doing so well. She made an effort to settle herself, took a slow sip of wine. "Why don't you tell me about this hay you're going to mow?"

He angled his head. He knew when a woman was yanking his chain, and he knew how to tug back. "I'll have the mower out tomorrow. You can come on by and see for yourself. Maybe lend a hand. I can always use an extra pair of arms—even skinny ones."

"That sounds fascinating, but I'm going to be busy. My equipment came in." She twirled her fork and neatly nipped pasta from the tines. "But later on, when I set up at your place, I'm sure I can find the time now and then to help you out. In fact, I'm looking forward to observing you in your natural milieu."

"Is that right?" He shifted, turning to face her. The hand he rested on the back of her chair brushed her shoulder on the way. And her quick, involuntary jolt did a great deal to smooth out his ego, which was still raw from their earlier encounter.

Deliberately he leaned closer, just a little closer. "If that's what you want, Rebecca, why don't you come on home with me tonight? We'll—"

"Shane, stop flirting with Rebecca." Regan shook her head as she looked down the table. "You're embarrassing her."

"I wasn't flirting. We were having a conversation." His lips curved, his dimple winked. "Weren't we, Rebecca?"

"Of sorts."

"Shane can't keep his eyes, or his hands, off the ladies." Too logy and sluggish to do justice to the meal, Savannah pushed back her half-finished plate. "The smart ones don't take him seriously."

"Good thing Rebecca's one of the smart ones," Devin put in. "I tell you, it's a sad thing to watch the way some women come sniffing around him."

"Yeah, I get real depressed about it." Shane grinned wickedly. "I can hardly hold my head up. Just last week,

Louisa Tully brought me out a peach pie. It was demoralizing."

Rafe snorted. "The trouble is, too many of them haven't figured out the way to your heart isn't through your stomach. It's through your— Ow!" He winced, laughing, when Regan kicked him hard under the table. "*Mind*. I was going to say *mind*."

"I'm sure you were," Regan said primly.

"Shane's always kissing somebody." Bryan shoveled in the last bite of his third helping, and used his napkin rather than the back of his hand to wipe his mouth only because he caught his mother's eye.

Enjoying herself now, Rebecca leaned forward to smile at the boy. "Is he really?"

"Oh, yeah. At the farm, at the ballpark, right in town, too. Some of them giggle." He rolled his eyes. "Con and I think it's disgusting."

Shane had always thought that fire was best met with fire, and he turned to his nephew. "I hear Jenny Metz is stuck on you."

Bryan flushed from his sauce-smeared chin to the roots of his hair. "She is not." But the humiliation of that, and the primal fear of girls, was enough to shut his mouth firmly.

Jared sent his stepson a sympathetic look and steered the conversation onto safer ground.

From her vantage point, Rebecca saw Shane lean over, murmur something to the hunched-shouldered Bryan that made the boy grin.

The sound of fretful crying sounded through one of the baby monitors almost as soon as the meal was over. After a heated debate, Rebecca started on the dishes. Babies needed to be tended to, as she'd pointed out. Children put to bed. She was better suited to washing dishes than to fulfilling either of those responsibilities. And—and that clinched it—was she a friend or a guest?

While she worked, she could hear voices from the living room and more sounds through the other monitor that stood in the kitchen. Some soft, some deep. Soothing, she mused. A kind of routine that dug roots, honed traditions. She could hear Rafe talking to Nate as he readied him for bed, Regan murmuring to the baby as she nursed him.

Someone—she thought it was Devin's voice—was calmly directing children to pick up the scattered toys. Jared poked his head in once, apologizing for skipping out on kitchen duty, explaining that Savannah was exhausted.

She waved him away.

She was sure that if anyone else had to face a mess like this, the piles of pots, pans, dishes, glasses would be daunting at best, tedious at worst. But for her it was a novel chore, and therefore entertaining.

Shane strolled in, thumbs hooked in his pockets. "Looks like I'd better roll up my sleeves."

"You don't need to pitch in." Rebecca was working the problem of fitting everything into the racks of the dishwasher into a geometric equation. "I've got it."

"Everybody else is tied up with kids or pregnant wives. I'm all you've got." So he did roll up his sleeves. "Are you going to put the dishes in there, or study it all night?"

"I'm working on a system." Fairly satisfied with it, Rebecca began to load. "What are you doing?"

"I'm going to wash the pans."

She paused, her eyes narrowing a bit as she recalculated. "That would be simpler." She caught a whiff of lemon from the soap he squirted into the hot running water. But when she bent over, her bottom bumped his thigh and had her straightening again.

"Close quarters around the sink," he said with an easy grin.

To offset it, she merely walked to the other side of the dishwasher and worked from there. "So, is flirting with women a vocation or an avocation?"

"It's a pleasure."

"Mmm... Isn't it awkward, in a small town, to juggle women?"

"I guess it would be, if you thought of them as rubber balls instead of people."

She nodded as she meticulously arranged dishes. It would be, she mused, interesting and educational to delve into the mind of a ladies' man. "I'll rephrase that. Isn't it awkward to begin or end a relationship in a small town where people appear to know a great deal about other people's business?"

"Not if you do it right. Is this another study, Rebecca?"

She straightened again, battling a flush because it had been just that. "I'm sorry. Really. That's a terrible habit of mine—picking things apart. Just say, 'Butt out, Rebecca.'"

"Butt out, Rebecca."

Because there had been no sting in the order, she laughed and got back to work. "What if I just say I think you have a wonderful and interesting family, and I enjoyed meeting all of them?"

"That would be fine. I'm fond of them myself."

"It shows." She looked up, lips curved. "And it almost makes me think there's more to you than a woman-chasing farm boy. I enjoyed watching all of you together, the interaction, the shorthand conversations, the little signals."

He set a pan into the drainer. "Is that what you were doing when I caught you at dinner? Making observations on the MacKades in their natural milieu?"

Her smile faded a little. "No, actually, I was thinking of

something else entirely." Suddenly restless, she picked up a damp cloth and walked away to wipe off the stove. "I do need to talk to you about making arrangements to work at the farm. I realize you have a routine, and a private life. I don't intend to get in your way."

But you will, he thought. He'd suspected it before, but that quick glimpse of sadness in her eyes moments ago had confirmed it. He was a sucker for a woman with secrets and sad stories.

"I told Regan you could come and work there, so I'm stuck with it."

She shrugged her shoulder. "It's important enough to me that I can't worry overmuch about it making you uncomfortable." When she glanced back at him, her eyes were cool again, faintly mocking. "You'll be out in the field most of the time, won't you? Baling hay, or whatever?"

"Or whatever." Damned if she wasn't pulling his strings, he thought. Both of her. For he was certain there were two women in there, and he had a growing fascination with each one.

Though he hadn't quite finished the pans, he picked up a towel, dried his hands. Maybe it was that slim white neck, he mused. It was just begging to be touched, tasted. Or it could be those odd golden eyes that hinted at all sorts of elusive emotions, even when they shone with confidence. Or maybe it was just his own ego, still ruffled from her mocking response to him that morning.

Whatever it was, he was compelled to test her, and perhaps himself, again.

He moved behind her, quietly. Following impulse, he lowered his head and closed his teeth gently on the sensitive nape of her neck. She jerked, came up hard against him with a shudder that seemed to rack her from head to toe. As surprised as he was pleased, he took her shoulders firmly in his hands and turned her to face him.

"Not so cool this time," he murmured, and crushed her mouth with a kiss of practiced skill and devastating intensity.

She hadn't had time to brace, to think, to defend. His mouth quite simply destroyed her. Her head spun, her knees jellied, her blood went on fast boil. Never in her life had so many sensations battered her at once. The smooth, warm demand of his mouth taking from hers, the hard, confident hands moving over her, the smell of lemon and soap and... man.

Her mind simply couldn't compute it, so her body took over. Some weak, accepting sound purred out of her throat. She couldn't stop it, couldn't stop the trembling or the heat or the sudden and baffling need to let everything she was melt into him. One shock of pleasure sparked another, then another, until there was nothing else.

His first reaction was of arrogant delight. Indifferent to him? Like hell she was. She was hot. She was trembling. She was moaning. The woman he kissed that morning had been cool and amused and mocking. Not this one. This one was...

Deliciously warm. He could have tasted that mouth endlessly, so smooth, so soft, so silky. He eased deeper, aroused by each throaty moan and murmur. His mind went blissfully blank with pleasure when he slid his hands under her sweater and found only Rebecca beneath it.

She quivered, her breath catching in her throat as he skimmed those rough palms over small, firm breasts. His thumbs scraped lightly over her rigid nipples, and he swallowed her gasps, absorbed her shudders.

The arms she'd lifted to twine around his neck went

limp, dropped slowly to her sides in a kind of helpless sur-render that excited unbearably, even as it warned him.

He eased back, clamping his hands on the stove at either side of her as he studied her face. Her cheeks were flushed, her eyes were closed, her breath was coming fast and harsh through lips erotically swollen from his.

He thought she would look just like that on the floor, with him mounting her. The image of that had him grip-ping the stove until his fingers ached.

Then she opened her eyes, and he saw that they were blind, drugged, and a little bit afraid.

"Well, well, well…" He said it lightly, mockingly, as much in defense as in triumph, as his stomach lurched with need. "I'd say we had a different result this time around."

She couldn't catch her breath, much less form a word. She only shook her head as her body continued to suffer from quick, lethal explosions.

"No theories this time, Doc?" He didn't know why he was angry, but he could feel his temper building. Build-ing, then spiking, as she stood there looking helpless, stunned, and more and more terrified. "Maybe we should try it again."

"No." She got that out. She thought her life might de-pend on the uttering of that single syllable. "No," she said again. "I think you proved your point."

He didn't know what his point had been—something about amusing himself, a test—but it certainly didn't apply now. Now he wanted her with a ferocity that was totally un-precedented. He believed desire was as natural as breath-ing, and should cause no more discomfort than the easy exhaling of air.

And yet he ached, fiercely ached.

"You… Let me by," she managed.

"When I'm ready. I'm waiting for your hypothesis—or would it be a conclusion now? I'm curious, Rebecca. How are you going to react the next time I kiss you? And which one of you am I going to find when I take you to bed?"

She didn't know—and wasn't sure she could tell him if she did. She was saved from what she was sure would have been abject humiliation when Rafe swung through the kitchen door.

He stopped, summed up the situation in a glance and scowled at his brother. "For God's sake, Shane."

"Get out."

"It's my damn house," Rafe shot back.

"Then we'll get out." He snagged Rebecca's arm and took two strides before panic gave her the strength to yank away.

"No." It was all she said as she walked past both men and out of the kitchen.

"What the hell's wrong with you?" Rafe demanded. "You had her pinned up against the damn stove. She was white as a sheet. Since when have you gotten off on scaring women?"

"I didn't scare her."

But he realized abruptly that he had, and that for a few moments he hadn't cared that he had. In fact, he'd been hotly thrilled that he could. That was new for him, and shaming.

"I didn't mean to. It got out of hand." Frustrated, he dragged his unsteady fingers through his hair. "Hell, I got out of hand."

"Maybe you'd better keep your distance until you can handle yourself."

"Yeah, maybe I'd better."

Because he'd been expecting an argument, Rafe's brows

drew together. He noted now that Shane was just about as pale as Rebecca had been. "You okay?"

"I don't know." Baffled, Shane shook his head. "She's the damnedest woman," he muttered. "The damnedest woman."

Chapter 5

As she was a meticulous woman, it took Rebecca hours to set her equipment to her specifications. There were sensors, cameras, recorders, computers, monitors. Cassie had been able to give her one of the larger suites for a couple of days, and she tried to be grateful for it. Yet it was confining not to be able to set up a camera or two on the first floor.

She doubted any of the other guests would welcome one in the rooms they slept in.

Still, she had space, and the thrill of occupying what had been Charles Barlow's room. The windows afforded a lovely view of the sloping front lawn, the late-summer flowers, the wild tiger lilies lining the edge of the road and the town itself. She imagined the master of the house would have enjoyed looking out, studying the rooftops and chimneys of the houses and shops, the quiet stream of traffic.

Everything she'd read about Charles Barlow indicated

that he had been the kind of man who would consider it his right, even his duty, to look down on lesser men.

She wished she could feel him here, his power, even his cruelty. But there was nothing but a charming set of rooms, crowded now with the technology she'd brought with her.

It was frustrating. She was positive every one of the MacKades had experienced something in this house, had been touched by what lingered there. Why couldn't she?

Her hope was that science would aid her, as it always had. She'd purchased the very best equipment suited to a one-person operation, and shrugged off the expense. Some women, she mused, bought shoes or jewelry. She bought machines.

All right, perhaps she was buying more in the shoes-and-jewelry line these days. Money had never been a problem, and didn't look to be one in the foreseeable future. In any case, she was entitled to her hobby, Rebecca told herself as she dipped her hands in her pockets. She was entitled to the new life, the new persona she was carving out.

A great many of her colleagues thought she had gone mad when word got out on what she planned to spend her free time studying. Her parents would be deeply annoyed— if she ever drew up the courage to face them with her new interest. But she wasn't going to let that matter.

She wanted to explore. Needed to. If she had to go back to being the boring, predictable, utterly tedious Dr. Knight, she *would* go mad.

Yet she'd learned a valuable lesson the night before. She wasn't quite ready to handle certain aspects of her new life. She'd been cocky, entirely too self-assured, and Shane MacKade had knocked the chip from her shoulder and crushed it to splinters. Lord knew why she'd thought she could deal with sex.

All he'd had to do was catch her off guard once, and she'd turned into a trembling, mindless mess. She'd spent some time being furious with him for causing it— after she got over being terrified. But she was too analytical to blame him for long. She had put on the mask of confidence, had even tried her hand at flirtation. It was hardly his fault that he'd believed the image and responded to it.

She would simply have to be more careful in the future, and rethink her plan to stay at the farm. The man was entirely too physical, too attractive. Too everything. Especially for a woman who had barely begun to explore her own sexuality.

Yes, she would be very careful, and she wouldn't dwell on those sharp and intense needs he'd stirred up in her— the way his mouth had felt on hers, the way his hands had moved over her bare skin. What it had felt like to be touched that way, by that man. So intimately. So naturally.

She let out a long, shaky breath and closed her eyes.

No, she wouldn't dwell on that. She was going to enjoy herself, start her paper on Antietam, make plans for the book she intended to write. And, if perseverance counted for anything, find her ghosts.

Moving to her computer, she sat and booted up.

I'm settled in the MacKade Inn now, in what were Charles Barlow's rooms during the Civil War period. There are other guests, and I'll be interested to hear if they had any experiences during the night. For the moment, all is quiet. I'm told that people often hear doors slamming, or the sound of weeping, even the report of a gun. These phenomena happen not only at night, but also during the daylight hours.

Regan has experienced them, and Rafe. There are

also reports of the scent of roses. This particular experience is most common. I find this interesting as the olfactory sense is the strongest.

In my brief meeting with Savannah MacKade, I learned that she has often felt a presence in this house, and the woods that border the land. I gather that both she and Jared are similarly drawn to the woods where the two corporals met and fought.

It's fascinating to me that people find each other this way.

Cassie and Devin MacKade are another example. In this case, they lived in the same small town all of their lives. Cassie married someone else and had two children, and from what I can glean, a truly horrific marriage. Still, she and Devin found each other and, from this outsider's perspective, seem as though they've been together always.

Both Cassie and Devin have stories to tell about the inn, and their experiences here. I'll have to go into them in depth in my official notes.

Shane MacKade is the only one who has no stories to tell—or rather none he's willing to tell. I'm not used to relying on my instincts rather than pure data, but if I were to trust them I'd say he holds back what he knows or feels. Which is contradictory, as he isn't a man who seems to hold back anything on a personal level.

I'd have to say he's one of the most demonstrative people I've even encountered. He's a habitual toucher, and by reputation one who enjoys the company of women. I suppose one would call him earthy, without the cruder connotations of the word. He is basically a man of the earth, and perhaps that explains why he scoffs at anything that hints of the paranormal.

To be honest, I like him very much. His humor, his obvious attachment to family, his unabashed love of the land. On the surface, he appears to be a simple man, yet—using those rusty instincts of mine—I sense complications underneath.

He would certainly make an interesting study.

However— "The lady doesn't come in here."

Fingers still poised on the keyboard, Rebecca glanced up and saw Emma in the doorway. "Hello. Is school out?"

"Uh-huh. Mama said to come tell you she has coffee and cookies if you want." Very much at home, Emma wandered in, gazing wide-eyed at the machines. "You have a lot of stuff."

"I know. I guess you could say they're my toys. Who's the lady?"

"She's the one who used to live here. She cries, like Mama used to. Didn't you hear her?"

"No. When?"

With calm and friendly eyes, Emma smiled. "Just now. She was crying while you were typing. But she never comes in here."

A quick, cold shiver spurted down Rebecca's spine. "You heard her, just now?"

"She cries a lot." Emma walked over to the computer and solemnly read the words on the monitor. "Sometimes I go to her room, and she stops crying. Mama says she likes company."

"I see." Rebecca was careful to keep her tone light. "And when you hear her crying, how does it make you feel?"

"It used to make me sad. But now I know sometimes crying can make you feel better when you're finished."

In spite of herself, Rebecca smiled. "That's very true."

"Are you going to take pictures of the lady?"

"I hope so. Have you ever seen her?"

"No, but I think she's pretty, because she smells pretty." Emma offered another quick, elfin smile. "You smell pretty, too."

"Thanks. Do you like living in the house, Emma, with the lady and everything?"

"It's nice. But we're going to build our own house, near the farm, because we're a big family now. Mama will still work here, so I can come whenever I want. Are you writing a story? Connor writes stories."

"No, not exactly. It's like a diary, really. Just things I want to remember, or read over sometime. But I'm going to write a story about Antietam."

"Can I be in it?"

"Oh, I think you have to be." She ran a hand over Emma's springy golden curls. It was lovely to discover that, yes, she did seem to appeal to children. And they appealed, very much, to her. "I hope you'll tell me all about the lady."

"My name's Emma MacKade now. The judge said it could be. So I'll be Emma MacKade in the story."

"You certainly will be." Rebecca shut down her machine. "Let's go get some cookies."

She hadn't intended to walk over to the farm. She'd set out to take a stroll in the woods—or so she'd told herself. To take some air, clear her mind, stretch her legs.

But she was out of the trees and crossing the fields before she knew it.

She couldn't say why it made her smile to see the house.

She hoped it was late enough in the day that Shane was settled in somewhere, or off with one of his lady friends. She knew that farm work started early in the day, so it seemed safe to assume it would be done by now.

She could see that part of a hayfield had been mowed, but there was no tractor, or whatever was used to cut it, in sight now. She was sorry she'd missed the action. Undoubtedly Shane MacKade riding through the fields on a large, powerful machine would make quite an interesting picture.

But it was really solitude she wanted, before she went back to her rooms and hunkered down with her equipment and notes for the rest of the night.

That was why she veered away from the house, rather than toward it.

She liked the smells here, found them oddly familiar. Some deeply buried memory, she supposed. Perhaps a former life. She was really going to start exploring the theory of reincarnation sometime soon. Fascinating subject.

Because she knew the story of the two corporals well, she wandered toward the outbuildings. She didn't know precisely what a smokehouse might look like, but Regan had told her it was stone, and that it still stood.

There were wildflowers in the grass, little blue stars, yellow cups, tall, lacy spears of white. Charmed, she forgot her mission and began to gather a few. Beyond where she stood was a meadow, lushly green, starred with color from more wild blooms and the flutter of butterflies.

Had she ever taken time to walk in a meadow? she wondered. No, never. Her botany studies had been brief, and crowded with Latin names rather than with enjoyment.

So, she would enjoy it now. Light of heart, she walked toward the wide field of high grass, noting the way the sun slanted, the way the flowers swayed—danced, really—in the light breeze.

Then her throat began to ache, and her heartbeat thickened. For a moment there was such a terrible sadness, such a depth of loneliness, she nearly staggered. Her fingers clutched tightly at the flowers she'd picked.

She moved through the high grass, among the thistles shooting up purple puffs on thick stalks, and the sorrow clutched in her stomach like a fist. She stopped, watched butterflies flicker, listened to birds chirping. The strong sun warmed her skin, but inside she was so very cold.

What else could we have done? she asked herself, shivering with a grief that wasn't her own, yet was stunningly real. *What else was there to do?*

Opening her hand, she let the flowers fall in the meadow grass at her feet. The tears stinging her eyes left her shaken, baffled. As carefully as a soldier in a minefield, she backed away from where her flowers lay in the grass.

Done about what? she wondered, a little frantic now. Where had the question come from, and what could it possibly mean? Then she turned, taking slow, deliberate breaths, and left the meadow behind.

All those strong, confusing emotions faded so that she began to doubt she'd ever felt them. Perhaps it was just that she was a little lonely, or that it was lowering to realize she wasn't a woman to gather wildflowers or walk in meadows.

She was a creature of books and classrooms, of facts and theory. She'd been born that way. Certainly she'd been raised that way, uncompromisingly. The brilliant child of brilliant parents who had outlined and dictated her world so well, and for so long, that she was fully adult before she thought to question and rebel. Even in such a small way.

And the life she wanted to create for herself was still

so foreign. Even now, she was thinking of going back, of keeping to her timetable, of sitting down with her equipment. No matter that it was something out of the ordinary that she intended to study, it was still studying.

Damn it.

Jamming her hands in her pockets, she deliberately turned away from the direction that would take her back to the inn. She would have her walk first, she ordered herself. She'd pick more wildflowers if she wanted to. Next time, she'd take off her shoes and walk in the meadow.

She was muttering to herself when she saw the cows, bumping together under a three-sided shed that was attached to the milk barn. Didn't cows belong in the fields? she wondered. There were so many of them crowded together there, munching on what she supposed was hay or alfalfa.

Curious, she walked closer, keeping some distance only because she wasn't entirely sure cows were as friendly as they looked. But when they didn't seem the least concerned with her, she moved closer.

And heard him singing.

"One for the morning glory, two for the early dew, three for the man who stands his ground and four for the love of you..."

Delighted with the sound, Rebecca moved to the doorway and had her first glimpse of a milking parlor.

Whatever she'd imagined, it wasn't this organized, oddly technical environment. There were big, shiny pipes and large chutes, the mechanical hum of a compressor or some other type of machine. A dozen cows stood in stanchions, eating contentedly from individual troughs. Some of them munched on grain as devices that looked like clever octopuses relieved them of their milk.

And Shane, stripped down to one of those undeniably sexy undershirts, a battered cap stuffed onto all that wonderful, wild hair, moved among them, still singing, or dropping into a whistle, as he checked feed or the progress of the milking machines.

"Okay, sweetie, all done."

Caught up in the process, Rebecca stepped closer. "How does that work?"

He swore ripely, bumping the cow hard enough to have her moo in annoyance. The look he aimed at Rebecca was not one of friendly welcome.

"I'm sorry. I didn't mean to sneak up on you. It's noisy." She tried a smile, and forced herself not to take a step in retreat. "I was out walking, and I saw the cows out there, and I wondered what was going on."

"The same thing that goes on around here twice a day, every day." It was an effort for him to readjust himself. He'd planned to avoid her for a few days, but here she was, pretty as a picture with those big, curious eyes, right in his milking parlor.

"But how do you manage it all by yourself? There are so many of them."

"I don't always do it alone. Anyway, it's automated, for the most part." Deftly he removed inflations from udders.

"Where does the milk go? Through the pipes, I imagine."

"That's right." He bit back a sigh. He didn't much feel like giving her a class in Milking 101. He felt like kissing the breath out of her. "From cow to pipes and into tanks in the milk house." He gestured vaguely. "It keeps it at the proper temperature until the milk truck pumps it out. I have to take these girls back to the loafing shed."

"Loafing shed?"

He did smile now, just a little. "That's where they loaf, before and after."

Rebecca made way, perhaps a bit more than necessary, as he herded the milked cows out. She wondered how he kept them straight, the ones still to be milked, the ones who had been. And when he herded more in, she realized the answer was obvious.

Their bags were huge. She muffled a giggle as he moved them into place. With approval for the efficiency and organization of the system she watched him pull a lever that poured grain from chutes to troughs.

"So they feed and milk at the same time."

"Food's the incentive." He paid little attention to her as he went about his business. "They eat, you milk half of them. You milk the other half while you set up the next group."

Quickly, and with little fuss, he hooked his new stock into their stanchions. "These are inflations. They go over the teats, do the work that used to be done by hand. You can milk a hell of a lot more cows a hell of a lot faster this way than with your fingers and a bucket."

"It must be more sanitary. And you use that solution— some sort of antiseptic, I suppose—on their..."

"Bags, honey. You call them bags." He nodded. "You want grade A milk, you have to meet the standards."

"How is the milk graded?" she began, then stopped herself. "Sorry. Too many questions. I'm in your way."

"Yeah, you are." But, as the machines did their work, he stepped toward her. "What are you doing here, Rebecca?"

"I told you, I was out walking."

He lifted a brow, hooked his thumbs in his front pockets. "And you decided to visit with the cows?"

"I didn't have a plan."

"I think it's safe to say you usually do."

"All right." He was, of course, on target, no matter what she'd told herself when she started through the woods. "I suppose I felt we'd left something unresolved. I don't want things to be difficult with you, since I'm dealing with so much of your family while I'm here."

"Umm-hmm..." He wasn't precisely sure which side of her he was dealing with at the moment. "I was pushy. Do you want an apology?"

"Unnecessary."

That made him smile again. He had a growing affection for that cocky tilt to her chin. "Want to try it again? I've got an urge to kiss you right now."

"I'm sure you have an urge to kiss any woman, just about anytime."

"Yeah. But you're here."

"I'll let you know if and when I want you to kiss me." As a means of defense, she turned, wandered, frowned intently at a container labeled Udder Balm. "The problem I have is that as long as we have this..."

"Attraction?" he put in. "Lust?"

"Tension," she snapped back. "It makes it difficult for me to follow through on my plan to work here. I do want to work here," she said, turning to him again. "But I can't if I'm going to have to deflect unsolicited advances."

"Unsolicited advances." Instead of being annoyed, he nearly doubled over with laughter. "Damn, Rebecca, I love the way you talk when you're being snotty. Say something else."

"I'm sure you're more used to women keeling over at your feet," she said coldly. "Or bringing you peach pies. I just want to be certain that you clearly understand the word *no*."

He didn't find anything amusing about that. She had the fascinating experience of watching his grin turn into a snarl. "You said no last night, didn't you?"

"My point is—"

"I could have had you, right there on my brother's kitchen floor."

The color that temper had brought to her cheeks faded away, but her voice remained steady and cool. "You overestimate your appeal, farm boy."

"Watch your step, Becky," he said quietly. "I've got a mean streak. You want to dissolve some tension so you can get on with your project. I've always found honesty goes a long way to cutting the tension. You wanted me every bit as much as I wanted you. Maybe you were surprised. Maybe I was, too, but that's the fact."

She opened her mouth, but found no suitable lies tripping onto her tongue. "All right. I won't deny I was interested for a moment."

"Honey, what you were was a long way up from interested."

"Don't tell me what I felt, or what I feel. I will tell you that if you think I'm going to be another notch on your bedpost, think again."

"Fine." In casual dismissal, he walked over to check on his cows. "*No* isn't a word I have any problem understanding. As long as you actually say it, I'll understand it."

Most of her nerves smoothed out. "All right, then, we—"

"But you'd better keep your guard up, Rebecca." He shot her a look that had all the nerves doubling back and sizzling. "Because I don't have any problem understanding a challenge, either. You want to play ghost hunter in my house, you take your chances. Willing to risk it?"

"You don't worry me."

His smile spread, slowly this time. "Yeah, I do. You're standing there right now wondering what in hell to do about me."

The Fall of Shane MacKade

"Actually, I was wondering how you manage to walk around upright, when you're weighed down with that ego."

"Practice." Now he grinned. "Same way you manage it with all those heavy thoughts inside that head of yours. I'm just about finished up here. Why don't you go on in, make us some coffee? We can talk about this some more."

"I think we've covered it." She moved just quickly enough to get out ahead of him. "And I don't make coffee."

For a skinny woman, he mused, she looked mighty nice walking away. "Don't you want me to kiss you goodbye, sweetie?"

She tossed a look over her shoulder. "Kiss a cow, farm boy."

He couldn't resist. He was on her in a heartbeat, swinging her up into his arms and around in a dizzying circle while his laughter roared out. "You're the cutest damn thing."

Her breath had been lost somewhere during the first revolution. For an instant, all she could think was that his arms were as hard as rock, and felt absolutely wonderful. "I thought you understood *no.*"

"I'm not kissing you, am I?" All innocence, Shane's eyes laughed into hers. "Unless you want me to. Just wanted to get a hold of you for a minute. I swear you weigh less than a sack of grain."

"Thank you so much for that poetic compliment. Put me down."

"You've really got to eat more. Why don't you hang around? I'll fix you some dinner."

"No," she said. "No, no, no."

"You only have to say it once." He cocked his head, enjoying the way the pulse in her throat beat like a bird's, just above the open collar of her silky white shirt. "Why are you trembling?"

"I'm angry."

"No, you're not." Intrigued now, he studied her face, and his voice gentled. "Did somebody hurt you?"

"No, of course not. I asked you to put me down."

"I'm going to. If I did what I wanted and carried you inside right now, I'd neglect my cows and break my word. I wouldn't want to do either." So he set her on her feet, but kept his hands on her shoulders. "It seems to me we've got something going here."

"I'd prefer to take my own time deciding that."

"That's fair." Because he was becoming fond of it, he skimmed a finger over her hair, tugged on one of the short, soft tresses. "It occurs to me that I've already decided. I really want you. Not being a psychiatrist or a heavy thinker, I don't have to analyze that or look for hidden meanings. I just feel it."

His eyes, green and dreamy, lowered to hers again, and held. "I want to take you to bed, and I want to make love with you. And I want it more every time I get near you. You can put that into your equation."

"I will." It was a struggle to concentrate when his hands were moving in gentle circles on her shoulders. "But it's not the only factor. Things would be…a lot less convoluted if we could back off from this while I'm getting my project under way."

"Less convoluted," he agreed, amused by the word. "And less fun."

Fun, she thought, feeling herself yearn toward him. It was a novel and interesting concept, when attached to intimacy.

He watched her lips curve just a little, felt her body soften, saw her eyes deepen. A knot of need twisted in him as he drew her closer. "Pretty Rebecca," he murmured, "let me show you—"

He could have committed murder when a sharp blast of a horn shattered the moment.

She stiffened, stepped back, as both of them looked over at the dusty compact that pulled up in front of the house. Rebecca had a clear view of the sulky-mouthed brunette who poked her gorgeous head out of the window.

"Shane, honey, I told you I'd try to drop by."

He lifted a hand in a casual wave, even as he felt the temperature surrounding him drop to the subzero range. "Ah, that's Darla. She's a friend of mine."

"I bet." The chip was back on Rebecca's shoulder, and it was the size of a redwood. She cocked a brow and curved her lips mockingly. He didn't have to know the mockery was for herself. "Don't let me keep you from your…friend, Shane, honey. I'm sure you're a very busy boy."

"Look, damn it—"

Darla called out again, her husky voice a little impatient. Shane saw, with unaccustomed panic, that she was getting out of the car. With anyone else, the meeting would have been easy, even amusing. With Rebecca, he had a feeling it would be deadly. She'd eat Darla for breakfast.

"Listen, I—"

"I don't have time to look, or to listen," Rebecca said, interrupting him, desperately afraid she'd make a fool of herself in front of the stunning woman picking her way over the lawn in thin high heels. "I have work to do. You and Darla have a nice visit."

She strode off, leaving Shane caught between the willing and the wanted.

Chapter 6

During her stay at the inn, Rebecca had established a pattern. She rose early enough to join the other guests for breakfast. It wasn't the food, as marvelous as Cassie's cooking was, that nudged her out of bed and downstairs. She wanted the opportunity to interview her companions under the guise of a breezy morning chat.

It was work for her to keep it casual, not to fall into the habits of analyst or scientist. She'd been rewarded over coffee and waffles that morning by a young couple who both claimed to have felt a presence in the bridal suite during the night.

Now, alone in her room late at night, the inn quiet around her, Rebecca read over the notes she'd hurriedly made that morning.

Subjects corroborate each other's experience. Sudden cold, a strong scent of roses, the sound of a female weeping. Three senses involved. Subjects excited by experience rather than frightened. Very clear and firm when reporting each phenomenon. Neither claimed a sighting, but female subject described a sense of deep sadness which occurred just after temperature fluctuation and lasted until the scent of roses had faded.

Interesting, Rebecca mused as she worked the notes into a more formal style, including names and dates. As for herself, she'd slept like a baby, if only for a few short hours. She rarely slept more than five hours in any case, and the night before she had made do with three, in hopes of recording an event of her own.

But her room had remained comfortable and quiet throughout the night.

After her notes were refined, and her journal entry for the day was complete, she switched over to the book she was toying with writing. *The Haunting of Antietam.*

She rather liked the title, though she could picture some of her more illustrious colleagues muttering over it at faculty teas and university functions. Let them mutter, she thought. She'd toed the line all her life. It was time she did a little boat rocking.

It would be a new challenge to write something that was descriptive, even emotional, rather than dry and factual. To bring to life her vision, her impressions of the small town, with its quiet hills, the shadow of the mountains in the distance, those wide, fertile fields.

She needed to spend some time on the battlefield, absorb its ambience. But for now she had plenty to say about the inn, and its original inhabitants.

She worked for an hour, then two, losing herself in the story of the Barlows—the tragic Abigail, the unbending

Charles, the children who had lost their mother at a tender age. Thanks to Cassie, Rebecca had another character to add. A man Abigail had loved and sent away. Rebecca suspected the man might have been of some authority in Antietam during that time. The sheriff, perhaps. It was too lovely a coincidence to overlook, and she intended to research it thoroughly.

She was so deep in her work that it took her several minutes to notice the hum of her equipment. Startled by it, she jerked back, stared at the monitor of her sensor.

Was that a draft? she wondered, and sprang up, shuddering. The temperature gauge was acutely sensitive. Rebecca watched with amazement as the numbers dropped rapidly from a comfortable seventy-two. She was hugging her arms by the time it reached thirty, and she could see her own breath puff out quickly as her heart thudded.

Yet she felt nothing but the cold. Nothing. She heard nothing, smelled nothing.

The lady doesn't come in here.

That was what Emma had told her. But did the master? It had to be Charles. She'd read so much about him, the thought filled her with a jumble of anger, fear and anticipation.

Moving quickly, Rebecca checked her recorder, the cameras. The quiet blip on a machine registered her presence and for an instant, an instant almost too quick to notice—something other.

Then it was gone, over, and warmth poured back into the room.

Nearly wild with excitement, she snatched up her recorder. "Event commenced at two-oh-eight and fifteen seconds, a.m., with dramatic temperature drop of forty-two degrees Fahrenheit. Barely measurable energy fluctuation lasting only a fraction of a second, followed by immediate rise in temperature. Event ended at two-oh-nine and twenty seconds, a.m. Duration of sixty-five seconds."

She stood for a moment, the recorder in her hand, trying to will it all to start again. She knew it had been Charles, she felt it, and her pulse was still scrambling. Dispassionately she wondered what her blood pressure would register.

"Come on, come on, you bully, you coward! You son of a bitch! Come back!"

The sound of her own voice, the raw intensity in it, had her forcing herself to take several deep breaths. Losing objectivity, she warned herself. Any project was doomed without objectivity.

So she made herself sit, monitored the equipment for another thirty minutes. Precisely she added the event to her records before shutting the computer down.

Too restless to sleep, she left her room. In the hall, she stood quietly, waiting, hoping, but there was only the dark and the stillness. She moved downstairs, lingering as she tried to envision the murdered Confederate soldier, the shocked Abigail, the terrified servants, the murdering Barlow.

They were all less substantial than thoughts to her.

She tried every room—the parlor where some said you could smell wood smoke from a fire that wasn't burning, the library, which both Regan and Cassie avoided as much as possible, because they felt uncomfortable there. In the solarium there was nothing but leafy plants, cozy chairs and the light of the moon through the glass.

She struggled against discouragement as she wandered into the kitchen. There had been a moment, she reminded herself. She'd experienced it. Patience was as important as an open and curious mind.

She was drawn to the window, and that open and curious mind drifted past the gardens and the lawn, through the trees, to the fields beyond. And the house where Shane was sleeping.

The urge was so strong it shocked her. The urge to go out, walk over that grass, over those fields. She wanted to go into that house, to go to him. Foolishness, she told herself. It was doubtful he was alone. She imagined he was snuggled up with that beautiful brunette, or some other equally appealing woman, for the night.

But still the urge was there, so powerful, so elementally physical, it brought an ache to her belly. Was it the place that pulled at her? she wondered. Or the man?

It was something to think about. Something she would have to gather the courage to explore. No more mousy, fade-into-the-corner Rebecca, she thought. No more spending her life huddled behind a desk or a handy book. Experience was what she'd come here for. And if Shane MacKade offered experience, she'd sample it.

In her own time, of course. At her own pace.

He saw her as a woman who could hold her own with him, and she was going to find a way to do exactly that.

He wanted to take her to bed.

How does that make you feel, Dr. Knight?

Frightened, exhilarated, curious.

Frightened, you say. Of the sexual experience?

Sex is a basic biological function, a human experience. Why would I be frightened of it? Because it remains unknown, she answered herself. So it frightens, exhilarates and stirs the curiosity. He stirs the curiosity. Once I have control of the situation—

Ah, Dr. Knight, so it's a matter of control? How do you feel about the possible loss of control?

Uncomfortable, which is why I don't intend to lose it.

She blew out a breath, shut off the questioning part of her brain. But she couldn't quite shut off that nagging urge, so she walked quickly out of the kitchen and went upstairs to bed.

But she dreamed, and the dreams were full of laughter...

A man's arms around her, the two of them rolling over a soft, giving mattress like wrestling children. Giggles muffled against warm lips, teasing fingers combing through her long, tangled hair.

Hush, John, you'll wake the baby.

You're making all the noise.

Quick hands sneaking under her cotton nightgown, finding wonderful spots to linger.

You've got too many clothes on, Sarah. I want you naked.

Mock slaps and tussles, more giggles.

I'm still carrying around extra weight from the baby.

You're perfect. He's perfect. God, I want you. I want you, Sarah. I love you. Let me love you.

While the laughter stilled, the joy didn't. And the soft feather bed gave quietly beneath the weight and rhythm of mating...

She was groggy the next day, not from lack of sleep, but from the dream that wouldn't quite leave her. For most of the afternoon she closeted herself in her room, using her modem to call up snatches of data on the population of Antietam, circa 1862.

Her printer was happily spewing out a list of names from census, birth and death registries when Cassie knocked on the door.

"I'm sorry to bother you."

"No, that's fine." Distracted, Rebecca peered through her glasses. "I'm trying to find Abigail's lover—if she had one."

"Oh." Obviously flustered, Cassie ran a hand through her hair. "But how would you be able to?"

"Process of elimination—ages, marital status." Remembering, she took the glasses off, and Cassie popped into focus. "You seemed awfully sure he didn't have a wife."

"No, he couldn't have."

"And he wasn't in the army, but you said something about him resigning some kind of post when he left town."

"It's so odd to hear you talk about it, about them, as if they were real and here."

Rebecca smiled and leaned back in her chair. "Aren't they?"

"Well, yes, I suppose they are." Cassie shook her head. "I get caught up in the story. I came to tell you I have to run to the hospital."

"Hospital?" Alarmed, Rebecca shot out of her chair. "Is one of the children hurt? Sick?"

"Oh, no, no. Shane—"

"He's had an accident." Rebecca's face went dead white. "Where is he? What happened?"

"Rebecca, it's Savannah. She's in labor." Curious, Cassie watched Rebecca sink bonelessly back into her chair. "I didn't mean to frighten you."

"It's all right." Weakly she waved a hand. "I'm supposed to know better than to jump to conclusions."

"Shane called a couple of hours ago, after Jared called him. I needed to arrange for a sitter before I could go. I'm going to drop Connor and Emma off with Ed at the diner. You haven't met Ed yet. She's just wonderful. She can't handle Ally, too, but there's day care at the hospital."

"Uh-huh." Rebecca had nearly recovered.

"I didn't want you to think you'd been deserted. There's some cold cuts and a pie in the kitchen, if you get hungry. I have to take the car, but I'm supposed to tell you that you can go over to the cabin, or the farm, and borrow one if you need to go out."

"I don't need to go anywhere." Calm again, she smiled. "Savannah's having her baby. That's wonderful. Is everything all right?"

"Fine, at last report. It's just that we all want to be there."

"Of course you do. Give mother and father my best. I'd be happy to keep Ally for you, if you like."

"That's awfully nice of you. But I'm nursing, and I don't know how long I'll be." Cassie nibbled her bottom lip as she began to organize things in her head. "We're not expecting any new guests, and I've left a note for the ones who are out and about today. I usually serve tea in about an hour, but…"

"Don't worry, we'll fend for ourselves. Go on, Cassie, I can see you're dying to be there."

"There's nothing like a new baby."

"No, I'm sure there isn't."

When she was alone, Rebecca tried to concentrate, but she could visualize it all. The whole MacKade family would be pacing the waiting room, probably driving the nursing staff to distraction. They'd be noisy, of course. One of them would pop into the birthing room to check the progress, and come out and report to the others.

All of them would enjoy every minute of it. That was what close families did, enjoy each other. She wondered if they had any idea how lucky they were.

She put in another two hours at the computer, easily eliminated half the male names on her list before hunger had her wandering down to the kitchen.

Some of the other guests had already sampled the pie Cassie had left. And someone had been considerate enough to leave coffee on. She poured a cup, thought about building a sandwich and settled for blueberries baked in a flaky crust.

When the phone rang, she answered automatically. "Hello. Oh, MacKade Inn."

"You've got a good, sexy voice for the phone, Rebecca."

"Shane?"

"And a good ear. We thought you'd want to know the MacKades just increased by one."

"What did she have? How is she?"

"A girl, and they're both terrific. Miranda MacKade is eight pounds, two ounces and twenty-one inches of gorgeous female."

"Miranda." Rebecca sighed. "That's lovely."

"Cassie's on her way back, but she might be a while yet, picking up the kids, telling Ed all the details and all. I thought you might be wondering."

"I was. Thanks."

"I'm in the mood to celebrate. Want to celebrate with me, Dr. Knight?"

"Ah..."

"Nothing fancy, I didn't have time to change before. I can swing by, pick you up. Buy you a beer."

"That's sounds irresistible, but—"

"Good. Half an hour."

"I didn't say—" She could only frown at the rude buzz of the dial tone.

She wouldn't primp. Sheer vanity had her doing a quick check in the mirror and giving her makeup a buff, but that was all he was getting. The leggings and thin fawn-colored sweater she'd worked in that evening were comfortable, and would certainly do for a casual beer.

If she dressed them up with big copper-and-brass earrings, it was for her own benefit. She'd begun to enjoy the ritual of decorating her body over the past few months.

She left a note for Cassie on her door, then walked out of the inn to wait for Shane.

Hints of the coming fall brought a tang on the air. The day had been hot and still, but now the air was cool. The darkness was soft and complete, as it was meant to be in the country.

Occasionally a car would rumble by on the road below the steep lane. Then silence would fall again, beautifully.

She'd been sure she would miss the noise of the city, the comforting grumble of life, the periodic and cheerful rudeness of it. In New York, she'd finally taught herself to join in that life, to spend time in the stores and museums, to brush up against people instead of shying away from them. It was a kind of therapy she'd prescribed for herself, and it had worked.

She'd stopped walking with her eyes on her own feet, stopped hurrying back to her own apartment, where she could be safe and alone with her books.

But she didn't miss it. She liked the quiet here, the slower pace and the opportunity to get to know people. Now she was going to have a drink with a very attractive man.

All in all, it wasn't a bad end to a productive day.

She watched the headlights come and veer toward the lane. Shifting her shoulder bag, she headed toward the truck.

"That's what I like to see, a woman waiting for me."

"Sorry to disappoint you." She hiked herself up and

into the cab of the truck. "I wanted to enjoy the incredible weather. It's starting to smell like fall."

"You look pretty." Reaching over, he flicked a finger over her earring and sent it dancing.

"So do you." It was absolutely true—the stubby ponytail, the faded work shirt, the easy grin. "Where are we going?"

"Just down to Duff's." Shane slung an arm over the back of the seat and set the truck in Reverse. "It's not much, but it's home."

It certainly wasn't much, Rebecca decided at first study. The tavern was badly lit, with glaring fluorescent lights over the pool table that were only softened by the clouds of smoke from cigarettes. A jukebox that blared out whiny country music. The decorations ran to scattered peanut shells, posters for beer and an oddly charming print of dogs playing poker. The air smelled stale, and a little dangerous.

She liked it.

On their way to the bar, a scarred affair guarded by a scrawny man with an irritable look on his face, Shane introduced her to half a dozen people.

She got the look outsiders are greeted by in a close-knit community—a combination of curiosity, distrust and interest. Someone called out for Shane to pick up a cue, but he shook his head and held up two fingers to the man behind the bar.

"How's it going, Duff?"

The skinny bartender grunted as he popped the tops of two bottles. "Usual."

"This is Rebecca, a friend of Regan's from New York."

"New York City's a hellhole."

"You've been there?" Rebecca asked politely.

"Couldn't pay me to set foot in it." He slid the bottles over the bar and went back to scowling at his customers.

"Duff's a real chatterbox," Shane commented as he led the way to a table. "And the happiest man in town."

"I could tell right off." She took her seat. "After all, I'm a professional."

Grinning, Shane tapped his bottle to hers. "To Miranda Catherine MacKade."

In concert, Rebecca lifted the bottle and sipped. "So, tell me all about it."

"Well, the couple of times I got in to see her, Savannah was a little cranky. She said MacKade men should be locked up—among other things that had to do with specific parts of the anatomy."

"Sounds fair, coming from a woman in labor."

"Yeah, well, Regan and Cassie weren't quite so nasty. Then again, Savannah's a little more out there. Anyway, she spit nails for a while. Then, after it was over, she was cooing rose petals."

"And Jared?"

"Went from sweating bullets to grinning like a demented fool. That's the way it goes every time we have a baby."

"We?"

"It's a family affair. You could have come."

"It sounds like Savannah had enough company." She tilted her head. "So, does it give you any ideas?"

"Huh? Oh." He leaned back, grinning. "It gives me the idea that my brothers are doing a fine job making families. No need for me to horn in. What about you? You thinking about settling down and hatching a brood?"

"Hatching a brood?" She had to laugh. "No."

Shane took a peanut from the plastic bowl on the table, cracked it. "So, what do you do when you're not shrinking heads or chasing ghosts or giving lectures?"

"I live in a hellhole, remember? There's always plenty to do. Muggings, murders, orgies. My life's very full."

He skimmed a hand over hers. "Anyone in particular helping fill it out?"

"No. No one in particular." She smiled sweetly, leaned forward. "How's Darla?"

He cleared his throat and bought himself a little time by sipping his beer. "She's fine. Dandy."

It wasn't worth mentioning that he'd nudged good old Darla along, despite her invitation to fix his supper—and anything else he might like. "Any progress on the hunt?"

"That's not a very subtle avoidance of the topic."

"I wasn't trying to be subtle." He laid his hand over hers again, snagging her fingers before she could draw them away. "Find any good ghosts lately?"

"Actually, I did." She had the pleasure of seeing the smile fade from his eyes.

"That's bull."

"No, indeed. I have some very nice documentation of an event. Registered a forty-two-degree temperature drop in less than two minutes."

He took another drink. "Your fancy equipment needs to be overhauled."

His reaction amused her, intrigued her. "You're very resistant. Do you feel threatened?"

"Why would I feel threatened by something that doesn't exist?"

One brow cocked up under her fringe of bangs. "Why would you?"

"Because I—" He caught himself, narrowed his eyes. She was smiling blandly and, he noted, very much in control. "Is that how you analyze your patients?"

"Do you feel like a patient?"

"Cut it out."

"Sorry." She threw her head back and laughed. "It was irresistible. I don't really do individual therapy, but you'd make a terrific subject. Want to try word-association?"

"No."

She arched both brows this time. "You're not afraid, are you? It's very simple. I say a word, you respond with the first thing that comes to mind."

"I'm not afraid of some silly parlor game." But he was irritated, just enough to jerk his shoulders. "Fine. Shoot."

"Home."

"Family."

It made her smile. "Bird."

"Feather."

"Car."

"Truck."

"City."

"Noise."

"Country."

"Land."

"Sex."

"Women." Then he brought their joined hands to his lips, nipped lightly at her fingers. "Rebecca."

She ignored the jingling spurt of her pulse. "It's the first thing that comes to your mind that counts. All in all, I'd say you're a very elemental man, set in your ways and happy with them. Consider that a thumbnail analysis."

"Why don't I try it with you?"

"As soon as you get your degree, farm boy." She waited a beat. "If you're hungry, why don't you try the peanuts?"

"I like your hand better." To prove it, he continued to nibble, all the way around to her palm. "It's long and a little bony. Like the rest of you."

In a casual move, she scooted her chair closer, leaned her head toward his. "Do you really think I'd let you seduce me over a couple of beers at the local tavern?"

"It's worth a shot." He brushed his lips over her wrist. "Your pulse is racing, Dr. Knight."

"A basic chemical reaction to stimulus. Nothing personal."

"We could make it personal." He glanced over his shoulder, saw that the pool table was free. "You up for a bet?"

"Depends on the type of bet."

"How about a game of pool, a friendly wager?"

"Pool?" Her brows drew together. "I don't know the rules."

Even better, he thought. "I'll explain them. You're supposed to be a quick study. Anybody smart enough to have a bunch of initials after their name should be able to learn a simple game."

"All right. What's the bet?"

"I win, we go out to my truck and neck. I'm really hankering for a taste of you."

She took a slow breath, made sure her eyes stayed cool. "And if I win?"

"What's your pleasure?"

She considered, then smiled. "When I move my equipment over to the farm, you'll help me with my project, on a purely professional level."

"Sure." With the confidence of a veteran hustler, he rose and led her over to the table. "Since you're a beginner, I'll spot you two balls."

"That's generous," she said, without having a clue whether it was or not.

Being a fair man, and one who rarely lost at this particular game, he explained the procedure carefully. That also gave him the opportunity to snuggle up behind her, his mouth at her ear as he gave her instructions on how to hold and use the cue.

"You want control," he told her, sniffing her hair. "But you don't want to force it. Keep the stroke smooth."

She tried to ignore the fact that her bottom was snug against him and, following his guiding hands, struck the cue ball.

"Nice," he murmured. "You've got good form. And great ears." He nipped at one before she straightened. But when she turned, rather than backing away, he set his hands comfortably on her hips. "Why don't we pretend we played and just go neck?"

"A bet's a bet. Back off, farm boy."

"I can wait," he said cheerfully. He could already imagine wrapping himself around her and steaming up the windows in the truck. "You want to break?"

"I'll leave that to you." She stepped away, chalked her cue as he did.

The rules were simple enough, she mused. You were either solid or striped, depending on which type of ball you managed to sink first. Then you just kept sinking them, avoiding the black eight ball. If you hit that in before the rest were dispatched—unless you struck it with another ball first—you lost.

Otherwise, whoever sank all their balls first, then the eight, won.

She watched Shane lean over the table, long legs, long arms, big hands. The look of him distracted her enough that she didn't see how he broke the triangle of balls, but she did see the results. Three balls thumped into pockets, and he called solids.

Lips pursed, she studied his technique, the speed and

direction of balls rolling over the green felt. She'd seen the game played, of course. There was a billiard table in the country club where her parents had a membership. But she'd never paid much attention.

It was obviously simple geometry and applied physics, she decided. Quick calculations, a steady hand and a good eye were all that was required.

Shane pocketed another two balls before he glanced at her. Her brow was furrowed, her head cocked. It was interesting to watch her think, he mused. It would be even more interesting to watch her feel. But it wasn't quite fair to run the table on her when she hadn't even had a chance to shoot.

To balance the scales a bit, he attempted a nearly impossible shot. He nearly made it, but his ball kissed the corner of the pocket and rolled clear.

"You're up, Doc."

He moved around the table to help her with her stance, but she shrugged him away. "I'd rather do it myself."

"Fine." He smiled at her with affection, and superiority. "You should go for the one with the yellow stripe. It's a clean shot into the side pocket."

"I see it." Muttering to herself, she leaned over the table, took careful aim, squinting a bit to keep the balls in focus, and sent it in.

"Nice." Genuinely pleased, he walked back to their table to fetch the beer. "You even left your cue ball in good position for the next shot. If you—"

She lifted her head, aimed a bland look in his direction. "Do you mind?"

"Hey." He lifted a hand, palm out. "Just trying to help. You go on ahead."

He did cluck his tongue a bit as she set up for a bank shot. Couldn't the woman see her three ball was clear? He lifted his beer to hide his grin. At this rate, he was going to have her exactly where he wanted in five minutes.

Then his mouth dropped open. She banked the ball against the side and sent it at a clean angle into the corner pocket. She didn't so much as smile, never glanced up, but went directly back to work.

A few customers roused themselves to wander over to watch, and to kibitz. They might have been as invisible as her ghosts.

She played systematically, pausing only briefly between shots, with her brows knit and her eyes unfocused, as she circled the table. He forgot the beer that was dangling from his fingers, suffered the elbow nudges and comments from onlookers as she quickly, quietly, and without a hitch, cleaned house.

To add insult to injury, she used one of his own balls, the one he could—and should—have sent home when he was feeling sorry for her, to knock the eight ball into the pocket and trounce him at his own game.

Lips pursed, she straightened, scanned the table. "Is that it?"

There were hoots of laughter. Several men patted her shoulder and offered to buy her a beer. Shane merely propped his cue on the table.

"Is this how you worked your way through college? Hustling pool?"

Flushed with success now that the work was done, she beamed at him. "No, I had numerous scholarships, and a generous college fund. I've never played pool before in my life."

"I'll be damned." He dipped his hands in his pockets, studying her. "You ran the table. That wasn't luck, beginner's or otherwise."

"No, it wasn't. It was science. The game is based on angles and velocity, isn't it?" Delighted with the fresh knowledge, she ran a hand through her hair. "Want to play again? I could spot you two balls this time."

He started to swear, but couldn't resist the laugh. "What the hell! We'll go for two out of three."

Chapter 7

"So we played pool." Rebecca was busily adjusting one of her cameras in Shane's kitchen while Regan looked on. "He's really very good. We ended up closing the place down."

Regan waited a moment, tugged her ear as if to clear it. "You played pool—at Duff's."

"Uh-huh. We were just going to play one game, then it was two out of three, and three out of five, and so forth. It's great fun. But I couldn't let all those men buy me beers. I'd have been flat on my face."

"Men were buying you beer."

"Well, they wanted to, but I'm not much of a drinker." Lips pursed, Rebecca stepped back to check the positioning. "Shane was awfully good-natured about it all. A lot of people get annoyed when you beat them at their own game."

"Excuse me." Regan held up a hand. "You *beat* Shane—that's Shane MacKade—at pool."

"Seven out of ten—I think. Do you know how to work this coffeemaker?"

Leave the woman alone for a few days and look what she gets into, Regan thought. "She can't make coffee, but she can beat Shane at pool. The only person I've ever known to beat Shane is Rafe—and nobody beats Rafe."

"Bet I could." Smug, Rebecca flashed a grin. "I'm a natural. Charlie Dodd said so."

"Charlie Dodd?" Measuring out coffee, Regan laughed. "You hung out with Charlie Dodd and the boys at Duff's, playing pool? What in the world were you doing there?"

"Celebrating Miranda's birth. Anyway, since I won the bet, Shane has to help me with my project. He's not terribly happy about it. He has a definite block about anything supernatural."

Curiouser and curiouser, Regan mused. "One minor detail."

"Hmm?"

"What if you'd lost the bet?"

"I'd have necked with him in his truck."

Regan splashed the water she'd been pouring into the coffeemaker all over the counter. "Good Lord, Rebecca, what has happened to you?"

A smile ghosting around her mouth, Rebecca looked dreamily out the window. "I might have enjoyed it."

"I've no doubt you would have." After blowing out a breath, Regan mopped up the spill and started again. "Honey, I don't want to interfere in your life, but Shane... He's very smooth with women—and he doesn't tend to take relationships seriously."

Rebecca caught herself dreaming, and stopped. "I know. Don't worry about me. I've been sheltered and secluded, but I'm not stupid." She leaned over to coo at the baby napping in his carrier. "I think I'm handling Shane very well, all in all. I may have an affair with him."

"You *may* have an affair with him," Regan repeated slowly. "Am I having some sort of out-of-body experience?"

"I hope you'll give me all the details, if you are."

Regan rubbed a hand over her face, told herself to be rational. But it was Rebecca, she thought, who was always rational. "You may have an affair, with Shane. That's Shane MacKade. My brother-in-law."

"Umm-hmm…" Unable to resist, Rebecca skimmed a fingertip over Jason's soft, round cheek. "I'm still considering it. But he's very attractive, and, I'm sure, very skilled." The fingertip wasn't enough, so she bent to touch her lips lightly to the same lovely spot. "If I'm going to have an affair, it should be with someone I like, respect and have some affection for, don't you agree?"

"Well, yes, in the general scheme of things, but…"

Rebecca straightened and grinned. "And if he's gorgeous and clever in bed, so much the better. A terrific face and body aren't everything, of course, but they are a nice bonus. I'd theorize that the stronger the physical attraction, the better the sex."

The coffeepot was gurgling away before Regan found the words. "Rebecca, making love with a man isn't an experiment, or a science project."

"In a way it is." Then she laughed and crossed over to take Regan by the shoulders. There seemed to be no way to explain, even to Regan, what it was like to feel this way. Free and able and attractive. "Stop worrying about me, Mama. I'm all grown up now."

"Yes, obviously."

"I want to explore possibilities, Regan. I've done what I was told, what was expected of me, for so long. Forever. I need to do what I want." With a little sigh, she took a turn around the kitchen. "That's what this is all about. Why do you think I chose the paranormal as a hobby? A first-year psych student could figure it out. All of my life has been so abnormal, and at the same time so tediously normal. *I* was abnormal."

"That's not true." Regan's voice was sharp and annoyed, and made Rebecca smile.

"You always did stand up for me, even against myself. But it is true. It's not normal for a seven-year-old to do calculus, Regan, or to be able to discuss the political ramifications of the Crimean War with historians, in French. I'm not even sure what normal behavior is for a seven-year-old, except in theory, because I never was one."

Before Regan could speak, she shook her head and hurried on. "I was pushed into everything so young. You can't know what it's like to go to school year-round, year after year. Even when I was at home, there were tutors and projects, assignments, and before I knew it my whole life was study, work, lecture." She lifted her hands, let them fall. "Earn a degree, earn another, then go home alone."

"I didn't know you were so unhappy," Regan murmured.

"I've been miserable all my life." Rebecca closed her eyes. "Oh, that sounds so pathetic. It's not fair, I suppose. I've had tremendous advantages. Education, money, respect, opportunities. But advantages can trap you, Regan. Just as disadvantages can. It seems petty to complain about them, but I am. Now I'm doing something about it, finally." With a kind of triumph, she drew in a deep, greedy breath. "I'm doing something no one expects from me, something to give my stuffy, straight-arrow colleagues a marvelous chance to gossip. And something that fascinates me."

"I'm all for it." But Regan was worried as she opened

cupboards for mugs. "I think it's wonderful that you've taken time for yourself, that you have an interest in something most people consider out of the ordinary."

Rebecca accepted the mug of coffee. "But?"

"But Shane doesn't come under the heading of Hobby. He's the sweetest man I know, but he could hurt you."

Rebecca mulled it over as she sipped. "It's a possibility. But even that would be an experience. I've never been close enough to a man to be hurt by one."

She moved over to the window to look out. She could see him, in the field, riding a tractor. Just as she'd imagined. No, it wasn't a tractor, she remembered. A baler. He'd be making hay.

"I love looking at him," she murmured.

"None of them are hard on the eyes," Regan commented as she joined Rebecca at the window. "And none of them are easy on the heart." She laid a hand on Rebecca's shoulder. "Just be careful."

But Rebecca felt she'd been careful too long already.

She couldn't even cook. Shane had never known anyone who was incapable of doing more at a stove than heating up a can of soup. And even that, for Rebecca, was a project of monumental proportions.

He didn't mind her being there. He'd talked himself into that. He liked her company, was certain he would eventually charm her into bed, but he hated her reasons for moving in.

Her equipment was everywhere—in the kitchen, the living room, in the guest room. He couldn't walk through his own house without facing a camera.

It baffled him that an obviously intelligent woman actually believed she was going to take videos of ghosts.

Still, there were some advantages. If he cooked, she cheerfully did the clearing-up. And it wasn't a hardship to come in from the fields or the barn and find her at the kitchen table, making her notes on her little laptop computer.

She claimed she felt most at home in the kitchen— though she didn't know a skillet from a saucepan—so she spent most of her time there.

He'd gotten through the first night, though it was true that he'd done a great deal of tossing and turning at the idea that she was just down the hall. And if he'd been gritty-eyed and cranky the next morning, he'd worked it off by the time he finished the milking and came in to cook breakfast.

And she came down for breakfast, he reflected. Though she didn't eat much—barely, in his opinion, enough to sustain life. But she drank coffee, shared the morning paper with him, asked questions. Lord, the woman was full of questions.

Still, it was pleasant to have company over the first meal of the day. Someone who looked good, smelled good, had something to say for herself. The problem was, he found himself thinking about how she had looked, had smelled, what she had said, when he went out to work.

He couldn't remember another woman hanging in his mind quite so long, or quite so strongly. That was something that could worry a man, if he let it.

Shane MacKade didn't like to worry. And he wasn't used to thinking about a woman who didn't seem to be giving him the same amount of attention.

It was simply a matter of adjustment—or so he told himself. She was a guest in his home now, and a man didn't take advantage of a guest. Which was why he wanted her out again as soon as possible—so that he could.

And if he just didn't think overmuch about how pretty she looked, tapping away at her keyboard, those little round glasses perched on her nose, the eyes behind them dark with concentration, her long, narrow feet crossed neatly at the ankles, he didn't suffer.

But, damn it, how was he supposed to *not* think about it?

When he banged a pot for the third time, Rebecca tipped down her glasses and peered at him over them. "Shane, I don't want you to feel that you have to cook for me."

"You're not going to do it," he muttered.

"I can dial the telephone. Why don't I order something and have it delivered?"

He turned then, his eyes bland. "You're not in New York now, sweetie. Nobody delivers out here."

"Oh." She let out a little sigh, took off her glasses. There was tension radiating from him. Then again, there was always something radiating from him. He was the most… alive, she decided…man she'd ever come across.

And right now he seemed terribly tense. Probably a cow problem. Sympathetic, she rose to go over and rub his shoulders. "You've had a rough one. It must be tiring working in the fields like that, hours on end, then dealing with the stock."

"It's easier on a decent night's sleep," he said through gritted teeth. Her bony hands were only tensing muscles that already ached.

"You're awfully tight. Why don't you sit down? I'll open a can of something, make sandwiches."

"I don't want a sandwich."

"It's the best I can do."

He spun around, caught her. "I want you."

Her heart lurched, did a quick, nervous jig in her throat before she managed to swallow it. "Yes, I believe we've established that." She didn't gulp audibly, didn't tremble noticeably. The temper in his eyes was easier to face than the passion beneath it. "You also agreed to a professional atmosphere."

"I know what I agreed to." His eyes, green and stormy, bored into hers. "I don't have to like it."

"No, you don't. Has it occurred to you that you're angry because I'm not reacting in the manner you're accustomed to having women react?"

"We're not talking about women. We're talking about you. You and me, here and now."

"We're talking about sex," she answered, and gave his arms a squeeze before backing away. "And I'm considering it."

"Considering it?" He could have throttled her. "What, like considering whether to have chicken or fish for dinner? Nobody's that cold-blooded."

"It's sensible. Deal with it." With a jerk of her shoulder, she went back to the table and sat.

Deal with it? he thought, boiling over. "Is that right? So you'll let me know when you've finished considering and come to a conclusion?"

"You'll be the first," she told him, and slipped on her glasses.

He battled back temper. It was a hard war to win, for a MacKade. Cold-blooded reason was what she understood, he decided. So he'd give it to her, and hoped she choked on it.

"You know, now that I'm considering, it occurs to me that you may be a little cool for my taste, and definitely bony. I like a warmer, softer sort."

She felt her jaw clench, then deliberately relaxed it. "A good try, farm boy. Uninterest, insult and challenge. I'm sure it works a good percentage of the time." She made herself smile at him. "But you're going to have to do better with me."

"Right now, I'll do better without you." Since he obviously wasn't going to win where he was, he strode to the door and out. All he needed was to decide which one of his brothers to go pick a fight with.

Rebecca let out a long breath and took her glasses off so that she could rub her hands over her face. That, she thought, had been a close one. How could she have known that the barely controlled fury, the frazzled desire, that absolutely innate arrogance of his, would be so exciting, so endearing?

She'd almost given in. The instant he whirled around and grabbed her, she might have thrown any lingering doubts to the winds. But...

There would have been no way to control any part of the situation, with him in that volatile mood. She would have been taken. And as glorious as that sounded in theory, she was afraid of the fact.

If he only knew she was waiting now only to settle her own nerves and to be certain he was calm. She knew that when Shane was calm, and amused, he would be a delightful and tender lover. Edgy and needy, he'd be demanding, impatient.

So they would both wait until the moment was right.

She sat back, her eyes closed. It was peaceful now, with that whirlwind Shane could create around him gone. She missed it, a little, even as she reveled in the quiet. She found it so easy to relax here, in this room, in this house. Even the creak of the boards settling at night was comforting.

And the smell of wood smoke and meat cooking, the hint of cinnamon and apple, the muffled crackle of the fire behind the door of the stove. Such things made home home, after all...

She froze, her eyes still closed, her body as tense as a stretched wire. Nothing was cooking, so why could she smell it? There was no fire, so why could she hear it?

Slowly she opened her eyes. For a moment, the room seemed to waver and her vision dimmed. A cast-iron stove, a fire in the raised hearth. Pies cooling on the wide windowsill, and the sun streaming in.

A blink, and it was gone. Tile and wood, the hum of the refrigerator.

Yet the scents remained, clear, strong. Like an echo deep in her mind, she thought she heard a baby's fretful crying.

"All right, Rebecca," she said shakily. "You wanted it. Looks like you've got it."

Rising quickly, she darted into the living room. Amid the cozy chairs, the rocker, the books stacked haphazardly on shelves, was equipment. There'd been no temperature drop registered, but energy was crackling. She didn't need a gauge to tell her, she could feel it. Electricity singing along her skin, bringing the hair on the nape of her neck stiffly up.

She wasn't alone.

The baby was crying. With a hand pressed to her mouth, she stared at her recorder. Would she hear that piping wail on tape when she played it back? Upstairs, one of the bedroom doors closed quietly. She could hear the squeak and roll of a rocker over wood, and the crying died.

The baby's being rocked, she thought, almost giddy with delight. Soothed, loved. That was what she felt through all the energy, all the excitement. Love, deep, abiding and rich. The house was alive with it.

Tears trailed down her cheeks as the warmth of it enfolded her.

When it was quiet again, when she was alone again, she picked up the recorder and reported. Back at her laptop, she detailed every instant of the event and copied it to disk.

Then she got a bottle of wine from the refrigerator and celebrated her success.

It was nearly midnight when Shane got back, and she was right where he'd left her. He'd vented most of his temper. No one had been much interested in a fight, but Devin had managed to joke him out of his foul mood.

He was afraid it might come back now that he was faced with her, sitting there smiling, her hair tousled from her hands, her glasses slipping down her nose.

"Don't you ever quit?"

"I'm obsessive-compulsive," she said, very carefully. "Hi."

"Hi." His brows drew together as he noted the flushed cheeks and sloppy grin. "What are you doing?"

"Nothing. I've been playing with the ghosts. They're very friendly ghosts, much nicer than the Barlows."

He came closer. There was a bottle of wine next to her computer, all but empty. And a glass half-full. He took another, closer look at her face and snorted out a laugh.

"You're plowed, Dr. Knight."

"Does that mean drunk? If so, I'm forced to agree with your diagnosis. I'm very, very, *very* drunk." She lifted the glass, managed to sip without pouring it down the front of her shirt. "I don't know how it happened. Prob'ly 'cause I kept drinking."

Lord, she was cute, sprawled in the chair, her eyes all bright and glowing. Her smile was…well, he thought, stupid. It was satisfying to realize that she could be stupid about something.

"That'll do it." Gently he braced a finger under her chin to keep her head from wobbling. "Did you eat anything?"

"Nope. Can't cook." That was so funny she sputtered with laughter. "Hi."

"Yeah, hi." It was impossible to be angry with her now. She looked so sweet, and so incredibly drunk. He slipped the glasses the rest of the way off her nose and set them aside. "Let's get you upstairs, baby."

"Aren't you going to kiss me?" With that, she slid gracefully from chair to floor.

With a good-natured oath, he reached down to pick her up. She might be drunk, but she had damn good aim. Her mouth fastened on his in a long, sucking, eye-popping kiss.

"Mmm… You're so…tasty." Riding on that taste, and on the wine swimming in her head, she flung out her arms to fasten them around his neck. "Come down here, okay? And kiss me again. It just makes my head go all funny, and my heart pound. Want to feel my heart pound?" She snatched his hand and slapped it over her breast. "Feel that?"

Yeah, he could feel it all right. "Cut it out." His system was jangled, and he had to hold on to honor with a slippery fist. "You're impaired, sweetie."

"I feel wonderful. Don't you want to feel me?"

This time his curse wasn't quite as good-natured. He hauled her up, and couldn't avoid the cheerful kisses she plastered over his face and neck.

"Stop it, Rebecca." His voice cracked with desperation as his body went on red alert. "Behave yourself."

"Don't want to. Always behaving. Tired of it. Let me just get this off for you." With more enthusiasm than finesse, she fumbled at the buttons of his shirt. "I love the way you look in your undershirt, all those muscles. Let me have them."

Now he was cursing bitterly as he carried her from the room. "You're going to pay for this. I swear. A hangover's going to be the least of it."

She giggled, kicking her legs, letting her hands run through his long, thick hair. She weighed next to nothing, but the muscles in his arms still began to quiver. His knees were going weak.

He nearly yelped when she bit his ear.

"Oh, I love this house. I love you. I love everything. Can we have wine in bed?"

"No, and you'd better—" He made the mistake of looking at her, and her mouth fused to his. Honorable or not, he was human. The heat ran through him, tormenting, tempting. With a long, desperate moan, he teetered on the stairs as he lost himself in those wonderful, willing lips. "Rebecca." Her name was a plea. "You're driving me crazy."

"I've always wanted to drive someone crazy. Then I could fix them, 'cause I'm a psychiatrist." Wiggling against him, she laughed uproariously. Her fingers tugged on the neck of the undershirt she'd uncovered, then snuck beneath, to flesh that was growing damp with sweat. "Kiss me some more, you know, the way you do when I can feel your teeth with my tongue. I just love when you do that."

"Oh, my God." As a prayer, it was perfectly sincere. He repeated it over and over again as he carried her to the guest room. It was his intention to dump her on the bed and make as quick and as dignified an exit as his scattered wits and aching loins would allow.

But she pulled, tugged and had him flopping onto the big soft bed with her. On top of her. "Feels good." She sighed. Then arched. "Oh, my."

He moaned, pitifully. What was left of his mind scrambled so that all of the blood drained out of it, and down.

He knew his eyes rolled back in his head when she latched those narrow hands on to his butt and squeezed.

"I'm not doing this." His breath was panting out with the effort to keep himself from ripping off her clothes.

"Are, too. Soon as we get these pants off."

His hand vised over hers when she reached for the snap of his jeans. He stared at that glowing, cheerfully seductive face and, with a titanic effort, reminded himself there were rules to the game.

"I want you to stop this, right now." None too gently, he hauled her arms up over her head and pinned them. The only problem with that was that the position pushed his body more firmly to hers. And, damn her, she wouldn't keep still. "Keep your hands off me, damn it."

She grinned at him, lazily experimenting with the sensations that worked their way through her alcoholic haze whenever she rocked her hips. "I promise not to hurt you." A snort of laughter escaped. "You look so fierce. Come on and kiss me."

"I ought to strangle you." But he did kiss her, as much from frustration as from need. And the kiss was raw and wild and just a little mean. When he managed to pull himself back, her eyes were heavy and glazed. But those tempting lips curved.

"Mmmore…"

His body ached, his head throbbed. "You're going to remember when I make love with you, Rebecca," he said tightly. "You're going to be stone-cold sober, and you're going to remember every instant of it. And before I'm finished with you, you're not going to know your own name."

"Okay," she murmured agreeably as her heavy eyes drooped. "Okay." Then she yawned, hugely, and passed out.

He lay there several minutes, fighting for breath, fighting for strength. He could feel the steady rise and fall of the breasts that were crushed under him, the clean angles of her body, the limp droop of the hands he still held imprisoned.

"You're not going to hate me in the morning, baby," he muttered as he levered himself away. "But I might just hate you."

As an afterthought, he tossed a quilt over her, and left her fully dressed, right down to her shoes, to sleep it off.

He didn't sleep at all. As he had been all his life, Shane was up before the sun. But this morning he wasn't whistling. He did no more than glower down the hall toward Rebecca's room before he trooped downstairs and outside to begin the morning chores.

If the two 4-H students who worked with him on weekday mornings noticed he wasn't his usual cheerful self, they were wise enough to make no comment. Cows were milked and tended, pigs were fed, eggs were gathered. There were bales of hay to be split and spread.

The dogs danced around, as was their habit, but after a short time it seemed they sensed things were not quite as they should be. So they slunk off to lie low under the back porch.

The sun was up by the time Shane came back into the house to clean up and start his breakfast. Physical labor had helped work off most of his black mood. His sense of the ridiculous was dealing with the rest. Here he was, a grown man, he told himself, with a reputation for charming the ladies. And he was more frustrated than he'd been as a green adolescent taking that first tentative step into female territory.

It was laughable, if you looked at it from a little distance.

Seeing the cool, sarcastic and quick-witted Dr. Knight wildly drunk was certainly worth the price of a ticket.

He thought about it as he fried up bacon. She'd certainly looked cute, sitting there with her glasses sliding off her nose and that stupid grin on her face. And a man couldn't complain overmuch about having a pretty woman wrap herself around him. No matter how frustrating it had been.

Of course, a different kind of man would have taken advantage of the situation. A different kind of man would have let her pull his clothes off, done the same courtesy for her. A different kind of man would have plowed right into that hot little body, and—

Because he was tormenting himself, he took several long, steadying breaths. She was damn lucky he wasn't a different kind of man. In fact, as he saw it, she owed him. Big.

That made him a bit happier as he poured himself a cup of coffee.

Then again, she was going to suffer plenty. As the smells of breakfast, the zing of caffeine, the simple beauty of the morning, worked on him, he decided he could even feel a little sorry for her.

She was going to wake up with a champion hangover and a lot of blank spaces. He was going to enjoy filling in those blanks, watching her cringe with embarrassment. It would even the scales somewhat. Enough, he thought, so that he could be compassionate. He'd give her some aspirin, along with the MacKade remedy for the morning after.

And if he got a couple of good laughs at her expense, well, she deserved them.

Poor baby, he mused, scrambling eggs briskly. She'd probably sleep until noon, then wake up, pull the covers over her pounding head and pray for a quick, merciful death.

All in all, it was a fair trade for the miserable night he'd spent.

He was very surprised when he turned the burner off under the skillet, reached for a plate and saw her standing in the kitchen doorway.

His brows lifted as he studied her. Definitely pale, he mused, heavy-eyed, still in her robe. Her hair was wet, which meant she'd probably tried to drown herself in the shower.

He grinned, just a little evilly.

"How's it going, Doc?"

Cautiously she cleared her throat. "Fine." She glanced toward the table. The evidence of her crime was still there. The bottle of wine, the glass still holding what she hadn't been able to gulp down. She was going to have to face it. "I guess I got a little carried away."

"You could say that." Looking forward to the next few minutes, he closed the cupboard door, perhaps a bit harder than necessary. She didn't wince at the bang, and that disappointed him. "Around here we'd say you were drunk as a skunk."

She did wince at that. "I'm not much of a drinker, as a rule. It was foolish, on top of an empty stomach. I want to apologize, and to thank you for getting me to bed."

His grin was rapidly fading. She was entirely too composed for his liking. "How's the head?"

"The head. Oh…" She smiled, relieved that he would care enough to ask. "Fine. I don't get hangovers. I must have a good metabolism."

He simply stared at her. Was there no justice? "You don't have a hangover?"

"No, but I could use some coffee."

She walked toward the pot. No stumbling, Shane noted as his resentment grew. No squinting away from the sunlight. Not even one quiet, pitiful moan.

"You drank the best part of a bottle of wine, and you feel fine?"

"Mmm... Hungry." She smiled at him again as she poured coffee. "I really was an idiot last night, and you were very understanding."

"Yeah." He was rapidly losing his appetite. "I was a brick."

He certainly had been, she mused, and he deserved an explanation along with her apology. "You see, I'd had this breakthrough, and..." The expression on his face warned her to fill in those details later. "You're angry with me. You should be. I was awful." She laid a hand on his arm. "Totally out of control. And you were so restrained and sweet."

"Sweet." He spit the word. "You remember what happened?"

"Of course." A bit surprised that he'd think she'd forget, she leaned back against the counter as she sipped her coffee. "I was—well, pawing you is the only way to describe it. Not my usual style. I'm very grateful you understood it was the wine talking. I wouldn't have blamed you for leaving me sprawled on the floor here." Because she was more amused at herself than embarrassed, her eyes laughed over her cup. "I must have been quite a handful. I can't imagine a ridiculously drunk woman is very tempting, but you were very decent, very patient."

She didn't even have the courtesy to be humiliated, he fumed. And, worse—much worse—she had the gall to make him into some sort of saint. "You were obnoxious."

"I know." Then she laughed and cut the last thread of

his control. "Still, it was an experience. I've never been so drunk—and don't think I care to be again. I was lucky I did it in private, and it was you who had to deal with me. Can I have a piece of this bacon?"

He was calm, he told himself, listening to the steady, if loud, beating of blood in his head. So he spoke calmly, quietly. "Are you sober now, Rebecca?"

"As a judge." She nipped at a slice of bacon. "And I'm going to stay that way for a long time."

Slowly, he nodded, his eyes on hers. "Head clear, all your faculties in order?"

She started to answer, but something in his tone tripped a warning bell. Warily she looked over at him. The dark, dangerous gleam in his eyes had her backing up a step. "Shane—"

He yanked her back and sent the coffee cup she still held flying. "So you weren't tempting?" His mouth, full of fury and frustration, crushed down on hers. "I was sweet?" he added, swinging her around until her back rapped into the refrigerator. "Understanding. Patient." Between snapped-off words, he continued to assault her mouth.

"Yes. No." How was she supposed to think, with all the blood roaring in her head?

"You damned near killed me." He jerked up her chin and plundered, shooting vicious spurts of fire into every cell of her body. "You know how much I wanted you? Get the picture?"

He gave her one, a very vivid one of hard, impatient lips, rough, ready hands, a body that was tight with tension and steaming with heat. She fought for breath, fought to stay upright as what was left of her mind went to mush.

She was melting against him again, soft, fragrant wax. His blood pumped in response to those soft, sexy sounds she made in her throat. Eager, helpless sounds that turned frustrated lust into a rage of desperate need.

"That's it," he muttered, and swung her up in his arms.

With a jolt of panic, she pushed a hand against his chest. "Wait."

"The hell I will." His eyes flashed at hers, all but searing her. "You'd better say no, loud and clear, and say it fast, Rebecca. Tell me you don't want me, don't want this. And make damn sure you mean it."

Under her palm she felt the furious beating of his heart, and her hand trembled. She'd thought it was fear, but it wasn't. Oh, no, it wasn't fear. It was longing.

"I can't." She let out a whoosh of breath. "I wouldn't mean it."

Triumph suited him. "I know."

Chapter 8

She wanted to remember everything, to seal somehow every moment, every sound, every taste, into her mind and heart. She wanted to be able to recapture this incredible feeling of being carried in strong arms, of being wanted, and wanted with such ferocity, by a beautiful man. Of being sampled every few steps by skilled and hungry lips.

She didn't care if he was gentle or rough, patient or frenzied. As long as he didn't stop wanting her.

Then he paused on the stairs, his mouth swooping down on hers in a way that made any thought of the future float away to make room for the all-encompassing present.

On a moan of sheer delight, she wrapped her arms around him and let her own greedy mouth savor the taste of his face, his neck. The tangy flavor of him poured into her until her head swarmed with sound, revolved with half-formed images. The sheer force of her appetite made her shudder. This, she thought, dizzily, was only the beginning.

It no longer surprised her to find that her fingers were fighting with the buttons of his shirt. She wanted to feel him, touch him, everywhere, all at once.

He was out of breath and laughing by the time he made it to his own bedroom. "This is a lot like last night." He tumbled to the bed with her. On top of her. "Only better."

"Can't you get this thing off?" She was laughing, too, hadn't realized it was possible when desire was squeezing every throbbing inch of her body with sweaty fists.

"Yours is easier." With one expert stroke, he parted her robe. She was milk-pale, narrow of torso. With a low animal sound, he took her breast in his mouth.

The shock of it screamed through her, incited an avalanche of new and unexplored sensations. Even as she struggled to clear her mind to record them, the hands that had been busy on his shirt dropped away to grip frantically at the neat spread beneath.

Each tug, each nip, of his clever and hungry mouth shot arrows of golden heat straight to her center. Each arrow erupted into a dozen more flame-tipped missiles that streaked under her skin, over it, with dizzying speed.

How could anyone survive these sensations? she wondered. How could anyone live without them?

He had her naked in seconds, and feasted on her.

There was panic now—panic at the thought that it was possible to die from pleasure. Her skin was hot and damp, quivering at each pass and stroke of those big, callused hands. Tossed by a tidal wave, she rolled over the bed with him, desperate to keep up.

He couldn't get enough. All that baby-smooth skin, those long, narrow bones, the small, apple-firm breasts. He could smell her shower on her, and simple soap had never been so arousing. He thought he could eat her alive, bite by ravenous bite.

She was writhing under him, wrestling over him, her hands fast and frantic. Those wonderful eyes, the eyes he could never quite seem to get out of his head, were dark as whiskey now, and vividly intense. Everywhere he touched, she responded as though she'd never been touched before. Shuddering, arching, flowing. A purr, a moan, a gasp.

No woman he'd ever known had ever made him feel so powerful, so free, so needy.

"Damn it." Dizzy with desire, he sat up to drag at his boots. She reared up, wrapping that wonderful naked body around his, making his vision waver as she raced hurried kisses over his neck and shoulder.

"Hurry." She pulled up his undershirt and ravished his back. "Oh, I love your body. I just... Mmm..." She slid her breasts over the flesh she'd exposed and drove them both mad.

With an oath, he flipped her over into his lap. His mouth found hers waiting and avid. Her need, as wild as his, poured into him like a shot of raw whiskey.

To please them both, he cupped her, and she was hot and wet. He felt her body stiffen, tasted the warm rush of impact as her breath caught and expelled. She went wild, nails scraping, hips pumping, dazzling him with her unrestricted greed for pleasure.

"I've got to be inside you." His voice was harsh, his body frantic. Near violence, he shoved her back on the bed, yanked at his jeans. He couldn't remember his hands ever fumbling before, but they did now, in his outrageous and overwhelming rush to possess. "I want to fill you. I want to watch you take me."

"Hurry." Her hands were already gripping his hips. Oh,

to feel like that again, to know he would send her flying again. "I can't stand it." She arched up to welcome.

He drove inside her, in one hard stroke. And froze. Shock, disbelief, terror, tangled with desperation when she cried out, when he felt himself ram mercilessly through her virginity. The muscles in his arms quivered from the strain, and his eyes, half-blind, locked frantically on hers.

"Rebecca. God. Don't move."

"What?" She was lost, delirious. Oh, the extraordinary feel of him inside her, inside her body, filling her with the sheer glory of invasion. "What?"

"For God's sake, don't move." He said it through gritted teeth as he fumbled for control. His body quivered on the tether he yanked ruthlessly to hold it in place. Sweet God, she was so hot, and tight, and wet.

"I'm not going to hurt you anymore." He couldn't get his breath, simply couldn't pull in enough air. "Just give me a minute."

"What?" she said again. With a primal instinct, she locked her legs around him and rose up.

"Don't—"

The animal took over, clawed aside everything but the urgent need to mate, and leaped free. Helpless to resist, he took her, plunging in deep, driving her to match his frenzied pace until the world seemed to contract to nothing but two bodies, linked. The hard slap of flesh on flesh, the explosive burst of air expelling from labored lungs, the musky smells of sweat and sex, and that glorious sensation of slicked bodies sliding. The dark pleasure swamped him, emptied him.

Weak, he collapsed on her and tried to gather his scattered wits. "I'm sorry" was all he could manage, and that was no more than a whisper. He had to move, knew he had to move, but he simply couldn't. No experience in his life had ever sapped him like this.

He told himself it was because she had been innocent and the guilt was draining him.

She was shuddering beneath him, quick, violent shudders that damned him. He was mortally afraid she was crying.

"Rebecca, you should have told me." There had to be some way he could soothe her, but this was simply beyond his experience.

"Told you?" she repeated, in a voice almost too faint to hear.

"I wouldn't have pushed you. I wouldn't have— Hell, I probably would have." He found the strength to ease back and look at her face. Her eyes were closed, her lips parted as the breath raced through them. "I hurt you. I must have hurt you."

Her eyes opened then. The gold was hardly more than a thin ring around the pupils. Shock, he thought, cursing himself again. But, to his confusion, those swollen lips curved.

"No, you didn't. It felt wonderful. I feel wonderful."

"But…"

"Does it always feel like that?" She let out a long, satisfied sigh. "So overwhelming, so…huge, as if nothing could stop you from getting from one incredible moment to the next. It's so…" She sighed again. "Primitive."

"I— No— Yes." What the hell was he supposed to say to that? To her? "I can't think straight yet."

Hearing that made her smile deepen. "I wasn't sure I'd be any good at it, but I was. Wasn't I?"

"You…" What the devil was going on? She wasn't crying, she wasn't upset at all. She looked like a cat who'd just dined on a platoon of canaries. More for his own benefit than for hers, he spoke slowly, carefully. "Rebecca, you'd never been with a man before."

"I wasn't particularly interested in a man before." She found the strength and started to lift her arms to circle him. Then her smile faded. "I wasn't good at it? I did something wrong? You're not feeling the way I'm feeling?"

"You destroyed me." Shane rolled off her to lie on his back and scrub his hands over his face. "I had no control. Even when I realized, I couldn't stop. I should have been able to stop."

"I'm sorry if I didn't do everything right." Stiff now with embarrassment, she sat up. "It was my first time, and I'd think you'd have some patience."

He swore at her and snagged her arm before she could climb regally from the bed. "Look at me. At me," he repeated, until her sulky eyes met his. "I'm not going to give you a damn grade, but I'll tell you this. I want you. Right now I want you again so much I could swallow you whole. It doesn't even seem to matter that I feel guilty that I was rough. If I'd known, I would have been gentle. I would have taken some care. I would have tried."

"You didn't hurt me, Shane." Something in her heart shifted as she lifted a hand to his cheek. "I didn't tell you because I thought it wouldn't happen if you knew. I thought you'd want someone with experience."

"Who the hell are you?" he murmured. "Why can't I understand you?"

"I'm still working on understanding myself." Leaning forward, she touched her lips to his, then sighed as he drew her close to cuddle. "This was the most beautiful first of my life. I want to feel this way again. You're an incredible lover."

"How would you know?" Surrendering, he nuzzled at her throat. "Ah, Rebecca?"

"Hmm?"

"Is something wrong with those academic types? How'd they manage to let you get away?"

She rubbed her curved lips over his shoulder. "If you'd known me even a year ago, you wouldn't ask. You wouldn't have looked at me twice."

"I always look at women at least twice. Any woman."

She chuckled, enjoying the feel of his muscles under her hands. "I was a mess, believe me." It didn't sting to admit it now, not now that she nestled in his arms, still groggy from loving. "A certified geek."

Amused, he drew her back. "Baby, no geek's ever had eyes like yours. I don't care what's in your brain, those eyes are pure sin."

She blinked. "They are?"

He laughed and hugged her hard. "We're going to have to make love a lot. It dulls your wits." He tipped her head back, kissed her lightly. "I've got work that can't be put off, or we'd get started right now."

Testing, she slid her hands over his chest. "Can you work fast?"

His heart stuttered. Before they could get into trouble, he snagged her hands and lifted them to his mouth. "I think today I can work real fast."

She had work to do herself, but stayed where she was when Shane went downstairs. He would have to eat a cold breakfast, she mused, and found herself wonderfully smug at the knowledge that he'd hungered for her more than for food.

She'd tempted him. Destroyed him, she thought, grinning at the ceiling. His words. What a powerful, wonderful thing it was to be a woman.

As much as she would have loved snuggling in bed with him all morning, she was glad to have the time alone. Now she would be able to relive and savor every moment, every sensation, every surprise.

Dr. Rebecca Knight, prodigy, lifelong nerd, academic wonder and social oddity, had a lover women would kill for. And, at least for a little while, he was all hers.

With a throaty sigh, she lay back amid the tumbled pillows, holding the excitement, the wonder, to her.

He had the face of some dark, clever angel, the hands of a working farmer and the body of... Well, why be conservative? The body of a god.

And if you went beyond the surface—which was outstanding—he was kind and sweet. Volatile, certainly, but that only added to the package. He was sturdy, the kind of man who did what had to be done, who worked hard, loved his family, respected his roots, laughed at himself.

For heaven's sake, he even cooked.

In her estimation, he was as close to perfect as the species came. And wasn't it a fine stroke of luck that she should fall in love with perfection?

She reared up in bed with a jolt. That was a textbook reaction, she reminded herself, swallowing panic. She was mixing emotion with a physical experience. Enlarging affection and attraction into a complicated equation. It was a very typical female response. Sex equals love.

She knew better than that. She was a psychiatrist.

Very slowly, she lay back again. Intelligence, training, even common sense, had nothing to do with it. She laid a hand on her heart gingerly.

Of course she was in love with him. She'd been in love

with him all along—the cliché of love at first sight. She'd ignored it, given it different names, fit her newly developed sophistication over it. But it had been there.

Well, what now? Not that long ago, she would have run like a rabbit. No doubt, if she greeted Shane with a declaration, *he'd* run like a rabbit. But wasn't it just one more new experience? An emotion to be added to the others she'd finally allowed herself to feel? The only sensible course of action was to accept it, and deal with whatever came next as best she could.

She had weeks left to enjoy what she could have, and enough experience to know how to live without what she couldn't have. It might hurt in the end, but she could accept that, too.

Much worse than pain, she well knew, was having nothing at all.

With the first days of September gleefully pouring out the last of the summer heat, Shane was sweaty when he headed for the house at midday. He was filthy, a little bloody where he'd scraped his knuckle on a bolt and afraid he might smell a bit reminiscent of the manure spreader he'd just finished with.

But he'd also worked hard enough, and fast enough, to carve out two good hours of free time. He intended to occupy Rebecca for every moment of them.

He knew he had a stupid grin on his face, and didn't care. He wanted her in bed again, quickly. He needed to see if it had just been the novelty of her, or something more. All he was sure of was that he'd never been so involved, so lost in a woman, as he had been with her.

Because he'd never found it otherwise, he believed love-making was meant to be a pleasure. But with Rebecca, it had gone beyond pleasure, into delirium. He was looking forward to taking the trip again.

There she was at the table, working away, her glasses perched, long fingers flying. He started to grin, and a spear pierced his heart, painfully, when she looked up and smiled at him, her face lighting up.

"You really are beautiful," he murmured, and discovered he was clutching the doorknob for balance. Had a woman, any woman, ever knocked him off his feet before?

She could only stare at him. No one had ever called her beautiful. And at the moment, he looked as though he meant it. Then he grinned, and the dazed look left his eyes.

"Now, if you could only cook."

"I managed some iced tea."

"That's a start." And it might do something to cool his suddenly dry throat. He took out the pitcher, poured a generous glass and gulped. Choked. "Ah, how many bags did you use, Doc?"

"About a dozen."

He shook his head and hoped his eyes would stay in their sockets. The stuff in his glass was as thick and strong as a trucker's fist. "Well, it ought to get the blood moving."

She snickered. "Sorry. I'm useless in the kitchen. It probably shouldn't have steeped for three hours, either."

"Probably not." Cautiously he set the glass aside. He wouldn't have been overly surprised if it simply marched away under its own power. "We can dilute it. I've got a fifty-gallon drum outside."

"I could make a sandwich." When she rose, he held up a hand.

"Thanks anyway. I'll do it. No, don't come near me. I smell like the wrong side of a cow."

Enjoying the little bubbles of anticipation bursting in

her blood, she traced her tongue over her lips. "You're awfully dirty," she said. She liked it. "And sweaty. Take off
your shirt."

A lightning bolt of desire flashed into his gut. "You're
very demanding. I like that in a woman." Still, he backed
up again. "I don't want to touch you. You're all neat and
tidy, and my hands are covered with things you wouldn't
want on that pretty sweater."

She looked down at them, then let out a little hum of
concern. "You're bleeding."

"Just scraped a knuckle. Let me wash up."

"I'll do it." She took his hand before he could turn on
the tap.

She bathed his hand herself, knitting her brows over
the scrape. He had the pleasure of standing there while
she soaped his hands, rubbed them gently between hers.

He began to fantasize about taking a shower with her.
Wet bodies, slicked skin, rising steam.

"I guess you'll live. But you should be more careful."
She sniffed, wrinkled her nose. "What *have* you been doing
out there?"

He grinned. "Spreading manure."

Her eyes popped wide. "With your hands?"

The intriguing little fantasy burst. He laughed so hard
he thought his ribs would crack. "No, darling, we've got
technology now, even out here in the boonies."

"Glad to hear it." She turned away, intent on helping him
with his lunch, and bumped solidly into the refrigerator.
"Damn it. I haven't done that in ages." Feeling ridiculous,
she snatched her glasses off. "I used to forget I was wearing them and walk into things all the time."

He sent her a curious look. "I didn't think you forgot
anything."

"Only about myself. Ask me about anything else, and I'll give you chapter and verse."

"Wool."

She turned and straightened, a platter of ham in her hand from the refrigerator. "Excuse me?"

"Maybe I'm thinking about buying some sheep. Tell me about wool."

"Don't be ridiculous."

He shrugged, reached for the bread. "I guess I found something you don't know about."

He didn't have to look to know her eyes had narrowed. He could hear it in her voice.

"An animal fiber forming the protective covering or fleece of sheep or other hairy mammals such as goats or camels. Wool is mainly obtained by shearing fleece from living animals. Cleaning removes the fatty substance, which is purified to make lanolin. Shall I go on?"

Amused, impressed, he studied her. "That's very cool. Where were you when I was in high school?"

"In a snooty boarding school in Switzerland, if my calculations are accurate."

"I imagine they always are," he murmured. The tone, the cool defense in it, told him this was something to be explored later. She spoke of boarding school the way he had once spoken of liver—as something highly detested.

"It's not just remembering facts," he said casually. "You obviously apply them. So how did you decide what to study?"

It was making her uncomfortable; she couldn't help it. However shallow and politically incorrect it might be, she preferred his interest in her body over his interest in her brain. "Initially, I was told what to study. My parents had a very specific blueprint for my education. Later, I concentrated on what held interest for me."

Her voice was cool and clipped, but he wasn't quite ready to let the subject go. He turned to get out the mustard. "You must have wowed your teachers."

She remained where she was, still holding the platter. "They were selected for their credentials in working with gifted children."

"My parents were relieved if I didn't get hauled down to the principal's office for a full week. Yours must have been thrilled with you."

"They're both very successful in their own right," she said flatly. "My father is one of the top vascular surgeons in the country, and my mother is a respected industrial chemist. They expected me to excel. Any other questions?"

Swampy ground again, he mused, sorry that he'd put that note of formality in her voice. He turned, looked at her and was equally sorry he'd put that distant look in her eye. Just now, he wanted to see her smile again.

"Just one," he said. "What have you got on under that shirt?"

Relief loosened the muscles that had knotted her shoulders. "The usual."

"Oh, yeah?"

She did smile as she set the platter on the table. "Maybe you'd like to see for yourself."

"That's just what I had in mind."

She nipped around the far side of the table as he came forward. "After lunch."

His lips curved; his eyes danced. He looked wonderfully dangerous. "I don't want lunch."

He circled; so did she. "You have to keep your strength up, to spread that manure."

"I had a big breakfast. A big, late breakfast." He feinted, nearly snatched her, but she slipped away, laughing. "You're quick."

"I know."

He faked again and, as she pivoted, snaked out an arm to wrap around her waist. When he lifted her off her feet, she squealed with laughter. "I'm quicker."

It was dizzying to realize he could hold her suspended with one arm. Dizzying and exciting. "I let you catch me."

"Bull." He kissed her, hard, then tucked his other arm around her to swing her in three quick circles.

"You're making me drunk again." Laughing, she clutched at his shoulders and enjoyed the ride.

"Good." He swung her again, again, caught up in the joy of it, the joy of her. The sound of her laugh was thrilling, familiar. The feel of her body against his, suddenly as vital as home...

"Put me down, you fool. John." Her head rolled back; the room spun. "Supper's burning."

She could smell it. The bottom of the pot would be scorched for certain. She could smell him—sweat and smoke and animal. Beneath her apron, the baby she carried quickened...

Panic and something else clogged Shane's throat. He set her on her feet, still supporting her as he shook her. "Rebecca. What is it?"

"It's happening again. Like last night." Her face was sheet-white, and her voice became faint and dreamy... "There's stew in the pot, burning in the pot. Did you bring in more wood for the fire?" With her eyes unfocused, she pressed a hand to her stomach. "This one's a girl. Johnnie's going to have a sister…."

Then, as if a light had been switched on, her eyes cleared, sharpened. "My equipment." She broke away and raced to the living room. "Look at this! Just look. It's registering higher than last night. There's so much energy. I can feel it on my skin—like electric shocks."

While he watched, saying nothing, she began to mutter to herself, checking dials, gauges, monitors. All business now, her movements brisk and precise, she turned to her recorder.

"Event commenced at thirteen-twenty and five seconds. Sharp sensory stimuli. Visual, olfactory." As if distracted, she ran a hand over her hair, then competently recounted everything that had happened.

"An overall sense of well-being," she finished, "of happiness. Love. It's possible sexual anticipation was caused by previous stimulation rather than the event, or was enhanced by previous stimulation." She tapped her finger on her lips, thinking. "End of event thirteen-twenty-four and fifty-eight seconds, which at four minutes and fifty-three seconds makes it the longest to date."

On a long breath, she set the recorder down. "And the strongest," she murmured.

"Previous stimulation?"

She pulled herself out of her thoughts and turned to Shane. "I'm sorry, what?"

"Is that what you're calling it? Previous stimulation?"

"Technically." She dragged her hands through her hair again until it stood up in spikes. "That was incredible, absolutely incredible. Last night I was sitting in the kitchen, and I could see it change. It was smaller, and there was a fire in a little stone hearth, pies on the windowsill. There was a baby crying, Shane." Excitement sparkled in her eyes and seemed to shimmer in the air around her. "I got the baby crying on tape. I recorded it."

Pressing her hands to her cheeks, she laughed. "I could hardly believe it myself, even after I played it back half a dozen times. That's why I got out the wine. A little toast that turned into several big ones. I meant to tell you this morning, but we got distracted."

"Distracted."

Finally, the edgy tone of his voice, the flat look in his eyes, pierced through her exhilaration. The glow faded from her cheeks. He was pale, his face set, his eyes hard.

"Why are you angry?"

"Because this is nonsense," he tossed back, preferring anger to the heady sensation of fear. "And because I don't like being called a distraction, or a previous stimulation."

"That's not it at all."

"Don't you start on me. Keep your degrees in your pocket, and don't poke in my brain."

"You're not angry," she said quietly. "You're scared."

For an instant, his eyes were lethal. "I've got things to do."

She darted after him, grabbing his arm when they got to the kitchen. "You said you'd help me, Shane. You gave me your word on it."

"Leave it alone." Toughly he shook her off. "Leave me alone."

She simply stepped into his path and blocked it. Another man, she knew, might have mowed her down. And Shane had the temper for it, as well as the strength. But he also had what made him Shane. "You had the same experience I did, felt the same things I did. I can see it in your face."

He reached out, picked her up and set her aside. "I said leave it alone."

"Who were John and Sarah?" She let out a breath when he stopped on his way to the door. "Her name was Sarah. Who were they, Shane? Who were we a few minutes ago?"

"I'm exactly the same person now as I was a few minutes ago. And so are you. If you're going to keep playing this game, leave me out of it."

"John and Sarah," she said again. "Was it John and Sarah MacKade? Would I find their names in your family Bible?"

He whirled back, stalked to the refrigerator. With one rigid hand, he jerked open the door, took out a beer. After twisting the top off violently, he tossed it aside and drank half the bottle down.

"My great-grandparents."

She let out a long, long sigh. "I see. And they lived here, in this house. They were the ones who tried to save the young Union soldier the day of the battle."

"So the story goes."

"What happened here just now—you've experienced similar things before."

He caught her quick look toward her computer and set his teeth. "No. No way in hell you're going to use me like some damn lab rat."

"All right, I'm sorry. This upsets you." She walked to him to run her hands up his arms. "But I think you need to know that for several years now I've had dreams. And now I know they were about this house, and those people."

He lowered his beer, but said nothing. Rebecca waited a moment, wondering if this kind of intimacy was more than either of them was prepared for.

"The dreams were one of the major reasons I began research into this field. They were—are—real, Shane. I've seen this room, this house, as it was more than a hundred years ago. And I've seen John and Sarah. I don't know if you have any old photographs of them to corroborate that. I can certainly describe them to you, at different periods of their lives here together. I can even tell you things she thought, felt, wanted. I think you can do the same with him."

"No." He said it flatly, finally. A lie for an honest man, a defense for a brave one. "I don't believe in any of that."

In frustration, she lifted her hands. "Do you think I'm making it up, that I'm making all of what just happened up?"

"I think you've got too many things crowded in that ma-jor-league brain of yours." To ease his hot throat, he took another swig of beer. "And I prefer reality."

She could have told him he was in denial, but that would only have made him angry—and possibly more resistant. Patience, she decided, patience and understanding, would be more productive all around.

"All right. We'll let it go, as long as you understand you can talk to me about it anytime."

"You're not my therapist."

"No, I'm not."

Her voice was entirely too reasonable. He slammed down the bottle. "I want you in bed, understand. That's what I want, that's what I need. Just you, just me." Grabbing her hand, he dragged her from the room. "Dreams are just dreams, and ghosts belong in bad movies. So you can just turn off that brain of yours. Distraction, my butt."

He was all but heaving her up the stairs, and she felt twin sensations of alarm and arousal. "It wasn't meant as an insult."

"Too many damn people inside you to suit me. I like it

simple." He let her go to sit down on the edge of the bed and pull off his boots.

"I'm not simple," she said quietly. "Not the way you mean."

"This is simple." Boots dispatched, he rose to pull off his shirt, unhook his belt. "I want you. I break out in a sweat just thinking about you. That's basic, Rebecca. That's simple."

It was love, every bit as much as need, that had her moving to him, wrapping her arms around him. "I'm here." She lifted her head and drew his mouth down to hers.

She gentled him, as he would a skittish animal. Soothing hands, welcoming lips. He told himself that if this was familiar, this sinking into her, this allowing her to smooth away his worries, it was because he had lain with her here only that morning.

But as he fell into the sweet, seductive rhythm of loving her, it was as if there had been no one before, would be no one after. Only the texture of her skin would stay in his memory, the taste of her mouth, the sound of her sigh.

And as she rose to meet him in that fluid movement of comfortable sex, part of his mind fretted that he would never want, could never want, anyone else.

Even as he tumbled over that last edge of pleasure, he held himself back from a bigger, more dangerous fall.

Chapter 9

I've now had three events at the farm. The last was during the night. I felt such grief, such tearing grief. There was a candle by the bed, burning. For a moment, I thought there was a figure standing by the window. Just standing, looking out at the night. While the grief was in me, it was also there, shimmering around that figure. A shared, yet separate, pain. I thought it was Shane, and started to get out of bed to go to him. But he was asleep beside me. And there was no one standing there at all.

I knew, clearly, that it was John and Sarah, and that their son was dead. I knew this even before Shane stirred restlessly beside me. He dreams, as I do, and he feels, as I do, but he doesn't want to speak of it. They're part of him, the people who lived here, who remain here in some fashion. Not only through blood, but through spirit. I wonder why they seem to be part of me, as well.

It upsets him, so I didn't tell him. Perhaps this is wrong. It's certainly unprofessional. But I'm learning that love has its own way. I love him so much, and in my own limited fashion would protect him from what haunts him.

I wonder what his feelings are for me, but I don't ask. I have to protect myself, as well. I can talk to him about anything but that. Anything at all. And I never run out of words. He's in the fields now. There is always so much work that must be done, yet he never seems to tire of it, or resent it. For myself, in this first, dizzying rush of love, I realize I could spend every second of every day with him and still not have enough time. It's a wonderful, liberating and humbling thing, this love. I'm so grateful I've had the chance to experience it.

If I could, I would take one moment, any single moment at all that I've had with him, crystallize it, preserve it and carry it with me. Then, in all the years to come, I could take it out, not just to remember, but to relive.

Love gives you the oddest fantasies.

Rebecca heard the bark of the dogs, and the voices. Like a woman hiding a secret treasure, she saved her document and changed screens. Devin opened the door, followed by boys and dogs and all the noise that comes with them.

"Sorry. Didn't mean to bust in on you."

"That's all right." Automatically she lowered a hand to rub at the dogs, who came to greet her. "I was just finished."

"Cassie's just like the rest of the women in the county. Figures Shane must be starving." He set a dish on the counter. "She sent over an apple cobbler."

"It's great," Bryan informed Rebecca. "We had some of the other one she made already." Obviously at home, he poked into the refrigerator.

"Are you writing your book?" Connor approached more slowly, his eyes on her laptop.

"Not right now. Do you use a computer?"

He was studying hers with naked envy. "We get to use them in school sometimes. But they're not like this one."

"This one's loaded. Want to try it?"

He goggled. "Really?" He looked at his father, then put his hands behind his back. "I don't know how to work this kind."

"Nothing to it." Recognizing the look in his eyes, she laughed and took his hand to draw him closer. "I can show you. I've got everything backed up."

"Now you've done it," Devin murmured. "He's going to start pining for one."

"I can get you a deal on a used one." With a grin, she rose and pointed at her chair. "Sit down and give it a go. You must know the basic functions."

"Sure." The first thing he did was type his name. Connor MacKade.

"Does it play any games?" Bryan wanted to know.

"Nope. It's just a workhorse."

Losing interest immediately, Bryan cast his eyes on the cobbler.

"Forget it," Devin warned. "We came by to give Shane a hand with the haying," he told Rebecca. "You can expect the rest to descend before long."

"Oh." She glanced toward the window. "He's out there now, mowing it."

"Baling it," Devin told her. "First you mow, then you rake, then you bale."

"Right."

"You guys head out when you're done here. And don't pester Dr. Knight."

She followed him out to the porch and paused outside the door. "Devin, you lived here a long time."

"Most of my life."

"Have you ever had any unusual experiences? Of a paranormal nature," she added when he flashed a grin.

"You're asking if I think the place is haunted. Sure it is."

She shook her head. "You say that so casually."

"I've lived with it. You get used to it."

"Not everyone."

He followed her gaze to where Shane guided the tractor over the mowed hay. "Shane's got a stubborn streak."

"So I've noticed."

"And when it comes down to it, he's got a sensitive nature." Devin grinned again. "He'd bloody my nose for that one. But he does. Lived on a farm all his life, but he suffers if an animal's in pain, or if he loses one. Can't take it as a matter of course. There's a lot of leftover emotion in this house. It gets to him."

"Yet he lives here."

"He loves it," Devin said simply. "Every stone. Can you picture him anyplace else?"

She looked out to the hayfield again, smiled. "No. No, I can't. I could help him with what's here. If he'd let me."

"Maybe you could." Devin sighed. He was used to women falling for Shane, but it was easy to see that Rebecca was different. He doubted that she'd walk away unscathed when the time came. "I'd better go give him a hand."

She made some sound of agreement, and watched for some time before she went back into the house.

Devin told himself it wasn't his business as he walked

across the field. In the easy rhythm of familiarity, he fell into step behind the baler. They worked together in silence until Shane shut off the motor.

"Rafe and Jared coming?"

"Should be on their way."

Shane nodded, squinted at the sky. "It's going to rain. We've only got another hour or two to get this in." But his gaze wandered to the house and stayed there.

"Damn it, Shane." Disgusted, Devin pulled out a bandanna and mopped his brow. "You're sleeping with her."

"Who?"

"Don't give me that. Aren't there enough women to dangle after around here without sniffing around Regan's friend? She's not even your type."

Shane worked to keep his temper in check. "You've always said I don't have a type."

"You know what I mean. That's a serious woman. Serious women have serious feelings. If she's not in love with you already, she will be. Then what the hell are you going to do?"

It cut just a little too close to the quick. Shane had always been careful to keep women from falling in love with him—seriously in love, in any case. And he knew he wasn't being careful with Rebecca.

"That's my business, isn't it? Mine and Rebecca's. I didn't push her into anything."

To drown out any more unwelcome advice, he cranked up the tractor again.

He wasn't going to talk about it, and he certainly wasn't going to worry about it. He meant to go on as he always had, and that meant, at this moment, getting the haying done before the rain hit.

He was grateful when the rest of his family showed up.

It meant extra hands to load the hay wagon, drive it to the barn and off-load it. It also meant everyone was too busy working to pester him about his private life.

A man was entitled to a private life.

He cooled down considerably when it looked as if the job would be done before the storm hit. And when he could see children playing in the yard, dogs racing around and women going in and out of the house. Then there was the soothing quality of the steady vibration of the tractor under him, the voices of his brothers, that sweet, strong scent of hay. The clouds rolling in from the west shadowed the mountain, and the winter wheat he'd planted would welcome the rain.

In the kitchen, someone would be cooking, he mused, glancing over his shoulder to check the progress of the hay wagon. It wouldn't be Rebecca. She'd be playing with one of the babies. And when he walked in, covered with hay dust, she'd look over and smile.

She had the prettiest smile.

By the time they were hauling bales from wagon to barn, Shane had convinced himself that Devin was not only out of line, he was off base.

"So." Rafe took a break, gulping down some of the ice water from the cooler just inside the barn. "I didn't get a chance to talk to Rebecca. How's the ghostbusting?"

"She's into it." Sharp prickles of dry hay poked through his work gloves as Shane heaved a bale. "She gets pretty intense about something that's just a hobby."

"Hey, some people play golf," Jared commented, loading the hay lift.

"At least there's a purpose to that. Get the little ball in the hole, win the game."

"It's a puzzle to her," Jared added. "She strikes me as a woman who likes to solve puzzles, find answers."

"Maybe I'll buy her a jigsaw puzzle," Shane muttered.

"Bothers you, huh?" Amused, Rafe put his back into the work again. "Hear any chains rattling lately? Any disembodied moans?"

"Kiss my butt."

"How's it going otherwise?" Jared asked, with a vague thought to defusing an argument. Rain was beginning to patter on the ground, and they still had work to do. "Hasn't been a woman living in the house since Mom died. Cramping your style?"

A smile curved Shane's lips. "Nope."

"Well, hell." Catching Shane's look, Rafe set down the bale he'd just lifted. "You're sleeping with her."

"What am I, wearing a sign?"

"Can't you keep it in your pants for once?" In disgust, Rafe sliced his baling hook down. "Regan feels responsible for her."

Guilt and fear only inflamed a ready temper. "Why the hell should anybody feel responsible? She's a grown woman."

"You going to get that last load up here?" Devin called from the loft.

"Shut up." Shane spared him a glance before he turned on Rafe. "It's none of his business, it's none of your business."

"Anything connected to Regan's my business. And Rebecca's connected. What do you know about her? Do you know how she was brought up? How she spent all her time in classrooms, with tutors, in boarding schools?"

"What difference does it make?" Irritated because he didn't know, knew far from enough, Shane ignored the rain, the work, and let out the frustration on his brother. "She's got a brain, she uses it."

"That's all she was ever allowed to use. She wouldn't stand a chance if you aimed for her."

"What's the problem here?" Devin stepped out into the rain. "Are we going to get this load in before it's soaked, or just leave it?"

"Back off," Shane snarled at Rafe. "And stay out of my personal life."

Jared sighed. "Looks like we're going to leave it."

"This about Rebecca?" Interested now, Devin plucked out a spear of hay and gnawed on it. "We should've figured he'd hit on her."

"I didn't hit on her."

"That's bull. She'd barely unpacked her bags and you were stalking her in my kitchen. I should've punched you out right then."

Shane's eyes narrowed. "Try it now. You've got it all figured out, don't you? Now that you've got your pretty wife and your pretty kids. All of you." There was more anger than he'd realized boiling inside him. "I live my life my way, not yours. So stick your advice and your judgments and anything else you've got up your—"

From the kitchen window, Rebecca watched the four men. She was puzzled. At first it had seemed they were having some sort of serious discussion—some logistical problem with the hay, she'd concluded. Then it had looked as though an argument were brewing.

"Something's going on out there," she commented, and Savannah, an infant over her shoulder, wandered to the window.

"Oh, they're going to go at it."

"At what?"

"Each other, what else?" She shook her head and called

to Regan and Cassie, who were busy at the stove. "Our boys are about to rumble."

"Fight?" Shocked to the core, Rebecca goggled. "You mean they're going to fight with each other? But why?"

Regan walked to the kitchen door, opened it. "It's just something they like to do from time to time."

"Do you think it's early enough to stop it?" Cassie wondered out loud.

"We can— No," Regan finished as the first blow was launched. "Too late."

With horrified eyes, Rebecca watched Shane's fist streak out and plow into Rafe's face. An instant later, they were rolling in the dirt. "But— But—"

"I'll make sure there's plenty of ice." Cassie turned away from the battle and went to the refrigerator.

"Why doesn't somebody stop them?" Regan demanded. "Jared and Devin are just standing there."

"Not for long," Savannah predicted.

As if on cue, Devin reached down. If his intention was to break it up, he failed miserably. Now there were three men wrestling in the mud the rain had churned up.

"This is ridiculous." By the time Rebecca reached the kitchen door, Jared had joined in the fray.

She couldn't see how any of them could tell who was fighting whom. She certainly couldn't. All she saw were arms and fists and bodies. All she heard were grunts and curses.

Outside of movies and television, she'd never actually seen anyone brawl. It was messier than she'd imagined, and certainly looked more painful.

"Isn't one of you going to do anything? They're your husbands."

"Well." Slowly Savannah ran a hand up and down Miranda's back. "We could put some money on it. I'll take Jared for five—it's a matter of loyalty."

"Five it is," Regan agreed. "Cassie?"

"All right—but Devin was up half the night. Ally's teething."

"No handicapping," Savannah declared. "Straight odds. You want to take Shane, Rebecca? Seems fair."

Totally baffled, she stared at the women. "Why, you're as bad as they are." She straightened her shoulders. "I'm going to put a stop to this, right now."

As Rebecca marched out, Savannah slanted a look at Regan. "To borrow Bryan's phrase, she's really stuck on him, isn't she?"

"I'm afraid so. It worries me."

"I think she's good for him." Cassie joined them at the door. "I think he's good for her, too. Both of them need someone, even if they haven't figured it out yet."

The only thing Rebecca figured as she marched toward the hay barn was that these four grown men—brothers, no less—were absolute fools.

By the time she neared the battlefield, she was soaked, her hair plastered to her head like a cap. She shook her head at the sight that met her eyes. The dogs had joined the party, racing around, occasionally leaping onto rolling bodies, then dancing away with delighted barks.

"Stop it." It halted the dogs, but not the men. Fred and Ethel sat politely, tongues hanging out, while the men continued to pummel each other. "I said stop this, right now."

Jared made the mistake of glancing over at the order and caught an elbow sharply on the chin. He retaliated by ramming a fist into the nearest belly.

Filled with righteous indignation, Rebecca slapped her hands on her hips. She didn't just hear grunts and curses now. They were laughing. Four baboons, she decided, laughing while they beat on each other.

She had a good carrying voice when she needed one. It had filled many a lecture hall. She used it now. "Stop this nonsense immediately. There are children in the house."

Devin paused, his filthy hand over Rafe's filthy face. "What?"

"Get up from there, all of you. You should be ashamed." Eyes hot, she scalded every one of them in turn. "I said get up. You." Choosing at random, she pointed a righteous finger at Devin. "You're a sheriff, for God's sake. You're supposed to uphold order, and here you are rolling in the mud like a hooligan."

"Yes, ma'am." Gamely he swallowed a chuckle and disengaged himself from the tangle of limbs. "Don't know what got into me."

"And you." That valiant finger aimed at Jared. "A lawyer. What are you thinking of?"

"Nothing." He rubbed a hand over his sore jaw before he rose. "Absolutely nothing."

"Rafe MacKade." She had the pleasure of seeing him wince. "A businessman, a pillar of the community. Husband and father. What kind of example are you setting for your children?"

"A poor one." He cleared his throat and got to his feet. He had the feeling that if he let the laugh loose she'd put him on his butt again.

"And you," she said, with such contempt in her voice that Shane decided to stay put in the mud. "I thought better of you."

"She sounds just like Mom," Shane murmured, and had his brothers nodding in respectful agreement. "Hey, I didn't start it."

"Typical response. Just typical. Is this how you solve your problems, your disagreements?"

He rubbed some of the dirt from his aching face. "Yeah."

"That's pathetic. You're all pathetic." Her authoritative look had three men shifting their feet and Shane grinning. "Violence is never the answer. There's no problem that can't be solved with reason and communication."

"We were communicating," Shane said, and earned a withering stare.

"I expect you to settle this like rational human beings. If you can't control yourselves, you'll just have to keep your distance from each other."

"Isn't she something?" Shane said, in a tone that had all three of his brothers studying him. "Have you ever seen anybody like her? Come on and kiss me, sweetie."

"If you think you can—" She let out a shriek as he swiped out a hand and had her sprawling on top of him. "You idiot. You brainless—"

Then she was flat on her back, covered by wet, hard male. His mouth, trembling with laughter, swooped onto hers. "She's the prettiest little thing."

He kissed her again, while mud oozed through her shirt.

"Get off me, you ape!" She bucked, wiggled and gave him a whack.

"Violence." He was shaking with laughter now, his battered, dirt-streaked face grinning down at her. "You see that?" he called out to his brothers. "She hit me. She isn't solving the problem with reason and communication."

"I'll communicate, all right." Her fist grazed his ear before his mouth fused to hers again.

And then he was kissing her senseless. The rain beat down, mud slicked her hands, and there was an audience of fascinated onlookers.

She just didn't care.

As he watched, Rafe found himself grinning. "I'll be damned," he murmured. "She's hooked him."

"I think you're right." Devin rubbed his bloody cheek on his muddy shoulder. "I've never seen him look at any woman that way. Think he knows it?"

"I don't think either of them have a clue." Delighted, Jared swiped wet hair out of his eyes.

"It's going to be a pleasure." Rafe hooked his thumbs in his pockets, rocking back on his heels. "A real pleasure, to watch Shane MacKade take the fall."

"Should we go inside and leave them alone?" Devin angled his head as he considered. "Or should we haul him off her and pound on him some more?"

Rafe touched his fingers to his eye. Shane's first punch had been a doozy. He was going to need some of the ice he was sure his wife was readying.

"I wouldn't mind pounding him some more, but she'd just get going again."

"I don't think we should leave them out here," Jared decided. "They could catch pneumonia."

"Not with all that heat." With a nod, Devin moved forward, and his brothers flanked him. Between them, they took arms and legs and hauled Shane into the air.

"Let go. You've got your own women. This one's mine." But they had him pinned, so he could only grin foolishly at Rebecca. "Baby, you're a mess. Let's go take a shower."

Eyes narrowed, Rebecca pulled herself to her feet. She knew she had mud in places best left unmentioned. With as much dignity as possible, she swiped her hands down her ruined slacks and through her filthy hair.

"Have you got him?" she asked calmly.

"Yes, ma'am." Recognizing the look in her eyes, Devin grinned. "I believe we do."

Shane knew the look, too, and tried to yank free. "Come on now, honey. Reason, remember? Violence isn't an answer. God, you're so pretty. I could gobble you right up. Why don't we—"

His breath whooshed out when she clenched a fist and rammed it into his stomach.

"Good one," he said weakly, then coughed and managed to draw another breath. "You show real potential."

"Idiot." With a toss of her head, she dripped her way to the house.

"Isn't she something?" Dazed with admiration and pain, Shane stared after her. "Isn't she just something?"

In the end, he tried flowers. After the chores were done, supper was eaten and his family had gone their separate ways, Shane calculated he needed a bit of an edge. He went out in the rain, in the dark, and picked wildflowers by flashlight.

When he came back, she was working at her computer. She did glance up; it was one of those cool, killing glances she'd aimed his way all evening.

He put the wet flowers on the table beside her and crouched down. "How mad are you?"

"I'm not angry." She was embarrassed, and that was worse.

"Want to hit me again?"

"Certainly not."

"It was just mud." He took her hand, brought it to his lips. "It looked good on you."

She would have tugged her hand away, but he was nibbling on it. "I'm trying to work."

"Wasn't the term you used *avoidance*?" When she turned her head to glare, he picked up the flowers and held them out. "I'm crazy about you."

She let out a sigh. What was so important about dignity, anyway? "You must be crazy to go out on a rainy night to pick flowers."

"It always worked with my mother. You reminded me of her today, when you were letting us have it. Of course, she'd have pulled us up by the scruff of the neck, and then lectured. I guess we were smaller then."

Unable to resist, Rebecca sniffed at the dripping blooms. "She must have been quite a woman."

"She was the best," Shane said simply. "They don't come any better. She and my father, well, they were terrific. You always knew somebody was there, ready to give you a kick in the butt or a helping hand, whichever you needed most." Reaching up, he stroked a finger over her cheek. "I guess that's why I don't really understand loneliness."

"Big families aren't always a buffer against it. It's the people in them." She scraped back her chair. "I'd better put these in water."

She wasn't going to tell him, he realized. She wasn't going to speak of her background, her family, unless he pushed. "Rebecca—"

"What were you fighting with your brothers about?" She asked it quickly, as if she sensed what he'd been going to ask.

"Stuff." Then he shrugged. If he wanted her to be honest, he had to be, as well. "You."

Stunned, she turned back. "Me? You're joking."

"It wasn't a big deal. Rafe said something to tick me off. That's usually all it takes." He crossed over, bent down to take a slim old bottle out of the bottom cupboard. "They think I'm taking advantage of you."

"I see." But she didn't. She took the bottle, filled it, then began to carefully arrange the flowers. "You told them we were intimate."

"I didn't have to." He had an idea of what she was imagining. Locker-room talk, snickers, bragging and nudging elbows. "Rebecca, I didn't talk about what's between us."

And he might have, probably would have, he realized, if it had been another woman. Frowning, he walked over to pour coffee he didn't want.

He didn't go around bragging about his relationships with women. But with his brothers, he would certainly have made some comment about a new interest. He'd kept his feelings about Rebecca to himself.

And it wouldn't have bothered him in the least to have Rafe or any of the others tease or prod about his exploits with a woman. Yet it had with Rebecca. It had hurt and infuriated and—

"What the hell is this?" he muttered.

"I thought it was coffee."

"What?" He stared into his mug. "No, my mind was wandering. Look, it wasn't a big deal. It's just the way we are. We fight." He smiled a little. "We used to beat on each other a lot more. I guess we're mellowing."

"Well." Thoughtful, she carried the flowers to the table, set them in the center. "I've never had anyone fight over me before—especially four big, strong men. I suppose I should be flattered."

"I have feelings for you." It came right out of his mouth, out of nowhere. Shaken, Shane lifted his mug and gulped down coffee. "I guess I didn't like the idea of somebody thinking I'd pushed you into bed."

Warmth bloomed inside her. A dangerous warmth, she knew. A loving one. She made certain her voice was light. "We both know you didn't."

"You haven't exactly been around the block. I wanted you. I went after you."

"And I put up a hell of a battle, didn't I?"

"Not especially." But he couldn't smile back at her. "I've been around the block, a lot of times."

"Are you bragging?"

"No, I—" He caught himself. There was amusement in her eyes, and understanding, and something else he didn't know quite what to do with. "I guess what I'm trying to say is that I'd try to go along with it if you wanted to rethink the situation, or take some time."

She swallowed a nasty ball of fear. Fear made the voice tremble, and she wanted hers to be steady. "Is that what you want?"

With his eyes on her, he shook his head slowly. "No. Lately I can't seem to want anything but you. Just looking at you makes my mouth water."

The warmth came back, pulsed, spread. She crossed the room, lifted her arms to twine them around his neck. "Then why don't you do more than look?"

Chapter 10

There were many places to talk to ghosts. An open mind didn't require a dark night, howling winds or swirling mists. This day was bright and beautiful. Trees touched by early fall were shimmering in golds and russets against a sky so blue it might have been painted on canvas.

There was the sound of birdsong, the smell of grass newly mowed. There were fields crackling with drying cornstalks, and, like a miracle, there was a lone doe standing at the edge of the trees, sniffing the air for human scent.

Rebecca had come to the battlefield alone. Early. She lingered here, near the long depression in the ground known as Bloody Lane. She knew the battle, each charge and retreat, and she knew the horrid stage of it when men had fallen and lain in tangled heaps in that innocent-looking dip in the land.

There was a tower at the end of it, built long after the

war. She'd climbed it before, knew the view from the top was glorious. From there, she would be able to see the inn, the woods, some of Shane's fields.

But it didn't call to her as this spot did. Here, on the ground, there was no lofty distance between the living and the dead.

She sat down on the grass, knowing she would feel only a sadness, an intellectual connection with the past. As compelling, as hallowed, as the ground was, she could only be a historian.

Ghosts didn't speak to her, not here. It was the farm that held the key for her. The farm that haunted not only her dreams now, but her waking hours, as well. She accepted that. But what was the connection there? What was the emotional link? A link so strong it had pulled at her for years, over thousands of miles.

That she didn't know.

She knew only that she was in love.

She lifted her face to the breeze, let it run its fingers through her hair as Shane often did. How could she be so content, and yet so unsettled? There were so many questions unanswered, so many feelings unresolved. She wondered if that was the way of love.

Was she still so passive, so undemanding of others, that she could settle so easily for what Shane offered? Or was she still so needy, so starved for love, that she fretted for more when she had enough?

Either way, it proved that a part of her, rooted deep, hadn't changed. Perhaps never would.

He cared for her, he desired her. She was pathetically grateful for that. He'd be shocked to know it, she was certain. She would keep that to herself, just as she kept this outrageous and overwhelming love for him to herself.

She had plenty of practice at restricting and restraining her emotions.

Common sense told her she was being greedy. She wanted all the love, the passion, the endurance, that lived in that house for herself. She wanted the stability of it, the constancy and the acceptance.

She was the transient, as she had always been.

But she wouldn't leave empty-handed this time, and that thought soothed. There wouldn't simply be knowledge received and given, there would be emotion—more emotion than she had ever received, more than she'd ever given. That was something to celebrate, and to treasure.

That should be enough for anyone.

Sitting alone, she gazed over the fields, the slope of the hill, the narrow trench. It was so utterly peaceful, so pristine, and its beauty was terrible. She'd studied history enough to know the strategies of war, the social, political and personal motivations behind it. Knew enough, too, to understand the romance that followed it.

The music, the beat of the drum, the wave of flags and the flash of weapons.

She could picture the charge, men running wildly through the smoke of cannon fire, eyes reddened, teeth bared. Their hearts would have pounded, roaring with blood. They had been men, after all. Fear, glory, hope and a little madness.

That first clash of bayonets. The sun would have flashed on steel. Had the crows waited, nasty and patient, drawn by the thunder of swords and boom of mortar?

North or South, they would have raced toward death. And the generals on their horses, playing chess with lives, how had they felt, what had they thought, as they watched the carnage here? The bodies piling up, blue and gray united by the stain of blood. The miserable cries of the wounded, the screams of the dying.

She sighed again. War was loss, she thought, no matter what was gained.

Always there would be a John and Sarah, the essence of the grieving parents for dead sons. War stole families, she reflected. Cut pieces out of hearts that could never truly heal.

So we build monuments to the wars, and the dead sons. We tell ourselves not to forget. John and Sarah never forgot. And love endured.

It made her smile as she rose. The grass was green here, and the air quiet. She decided that the world needed places of loss to help them remember what they had.

She went home to write.

It was nearly time for evening milking, Rebecca realized, and she laughed at herself. How odd that she would begin to gauge the day by farm chores. With a shake of her head, she hammered out the next sentence.

Why had she spent all her life writing technical papers? she wondered. This flow of emotion and thought and imagination was so liberating. Damned if she didn't think she might try her hand at a novel eventually.

Chuckling at the thought, she tucked it into the back of her mind. There were plenty of people who would consider her present topic, the supernatural, straight fiction.

When the phone rang, she let the next thought roll around in her head as she rose to answer. Absently she reached for the coffeepot and the receiver at the same time.

"Hello?"

"Dr. Rebecca Knight, please."

She stiffened, then ordered herself to relax. Why should

it surprise, even annoy, her that her voice hadn't been recognized? "This is Rebecca. Hello, Mother."

"Rebecca, I had to go through your service to track you down. I assumed you were in New York."

"No, I'm not." She heard the door open and worked up a casual, if stiff, smile for Shane. "I'm spending some time in Maryland."

"A lecture tour? I hadn't heard."

"No, I'm not on a lecture tour." She could easily visualize her mother flipping through her Filofax to note it down. "I'm...doing research."

"In Maryland. On what subject?"

"The Battle of Antietam."

"Ah. That's been covered very adequately, don't you think?"

"I'm coming from a different angle." She made way so that Shane could get to the coffee, but didn't look at him. "Is there something I can do for you?"

"Actually, there's something I can do for you. Where in the world are you staying, Rebecca? It's very inconvenient that you didn't leave word. I need a fax number."

"I'm staying with a friend." She turned her back, avoiding Shane's eyes. "I don't have a fax here."

"Surely you have access to one. You're not in the Dark Ages."

Now she did glance at Shane. He smelled of the earth, and carried a good bit of it on his person. "Not exactly," Rebecca said dryly. "I'll have to check on that and get back to you. Are you in Connecticut?"

"Your father is. I'm at a seminar in Atlanta. You can reach me through the Ritz-Carlton."

"All right. Can I ask what this is about?"

"It's quite an opportunity. The head of the history department at my alma mater is retiring at the end of this semester. With your credentials and my connections, I don't see that you'd have any difficulty getting the position. There's talk of endowing a chair. It would be quite a coup, given your age. At twenty-four, I believe you'd be the youngest department head ever placed there."

"I was twenty-five last March, Mother."

"Nonetheless, it would still be a coup."

"Yes, I'm sure it would, but I'm not interested."

"Don't be ridiculous, Rebecca."

She closed her eyes for a moment. That tone, that quick, dismissive tone, had whipped her along the path chosen for her all her life. It took a hard, wrenching effort for her to stand her ground.

"I'm afraid I'll have to be." And where had that cold, sarcastic voice come from? Rebecca wondered. "I don't want to teach, Mother."

"Teaching is the least of it, Rebecca, as you're quite aware. The position itself—"

"I don't want to be the dean of history, or the history chair, anywhere." She had to interrupt quickly, recognizing the old, familiar roiling in her stomach. "But thank you for thinking of me."

"I'm not happy with your attitude, Rebecca. You are obligated to use your gifts, and the opportunities your father and I have provided for you. An advancement of this stature will make your career."

"Whose career?"

There was a sigh. Long-suffering. "Obviously you're in a difficult mood, and I can see that gratitude won't be forthcoming. I'll depend on your good sense, however. Get me your fax number as soon as possible. I'm a bit rushed at the moment, but I'll expect to hear from you by the morning. Goodbye."

"Goodbye, Mother."

She hung up and smiled at Shane brightly, overbrightly, while the muscles in her stomach clenched and knotted. "Well, cows all bedded down?"

"Sit down, Rebecca."

"I'm starving." Terrified he would touch her and she would fall apart, she moved away. "I think there's still some of that chocolate cake one of your harem dropped off."

"Rebecca." His voice was quiet, and his eyes were troubled. She kept pressing a hand to her stomach, he noted, as if something inside hurt. "I think you should sit down."

"I can make more coffee. I've figured this thing out." She started to reach for the canister, but he stepped forward, took her shoulders gently. "What?" The word snapped out, her body jerking.

Careful, he thought, disturbed by the brittle look in her eyes. "So, you're from Connecticut."

She hesitated, then shrugged her shoulders under his hands. "My parents live there."

"That's where you grew up."

"Not exactly. I lived there when I wasn't in school. You don't want to drink that," she added, glancing at the pot. "It's been sitting for hours. I'd said I'd make fresh."

"What did she say to upset you, baby?"

"Nothing. It's nothing." But he kept holding her, kept looking at her with boundless patience and concern. "She wants me to campaign for a position at her college. It's a very prestigious position. I'm not interested. It's a divergence of opinion, and she's not used to me having an opinion."

It was simple enough, he thought, or it should have been.

But there was nothing simple about her reaction. "You told her no."

"It doesn't particularly matter. It never did, on the rare occasions I actually got up the courage to say it. I expect my father will be calling shortly, to remind me of my obligations and responsibilities."

"Who are you obligated to?"

"To them, to education, to posterity. I have a responsibility to use my talents, and to reap the rewards. It's just a variation on 'Publish or perish,' the battle cry of academia. Let's forget it."

He let her move away, because she seemed to need it. Her hands were steady as she measured out coffee, and her face was blank while she filled the pot.

Then, with a shudder, she set everything down. "I can't believe I'm doing this. This is how I got ulcers."

"What the hell are you talking about?"

"Ulcers, migraines, insomnia and a near miss with a breakdown. Isn't this why I studied psychiatry?"

She wasn't talking to him, Shane realized, so he said nothing. But he was beginning to burn inside.

"Repression isn't the answer. I know that. It's one of the things that punish the body for what's closed up in the mind. It's always so much easier to analyze someone else, always much harder to see things when it's yourself."

Her rigid hands raked through her hair. "I'm not going to be directed this time. I'm not going to be hammered at until I give. The hell with them. The hell with them. They never did anything but make me into a miserable, neurotic freak."

She whirled back to him. Her face wasn't blank now, it was livid. "Do you know what it's like to be four years old and expected to read Dante in Italian, and discuss it? To sit at the dinner table, when you weren't shuffled off somewhere else, and be quizzed on physics or converse about the Renaissance—in French, naturally?"

"No," he said quietly. "Why don't you tell me what it's like?"

"It's horrible. Horrible. To have your own parents regard you as a *thing,* a rousing success of genetics. I hated it, but what choice do you have when you're a child? You do what's expected of you. Then you get in the habit and you keep right on doing it even when you're not a child. One day you look in the mirror, and you see something so pathetic it hurts to look. And you wonder, why not just end it?"

The anger inside him turned to dry-mouthed shock. "Rebecca."

Impatient, she shook her head. "Maybe you fantasize about it, even obsess. And you're clever, you're so damned clever that you can find the most effective, the most painless way, to accomplish it. And, of course, the most tidy."

He didn't speak now. She'd shaken him down to the bone, and he was chilled to the marrow. This woman, this beautiful, precious woman, had considered ending her life.

She rubbed absently at the headache that throbbed dead-center in her forehead. "But you're too intelligent, too well-programmed, to tolerate that kind of waste. It frightens you a little to realize you could actually do it, so you decide—being a practical person—to study human behavior, psychiatry, instead. A much more productive outlet, all in all."

"How old were you?" he managed, but had to take a steadying breath before he could go on. "How old were you when you..."

"Researched suicide?" she said calmly. "Twelve. A dangerous age, all those hormones to deal with. A shock to the regimented system. You have to remind yourself that life, however miserable, is all you've got, and go on with it. It's easier to go on with it if you just close up, close off, lock yourself behind books and theories, credentials and degrees. Until you realize that's just a different kind of suicide."

She took a long, shuddering breath. "I'm tired," she murmured, rubbing her hands over her face. "They make me so tired."

Ulcers, a breakdown. Dear God, suicide. What the hell had they done to her? He wanted to tear them apart. All of them. Any of them who had ignored her heart to get to her mind. He wanted, desperately, to go back in time and find that young girl, to give her everything she'd needed and deserved.

But he could only reach out to the woman.

"Come on." He went to her, held her, close and gentle, despite the storm raging inside him. She needed his calm, not his fury. "Just lean on me awhile."

"I'm all right."

"No, you're not. But you will be." He damn well would see to it. "Hold on to me, baby."

So she did, and it was so easy. "She didn't do anything wrong, not really. We haven't seen each other in more than a year. I doubt she or my father would recognize me if we passed on the street. The change would surprise them."

He rubbed his cheek over her hair. She felt so fragile. Why hadn't he seen that before? Where hadn't he looked to see this hurt, vulnerable side of her?

"It doesn't matter what they think, only what you want."

"You can't always have everything you want. Once I wanted them to love me. I'd have done anything if they'd just said they loved me. You know the problem with a memory like mine? You can't forget things—even when you want to. I remember when they first sent me to boarding school. I was so frightened, so lonely and unhappy. They put me on a plane, didn't even go with me. I was six years old."

"Oh, baby, I'm so sorry."

"They could see I had an adult mind, but they never considered the child's heart. Well, I'm grown-up now. I should handle it better."

"You're handling it fine."

"Not fine, but better." She eased back a little. "I'm sorry. If you'd come in an hour later, I'd have been over it."

"I want you to tell me what you feel." Very gently, he lowered his head and touched his lips to hers. "I want to know who you are, and how you got there. I haven't been able to figure you out, Rebecca. All those different pieces of you that never quite seem to fit. Now they're starting to. Do me a favor?"

"What?"

"Don't call her back. Let her stew."

She smiled a little. "That's rude."

"Yeah. So?"

"She'll just call again. My father will call. They—" To prove her point, the phone rang. "There you are."

He tightened his grip before she could move. Nothing was going to put that shattered look back on her face while he was here to protect her. "I don't hear anything."

"The phone."

"We don't have a phone." Thinking only to give her peace, he kissed her again. And brought himself some, as well. "And we're not here, anyway."

"Where are we?"

He scooped his arm under her knees, picked her up. "Anywhere you want to go." As the phone continued to shrill, he carried her out of the room. "As long as it takes a real long time to get there."

When he reached the bedroom, he set her on her feet. The phone had stopped ringing, and he took it off the hook, then set the receiver in a drawer to muffle the buzz.

"That ought to do it."

"You don't even have an answering machine. It'll drive them crazy."

"Good." He'd have liked an opportunity to speak to either of her parents himself. But that could wait. At the moment, he had only one priority, and that was erasing the troubled look in Rebecca's eyes. "So, where do you want to go?"

She shook her head, her smile puzzled. "I thought we were there."

"This is just the starting-off point." He ran a finger down the vest she wore over a mannish shirt. "A tropical island? A—what do you call it?—mountain chalet? We could be snowed in. A castle, maybe." He brushed his lips over her brow. "Let's pretend."

"Fantasizing is often a—"

His lips slid down to hers. "Let's pretend. A long, empty beach, white sand, palm trees. Smell the flowers." Gently he kissed her eyes closed. "Hear the surf. Let's go there. I love the way your skin looks in the moonlight." He nibbled at her lips as he slipped the vest aside and, slowly, so slowly, undid the buttons of her shirt. "There's moonlight on the water, on you. Pretty Rebecca." Lightly he cupped her breasts. "Come away with me."

"Anywhere," she murmured, and let him take her.

"There's no one but us." He drew off his shirt, always

keeping contact with his mouth, on her lips, her cheek, the curve of her ear. "And nothing to do but make love. I want to make love with you, Rebecca. Only you, Rebecca. Day and night."

The words were seducing her. Words were powerful, she knew, and his were captivating her. His skin was under her hands now, wonderfully smooth and warm. His heart beat slow and thick against hers. She would have sworn she heard the waves hiss and rise on the sand.

"In the surf," she said dreamily as those wonderful hands glided over her. "With the water flowing up, then away."

"That's right. Your skin's wet and cool. Slick," he said as he continued to undress them both. "And it tastes of salt." Still murmuring, he lowered her to the bed. "There's starlight in your eyes." He could see it, though the last rays of the sun slanted through the windows. "Silver sparkling in the gold. We can stay as long as you like. As long as you want."

His mouth slid over hers, coaxing, giving, taking just a little more when her lips softened on a sigh. Beneath his, her body was soft, yielding, surrendering. She was with him now, he knew. Pulse to pulse. He wanted to show her what it was to be cherished.

So his hands were gentle, his lips tender, and each move, each shift, was fluid and patient. Loving. He lingered where he knew it pleased her most, going quietly, easily, sinking a little deeper with each stroke of his hands into the fantasy he'd created for her.

She was floating. It could have been water sliding over her, so sensitive were his hands. And the gift he brought to her was a liquid yearning as much of the soul as of the body.

She dreamed there was sand beneath them, wet and

smooth. And the wind at the windows was the musical murmur of surf. The dim light seemed to be rich and silver with the full, rising moon. The exotic perfume of island flowers, the midnight sea that stretched forever, the romantic song of tropical birds.

And her lover was there, holding her.

"Where are you, Rebecca?"

"With you."

"Stay with me."

She wrapped her arms around him.

He loved her endlessly, building the pace, letting the current take her up, over. When she tumbled down, he was there to catch her, to begin the journey all over again. Knowing she was lost in him, in them, was the most exciting thing he'd ever experienced. Each sigh, each moan, each catch of her breath, poured through him like wine.

Whispering her name, he drew her up until they were torso to torso and the pace had to quicken or he would go mad. He found her breasts, drawing them hard into his mouth when she arched back. When she cried out his name, it was like music, with a driving beat that burned in the blood.

He had shown her she was cherished. Now he would show her she was craved.

All she could think was that the storm was coming.

Now it was wild, windy, and the waves lashed against her, threatening to drag her under, into the swirling dark. And she would go, willingly, as long as she could stay with him. So, she clung to him, her mouth desperate on his, her body straining toward each shattering fall. She plunged her hands into his hair, took greedy handfuls of it when he lifted her up to race lips and teeth down her body.

She was drowning, and glorying in it. From some dim

corner of her mind, she heard her own voice begging him for more.

The moonlight was gone. Now there was only the flash of lightning, the bellow of thunder. Still he held her up, assaulting her system, destroying her nerves. She could feel the muscles in his arms quiver when he shifted. And he was under her.

"Look at me." His voice was rough, raw, his fingers dug deep in her hips. "Look at me. I want to see your eyes."

She opened them, and through her wavering vision saw his face. It was tensed, strained. Beautiful. "Come inside me. Now, for God's sake, Shane. I need you."

"Who are you?"

"Yours," she said, then cried out when he lowered her onto him.

She couldn't breathe, was sure her heart had stopped. Her body curved back like a pulled bowstring. Staggered, undone, she stroked her hands up her own quivering body, from belly to breasts, then up over her hair, where they linked as if to anchor her.

He'd never seen anything more beautiful, more arousing, more exciting, than Rebecca lost in pleasure. He watched her head fall back, saw the intensity of the climax that ripped through her. To savor the moment, he held himself still, let her absorb every instant of that first assault of sensation.

Then she began to rock, and that rhythmic demand spurred him to match it. Faster, until speed was all that mattered. When he could no longer wait for her, he clutched her hands, took her and dragged her under with him.

When his mind cleared a little, he realized that the sun had set and the room was soft with shadows. And that he had never in his life felt more content.

He waited until she lay still, her body sprawled limply over his, her breathing almost steady.

"So, where do you want to go now?"

Her laugh started out low in her throat, then rumbled out, the way he liked it best. "Why don't we try that mountain chalet? Snow would be a nice change of pace."

"Good thinking. After dinner, we can—"

"After dinner, hell." Eyes wicked, she lifted her head and began to nibble on him.

"Ah, listen, baby, I…" His breath hitched when she slid down and scraped her teeth over his nipple. "Maybe if you could give me a few minutes to…" Her hand slid lower, much lower. His oath was soft, reverent.

"You've got a reputation to uphold," she murmured, deciding she liked the idea of playing seductress with an exhausted man. "I've heard around town that you're…let's say insatiable."

"Yeah, well. People exaggerate. A little." Ten minutes, he thought. No, five, he told himself, watching her neat, narrow, naked body slither over his. He just needed five minutes to recover. "Listen, why don't we— Man, you're getting good at that."

She looked up, laughing, thrilled with herself. "I have a photographic memory, in case you've forgotten, and a very quick mind."

"You're telling me. Anyway, why don't we take a shower, or maybe a little nap? I don't think I'd be much good to you at the moment." He gulped in air when her busy mouth trailed lower. He wondered if his eyes crossed. "Then again, maybe I could handle it after all."

"I think we can count on it."

They did take a shower, later. She watched Shane stick his head under the spray and groan in appreciation. From behind, she wrapped her arms tight around him and pressed her mouth to his wet back.

"Jeez, woman, do I look like a rabbit?" But he turned to her, always willing to try.

"No." Laughing, she lifted her hands to his streaming hair. "That was to thank you."

"Okay." He dumped shampoo on her hair and scrubbed. "For what?"

She blinked as lather dripped, stinging, into her eyes. "You must have been tired and hungry when you came in. But you wanted to take my mind off things."

"Yeah, it was a hardship, all right. I don't know how I got through it." Amused, he nudged her under the spray.

"I mean it." She sputtered, tried unsuccessfully to wipe her eyes. "You were wonderful. I'll never forget it."

"That's what they all say." He grinned when she turned and gave him a narrow-eyed stare. "Kidding."

"You know, of course, that most accidents in the home occur in the bathroom."

"I've heard that. Gotta watch your step."

"Watch yours."

He put his hands on the tile and boxed her in. "Remember the first time we made love in here? Sure you do, you don't forget anything."

She lifted her brows. "You're not going to distract me that way."

"I could if I wanted." He lowered his mouth to hers. "But if I don't eat, I'm going to fall down."

"How about if I make you soup?"

He looked pained. "Do you have to?"

She sniffed, ducked under his arm and stepped out of the stall. "Cook your own dinner then."

"You know what I've noticed?" Casually he turned off

the shower, reached for a towel. "You pick up things in a snap. I mean, you ask a million questions, figure it out, file it all away. I'd bet you could go out there in the morning and handle the milking without a hitch."

"Don't get any ideas," she warned him, and toweled off, then bundled herself into a robe.

"I've seen you work a crossword puzzle in something under two minutes. That time we went to the market and you bought groceries, you had the money out before the total came up. To the penny."

She shrugged, picked up a comb from the side of the sink and ran it through her hair. "So, I'm good at parlor tricks."

"You could probably build a nuclear reactor in the living room if you put your mind to it. But you can't fry an egg." Watching her, he wrapped the towel around his hips. "Or, more accurately, you don't want to fry an egg, so you don't bother to figure it out."

She flicked a glance over her shoulder. "Caught me. Now what's your point?"

"I'll cook, and you build the nuclear reactors."

She smiled, but he saw the hint of clouds in her eyes. "Rebecca." Patient, he cupped her face in his hands. "Your brain is only one of the very appealing things about you. I like watching you think almost as much as I like watching you when you can't think. Whatever it took to get you to this point doesn't matter. Because you're here."

She let out a sigh. "It's hard to stop wishing you could be normal."

"Baby, you are normal. It doesn't mean you can't be special."

That was so simple, she thought. And so sensible. And so like him. Rising on her toes, she touched her lips to his. "Thanks."

"Anytime."

She blew out a breath. "Okay, let's go downstairs. You can give me my first cooking lesson."

Chapter 11

"I really appreciate the time, Savannah."

Savannah stretched out her long legs and glanced at the tape recorder Rebecca had set on the table between them. "It's no problem. I've got the time."

Rebecca scanned the living area of the cabin. It was bright and cluttered. Layla sat on the rug nearby and made engine noises as she raced a large plastic truck. "A woman with an active son and two kids in diapers can't have much time to spare."

"It only gets crazy around here ten or twelve times a day." Savannah slid a glance toward her daughter. "This seems to be a lull."

"How do you manage?" Rebecca blurted out. "I mean, three children—a new baby, your work, your home, your life."

"The first trick is to enjoy it. And I do. Since they're

not here to get cocky about it, I'll tell you that my men do their share."

"You have a beautiful family." Hearing the wistfulness in her own voice, Rebecca shook it off. "Let me explain what I'm after. The book I'm working on deals with Antietam specifically, the battle, of course, but the angles I'm most interested in are the legends that surround this area, and personal experiences."

"Ghost stories."

"To some extent. The MacKade connection," Rebecca continued. "Regan and Rafe. They were both drawn to the inn, shared extraordinary experiences. Rafe came back to town for the inn, and Regan was drawn to it through him. The inn also played a major part in Cassie's and Devin's lives and their relationship. I've interviewed each of them separately, and each corroborates the other's feelings and experiences. Some of those experiences were shared, some separate, but all seem to touch on the story of the two corporals."

"And you want me to tell you mine."

"Yes. I interviewed Jared this morning in his office. Oh, and I wanted to tell you I loved your paintings. Especially the one of the woods."

"Thanks. It was—is—the woods for us. If you want to use the word *connection,* I suppose that's ours." Savannah narrowed her eyes as she thought back. "The inn has a very strong pull. What Regan and Rafe have done there, and with Cassie and Devin living there, it's, I don't know, funneled off a great deal of the sadness. It was a sad place for a long time. But Regan tells me you tracked down some information on the Confederate corporal."

"Franklin Gray, yes."

"You said that Abigail had him identified and sent home

to his family." Thinking of it, Savannah nodded. "That was very brave of her. And very kind."

"Abigail had children of her own. She must have imagined what that boy's mother would have felt. The never knowing. The Yankee boy's family would never have known. The other corporal…" Rebecca sighed, with just a hint of frustration. "That's all I've ever been able to pin down on him so far—he fought for the Union and was a corporal. At least that's the information that's been passed down through the MacKades."

"What the MacKades did for that wounded boy was brave and kind, too," Savannah commented. "But you need to find him, don't you? To learn his name, see his grave. To settle it."

"I suppose I do. They were killed so long ago, yet it seems…unfinished. They fought and died at each other's hands, two ordinary young men who never really lived. But their deaths affected so many other people. And it seems they still do. Isn't that part of what you feel in the woods, Savannah?"

Savannah tilted her head. "What do you consider the strongest emotions, Rebecca?"

"Love and hate. Everything else stems from that."

"Yeah." Pleased, Savannah smiled. "That's good, for an egghead. Anyway, that's what I felt in the woods. Love, I suppose that was for Jared, and for home. Hate—it was more the fear and violence that hatred leaves behind. Why were we both drawn there, and drawn most strongly to the spot where those two young boys fought more than a century ago? Connections?" She lifted her shoulders. "A need to settle it, or soften it, or understand it."

"And did you?"

Savannah lifted a brow. "Did Jared tell you that the first time we made love was in those woods?"

"No. No, he didn't."

"He probably thought it would embarrass you." A slow, warm smile, utterly female, curved Savannah's lips. "The cabin was empty, there was a perfectly good bed upstairs, but we went to the woods. Because it was right for us, because we were...connected. Because love heals."

Rebecca thought of Shane and his tender gift to her. "Yes, it does."

"I've sat there and I've heard the rustle of leaves under boots, heard the shuddering breaths of frightened boys, the war cries, the crash of bayonets. I heard them before I'd heard the story."

Rebecca's eyes narrowed with new interest. "You didn't know about the two corporals when you came here?"

"No. Jared told me about it later, but I already knew. No, felt it."

"Do you consider yourself psychic?"

Now Savannah chuckled. "No more than anyone." A fretful wail had her glancing toward the stairs. "Feeding time," she murmured. "Be right back."

"Baby," Layla said as her mother headed upstairs. Toddling over, she handed Rebecca a doll. "Baby."

"Pretty baby." Understanding, Rebecca kissed the doll, then the child. "Almost as pretty as you."

With a grin that had the MacKade dimple winking, Layla squeezed the doll fiercely, then passed it back. "Mama." She danced in place, then squealed with delight when Savannah came down with Miranda fussing in her arms. "Baby! My baby!"

"Come and see," Savannah invited, settling down. Her

free hand brushed over Layla's dark hair as the child bent over the infant.

"Baby, baby, baby," she cooed, placing wet kisses over Miranda's red, furious face.

"The baby's hungry," Savannah explained, and rolled her eyes at Rebecca. "And boy, does she let you know it!"

Rebecca watched as Savannah chattered with both of her daughters, fingers expertly unfastening buttons. The baby rooted, one tiny hand kneading a breast while her busy mouth found the nipple.

The envy, pure and primal, that swarmed through Rebecca shocked her. Because of it, she swallowed the questions that sprang to her mind. How does it feel to feed your child from your own body? Is it the intimacy of it that makes your eyes go soft?

"Would you rather finish this later?"

"No, this is fine."

"Regan looks like a Madonna when she nurses," Rebecca murmured. "You don't." Savannah's lifted brow had her laughing a little. "That's not an insult. I bought these tarot cards—part of my research. The Empress is a card of fertility, female power. That's what you look like."

"I can live with that."

"Well." Taking a deep breath, Rebecca got back to work. She asked her questions, moving Savannah from generalities to specifics, then moving her on to more esoteric matters. By the time she was finished, the baby was sleeping again, her mouth milky and slack.

"I'd like to ask a question now." Savannah rose to tuck Miranda into a cradle beside her chair.

"Sure."

"What exactly do you intend to do with all this? A book,

I know, but I don't quite understand how you'll handle what I've told you. What we've all told you."

"I want to focus on the experiences of you three couples. And the influence of the legends on your lives. It's intriguing, and it's romantic, the way the past overlapped your present, and your future. Six people who've become three families," she explained, hands gesturing to illustrate. "Three families who are essentially one family. All of your relationships were affected by what happened here long before any of you were born. So, how much does the past influence us? How much does the power of place, the strength of who and what was, play on those open to accept it?"

"And you'll add your data to that, your evidence and your theories."

"That's right."

"And your reputation?" Savannah turned back. "What are all those institutes and the suits who run them going to say about Dr. Knight's interest in the occult?"

"Some will shake their heads and think it's too bad a brilliant young scientist lost her mind. Others…well, there are some excellent and serious studies being done on the paranormal at some of those institutes. And—" she smiled "—since I'm doing this for me, I don't really care what they think."

Savannah sat again, gathered Layla up in her arms. "Why haven't you talked to Shane?"

"Excuse me?"

"You said you'd interviewed all of us, and intend to use all of us in this book. But you never mentioned Shane."

"He's not comfortable with it." Rebecca busied herself tucking her tape recorder back into her bag. "He's been very tolerant of what I'm doing, but he doesn't like it. In any case, he doesn't fit into the equation. Six people, three couples. The connection."

Nodding, Savannah ran her tongue around her teeth. "You know, math isn't my strong point, but I figure eight people, four couples." She gave Layla a pat as the child wiggled down from her lap and went off to look for other entertainment. "What about your connection? You, Shane, the farm."

"It doesn't really apply."

"Of course it does. It's obvious you're in love with him."

"Is it?" Rebecca managed to say, relatively calmly. "You're mistaking attraction, affection and a physical relationship for— Hell. Are you sure you're not psychic?"

Poor thing, Savannah mused, sympathizing with any woman who'd tumbled for a MacKade. Poor, lucky thing. "You're a fairly controlled sort of woman, Rebecca. You don't advertise your feelings on your face. But I see things." Savannah waved a hand. "I'm an artist, and I have shamans for ancestors. You can chalk it up to that, or to the fact that one woman in love often recognizes another."

Rebecca looked down at her hands. "I don't know whether to be relieved or worried with that rundown."

"I like you. I don't like everyone. I'm selective. Actually, I didn't think I'd like you at all." Comfortable, she stretched out her legs again. "A professional intellectual, scientist, all those initials after your name. I got my high school equivalency when I was carrying Layla, and when Regan talked of you, all I saw was this enormous brain wearing horn-rim glasses."

The image had Rebecca snorting out a laugh. She'd come a good ways, she thought, when such a description brought amusement rather than pain. "If you sketch me that way, I'll hang it in my apartment."

"That's a deal. Anyway, I did like you. Do like you. If I'd sat down and tried to piece together the woman who would suit Shane, she wouldn't have been anything like you. And I'd have been wrong. The farmer and the savant." The phrase made Savannah grin. Poor Shane, she thought. Poor, lucky Shane. "In this case, it works. What are you going to do about it?"

"Enjoy it. While it lasts."

"And that's enough?"

"It's more than I've had before." There would be a price, of course, she thought. She was willing to pay it. "I'm a practical woman, Savannah."

"Maybe. But how brave are you, and how dedicated? Are you really going to write a book, take all that time, put in all that effort and leave out a piece of it? Your piece, and Shane's? Can you ignore that connection?"

Could she? Rebecca asked herself as she walked back to the farm through the woods. For the book, yes. She could and would do that for Shane. Personally, she'd accepted that the connection between them would remain with her forever.

Yet she could leave, would leave. It would hurt, but she would survive it. Intellectually, she knew no one really died of a broken heart. Emotionally, she suspected some could.

But it would be easier to live when she'd had love than it had been to exist without ever knowing it.

She knew her Greek tragedies well. There was always pleasure, and there was always payment.

Her bill, so to speak, was coming due, she knew. If Savannah could read her heart so easily, others would. Shane might, and then the payment could become too high to bear.

He meant too much to her for her to put him in an awkward position. She would have to start considering that first step away.

Tomorrow was the anniversary of the battle. She felt it important, even imperative, that she stay on the farm through the day, and perhaps the next. Then it would probably be best if she moved back to Regan's. A few days, a short transitory period before she went back to New York.

She stepped through the trees and looked at the farm. There was smoke coming out of the chimney from the living room fireplace. It was just chilly enough to warrant one. She could see the house itself, strong stone, painted wood, the silos and sheds and buildings.

It would, she realized, be almost as wrenching to leave the place as it would be to leave Shane. She'd been happier here than she'd ever been in her life. She'd found love here.

So she would be grateful, rather than regretful.

Walk away, a voice nagged in her brain, *rather than risk.*

Suddenly chilled, she rubbed her arms and began to cross the fallow field.

She saw the car zip up the curve of the lane and park at the side of the house. A quick, friendly toot of the horn, and the dogs were scrambling to greet the redhead who climbed out.

The air was clear enough to carry the woman's laugh to where Rebecca stopped. And the distance wasn't so great that she couldn't see Shane's lightning grin as he came around the side of the house to meet the woman.

Jealousy ebbed and flowed, ebbed and flowed, in a nasty, unpredictable tide as Rebecca watched them embrace easily. As the woman's arms stayed linked around Shane's neck.

Oh, no, you don't, she warned silently. He's still mine. He's mine until I walk away.

They stayed close together as they spoke, and there was more laughter, another quick kiss, before the woman stepped away and got back into her car.

Shane ruffled both dogs, straightened, waved. Rebecca knew the moment he spotted her in the field, and began to walk toward the house again. The car darted down the lane between them, then disappeared around the curve.

"Hey." He tucked his thumbs in his front pockets. "How's Savannah?"

"Fine. I had a chance to look at some of her paintings. They're wonderful."

"Yeah." With his instincts warning him to proceed with caution, Shane tried to read Rebecca's face. "Ah, that was Frannie Spader. You met Frannie."

"I thought I recognized her." Because they wanted attention, and because it was a good ploy, Rebecca bent to pet the dogs.

"She just dropped by."

"So I saw. I want to transcribe this interview."

"Rebecca." He touched her arm to stop her. "There's nothing going on here. She's a friend. She stopped by."

It was pure self-defense that had her arching a brow. "Why do you feel you have to clarify that?"

"Because I— Look, Fran and I used to be... We used to be," he finished, furious with himself. "Now we're not, and haven't been since...well, since you came to town. We're friends."

Oh, it was satisfying to watch him squirm. "Do you think I require an explanation?"

"No. Yes." Damn it. He imagined himself strolling along and coming across Rebecca hugging another man. Someone would have to die. "I don't want you to get the wrong idea, that's all."

"Do you think I have the wrong idea?"

"Will you cut that out?" he demanded, and paced away, then back again. "I hate when you do that. I really hate it."

"When I do what?"

"Make everything a question. How do you feel, what do you think?" He whirled back to her, eyes shooting sparks of temper. "Damn it, if you had a question, it should have been 'What in the hell were you doing kissing another woman?'"

"Do you feel a show of jealousy would be appropriate?" When he only scowled at her, she shrugged. "I'm sorry I can't accommodate you. Clearly, you had a life before I came here, and you'll have one after I'm gone."

"That's it. Throw the past in my face."

"Is that what you think I'm doing?"

He snarled. "Can't you fight like a regular person?"

"When there's something to fight about. Your friends are your business. And as I have no idea how many of those... friends I might run into every time I go into town, it would be remarkably unproductive of me to worry about it."

His brain was screaming out for him to let it go, but his mouth just refused to obey. "Look, Rebecca, if I'd slept with as many women as some people think, I'd never have gotten out of bed. And I haven't had sex with every woman I've gone out with, either. I don't— Why the hell am I telling you this?"

"That was going to be my next question. And, in my opinion, what you're doing is projecting—your feelings, your anticipated reaction to a situation, onto me. Added to that is a sense of guilt, and annoyance resulting from that guilt. In transferring the annoyance from yourself to me, you—"

"Shut up." His eyes as volatile as a storm at sea, he grabbed her face in his hands. "She came by to see if I wanted to go out later. I told her no. She asked if I was involved with you. I told her yes, very involved. We talked for another minute, she said she'd see me around. That's it. Satisfied?"

Her heart was tripping lightly, quickly, in her chest. But her voice was cool, and faintly curious. "Did I give you the impression that I was dissatisfied?"

His eyes narrowed, flashed. Rebecca found it very satisfying. Almost as satisfying as his frustrated oath as he turned on his heel and stalked away.

Nice job, Dr. Knight, she told herself. She didn't think Shane was going to be kissing anyone else for a while. Humming to herself, she strolled into the house.

She really did have work to do, she thought, and patted one of her video monitors as she passed. But she could take just a moment to savor the sense of smugness.

The poor guy had been so predictable. Classic reactions. Alarm at the thought that something, however innocent, could be interpreted badly. The added weight of his infamous career as a ladies' man. Not a womanizer, she mused. One day she might explain to him the difference between a man who loved and appreciated woman and one who used them.

And then, she thought, snickering on her way to the kitchen, his sense of unease, then irritation at her reasonable reaction. Direct hit on the ego.

It was so much more interesting to study the games men and women played with each other when you were in the middle of the field than when you were observing from the stands.

She might just do a paper on it, she mused, going to the window. Once she'd carved out enough emotional distance.

By then she would know not only what it was like to fall in love, to be in love, but what it felt like to lose at love.

One day she might find the courage to ask him what she had meant to him, what the time they had spent together had meant to him in the scheme of things. Yeah, she thought, amused at herself. She might find the courage for that in a decade or two.

Telling herself it was now that mattered, and wondering if the little incident would garner her more flowers, she decided to try her hand at cooking dinner solo.

It was really all just formulas, after all. And she had Regan's formula—no, recipe, she reminded herself—for fried chicken in her bag. Digging it out, she read it through once and committed it to memory. Since Shane's kitchen didn't run to aprons, she tucked a dishcloth in the waistband of her slacks, and got down to some serious experimenting.

It was actually soothing, she discovered as she coated chicken with herbed flour. At least on a casual level. She imagined that if anyone had to plan and cook and deal with the time and mess every day, day after day, meal after meal, it would be tedious.

But, as a hobby, it had its points. If she could just keep this particular hobby from becoming a vocation, as so many of her others had, she'd be just fine.

When she had chicken frying in hot oil in a cast-iron skillet, she stepped back and congratulated herself. It smelled good, it sounded good, it looked good. Therefore, according to basic laws, it should taste good.

Wouldn't Shane be surprised, and perhaps even more baffled, when he came in and found dinner cooking?

It was milking time, she thought, poking at the crisping chicken with a kitchen fork. And night was coming earlier, as the days shortened toward the still-distant winter...

* * *

Would she see the camp fires burning if she looked out the window? The soldiers were so close, close and waiting for dawn and the battle.

She wished John would come in. Once he was in and the animals were settled, they could shut up the house. They would be safe here. They had to be safe here. She couldn't lose another child. Couldn't live through it. Nor could John. She pressed a hand over the one covering her womb, as if to protect it from any threat, any harm. She desperately hoped it would be a son. Not to replace the one they'd lost. Johnnie could never be replaced, never be forgotten. But if the babe she carried was a son, it would somewhat ease the worst of John's grief.

He suffered. He suffered so, and there was no comfort for it. She could love him, tend him, share the grief, but she couldn't end it. The girls tried, and God knew they were a joy. But Johnnie was gone. Every day the war went on was another painful reminder of that loss.

Maybe it would end here. She turned the chicken in the pan, as she'd done so often in her life. Would that be some sort of justice, for this horrible war to end here, where her son had been born?

Was the man who had killed her son out there, right now, sitting, waiting, in the Union camp? Who would he kill tomorrow? Or would it be his blood that would seep into the land she had walked over for so many years?

Why wouldn't they go away? Just go away and leave the living in peace with their sorrows...

Hot grease popped out of the pan and seared the side of Rebecca's hand. She barely felt it as she staggered backward. Emotions, thoughts, words, sounds, reeled in her head.

Possession, she thought, dimly. This was possession. And, for the first time in her life, she fainted.

Primed to fight, Shane burst through the door. "And another thing—" he began, before he saw Rebecca crumpled on the kitchen floor, before his heart stopped.

He streaked forward, dropped down beside her to drag her into her arms. "Rebecca." His hands were running over her face, chafing her wrists. "Rebecca, come on now. Snap out of it." Terrified into clumsiness, he rocked her, kissed her, begged her. Until her eyes fluttered open.

"Shane."

"That's right." Relief poured through him in a flood. "Just lie still, baby, till you feel better."

"I was her," she murmured, fighting off the fog. "I was her for a minute. I have to check my equipment."

"The hell with your equipment." It was pitifully easy to hold her in place. "Do as you're told and lie still. Did you hit your head? Are you hurt anywhere?"

"I don't... I don't think so. What happened?"

"You tell me. I walked in and you were on the floor."

"Good Lord." She took a deep, steadying breath and let her head rest in the crook of his arm. "I fainted. Imagine that."

"I don't have to imagine it. You just scared ten years off my life." Now, naturally, there was fury to coat over the fear. "What the hell are you doing fainting? Did you eat today? Damn it, you never eat enough to keep a bird alive. You don't get enough sleep, either. Down four or five hours, then you're up prowling around, or clacking away at that stupid computer."

He was working himself up into a rare state, but he

couldn't stop. "Well, that's going to change. You're going to start taking care of yourself. You're nothing but bones and nerve. Didn't they teach you anything about basic bodily needs in those fancy schools? Or don't you think they apply to you?"

She let him run on until her head stopped spinning. He was ranting about taking her to the doctor, checking her into the hospital, getting vitamins. Finally, she held up a hand and put it over his mouth.

"I've never fainted before in my life, and since I didn't care for it, I don't intend to make it a habit. Now, if you'll calm down a minute and let me up, the chicken's burning."

He said something incredible and unlikely when applied to burning chicken, but he did haul her into a chair. Moving quickly, he flicked off the heat. "What the hell were you doing?"

"I was cooking. I think it was going to be fairly successful, too. Maybe it can be salvaged."

He grunted, turned to the tap and ran a glass of water for her. "Drink."

She started to tell him he needed it more than she, then decided against it. Obediently she sipped water. "I was cooking," she said again, "and letting my mind wander. Then the thoughts weren't mine any longer. They were very clear—very personal, you could say. But they weren't mine. They were Sarah's."

Ice skidded up his spine. "You're just letting yourself get too wrapped up in all this stuff."

"Shane, I'm a sensible woman. A rational one. I know what happened here. She was cooking chicken." With a shake of her head, Rebecca set the glass on the table. "Isn't it odd that I would have decided to try Regan's recipe tonight, September 16? Sarah was cooking chicken the night before the battle."

"So now you know what they ate."

"Yes," she said, facing down his sarcasm. "Now I know. She was frying it, worried about her family, thinking of her son and the baby she carried. Wondering who would die in the morning. Soldiers were camped not far from here, waiting for dawn. She was frying chicken, and her husband was out with the animals. She wanted him to come in, to come inside so that they could close it all out and just be together. She worried about him. She'd have done anything to ease his mind."

"I think you're working too hard," Shane said carefully. "And I think you've let the fact that the anniversary is to-morrow influence you."

Steady again, she rose. "You know that's not true. You know what's here and you've decided not to face it. That's your choice, and I respect that. Even though I know some nights you dream, and the dreams trouble you, I respect your decision and your privacy. I expect you to show my work and my needs the same respect."

"My dreams are my business."

"I've just said so. I'm not asking you to tell me any-thing."

"No, you never ask, Rebecca." He jammed his hands into his pockets. "You just wait and whittle a person down with waiting. I don't want any part of this."

"Do you want me to go?"

When he didn't answer, she braced herself, spoke calmly. "I suppose I'll have to ask. It's important to me to be here in the morning. I can't give you clear, rational data on why, only my feelings. I'd appreciate it very much if you'd let me stay, at least another day."

"No one's asked you to go, have they?" He snapped the words out, furious with himself now. Why should he panic at the thought of her packing up? There had never been any promises. He didn't make them, didn't want them. "You want to stay, stay—but leave me out of it. I've got some work to finish up, then I'm going out."

"All right."

He wanted desperately for her to ask him where, and would have snapped her head off if she questioned him. Of course, she didn't, so he couldn't. All he could do was walk out, when all he wanted to do was stay.

Chapter 12

He thought about getting drunk. It wasn't a problem-solver, but it did have its points. It was a shame he wasn't in the mood for it. Arguing with someone was a better idea, and since Rebecca wasn't going to accommodate him, he headed for town, and Devin.

He'd always been able to count on Devin for a good fight.

Shane figured it was a bonus when he found not only Devin in the sheriff's office, but Rafe, too.

"Hey, we were just talking about getting together a poker game." Rafe greeted him with a slap on the shoulder. "Got any money?"

"Got a beer around here?"

"This is a place of law and order," Devin said solemnly, then jerked his head toward the back room. "Couple in the cooler. You up for a game?"

"Maybe." Shane stalked into the back room. "I can do

what I want when I want, can't I? I don't have to check with a woman, like you guys do."

Devin and Rafe exchanged looks. "I'll give Jared a call," Rafe said, picking up the phone as Shane came back in guzzling beer.

While Rafe dialed the phone and murmured into it, Devin propped his feet on his desk. "So, what's Rebecca up to?"

"She doesn't have to check with me, either."

"Ah, had a little spat, did you?" Enjoying the idea, Devin crossed his arms behind his head. "She kick you out?"

"It's my damn house," Shane shot back. "And Reasonable Rebecca doesn't spat. She changes," he went on, gesturing with the beer. "Right in front of your eyes. One minute she's tough and smart and cocky. The next she's soft and lost and so sweet you'd kill anybody who'd try to hurt her. Then she's cool— Oh, she's so cool, and controlled, and—" He gulped down beer. "Analytical. How the hell are you supposed to keep up?"

"Well," Devin mused, "you can't call her boring."

"Anything but. She thinks she is, at least some of the time. Hell, I don't know what she thinks she is." Shane brooded into the bottle. "Just today, she comes across Frannie kissing me. Does she get mad, does she start a fight, accuse me of anything? No. Not that it wasn't perfectly innocent, but the point is that if you're sleeping with somebody you shouldn't like the idea of them kissing somebody else. Right?"

Rafe had hung up the phone and was watching his brother carefully. "I'd agree with that. You agree with that, Dev?"

"Pretty much, yeah."

Pleased with the unity of spirit, Shane lifted the bottle

again. "There you go. But Dr. Knight, she's as cool as you please. Studying me like I'm a smear on a lab slide again. I hate when she does that."

"Who wouldn't?" Rafe said, and sat down to enjoy himself.

Soothed by brotherly understanding, Shane finished off the first beer, then popped open the second. "And another thing—how come she doesn't ask where all this is leading? Tell me that. Women are always asking where all this is leading. That's how you keep things from getting too intense, by setting down the cards, you know."

"Is that how?" Devin smiled serenely.

"Sure. But she doesn't ask." He chugged down beer. That was why things had gotten so intense. He needed to believe that. "And you'd think she'd get in the way, wouldn't you? You'd think she'd get in the damn way, living there, but she just sort of fits."

"Does she?" Devin grinned and winked at Rafe.

"Sort of. I mean, there she is at breakfast in the morning, and she's always got something to talk about. She works in the kitchen most of the time, but she never gets in the way, and you start expecting her to be there."

Rafe looked around as the door opened and Jared walked in with a large brown bag. Jared set it on Devin's desk and took out a six-pack. "We playing here?"

"Maybe later." To keep the interruption at a minimum, Devin gestured Jared to a chair. "Shane's on a roll."

"Yeah." Jared looked at Shane. "What's he rolling about?"

"Rebecca. You were saying?"

"The bedroom smells like her," Shane muttered. "She doesn't leave any of her stuff laying around, and it still smells like her. Soap, and that stuff she rubs on her skin."

"Uh-oh," Jared said, and helped himself to a beer.

"You know, her parents sent her to boarding school when she was six. Practically a baby. She never had a chance to be a kid. Sometimes when she laughs, she looks a little surprised by the sound of it." He paused, thought about it. "She's got a great laugh."

Jared turned to Rafe. "She kick him out?"

"He says not."

"It's my damn house," Shane reminded them all. "My house, my land. I'm the one who says what goes on around there. If I don't like that stupid, idiotic, ridiculous equipment of hers, then that's it. I don't like that she's wrapped herself up in all this bull, and she's wearing herself down. I'm not coming in and finding her in a heap on the floor again."

"What?" Amusement fled as Devin straightened in his chair. "What happened?"

"She fainted—far as I can tell. She says she had an encounter with our great-grandmother." He downed beer to wash both worry and unease out of his system. "Yeah, right. They're both frying chicken the night before the battle. I'm not getting involved in that."

"Is she all right?" Rafe asked.

"Would I be here if she wasn't?" He raked his fingers through his hair and fought to block out the image of her pale, small, still form on the kitchen floor. But he couldn't. "She scared the hell out of me, damn it. Damn it." He squeezed his eyes shut for a moment, rubbed the heel of his hand over his aching heart. "I can't take her being hurt. I can't stand it. The woman's ripping at me."

With an effort, he pulled himself back, took another gulp from the bottle. "She bounces back," he muttered. "I've never seen anybody bounce back like she does. She's fine now, dandy, back in control. She's not pushing me into getting hooked up with that business. She's not going to hook me into anything."

"Brother." With some sympathy, Jared opened another beer and passed it to Shane. "You're already hooked."

"Like hell."

"At a guess, how many times do you think about her in a given day?"

"I don't know." Annoyed, Shane decided getting drunk wasn't such a bad idea after all. "I don't count."

In lawyer mode now, Jared briskly cross-examined the witness. "Anyone else you've thought about that much, that often?"

"So what? She's living with me. You think about somebody who's in the same house day and night."

Rafe studied his nails. "It's just sex."

"The hell it is." Like a bullet, Shane was out of his chair, fists ready. "She's not just a warm body." He caught himself, and his brother's sly grin. "I'm not an animal."

"That's a switch." Unconcerned, Rafe sampled his own beer. "How many other women have you wanted since Rebecca came along?"

Zip. Zero. Zilch. Terror. "That's not the point. The point is…" He sat again, brooded into his beer. "I forgot."

"The point is," Devin said, picking up the threads, "you've lost your balance and you're falling fast."

"He's already hit," Jared put in. "He just doesn't have the sense to know it. But, being a sensible woman, Rebecca might not fall so easy, especially for you."

"What the hell's wrong with me?"

"As I was saying," Jared continued. "She's got a life in New York, a career, interests. You might have a problem keeping her from wriggling away. You'll have to be pretty slick to convince her to marry you."

Shane choked, coughed and gulped more beer. "You're crazy. I'm not marrying anybody."

Rafe only smiled. "Wanna bet?"

Because Shane was terribly pale, Devin took pity on him. "Have another beer, pal. You can bunk in the back room and sleep it off."

It seemed like an excellent suggestion.

She didn't sleep. It wasn't only because Shane wasn't there and the house seemed to come alive around her. It was the wait for morning, through the longest night of her life.

She worked. It had always helped her through crises, small and large. She packed. The systematic removal of her clothing, the neat folding of it into suitcases, was a sign that she was ready to go on with the rest of her life.

If she had a worry, it was that she and Shane would part on uneasy terms. That she didn't want. When he came back, she told herself, she would try to put things back into perspective and achieve some kind of balance.

But he didn't come back, and the hours passed slowly to dawn.

When the sun had just begun to rise, and the gray mist hung over the land, swallowing the barn, she stepped outside.

It was impossible for her to believe, at that moment, that anyone wouldn't feel what she felt. The fear, the anticipation, the rage and the sorrow.

It took so little imagination for her to see the infantry marching through that soft curtain of fog, bodies and bayonets tearing it so that it swirled back and reformed. The muffled sound of boots on earth, the dull glint of brass and steel.

That first burst from the cannons, those first cries.

Then there would be hell.

"What are you doing out here?"

Rebecca jolted, stared. It was Shane, stepping through that river of mist. He looked pale, gritty-eyed and angry enough that she resisted the need to rush forward and hold him.

"I didn't hear you come home."

"Just got here." She hadn't slept. He could see the fatigue in her eyes, the shadows under them, and detested the stab of guilt. "You're shivering. You're barefoot, for God's sake. Go back inside. Go to bed."

"You look tired," she said, knowing her voice was more brittle than cool.

"I'm hung over," he said flatly. "Some of us humans get that way when we drink too much. Aren't you going to ask me where I've been, who I've been with?"

She lifted a hand, rubbed it gently over her heart. It still beat, she thought vaguely, even when it was shattered. "Are you trying to hurt me?"

"Maybe I am. Maybe I'm trying to see if I can."

She nodded and turned back toward the house. "You can."

"Rebecca—" But she was already closing the door behind her, leaving him feeling like something slimy that had crawled from under a rock. Cursing her, he headed toward the milking parlor.

They stayed out of each other's way through the morning. Rather than work in the kitchen, she closed herself in the guest room and focused fiercely on the job at hand. So they would part at odds, she thought. Perhaps that was best. It might be easier, in the long run, to hide behind resentment and anger.

From the window in her room, she saw him. He didn't seem to be working. Marking time, she decided, until she cleared out. Well, he would have to wait a little longer. She wasn't leaving until the day was over.

"Where are you, Sarah?" she murmured, pacing the room, which was beginning to feel like a cell. "You wanted me here. I know you wanted me here. For what?"

As she passed the window, she looked out again. He was walking across the yard now, past the kitchen garden, where he had late tomatoes, greens, squash. He stopped, checked something. For ripeness, she supposed.

It was painful to look at him. Yet too painful to contemplate looking away. Had she really believed she could take the experience of love and loss as some sort of adventure—or, worse, as an experiment on the human condition? That she could examine it, analyze, perhaps write about it?

No, she would never, never get over him.

When he straightened from the little garden and walked toward one of the stone outbuildings, she turned away. No, she wouldn't wait until the end of the day after all. That was too cruel. She would speak to him again, one last time, and then she would go.

She'd send for the equipment, she told herself as she went downstairs. She would make her exit with dignity, albeit with dispatch. To Regan's, she told herself, breathing carefully. To run back to New York just now would look cowardly. It was pointless to make him feel bad, to let him know he'd had her heart and broken it.

Let him think that it had simply been an experience, one that was over now, one they could both remember fondly.

She was never coming back. At the base of the stairs, she stopped to press her hand to her mouth. Never coming back to this town, this battleground, this house. Though she would be in full retreat, she would not run.

She never glanced at the monitors, the gauges. Down the hall, she trailed her fingers over wood and paint, as if to absorb the texture into memory.

At the kitchen doorway, the power punched like a fist...

Stew cooking. The distant pop of gunfire...

Weak, she leaned against the wall as the door opened.

She knew it was Shane. The rational part of her mind recognized the shape of him, the stance, even the smell. But with some inner eye she saw a man carrying a bleeding boy....

My God, my God, John. Is he dead?

Not yet.

Put him on the table. I need towels. Oh, so much blood. Hurry. He's so young. He's just a boy.

Like Johnnie.

So like Johnnie. Young, bleeding, dying. The uniform was filthy and wet with blood. The new stripe of his rank was still bright on the shoulder of the tattered jacket. There was a rustle of worn paper from a letter in the inside pocket as she peeled the uniform away to see the horror of his wounds.

Just a boy. Too many dying boys...

Rebecca saw it, could see the scene in the kitchen perfectly. The blood, the boy, those who tried to help him. There, the letter in Sarah's hands, the paper worn where it had been creased and recreased, read and reread. The words seemed to leap out at her...

* * *

Dear Cameron...

"They couldn't save him," Shane said carefully. "They tried."

"Yes." After the breath she'd been holding was expelled, Rebecca pressed her lips together. "They tried so hard."

"At first, he only saw the uniform. The enemy. He was glad that a Yankee had died there. Then he saw the face, and he saw his son in it. So he brought him home. It was all he could do."

"It was the right thing to do, the human thing."

"They wanted that boy to live, Rebecca."

"I know." Her breath shuddered out, shuddered in. "They fought as hard as they could. All the rest of that day, through the night, sitting with him. Praying. Listening to him, when he could speak. Shane, there was too much love in this house for them not to try, not to fight for that one young boy's life."

"But they lost him." Eyes grim, Shane stepped forward. "And it was like losing their son again."

"He didn't die alone, or forgotten."

"But they buried him in an unmarked grave."

"She was afraid." Tears trembled out, rolling down Rebecca's cheeks. "She was afraid for her husband, for her family. Nothing meant more to her. If anyone found out that boy had died here, and John a Rebel sympathizer who'd lost a son to the Yankees, they might have taken John from her. She couldn't have stood it. She begged him not to tell, to dig the grave at night so no one would ever know. Oh, she grieved for that boy, for the mother who would never know where or when or how he died. She read the letter."

"Yeah, then they buried the letter from his mother with him."

"There was no envelope, Shane. No address. Nothing to tell them where he had come from, or who was waiting for him to come home. Just the two pages, the writing close and crowded as if she'd wanted to jam every thought, every feeling into them." A breath shuddered out. "I saw it. I could read it, just as Sarah did... Dear Cameron."

Shane's eyes went dark, his stomach muscles tightened, twisted. "That's my middle name. Cameron was my grandfather's name. Cameron James MacKade, John and Sarah's second son. He was born six months after the Battle of Antietam." Shane took a steadying breath. "The name's come down through the MacKades ever since. Every generation has a Cameron."

"They named their child after the boy they couldn't save." Helplessly Rebecca rubbed the tears from her cheeks with the flats of her hands. "They didn't forget him, Shane. They did everything they could."

"And then they buried him in an unmarked grave."

"Don't hate her for it. She loved her husband, and was afraid for him."

"I don't hate her for it." Suddenly weary, Shane scrubbed his hands over his face. "But it's my life now, Rebecca, my land. I can't change what happened, and I'm sick of being haunted by it."

She offered a hand. "Do you know where he's buried?"

"No, I've always shut that part out." As he'd tried, most of his life, to shut it all out. All those wavering memories, those misty dreams. "I never wanted any part of this."

"Why did you come in now, tell me now?"

"I don't know, exactly." Resigned, he dropped his hands. "I saw him, beside the smokehouse. Bleeding, asking me to help him." He drew a long breath. "It's not the first time. I couldn't not come in, not tell you anymore. You're part of it. You knew that all along."

"He's buried in the meadow," she murmured. "Wildflowers grow there." She reached for his hand again, tightened her fingers on his. "Come with me."

They walked out toward the meadow, through the bright wash of sun. The mountains were alive with color, and the flowers underfoot were going to seed. There was the smell of grass and growing things. When she stopped, the tears still fell quietly.

For a moment, she could say nothing, could only stare down at the ground where she had once dropped her first clutch of wildflowers.

"They did their best for him. Not far from here, another man killed a boy simply because of the color of his uniform. These people tried to save one, despite it." She leaned into Shane when he circled her shoulders with his arm. "They cared."

"Yeah, they cared. They still can't leave him here alone."

"We make parks out of our battlefields to remember," she said quietly. "It's important to remember. He needs a marker, Shane. They would have given him one, if they could have."

Could it be as simple as that? he wondered. And as human? "All right." He stopped questioning and nodded. "We'll give him one. And maybe we'll all have some peace."

"There's more love than grief here," she murmured. "And it is yours, Shane—your home, your land, your heritage. Whatever lives on through it, through you, is admirable. You should be very proud of what you have, and what you are."

"I always felt as though they were pushing at me. I resented it." Yet it had eased now, standing there with her in the sun, on his land. "I didn't see why I should be the one to be weighed down with their problems, their emotions." He looked over the fields, the hills, and felt most of his weariness pass. "Maybe I do now. It's always been more mine than any of my brothers'. More even than it was my father's, my mother's. We all loved it, we all worked it, but—"

"But you stayed, because you loved it more." She rose on her toes and kissed him gently. "And you understand it more. You're a good man, Shane. And a good farmer. I won't forget you."

Before he realized what she was doing, she'd turned away. "What are you talking about? Where are you going?"

"I thought you might like some time alone here." She smiled, brushing at the tears drying on her cheeks. "It seems a personal moment to me, and I really have to finish getting my things together."

"What things?"

"My things." She backed away as she spoke. "Now that we've settled this, I'm going to stay with Regan for a few days before I go back to New York. I haven't had as much time to visit with her as I'd planned."

She might as well have hit him over the head with a hammer. The quiet relief he'd begun to feel at facing what had haunted him was rudely, nastily swallowed up by total panic.

"You're leaving? Just like that? Experiment's over, see you around?"

"I'm only going to Regan's, for a few days. I've already stayed here longer than I originally intended, and I'm sure you'd like your house back. I'm very grateful for everything."

"You're grateful," he repeated. "For everything?"

"Yes, very." She was terrified her smile would waver. Quick, was all she could think, get away quick. "I'd like to stay in touch, if you don't mind. See how things are going with you."

"We can exchange cards at Christmas."

"I think we can do better." Through sheer grit, she kept that easy smile on her face. "Farm boy, it's been an experience."

Mouth slack with shock, he watched her walk away. She was dumping him. She'd just put him through the most emotional, most wrenching, most stunning experience of his life, and she was just walking away.

Well, fine, he thought, scowling at her retreating back. Dandy. That made it clean. He didn't want complications, or big, emotional parting scenes.

The hell he didn't.

She'd reached the kitchen door and just stepped over the threshold when he caught up with her. A tornado of temper, he snagged her shoulders, whirled her around.

"Just sex and science, is that it, Doc? I hope to hell I gave you plenty of data for one of your stinking papers."

"What are you—"

"Don't you want one last experiment for the road?"

He dragged her up hard against him, crushed his mouth down on hers. It was brutal, and it was fierce. For the first time, she was afraid of him, and what he was capable of.

"Shane." Shuddering, she wrenched her mouth free. "You're hurting me."

"Good." But he released her, jerking away so that she nearly stumbled. "You deserve it. You cold-blooded—" He managed to stop himself before he said something he wouldn't be able to live with later. "How can you have slept with me, have shared everything we've shared, and then just turn around and walk, like it meant nothing to you but a way to pass some time?"

"I thought—I thought that's how it was done. I've heard people say that you stay friends with all the women you've—"

"Don't throw my past up at me!" he shouted. "Damn it, nothing's been the same since you came here. You've tangled up my life long enough. I want you to go. I want you out."

"I'm going," she managed, and took one careful step, then another, until she'd reached the doorway.

"For God's sake, Rebecca, don't leave me."

She turned back, steadied herself with one hand against the jamb. "I don't understand you."

"You want me to beg." The humiliation was almost as vicious as the temper. "Fine, I'll beg. Please don't go. Don't walk out on me. I don't think I can live without you."

She put a hand to her head as she stared at him. All she could see was all that emotion swirling in his eyes. Too much emotion, impossible to decipher. "You want me to stay? But—"

"What's the big deal about New York?" he demanded. "So they've got museums and restaurants. You want to go to a restaurant, I'll take you to a damn restaurant. Now. Get your coat."

"I—I'm not hungry."

"Fine. You don't need a restaurant. See?" He sounded insane, he realized. Hell, he was insane. "You've got that fancy computer, the modem and all those gizmos. You can work anywhere. You can work here."

She wasn't used to having her brain frazzled. In defense, she latched on to the last thing he'd said. "You want me to work here?"

"What's wrong with that? You've been getting along here, haven't you?"

"Yes, but—"

"Leave your equipment set up everywhere." He threw up his hands. "I don't care." In a lightning move, he leaped forward and lifted her off her feet with hands under her elbows. "I don't care," he repeated. "I'm used to it. Set up a transmitter in the hay barn, put a satellite dish on the roof. Just don't leave."

The first hint of a smile curved her lips. Perhaps relationships weren't her forte, but she believed she was getting the idea. "You want me to stay here?"

"How many languages do you speak?" Sheer frustration had him shaking her. "Can't you understand English?" He dropped her back on her feet so that he could pace. "Didn't I just say that? I can't believe I'm saying it, but I am. I'm not losing you," he muttered. "I'm not losing what I have with you. I've never felt this way about anyone. I didn't want to, but you changed everything. Now you're in my head all the time, and the thought of you not being where I can see you or touch you rips my heart out. It rips my damn heart out!" he shouted, spinning toward her with blood in his eye. "You've got no right to do that to somebody, then leave!"

She started to speak, but the look on his face when she opened her mouth stopped her cold.

"I love you, Rebecca. Oh, God, I love you. And I have to sit down."

His knees were buckling. He was sure he'd crawl next. To get some control, he pressed the heels of his hands against his eyes. Whatever the humiliation, he would take it, as long as she stayed.

Then he looked up, looked at her. And she was weeping. His heart stopped thudding, split apart and sank.

"I'm sorry. I'm sorry. I've got no right to treat you this way, talk to you this way. Please don't cry."

She took a sobbing breath. "In my whole life, no one has ever said those words to me. Not once, in my whole life. You can't possibly know what it's like to hear them from you now."

He rose again, resenting everyone who had ever taken her for granted, including himself. "Don't tell me it's too late for me to say them. I'll make it up to you, Rebecca, if you let me."

"I was afraid to tell you how much I love you. I thought you wouldn't want me to."

He took a moment before he tried to speak, a moment to let what she'd said seep in and heal his dented heart. "I want you to. I need you to. You're not going."

She was shaking her head when he pulled her into his arms. "I'm not going anywhere."

"You're in love with me."

"Oh, yes."

"Thank God." He covered her mouth with his while joy fountained through him. "I've been falling for you since I picked you up at the airport. You were so snotty, I couldn't resist you." A thought intruded, made him wince. "Rebecca, last night—"

"It doesn't matter."

"Yes, it does. I was with my brothers, down at Devin's office. I got drunk and slept it off on the cot in the back room. I was angry about what was happening here, and what had happened inside me, for you. Stupid." He lowered his brow to hers. "I didn't know if you just let go a little, it could all be so right. You were always meant to come here. Do you believe that?"

"Yes." She cupped her hands on his cheeks. The full power of it struck her like light. "We're connected."

"That's one way to put it. I like 'I love you' better. I really like that. Who'd have thought?"

"I like it, too, better than anything." Blissful, she snuggled into his arms. "And I won't leave my equipment spread around the house. Since we're going to be living together, we need some sense of order."

"Living together." He tipped her face back, kissed her forehead, her nose, her lips. "Wrong. We've already been there, sort of. You're going to marry me."

"Marry." Her head spun. "You." Her legs turned to water. "I have to sit down now."

"No, you don't. I'll hold you up." That lightning Mac-Kade grin flashed before he began to trace kisses over her face, move his hands up and down and over her. Damn, but she was cute when that brain of hers clicked off. "Marry me, Rebecca," he murmured. "You might as well say yes. I'll just talk you into it."

Marriage. Family. Children. Shane. Why would he have to talk her into something she wanted more than anything in the world? "I can't think."

"Good." They'd keep it that way awhile, he decided, and nipped gently at her jaw. "I love you. Mmm…pretty Rebecca, I love you. Say, 'I love you, too.'"

The muscles in her thighs went lax. "I love you, too."

"Marry me, Rebecca." His curved lips skimmed over hers, down her chin and back again. "Be my wife, have my children, stay with me. Say yes. Say, 'Yes, I'll marry you, Shane.'"

"Yes." The strength came back into her arms as she threw them around his neck. "Yes, I'll marry you, Shane."

He nibbled around to her ear. "Say, 'I'll cook for you night and day, Shane.'"

"I'll—" Her eyes popped open. The most momentous event of her life ended in laughter. "Sneaky. Very sneaky, farm boy."

"It was worth a shot, Becky." Laughing with her, he gathered her into his arms and swept her in circles. "But I'll take the best two out of three."

Epilogue

Sunlight glinted off snow and the ice that crusted over it, so that the land sparkled clean and pure. They would all be there soon, Rebecca thought. All the MacKades, with their noise and their energy. And they would come here, to the meadow where a simple stone marker rose out of the untrampled snow and cast its thin gray shadow over white.

But she had come first. She and her husband. The word, even after three months of marriage, still made her heart trip with pure joy. Shane Cameron MacKade was her husband. This day, the first day of the new year, she had love, she had a family, and the future was hers.

She slipped her hand in his, the hand that carried the simple gold band she'd wanted on her finger. And together they stood.

"It's what they all wanted," Shane said quietly. "Acknowledgment for a life that ended too soon. Acknowledgment is a kind of peace, don't you think?"

"That's what you feel here now, in the air. And I'll find his family's descendants." She turned her head, smiled up at Shane. "It'll take time—but we have time."

"I'll help you." He tipped her face up for a kiss. "We all will. It's a MacKade project. And you've got to finish putting your book together. I want the first copy, hot off the press, of *The Legends of Antietam* by Rebecca Knight MacKade."

"That's Dr. MacKade to you," she said and chuckled against his lips. "I'll finish the book very soon now." She turned again, touched a hand to the cool stone that marked a young man's grave. "And we'll finish the rest, together. It's what they wanted from us—John and Sarah."

"I can still feel them. In the house. In the land."

"We always will." Content, Rebecca snuggled into his arms as the wind kicked up and sent snow flying. "But it's different now. Settled."

"Settled." He smiled, resting his cheek on the top of her head. It was a word he'd never expected to apply to himself. But how well it fit, how well she fit. "I love you, Rebecca."

"I know." Still her heart swelled just hearing it. "I love you."

It was the perfect time, she thought. The perfect place. Though she stayed in the circle of his arms, she tilted her head back. She wanted to see his face when she told him, to see what came into his eyes. She drew a breath because the words, the first time they were said, were so precious.

"We're going to have a baby."

His eyes went totally blank, and that made her lips curve. "What?"

How lovely, she thought, to have the chance to say it again. "We're going to have a baby, in a little over eight months." Her smile spread, her eyes filled as she took his limp hand and pressed it to her stomach. "We're going to have a baby," she said a third time.

"You're pregnant." His breath came out in a whoosh, and his eyes were no longer blank. Shock, joy, delight. Everything she'd wanted to see raced into them. "We're pregnant." His gaze dropped down to their joined hands covering a miracle. "Our baby."

"Our baby." Then she let out a rich laugh as she was spun off her feet and into wild circles that sent snow flying into the sunlight.

He stopped as abruptly as he'd begun, and now concern and a touch of fear showed on his face. "You're feeling all right? You're not sick? You don't eat enough. You've got to start eating. Are you sure you feel all right?"

"I feel wonderful. Invincible." She touched her lips to his. "I feel loved."

"Rebecca." His mouth lingered, then gently deepened the kiss, and the arms that cradled her gathered her closer yet. "You are loved." Emotion flowed through him as she nestled her head on his shoulder. His wife. His child. "It's a circle," he murmured, looking down at the stone marker again. "Season to season."

"Yes. If it's a boy, I'd like to name him Cameron."

"It feels right. It all feels so right." He heard his dogs barking in the distance, quick yelps of joy and recognition. "That's the family coming." He kissed her once again, then turned from the snow-draped meadow, boots crunching as he walked back toward the house. "I can't wait to tell them another MacKade's on the way. We need champagne or something. Oh, you can't have any alcohol. Well, we'll come up with something." He glanced down, grinning like a fool. "Hey, that's why you didn't drink anything for New Year's Eve."

"Yes, that's why." She cocked a brow at him. She wondered if he knew he was rambling, and being simply so adorable she wanted to shout with laughter. "Shane, you can put me down now," Rebecca told him.

He only held her closer. "No, I can't."

"You don't have to carry me all the way into the house."

"Yes, I do." His eyes met hers and he laughed. "I've got you now, Rebecca MacKade. I'm not letting go."

* * * * *